A DANGEROUS KISS

Norah looked up to find they were in the dimness near the end of the hall and her room, and she stopped. "This is my room." She waved a hand toward her door. "It's comfortable and it's far from the earl's quarters and the rest of the family."

"I'm afraid you're wrong," Barclay said with a wry smile. "*I* am the rest of the family." He motioned to the door across the hall from her room and his voice lowered. "And that is my room."

Dearest Heaven, she had chosen the room directly across from the one occupied by the very person she hoped to avoid as much as possible during her tenure here.

He was now facing her, his arms at his sides, his eyes that dangerous liquid amber. She held her breath for a moment, wondering if he was getting closer or if it was just her imagining it.

His head lowered and his lips touched hers with a gentle pressure that gradually deepened and spread to cover her mouth. His lips were on hers like—Sweet Jesus!—he was kissing her! She stood rigid, shocked to immobility, and drank in sensations unlike anything she had imagined.

Not even when she sneaked old Ovid's racy sonnets into her room at the academy and tried to glean from them the truth about the unthinkable between a man and a maid . . . had she guessed the warmth-generating pleasure of a man's lips on hers. Some things, she had learned recently, had to be experienced to be understood.

Also by Betina Krahn

The Reluctant Heroes series:
Hero Wanted
White Knight Needed

The Sin & Sensibility romances:
A Good Day to Marry a Duke
The Girl with the Sweetest Secret
Anyone But a Duke

Three Nights with the Princess
Behind Closed Doors
Rapture's Ransom
Passion's Storm
Rebel Passion
Hidden Fires
Passion's Treasure
Love's Brazen Fire
Midnight Magic

NEW YORK TIMES BESTSELLING AUTHOR

BETINA KRAHN

White Knight Needed

ZEBRA BOOKS
KENSINGTON PUBLISHING CORP.
www.kensingtonbooks.com

ZEBRA BOOKS are published by

Kensington Publishing Corp.
119 West 40th Street
New York, NY 10018

All Kensington titles, imprints, and distributed lines are available at special quantity discounts for bulk purchases for sales promotion, premiums, fund-raising, educational, or institutional use.

Special book excerpts or customized printings can also be created to fit specific needs. For details, write or phone the office of the Kensington Sales Manager: Attn.: Sales Department. Kensington Publishing Corp., 119 West 40th Street, New York, NY 10018. Phone: 1-800-221-2647.

Zebra and the Z logo Reg. U.S. Pat. & TM Off.

First Printing: April 2022
ISBN-13: 978-1-4201-5197-8
ISBN-13: 978-1-4201-5198-5 (eBook)

10 9 8 7 6 5 4 3 2 1

Printed in the United States of America

In Loving Memory of

Zebulun Krahn

November 1978–December 2020

One

London 1883

Stares and whispers fell at Barclay Howard's broad back as he exited his carriage and proceeded down Gordon Street. He paid little heed. He was used to them by now.

Three fashionably dressed young ladies stood by the door of a nearby milliner's shop watching him with widened eyes. He recognized one as a young beauty to whom he had been introduced at his best friend's recent birthday celebration. He squared his shoulders and continued on his way, oblivious to the pedestrians who scrambled off the pavement into the street to avoid him. Why should he acknowledge snobbish, overbred females when they wouldn't give him the time of day, much less a hand in marriage?

He had better things to do, like attending a lecture that could very likely change his life. He realized he was scowling and relaxed his face as he turned down the narrowing lane that led to Lightner Hall.

The large, square brick building was of a design that conveyed a simplicity and utility in keeping with the nature of the wisdom dispensed inside. The only bit of architectural dash about the place was a gracefully carved stone lintel surrounding the open front doors. On the pavement outside the hired hall were sandwich boards advertising upcoming lectures and demonstrations intended for those whose taste in diversions were a step above corner pubs and raucous music halls.

He entered the small lobby and paid for admission—an entire pound—a surprising sum for the privilege of listening to people just talk, ironically about "free" love. The man and woman selling tickets glanced nervously at each other, waved him toward the doors of the lecture hall, and began to pack up their cashbox as soon as they took his money.

He took a seat in the back row, because sitting closer to the front always blocked the view for people behind him, and he did try to be courteous. The chairs, as often happened, were small and hard. He had to turn slightly to wedge his broad shoulders against the curved back and had to tuck his muscular legs to the side to avoid blocking the aisle. With a deep breath, he looked around at his fellow seekers of enlightenment.

They were a surprisingly fusty group, these "free-lovers" . . . a sea of tweeds and meerschaum pipes, sensible brogans and graying beards. The women weren't much better. Most wore Puritan-dark dresses and dour expressions . . . they looked like they might be carrying rolling pins hidden in their skirts. A pair of younger females caught his eye until they turned. Sour expressions and protruding teeth made him decide to look elsewhere.

This was hardly the free-spirited group he had expected. But as the moderator called the hall to order and introduced the first speaker, Barclay made himself concentrate on what he might learn . . . though he had already learned that this was probably not the place to find "free love" partners.

The first speaker was a woman in a black woolen ensemble with a white standing collar that made her look absurdly like a village vicar with a bun. She opened with a barrage of questions about "women in bondage," which widened Barclay's eyes. *Briefly*. It was a disappointment to realize she was talking about the restrictions and limitations that marriage placed on women. The state of current laws, she said, treated women as little more than property to be managed or brood mares to be bought and sold with dowries. There were polite grunts and nods from men present and "Hear! Hears!" from the women.

Really? Barclay looked at the women attendees in dismay. Who in their right mind would think of these females as oppressed or—*shudder*—breeding stock? He scowled, thinking of his best friend's birthday celebration and the formidable doyens and haughty debs who attended. It was hard to imagine any of them being led around by a halter.

By the time she finished with salvos against a society that kept women bound in marriages despite abandonment by husbands "gone to green" or forced them into infirmity by ceaseless childbearing, Barclay was eyeing the door. Clearly her notion of "free love" and his expectations were oceans apart. He started to wonder if the flyer advertising this lecture was some sort of joke.

Just then, one of the doors opened and a woman in a short cloak slipped inside the hall. He was struck by an air of urgency about her and a hint of trembling in her clasped hands. As she looked over the hall, he caught a glimpse of her face . . . a pale oval with delicate features framed in a halo of light hair. She hurried down the far side aisle away from the door and took an empty seat in a group of women dressed like nuns on holiday. He watched her for a moment longer, wishing she would turn again so he could confirm his brief impression of her face.

The second speaker, an august-looking man of middle years, was introduced and began a broadside against the exploitation of women and girls for money . . . which sounded rather lasciviously like prostitution. It turned out he meant hazardous factory work at low wages that trapped women and children in shortened lives of desperation. It was more decent to give women alternatives, he railed . . . allow them to decide when to have and raise children . . . allow them to control their own "fecundity."

Barclay knew the definition, but he had never heard the word spoken aloud. So that was how it sounded.

There were ways, the speaker insisted, safe and practical ways for married couples—women in particular—to limit the number of their pregnancies and better care for the children they did bear.

Pregnancy? That was another term not used in polite society. Something a physician might say to a colleague, but never to a patient.

Just then, he heard voices from outside as the rear door opened again. Out of the corner of his eye he saw a man enter and stand glowering at the assembly. The fellow was a stocky, ruddy-faced sort with narrowed eyes, and he was breathing hard, as if he'd been running. At that exact moment, the young woman who had arrived late turned to look at the door. Barclay caught the shock on her face as she saw the man, then turned away and pulled the hood of her cloak closer around her face.

She was evading the man, he surmised. Had she meant to attend the lecture, or had she just slipped into the hall to escape the brute? He glanced at the man, taking in thick, gloveless hands that were clenching repeatedly at his sides. Every nerve in Barclay's body came alive. He looked to the young woman, who glanced again over her shoulder and then looked around frantically. *Searching for an exit. Clearly.*

His own hands clenched into fists and his jaw tightened.

A long moment passed as her pursuer edged slowly along the back wall toward her side of the hall. The man could scarcely haul her kicking and screaming out of a lecture on the mistreatment of women. She wisely kept her seat, sensing that there was safety in such a venue. For the moment, the pursuit was a stalemate and the lecture continued.

There was more talk of money and women . . . economic slavery, the fellow called it. The laws of the land kept women shackled and children doomed to a life of mere subsistence. Under the guise of protecting them and preserving order, society enslaved women and children while giving them no say in their futures.

Barclay thought of the irony presented in the case of the young woman trapped in a free-love lecture by a man pursuing her. Who was she running from? A father? A husband? A bully from a brothel? Again she glanced over her shoulder, and something about her pale face and delicate features tugged at his most dominant instincts. He uncurled his legs and leaned forward, resting his arms on the back of the empty seats in front of him. The moment the presentation was over he intended to—

Raised voices filtered in from outside the main doors, growing quickly louder. He glanced at the heavy wooden panels with a frown, and a moment later both doors flew open and a sea of dark blue uniforms filled the opening.

A man in a derby and a checkered suit led a dozen constables into the hall, where he stopped and issued an order in a booming voice.

"Stay where ye are! Yer all under arrest on charges of offendin' th' moral decency!"

A mad scramble ensued. Half of the audience rushed forward to defend the speakers, while the other half scrambled for the far doors that presumably led to an adjoining street. Barclay was instantly in motion, rushing toward the young woman, tossing chairs out of his way and into the path of determined constables. Luckily, the girl's pursuer was pinned against the rear wall of the chamber by bobbies, and in several furious strides, Barclay was at the girl's side and taking her by the arm.

"Let me go! What are you—"

"Out the nearest door," he growled, shocked by her resistance. "Unless you want to spend the night in jail."

That must have registered. Her struggling slowed enough for him to usher her to the nearest door—which led into a narrow, dead-end alley. Clearly that was why most of the other patrons had chosen to escape through the other side of the hall. He spotted daylight at the far end of the alley and took her by the wrist. "This way."

Two steps were all he managed before he was jolted to a stop. She had planted her feet to resist and glared at his hand on her arm.

"What are you doing? We have to go nowwww—" A sharp pain shot through his hand and he released her with an "Owww!" He drew back, staring at his hand in horror. Blood appeared in a puncture wound, and when he looked at her, she was gripping a large hatpin poised for another strike.

"Why the devil did you do that? I was taking you to the

street to avoid the constables." He reached for her hand and she struck again—but this time he drew back too quickly for her and she stabbed only air.

"How dare you set hands to me?" she said, scanning both him and the narrow alleyway to the street beyond, most of which he was blocking.

He pulled out a handkerchief to wrap around his hand, feeling confounded. "I was trying to help."

"I don't need your help," she said, her voice thin and a bit tremulous. "Stay away from me." She brandished the hatpin as she pressed her back against the brick wall to slide past him. "Or I'll scream."

When she was directly across from him—mere inches away—he got a good look at her face and a pair of startling eyes. Green as grass they were, and her skin was as smooth as cream. Her hair had a red-gold tinge, from what he could see of it, and she had full, nicely curved lips.

With vengeful gallantry he backed away and bowed, sweeping his uninjured hand toward the street, inviting her to flee.

She slid farther away, watching his mocking gesture, then turned and ran toward the mouth of the alley—where two coppers intercepted her and managed to block her blow and seize her weapon before it did them damage. One grabbed her arms and dragged her forcefully toward a waiting police wagon, snarling that she was under arrest.

"Hey!" Barclay shouted, rushing after them. "You can't just arrest a woman on the—"

"Yeah, we can," said the constable's comrade, coming from Barclay's side with a truncheon already completing an arc toward the back of his head. The blow sent Barclay to his knees. Swirling dark spots in his vision melted together and the last thing he heard was a rough voice declaring, "An' we can pinch you, too, ye bloody great toff!"

Norah Capshaw found herself with a clutch of older women who had also been stuffed into a Black Maria and hauled off to a nearby police station. The others seemed either outraged or oddly resigned to their fate. She was the only one with tears rolling down her cheeks, and a couple of the women noticed. One of the others, called Hermione, came to squeeze in beside her on the dirty bench and offered her a handkerchief. With some reluctance, Norah accepted it and dabbed her eyes.

"Your first time?" Hermione asked, leaning closer. "Getting 'pinched'?" Hermione studied her confusion and clarified: "Being arrested."

Norah was shocked. "Well . . . yes."

"Don't be afraid, dear," Hermione said, taking her hand. "We'll be with you. They're bullies, these coppers, and like throwing their weight around. But they know better than to cross the line with us."

Norah's disbelief must have shown in her face, for the sweet-looking older woman produced a mischievous smile.

"It's my fourth," she said, leaning into Norah with a nod. She almost sounded proud of it. "I'm Hermione Barton, by the way."

"Four times . . . arrested?" Norah repeated.

A tall, severe-looking woman across the jail wagon spoke up. "Five for me." She smiled tautly. "Lucrecia Haygood, here."

"Four for me, too." A short, older woman with a long

nose nodded defiantly. "Essie Delbarton. Still alive and kickin'."

Norah nodded as the rest introduced themselves.

"We've all been arrested before, dear," Hermione declared. "On ridiculous charges. 'Offending the public decency.' Balderdash. Complete codswallop."

"They just don't want women to speak up about how badly we're treated," Lucrecia declared irritably.

"Or that we have power ourselves and can make the world a better place if we seize that power and use it," plump Essie added.

"But they arrested us for just sitting and listening," Norah said, looking at the women in the police van with her. "How is that indecent?"

"They were talking about pregnancies, dear . . . about how married couples can limit or space childbearing to improve their health and the health of their families. Birth control, my dear. Annie Besant and Charles Bradlaugh published that American pamphlet on how couples—in the privacy of their own homes—can plan or prevent pregnancies. They were arrested on morals charges but managed to be acquitted in the courts. Since then, the Society for the Suppression of Vice has been on a tear—proclaiming even the mention of birth control obscene and undermining of the public morality."

"As if mentioning it were a greater threat to the public morals than the brothels men sneak out to at night," Lucrecia said with a scowl.

"Hypocrites," declared Maxine-call-me-Max, a handsome woman in a fashionable ensemble of fitted jacket and tie. "The same top-lofties who sit on the committee are the ones who treat their wives like property and keep mistresses in bondage to their baser urges. Power, my girl. It's all about men and their power."

Norah sat dumbfounded as they continued their scandalous talk and introduced themselves and their arrests as if they were proud of their unlawful activities. By the time they reached the station, were "processed," and put into an odoriferous cell, she knew their names and had learned that five of the eight were widows . . . left without means of support.

Seated on battered wooden benches along the dingy walls, the women were soon telling stories of their experiences in the working world. They had found ways to get by . . . sharing living quarters, working at difficult jobs, or diligently learning a trade. Two things they universally refused to do were factory work and household service, which they deemed demeaning or dangerous or both. They'd had enough of taking orders in their lives and all relished their independence.

Norah was astounded by their openness and camaraderie. Never, in her ladyish education, had she come across such audacious ideas. She and her fellow students at Trinity Academy had been entrenched in a course of classical studies and socially useful accomplishments like marriage, the arts, and hospitality. Matters of law, money, and independence were as foreign to her as speaking Chinese . . . at least until three months ago, when her aged guardian died. That was when she'd had to leave the academy and learned she was penniless and on her own. With no warning, she was forced to look for work that would pay enough to keep body and soul together.

Now—sitting in a jail cell with a group of opinionated women—she was once again plunged into an experience she was wholly unprepared for. Listening to them, she felt like a child pressing her nose against a shop window displaying things she had never imagined existed.

When they turned to her for her story, she swallowed hard, dabbed her eyes again, and felt something in her middle relax. Maybe these women would understand her plight.

"My mother died when I was quite young and my father only lasted a few years more. Having no other family, I was given into the care of a legal guardian, who sent me off to a boarding school and then on to a women's academy in Oxford. My guardian died three months ago, and I learned that my parents' legacy had run out years ago. My guardian, Mr. Rivers, had continued to pay my academy fees out of his own pocket. I suppose I was fortunate he cared enough to continue my education."

She looked down at the handkerchief she was worrying into a knot.

"That or he simply didn't know what else to do with you," Lucrecia said flatly.

Hermione gave her friend a sharp look, then turned back to Norah.

"I'm sure he wanted to prepare you for what was to come. So what are your plans, dear?"

Norah looked around at the tired but expectant faces of women whose circumstances, surprisingly, were not so different from her own. They had not only survived, they had grown stronger in conquering the difficulties they'd encountered. She felt embarrassed to admit: "I'm not certain what my plans are. I currently have a position as a tutor in an evening school for adults. It's not the best fit, but it is better than being a typewriter . . . which I did for a few days . . . until my employer decided I owed him more 'personal' duties. When I refused he fired me. Before that I worked at a library in acquisitions. It turned out some of the books I ordered from the Continent were salacious in content and had scandalous illustrations. I was fired."

"So this is your third job in three months?" Hermione was wide-eyed.

Norah nodded. The silence that followed stopped her breath.

Then Essie grinned, and her grin turned into a chuckle . . . which elicited laughter all around the cell. Norah's face flamed and she hid it in her hands.

This was a new low—

"Oh, my dear, don't be embarrassed." Hermione pulled her hands from her face and dipped to catch her lowered gaze. "That has happened to all of us at one time or another." There were murmurs of agreement around them. "We've all had trouble finding a place in the world. It's just that three jobs in three months . . . that's something of a record. You're our new heroine."

Norah looked up and found luminous eyes filled with sympathy watching her. Their laughter had been from surprise, she realized, and perhaps a release of tension.

Hermione engulfed her in a hug, and the others came to stoop beside her and give her hugs or pats and quiet words of encouragement. By the time they were through Norah felt better, though she couldn't say why. Acceptance by a bunch of rebellious older women was hardly a status to which she would have aspired. But here she was, in dire circumstances, telling them her failures and feeling better for having their understanding.

The rest of the night passed slowly as the women settled

in and leaned against one another to avoid the wretched walls and get what rest they could. Norah, however, had never felt less like sleeping. Her mind buzzed with thoughts ignited by their stories, opinions, and dauntless humor.

They advised her not to fret about the morning. The authorities didn't worry so much about the attendees at such gatherings, they said. It was the speakers they intended to take before the courts. The women had no notion of how long they might be held or what fines or imprisonment they faced. That, Hermione said, was tomorrow's problem, and she patted Norah's hand and offered her a shoulder to doze on.

As she closed her eyes, the image of the man who had dragged her out of the lecture hall came to her again. Tall, broad, forceful—a big, dark brute. But now she wondered if he honestly had been trying to help her.

Then the ruddy face and glower of the other man— the one pursuing her—rose in her mind. The bounder had followed her all day—at the green grocer's in the milliner's shop, on the street. His stare was unnerving and he was clearly maneuvering to get her alone, to the point of trying to set hands on her.

Why? What could he possibly want with her?

Two

Barclay awakened in a dim, stench-filled cell with a throbbing head and a back stiff from lying heaped and twisted on a wooden bench. His cellmates were a handful of lecture attendees and a number of gritty characters who could only be described as scrapings from London's grim underbelly. He no longer had his watch, and a quick check of his pockets revealed they had been thoroughly picked—whether by his fellow inmates or the coppers themselves, he had no way of knowing. What he did know was that he was getting out of this place as quickly as possible.

When a turnkey brought them some bread and a pail of water, he seized the opportunity to send for his solicitor. By noon, Mr. Anglesmith had paid whatever fine had been levied against him and he was free to go.

Annoyed as he was at being rendered unconscious—a first in his experience—he refused to leave the station until he had his beloved pocket watch back. After a search authorized by the red-faced precinct captain, they managed to find it in a box filled with contraband in the station's storage room. With vengeful pleasure, he had Anglesmith pay the fines for the rest of the men and women arrested in the lecture hall raid. He smiled as he watched the desk sergeant's irritation when the men and women filed past him and out through the main entrance.

And there she was . . . the fair-haired woman he had tried to help. His hand was still sore, but it was nothing compared to the headache the coppers had given him. For hours in that dank cell, the memory of her had tramped through his thoughts, but when he hurried out the precinct doors and headed for her, he was stopped by a handful of older women whose fines he had just anonymously paid. They gathered between him and her like sheepdogs protecting a lamb.

He glowered, which was usually more than enough to clear his path. But they held fast and had the temerity to make shooing motions and tell him to move along. Before he knew it, the young woman was hurrying away from both him and her guardians, as if pursued by a predator.

His fists curled and his face heated, he saw people staring wide-eyed and hurrying past him on the pavement. Once again his imposing stature and face did him a disservice. Burlap—that was what he was—in a world that prized only silk.

Stupid of him to think that his chivalrous behavior would be recognized or appreciated in any way. He stalked off toward the cab Anglesmith had hailed for him, ignoring the pedestrians who scrambled out of his path.

"Females. They hold the keys to love and happiness and are damned stingy with them," he said irritably to Anglesmith as they climbed aboard the cab.

The bespectacled, fortyish lawyer nodded and looked

pained by Barclay's conclusion. Anglesmith was a good listener.

"Always ready to judge us," Barclay continued after giving the driver his address. "Repulsed or enamored by what is on the outside of a man . . . forgetting that it's his insides—heart and mind—that make him worthy."

Anglesmith nodded in sympathy. He was a bachelor himself. "They cannot help themselves, I fear. It's bred in their bones."

Barclay leaned to the side of the cab to look back for his disappearing female, finding her no longer in sight.

Fine. Let her go. Why should he apologize for trying to help her?

The ride to his home in Mayfair was uneventful, but the moment he arrived, that changed. A caller waited in the salon, and Haskell, his butler, hurriedly whispered that the man had insisted on staying and waiting no matter how long it took. He handed Barclay a card with the names of the fellow and the York legal firm he represented. The names seemed familiar and before he headed into the salon, he sent Haskell to stop the cab carrying Anglesmith away to tell the solicitor he was needed inside.

Straightening his vest and coat, he gave the latter a sniff and deemed it smelly but probably fitting for an interview with his grandfather's lawyer. Bracing for whatever legal tangle he now faced, he strode into the salon.

"Henry Westerman, Esquire," the fellow said gravely, approaching Barclay with an offered hand. "From Maren, Lister, and Dowd, Solicitors at Law. We handle the Earl of Northrup's affairs, and it seems—"

"My grandfather has a demand of some kind or other," Barclay finished for him. He ignored the man's hand and widened his stance. Could this day get any worse?

"Well, yes, in a manner of speaking, sir. I have come to deliver certain provisions of the earl's will and see them carried out."

"Provisions of his will? What do you mean, 'carried out'?"

"Please forgive my abruptness, Mr. Howard. I assumed you would already know." The fellow had paled visibly. "I regret to inform you that your grandfather has passed from this mortal plane." When Barclay just stared, unblinking, the man frowned. "He died. The earl—your grandfather—is dead. These four days now."

"If this is some kind of a joke, it is a most distasteful one," Barclay declared, his deep voice rising. "If you knew my grandfather, you would know he is immune to ordinary human constraints, including *mortality*."

"A notion he subscribed to himself, I am told," Westerman declared, looking askance at Anglesmith striding into the salon. "Sadly, in error."

"Why was I not contacted straightaway? When is the funeral?"

"Your grandfather considered funerals 'costly nonsense' and left instructions that he be put straight into the family mausoleum."

Barclay looked to Anglesmith with relief. "A good thing Haskell was able to catch you. Westerman here says my grandfather has died, and informs me I am required to fulfill some provision in his will. I need you to look over whatever documents he has brought." He turned back to Westerman. "My personal solicitor, James Anglesmith."

The men shook hands, and Anglesmith's gaze fell expectantly to the briefcase lying on the settee beside the solicitor. Westerman pulled out a sheaf of documents and held them a moment before surrendering them to Anglesmith for inspection.

"The most immediate provision is that guardianship of the new earl passes to you, sir," Westerman continued, looking a bit apologetic. "And that your continued income from the estates is conditional upon you taking personal charge of the young earl . . . your first cousin, I believe."

Barclay's jaw dropped. He was being ordered to take charge of the new earl or be cut off financially? It must be true. His grandfather had passed. The devious old cod knew how to force compliance with his wishes and had never flinched from out-and-out blackmail when it suited him. Why should mere death change that?

"This provision involves your presence at the Northrup estates for the handover. And there are a few items the old earl insisted you have."

"I am to be the new earl's guardian? What about his mother?"

Westerman looked uncomfortable for a moment before answering. "She renounced all claim to the boy not long after he was born and took herself off to the south of France. She has not seen the child since and shows no interest in him. When the boy's father died two years ago, the old earl claimed the child as his heir and was named guardian. That guardianship passes to you, Mr. Howard, according to your grandfather's wishes."

Barclay steadied himself and drew a deep breath. "I need a drink."

Neither solicitor accepted his offer of a brandy; it was barely past noon. He stood by the long salon window, sipping and staring out into the park at the center of the fashionable square. He would likely never be a husband, but as of today he would be forced into the role of a father. How could the old man thrust such a thing upon him without a hint of warning?

His thoughts turned to the task now required of him. He would have to go to see the boy and make arrangements for his care and education. A good intellect ran in the Howard line, so proper schooling would be a must . . . a place with a rich and challenging curriculum. Not military—he would need something to bend him toward public service of a different kind. He would someday take his seat in the House of Lords and had to be prepared for such duties. Seeing to that preparation would be Barclay's responsibility for the next . . . what . . . six years? His eyes widened. Eight years?

"Just how old is this boy?" he asked, turning to the solicitors.

They had spread documents over settees, chairs, and the low table before the hearth. Anglesmith looked to Westerman, who answered briskly.

"Six years. The young earl is still in short pants, sir."

Barclay staggered back and bumped a shoulder into the window frame. At least *twelve years* then . . . a bloody life sentence!

"Only *six*?" He fairly choked on the word. "He's practically a babe. He needs a nanny, not a guardian."

"I believe he has one, sir," Westerman said with a strained smile.

"He won't be accepted into a school for years!" Barclay protested.

"Some schools do take boys at the age of eight," Anglesmith put in.

"If they are prepared and compliant." Barclay put down his glass and paced to the fireplace. "Has he been tutored?"

"I cannot say, sir. I have not met the young lord."
Westerman seemed to choose his words carefully. "I have
heard . . . he is . . . precocious."

Upon being freed from jail, Norah used the last of her
funds to pay for omnibus fare to the Diligence Adult
School, where she tutored. The minute she walked into
the building she was directed to the headmistress's office
and prepared herself for a difficult interview. Mrs. Guidry,
the founder and administrator of the school, where adults
came to learn basic literacy skills, was a stickler for prompt-
ness and diligence . . . thus the school's name.

Most of their classes were held at night to accommodate
working adults and, unfortunately, last night Norah was not
present to undertake their instruction. She had spent her
time on the omnibus trying to think of an acceptable
excuse for missing her assignment. Could she honestly
claim illness? It wouldn't be a full lie. She *had* been sick
with worry.

But starchy Mrs. Guidry took one look at her rumpled
clothes and shame-stained cheeks and narrowed her judgmental eyes. No amount of protesting or pleading would
convince her that Norah's absence hadn't been caused by
some kind of sordid activity. She was sacked on the spot
and even denied what wages she was owed because of her
"disregard for the reputation of the school." The woman
set her hulking son to escort Norah out of the building,
and that was that.

Penniless now and afoot, Norah had to walk the four
miles to her lodgings, dodging men and vehicles along
the way. Her hatpin had been confiscated by the police
and she was in no mood for dealing with men's streetside

admiration. When she finally reached her lodgings and trudged up the two flights of stairs, she stopped at the top to stare in disbelief at the trunks and boxes stacked in the hallway outside her door.

Her trunks, her boxes. Everything she owned.

She tried her door and learned her key no longer worked to admit her. Frantic, she rushed downstairs to the landlord's door and banged on it with the side of her fist. When it opened a crack the landlord's grizzled face and bloodshot eyes glowered at her.

"What have you done—throwing my things out into the hall and locking me out of my room?"

"Ye ain't paid yer rent and ye don't get to float another month on me good graces. Find yerself another roost, girlie. Yer done here."

The door slammed in her face.

She raced back up the steps and stood in the middle of her possessions, emotions exploding in her. Where could she go? What could she do? Three jobs in three months with nary a reference to be had. She thought about the women she'd met in jail, and their determination to fend for themselves. She had no idea how to contact Hermione or the others.

Why was she being punished so for things beyond her control?

Tears began to roll down her cheeks, and sobs soon followed. She wasn't one to shrink and weep, but honestly, how much difficulty was one expected to bear without even a glimmer of hope? She was alone and devastated by loss and—

A figure loomed beside her, and she looked up with a start to find a young woman—a pretty young woman—

staring down at her in concern. It took her a moment to recognize the girl who lived in the flat across the hall.

"The bloody bastard's turned ye out," the girl said, scowling.

Norah didn't trust herself to speak, but nodded as angry tears scalded her cheeks.

"Ye got a place to go?" she asked.

Norah shook her head and squeezed her eyes shut, humiliated.

There was a pause and then the girl spoke again.

"Well, ye do now. Ye can stay with me 'til you're on your feet." She picked up a hat box and headed for her door. "Come on. Help me get yer things inside. He'll be havin' a fit that they blocks the stairs."

When Norah looked up the girl smiled.

"I'm Goldie, by the by."

When the girl opened her door and beckoned her to follow, Norah rose and—lacking any alternative—accepted the help Goldie offered.

Inside Goldie's small flat they stacked Norah's belongings against a wall, and the girl offered her a cup of tea. Her lodging was a cold-water flat like the one Norah had just been evicted from, but Goldie managed to get hot water from an acquaintance on the first floor. The tea was warm and welcome, and the sympathy in Goldie's face opened the gates holding back Norah's story. She started with being orphaned and sent away to school and progressed to be arrested, sacked, and now evicted.

"Ye were sent away to school," Goldie said. "Don't ye have schoolmates to ask for help?"

"I couldn't approach any of those girls or their families.

They're all about social connections, and when you don't have any . . ." Norah halted.

"Ah." Goldie nodded and emptied the teapot into Norah's cup. "So, ye have to find another job." When Norah nodded, she looked thoughtful. "What can ye do?"

Norah gave a heavy sigh. "I can read Latin, French, and some Italian. I can typewrite and have studied the French philosophers and the works of English writers. I can arrange flowers and organize a dinner party for twenty. And I play the piano exceedingly well."

Goldie perked up. "Piano? I know a place what needs a player."

"Truly?" Norah sat straighter, hope burrowing out from under her heap of troubles. "Where?"

"Where I work. Fanwell Hall." When Norah didn't recognize the name, Goldie continued: "It's a music hall. Sometimes we got a band of fiddle players, but most days we just have a piano. There's singers an' dancers. Ye know a few songs?"

"I do, though I prefer to—"

"Tell ye what . . . come with me to the theater tonight and talk to the manager, Marcus Thibault. He gets a bit handsy at times, but he's not a bad sort, really." She looked Norah over critically and folded her arms. "But ye'll need something wi' more flash to wear."

"I'm not certain I have 'flash,' whatever that is," Norah said, heading for one of her trunks. "But I do have a dinner dress or two that might serve." Opening her trunk, she sorted through her carefully folded clothes to pull out a dark teal dress with a fashionable bodice and a tiered skirt that didn't require a bustle. She held it up to herself and turned to Goldie. "Will this do?"

"It'll do fine!" Goldie ran her fingers appreciatively over the soft fabric. "Just the thing." Then she surveyed Norah's sensible chignon. "We'll put your hair up . . . maybe a ribbon around your throat . . ."

Norah gave herself over into Goldie's capable hands, telling herself that she would do what was needed to keep body and soul together, even if it meant playing piano in a music hall. And she prayed that tonight her luck would finally change for the better.

Three

It was dusk and streetlamps were being lighted when Barclay strode into his club and down the stairs to the bar on the lower level. He had walked the damp streets for two hours, trying not to think of his unwelcome turn of fortune and yet unable to think of anything else. For the next three or four years he would be out of London and out of the public eye. Not that he was ever the thing in society—or even acceptable, despite his pedigree. But now he would be forgotten like a bad ague.

Thus, he was surprised to be greeted by fellow club members, young and old, with condolences and a black armband, which was hardly visible on the sleeve of his black coat. They had somehow heard of the earl's demise and offered sympathies on his titled grandfather's death. Brandy flowed magically into his glass, and he was forced to toast again and again the old man's legendary thrift and stubbornness. By eight o'clock he realized he had drunk far too much and was still damnably sober. His tolerance for spirits was both a blessing and a curse, especially tonight. He would love to just sink into a soft chair, banish all thought, and put off all decisions and preparations until tomorrow.

Strangely, men who rarely spoke to him now treated him like he was an old friend as they talked and laughed and reminisced about his grandfather. Though no one mentioned it, he couldn't help wondering if they were being cordial because they thought he might be inheriting the title. Surely they knew better. These men tracked heirs to titles more closely than they did their own offsprings' paternity. They had to know he was not in line for the coronet.

They were all solidly in their cups by the time someone suggested they move the gathering to a nearby music hall, where the dancers were scantily clad and known to sometimes "accompany" patrons afterward.

Pretty women? He could use such a diversion just now.

His companions pulled him into a growler and then into a gaudy music hall, where they found patrons singing along to a rotund fellow with an impressive baritone. It was hard to tell precisely what the lyrics were and the tune wasn't all that clear; there seemed to be no end to variations from the gin-soaked audience. But his party barreled in to the left side of the darkened theater and were soon singing along. After another song the curtain closed and the audience began stomping their feet and demanding the next act.

The master of ceremonies appeared and quieted the house with upraised hands and the announcement of the next act . . . a visit to fairyland. The crowd roared with anticipation. When the curtains parted a number of scantily clad young women were poised before a painted backdrop of a meadow with oversize flowers. They held their poses for what seemed a long time before the music started. The tempo was so slow that the "fairies" glanced at one another and frowned, seeming confused.

At length they began to move, but the music seemed to be out of time with their motions. Some tried to slow and prolong their movements to fit the accompaniment, while others insisted on performing as usual, at a faster pace. They bumped into one another and the performance took on a frantic quality that produced spurts of laughter and gin-laced jeering from the audience.

A voice could be heard shouting at the pianist to "speed it up." Then came additional exhortations: "Faster, dammit—faster!"

The result was the quickest, most erratic bit of Mozart ever performed. The audience didn't seem to know the music or care about its genius—they only knew the dancers were not giving them the tantalizing display they expected. From there the mood grew downright volatile.

Barclay, now more damnably sober than ever, rose and moved to the side aisle to see what the shouting was about and spotted the stage manager blustering at the pianist . . . a woman.

The light hair, the erect posture . . . he stalked closer to see her better as memory rose inside him. When the first rotten vegetable hit the floor beside her, she tossed a frantic glance over her shoulder at the well-oiled crowd and he glimpsed her face.

Her. The young woman who'd refused his assistance at the lecture. *Her* with the red-gold hair, amazing green eyes, and hatpin from hell.

When the first glob of vegetable matter struck her, she flinched but continued playing her bizarre rendition of one of humanity's finest compositions. The stage manager scurried along the orchestra pit just below the footlights, alternating between shouting at the pianist and at the dancers, demanding the performers finish their number. When overripe vegetables hit the floorboards near the dancers, several fled the stage.

Audience members began shouting, some at the dancers and others at their unappreciative neighbors. Voices and tempers rose, some hotly demanding the others "clam up" and others taking exception to being ordered to "shut yer gob!"

Fists came up and the theater exploded into a bare-knuckle brawl. The manager wheeled on the pianist, seized her by the arm, and shouted at her, while dodging nasty substances from the audience.

Barclay was in motion before he had time to think better of it.

He reached the piano and yanked the stage manager away from her. The man took a swing at him, but the impact barely registered. Barclay's weighty fist, however, sent the stage man sprawling on the floor of the orchestra pit, just as the first shrill sounds of constables' whistles cut through the commotion.

He turned back to the young woman, grabbed her wrist, and dragged her toward the door.

"Let me go! What do you think you're doing?" she declared, trying to pull away.

He halted at the door and glowered at her.

"Rescuing your ungrateful hide . . . *again*." His eyes narrowed and flicked toward the bobbies swinging truncheons at the men bashing one another. "Unless you'd rather spend more nights in jail."

Her eyes widened on the spectacle of constables working their way through the crowd, blowing whistles and meeting force with force. She looked up at Barclay with a jolt of recognition and her resistance shriveled. The next moment he was pulling her through a side door and into an alley where several cabs and carriages were waiting.

Norah wrenched her wrist free and clasped it with her other hand as they reached the street. *Him*. Again. The man who'd shoved her out the side door of that lecture hall yesterday. *The man she stabbed with her hatpin*. What was he doing here? Had he followed her? How else would he have known she was here?

It took her a moment to feel the heat of his hand at the small of her back and realize he was ushering her forcefully down the pavement toward a large four-seater cab. Alarm ignited in her.

"Unhand me," she declared, wheeling to confront him. But nothing could have prepared her for facing a tall, dark-haired man with a chest like a wall and a face that looked like it was hewn from old oak. She had thought of him as a large, dark specter since their last encounter, but now he took on human attributes that she found no less intimidating. Her voice shrank around her words. "I am perfectly capable of taking care of myself."

"I could see that. The manager was quaking in his shoes," he said irritably, tossing a coin up to the driver of the vehicle. "Take her wherever she needs to go."

He reached for the growler's door just as the side exit of the theater flew open and a handful of gents rushed out ahead of snarling constables. He grabbed her by the waist and tossed her up the steps into the cab, then barked at the driver to "Go!" Before the door closed the men escaping the hall were nearing the cab and her rescuer bashed a couple of them to keep them away before jumping on the step of the cab himself.

"Drive!" he shouted at the cabbie, and the fellow slapped the reins and the carriage lurched, throwing Norah back against the worn seat.

She saw her rescuer hanging on to the side of the cab and gasped as he struggled to wrench open the door and climb inside. When he dropped onto the seat beside her, she felt the cab rock. He was breathing heavily when he turned to look at her, and though she was determined not to show how frightened she was, she fled to the rear-facing seat across the coach.

"You will never get away with this," she managed through dry lips.

"With what?" he asked, glowering. "Rescuing you? I am well aware there will be consequences in helping you, *Miss Hatpin*."

The way he said it made her draw a sharp breath. She had stabbed him yesterday. Was this his bit of revenge?

"With abducting me," she charged.

He sat in silence for a moment, seeming to study her in the darkened cab while she wondered how much damage she would suffer if she flung herself out of the cab onto the street.

"What in God's name possessed you to play a dirge to accompany a troop of dancing girls dressed like threadbare fairies?" he demanded.

She blinked. It took her a moment to realize that, of all things, the beast was criticizing her musical performance!

"It was not a dirge," she protested. "They asked for accompaniment for a dance, and Mozart wrote that piece for the ballet."

"A dying swan or frog prince under a curse, surely. You

should have chosen something more suitable . . . like Beethoven. That could be speeded up nicely. *Bum, bum, bum, BUM . . . Bum, bum, bum, BUM . . .*"

"If you need battle drums or lightning and thunder." She huddled as far back into the opposite corner as she could, wishing she had the shawl she had worn to the theater. There wasn't enough space between them for her comfort, but she refused to let him see how he unnerved her. "Beethoven's Fifth is not music for gamboling fairies."

"Neither is a Mozart ballet in a music hall." His face smoothed. "Where did you learn to play Mozart anyway?"

"I studied piano for years, thank you. Some at boarding school, some at Trinity Academy."

"Trinity Academy? In Oxford?" He raised one eyebrow and appeared to file that answer away.

She could almost feel his gaze searching her in the flashes of light from the streetlamps they passed.

"Who was the man pursuing you yesterday?" he demanded.

She stiffened, surprised. "What business is that of yours?"

"Curiosity." His voice dropped. "Who are you running from?"

"I have no idea." That was Heaven's own truth, and one that had her looking over her shoulder for two long days.

"Come now. A husband . . . irate father . . . lover?"

"I have none of those. Nor am I a debtor, a soiled dove, or a housemaid with a purloined brooch." She was sick of half-truths and excuses. "All I know is . . . I was at the green grocer's and realized the brute was staring at me. I left without the apple I wanted, but he followed me. I ducked into a milliner's shop and waited a bit. When I left he was waiting for me. I escaped in a crowd watching a street musician, but he found me and tried to pull me into an alley. I fought and ran and managed to slip into that lecture."

"You're not a 'free lover'?" he said. His luminous gaze took on a more personal and alarming intensity.

"What? Absolutely not." She was shocked by the assumption, though on second thought, it made sense. The speaker in the hall was talking about the burdens and restrictions marriage placed on women . . . how they should be free to choose whom and when to *love*.

"Then what are you?" He tilted his head. "A suffragette?"

She thought for a moment, trying to decide how to answer without placing herself in more danger. "That is none of your concern."

After a moment he sat back in the seat and took a deep breath.

"Correct," he growled, his voice sounding like boulders grinding together. "However, I've rescued you twice now. I believe I am owed at least an answer or two."

"Rescued?" She sat back, only half aware that she was running her hands up and down her bare arms. "I spent last night in jail."

"As did I, after my attempt at gallantry failed," he said with dangerous-sounding annoyance. "And I did pay your fine."

That surprised her. She had assumed they were simply released. That thought seemed embarrassingly naïve. She still had much to learn about the workings of the world.

"If you are expecting recompense, I fear you will be disappointed." She raised her chin. "As a result of that incarceration, I lost my position."

"What position was that?" His gaze settled on the way she attempted to rub warmth into her bare arms.

"I am—was—a tutor at an adult school." In spite of her determination to seem collected and self-sufficient, she shivered.

He sat forward abruptly, removed his coat, and held it out to her.

"No, thank you," she said, lifting her chin.

His eyes narrowed and he leaned across the seat with the open coat. Her strangled scream escaped as the garment closed over her. He moved back to his side of the cab before she could protest further. It was shocking how easily the warmth of the coat seduced her outrage and his retreat to the other side of the cab lowered her tension. What was he doing? What did he want from her? Heaven above, the warmth felt good.

"It's beyond stubborn to refuse help when it is offered," he said, stretching out his legs onto the opposite seat. "Would you rather have stayed in jail?"

"Of course not." She managed a deeper, calmer breath. "I would not, however, be beholden to anyone."

"Ah." He nodded. "Well, you needn't feel beholden, Your Majesty. I would have done the same for any half-mad female arrested without cause or pelted by rotten vegetables."

She could have sworn there was a smile tugging at the corner of his well-formed lips. Soon it appeared fully and she found herself staring at it . . . then at big brown eyes . . . light brown with a hint of inner lights . . . perfectly suited to his rugged features. Her first impression of him had been of a dark, intimidating brute. Now she could see more refined elements, including his well-tailored clothing.

Gallantry, he said. Did he consider himself a gentleman? At least the beast was in no hurry to ravish her.

"Who are you?" she demanded.

"A man who is out of place and time. A man whose destiny is at odds with his dreams." He gave a one-sided smile. "In short, a man who has read too many books."

It was a disarming statement and struck her as words she might have used if asked to describe herself. For a moment her anxiety was nudged aside by interest.

"Why did you follow me to the theater tonight?"

"Follow you?" He seemed truly offended by the notion. "I was at my club tossing back a few when an acquaintance suggested we adjourn to a music hall. Imagine my surprise when I saw the young woman who stabbed me causing a riot with her lack of skill at the keyboard."

Was that possible? It was mere coincidence? And how dare he disparage her skill when he had only heard her playing under duress!

"I don't believe you," she said flatly.

He made a sound that seemed part laugh, part growl. "Of course you don't." She could feel him assessing her. "You don't know who to trust."

The truth of that stunned her. Whoever he was, he was astute and observant, which made her even more eager to be away from him. She had had enough judgment pronounced on her in recent weeks to last a lifetime.

"Name your street and I'll see you home."

She said nothing for a moment, searching him, wondering at his true intentions and remembering how easily he'd dealt with the men rushing the cab. If he wanted to hurt her or ravish her, there was probably little she could do about it. He had given her his coat for warmth and was sitting calmly on the other seat. Still, she was wary of revealing too much.

"Dallywell Street," she said, her heart began to pound.

He leaned forward to call the location to the driver. It didn't seem to register with him that she hadn't been precise. Perhaps he thought it a short street or intended to ask for a number when they reached it.

Most of the rest of the way to her lodgings was spent in silence. She knew he was watching her, but to be fair, she also watched him. His big hands rested on his knees or were tucked under his folded arms. His dark hair was short and a bit unruly in places. His garments were cut to accommodate his broad shoulders and muscular legs. Not that she studied his legs; God forbid. But it was hard to miss the size and solidity of the limbs taking up so much space in the footwell.

Had he truly been trying to help her? And why did the notion of a strange man trying to help her seem so foreign? Had her cloistered upbringing, recent employment fiascos, and the talk of those audacious women in jail combined to make her expect the worst of men?

The cab slowed and turned onto a narrow street and she looked out to confirm that it was indeed Dallywell Street. She wondered if Goldie was home and how she would get into the flat if she wasn't. Then it struck her: Goldie had danced in the fairyland debacle! Would her new friend toss her out on the street for the chaos she had caused?

"Here." She moved to the cab door and seized the

handle before he could slide across the seat to do it. "Just let me out here."

He called to the driver to stop, and a moment later she thrust his coat at him and fled down the coach steps. Hugging herself against the chill, she walked toward her lodgings. The cab sat for a moment before starting to roll slowly down the street behind her. When she darted in the street door to her building she paused for a moment to let her eyes adjust to the light from the low-burning lamp in the hallway. The worn stairs were shrouded in gloom and there were few sounds coming from nearby flats. She started up the steps, glancing behind her, half expecting to see her big rescuer entering the building. But she was alone.

With a sag of relief, she turned to climb toward Goldie's flat and looked up to find a face looming over the top of the third-floor railing. The features were indistinct, but something about the shape of the man and the flat cap he wore caused her to freeze.

"Stay where ye be!" His voice roared down the stairs at her, followed quickly by the thump of brogans on wooden steps. The masher she'd escaped the day before had followed her to her lodgings!

Panic seized her and she whirled and flew down the few steps and out the door. The cab was not far away, wheels turning slowly. He wasn't gone yet! She ran for the cab calling, "Wait!"

His face appeared at the open window and the cab halted. The door opened and a moment later she scrambled frantically inside.

"Stop, ye bloody tart!" came an accented order from behind her.

"Drive!" Her erstwhile rescuer ordered the cabbie, and

the vehicle lurched into motion. She was flung back against the rear seat and thrust out her arms. Her hand connected with her rescuer's arm and she drew back, though not before she sensed how hard it was.

When they headed toward a broader street at a fast clip, she righted herself enough to look out the window. Her pursuer was running after them. There was enough light from the lone streetlamp for her to see him stumble to a stop and kick at the cobblestones—very likely using language she would cringe to hear.

Pressing a hand to her heart, she glanced at the formidable man who had taken her in yet again. What made her think she was safer with him than with the Scotsman who pursued her?

"It was him? The man from the lecture hall?" he asked.

She nodded and took a breath. "He has learned where I live."

"And you have no idea what he wants from you?"

She shook her head and looked up at him. His eyes were luminous in the dim glow of the carriage lamps and she found herself staring.

"Where do you want to go?" he asked.

Her distress must have been too obvious. Her rescuer frowned.

"Where is your family? I'll see you there."

She swallowed hard and squeezed her hands together. It had been a long time since she had felt that loss as keenly as she did tonight. She was alone. Friendless. Without resources. The loss of her family—her sweet, vaguely remembered mother and doting father—still had the power to make her feel fragile and untethered.

Her voice sounded forced. "I have no family."

What possessed her to confess her deepest vulnerability to the man?

She lowered her gaze, and for a time the only sounds she heard were the clop of horse hooves and the rumble of carriage wheels echoing off nearby buildings. Then he called an order to the driver, who answered in the affirmative and slapped the reins.

"Where are you taking me?" she demanded, looking up, feeling the chill invading her bones again. She wrapped her arms around her and couldn't help a brief glance at the coat lying on the seat between them. A moment later he picked it up and draped it over her. It was missing his warmth this time and she felt an unreasoning pang of disappointment.

"To safety."

Curse him. Being gallant, was he? Likely trying to soften her up for what was to come. But, in truth, what alternative did she have? At some point she would have to bend to the will of fate and accept help from someone. Why in Heaven's name did it have to be *him*?

It struck her that he had rather cannily avoided giving her his name. Did that mean he had something to hide? Or that, come tomorrow, he would not want her to know his name?

"You don't believe me." He assessed her suspicion.

"As you said . . . I am a bit short on trust just now. You haven't even given me your name."

He drew a deep breath and expelled it slowly.

"Barclay Howard." He watched her reaction closely.

"Well, then, Mr. Howard, I think we should be quite clear about what will happen tonight. I will not be used for amusement or to satisfy some vile appetite. If I go with you, I insist you respect my person and allow me to reach the morning unmolested. If you find such expectations unreasonable, stop the vehicle and I will take my chances on the street."

"I find them insulting," he said, raising that eyebrow again, "after I rescued you. Twice. And I would have you know, I make it a rule not to pounce on my houseguests in a frenzy of animal passion." He looked her up and down. "I believe I can resist whatever temptation you think you present."

She had gone too far, she realized. Poking a beast was never a good idea. Especially a beast who could easily have her for a late-night treat.

Four

"Your name?" Barclay said as the cab slowed to a stop in front of a handsome town house in what was clearly a more affluent part of London. "I insist on knowing the identity of my overnight guests."

"This is where you live?" She looked up at the smartly appointed entry, with its granite steps, black doors, shining brass knockers, and potted shrubs trimmed into fanciful swirls.

He watched her appraise his home with surprise and felt a pang of disappointment. She, like most of society, must have assumed he lived in a *cave*.

"It is. And because you're a hunted woman, it's the safest place for you tonight." He paused for a moment, then asked again, "Your name?"

"Norah," she said quietly, as if in a confessional.

"Norah what?" He watched her shrinking beneath his coat.

"Capshaw."

"Well, Norah Capshaw, my handsome house has never been cracked or burgled . . . never even had the windows jimmied. You will be as safe here as in a bishop's pocket."

He made the mistake of grinning broadly. When she drew back his grin hardened into something more like a grimace. She pressed herself into the corner of the cab and he cursed silently. What the hell was the matter with him, grinning like a wolf? Women always recoiled at the sight of his teeth.

He exited the cab and waited stiffly for her to emerge. He noted her reluctance to take the hand he offered to help her down. When her feet touched the pavement he released her and headed up the steps to the lacquered doors that seemed to open magically before him. She hesitated another moment before lifting her skirts and following.

"Haskell, warm a guest room for the lady," he ordered the butler. She stood in the doorway as if she was considering bolting back out into the night. "And have Murielle do something with the stains on Miss Capshaw's dress." He glanced at her anxious form and lowered his voice. "And get her a sherry or some warm milk. She has 'nerves.'"

"Very good, sir," Haskell answered with a nod, and then turned to Norah. "Welcome, miss." He held out his hand for his master's coat.

"I'll have a fire in the study," Barclay declared before setting off to his customary retreat. With every step he felt the press of disappointment turning into annoyance.

This was what he got for attempting good deeds. Scorn. Distrust. Judgment. Well, let her think him a beast and an opportunist. She would escape his hospitality tomorrow, unscathed, and he would focus on preparing for a long stay at his grandfather's gloomy mansion. He had more pressing things to concern himself with than one female's hysteria over being pursued.

He turned up his reading lamp and dropped into his favorite wing chair in the book-lined study.

It had been a most eventful day . . . waking up in jail, learning his grandfather was dead and he was now guardian to a six-year-old earl, drinking himself pie-eyed with his fellow club members, and then rescuing a green-eyed fury for a second time. Small wonder his innards were in such turmoil.

He rubbed his irritated belly and pulled a book from the top of the stack on the side table by the chair, thinking to lose himself in the printed—*Ivanhoe*. He groaned. A damned romance. Two women madly in love with the same heroic knight . . . one of whom was destined for disappointment. He'd been obsessed with the story since his best friend, Rafe Townsend, had to compete with Sir Walter Scott's fictional hero for the hand of the woman he wanted to marry. He had sympathized with Rafe's dilemma of not measuring up against a hero who didn't—never would—exist in the real world. How did a man fight an ideal? For tall, elegant, handsome Rafe, "not measuring up" was an entirely new experience.

He, on the other hand . . . oversize, overmuscled, and overeager Barclay Howard . . . had never measured up to society's expectations. Now disappointment just rolled off his shoulders. Mostly. He tossed that volume onto the floor by the chair and reached for a different book.

But his thoughts cycled back.

What was it about the woman now occupying a bed in his house that made him want to help her even when she was angry and judgmental? Why had he ordered the cab to pause outside her building to make certain she was in and safe? What business was she of his?

Ridiculous questions.

Her face had been etched in his mind ever since she stabbed him with that damnable hatpin. Her burnished hair, her green eyes, her sweet features . . . there was something about her that kept invading his thoughts. He had seen a number of London beauties in the last few years—all turning a cold shoulder his way. But never in those fruitless introductions and distanced admirations had he been struck so potently by a woman's face and form.

Or was it something else—her vulnerability or determination in difficult circumstances—that captured him? He gave a huff. More likely, it was her height. When she squared her shoulders and stood erect, she came all the way up to his chin. He was more used to staring down at smart hats or the tops of ladyish coifs than looking women in the eye.

He pulled another book from the stack beside him.

Lady Audley's Secret.

He winced. A novel with a beautiful heroine of dubious origins and even more dubious deeds.

Just what he didn't need.

He tossed that aside, too, and settled for a travelogue on the beauties of the Scottish highlands and the oddities of the rugged Scots who inhabited them. It turned out to have a few good chuckles in it, too, regarding the dress, the manners, and the food preferences of the folk.

He shed his shoes and transferred to a horizontal position on the tufted leather sofa to continue reading. But his eyes grew heavy and the book drooped to his chest. The last thing he recalled as his mind wandered into beckoning darkness was the shock on Norah Capshaw's face when she stepped into his house and saw the handsome entry hall.

"This way, miss." The butler had showed Norah up the stairs and down a hallway, past what appeared to be bedchambers. Servants appeared out of nowhere, one with a canvas sling filled with wood to start a fire, one with a bed warmer to turn back the thick comforter on the four-poster bed and warm the sheets, and a third to bring hot water to the room for evening ablutions. They were clearly diligent and seemed respectful. Strangely, none of them seemed to find her presence there unusual.

"Excuse me," she said to the housemaid arranging water and toweling for her use. "Whose house is this?"

It shamed her to have to ask because she was clearly spending the night. But she lifted her chin and brazened it through.

"The master's," the woman said, looking puzzled. "Master Barclay. The Earl of Northrup's grandson. His mother was a Montgomery, who—"

"Tut-tut, Murielle—no call for gossip," the butler chastised her, then turned to Norah. "Would you care for some food, miss? A cold plate, perhaps? Some tea or warm milk? A sherry to ward off the chill?"

"No . . . nothing, thank you."

The butler nodded and motioned the others out of the room.

"Murielle will help you with your gown, miss." The butler backed toward the door, leaving her in the housemaid's care.

Norah eyed the bed, the fire now in full bloom in the

hearth, and the expectant housemaid. The idea of shedding her dress was intimidating.

"I'll undo you, shall I? I'll have ye right as rain come morning."

She felt unsettled about parting with her clothes in a strange man's house, but Murielle was one insistent creature. Orders were orders, she declared. Norah relented when the woman produced a dressing gown from a wardrobe—a man's dressing gown—for her to wear instead.

Murielle made quick work of removing her dress and offered to help with her stays and petticoats. Norah declined, wrapped herself in the voluminous robe, and watched Murielle whisk her only respectable garment out the door.

No key was evident for the lock, so the minute the maid left she pushed a small chest of drawers over to block the door. The washstand was next, though it sloshed water from the pitcher into the basin on the way. She was going to sleep in that dressing gown and her blessed clothes at the hearth, no matter how well-warmed that bed might be.

She pulled the shawl collar of the dressing gown tighter around her neck and went to the hearth to warm her icy hands and stockinged toes.

The Earl of Northrup. That explained a thing or two. She remembered the other girls at school talking of the old nobleman and his odd family. Scandals kept them out of polite society . . . there was an aging heir and an actress who gave him a son, and a beast of a man whose attentions terrified young debs.

Her eyes widened as she looked around the lovely guest room and recalled Barclay's wolfish grin in the cab. She had just met "the beast" and could see why he had such a reputation. His teeth were straight and even except for his canines, which were longer and gave his smile a feral cast. Combined with his raw muscularity and imposing stature, that wicked grin had given her goose bumps more than once.

She was exhausted but had never felt less like sleeping. What did he have planned for the night? And what could she do if what he planned truly was beastly?

The next morning found Norah sleeping soundly in the four-poster bed, swathed in a thick comforter and pristine cotton sheets. She hadn't bothered to take down her hair or do more than wash her face before transferring her aching bones from the hearth to the bed in the middle of the night. Now, something had awakened her, and she lay in bed for a moment, taking stock of her condition and regretting both her neglectful toilette and having worn her stays all night.

She gradually became aware of raps on the door and finally sat bolt upright. A woman's voice had said something that sounded like "breakfast." How long had the maid been trying to rouse her? Before she could wipe the sleep from her eyes and answer, the knocking stopped. She was starving and she wanted coffee badly enough to bound out of bed and rush to answer the summons. She pushed the furniture away from the door, but the hall outside was now empty. Her stomach growled in protest.

If she wanted sustenance, it appeared she would have to brave the unknown house in a borrowed dressing gown and pretend it was as normal as pie. She ran her hands over her mussed hair, squared her shoulders, and tightened the wrap of the robe, realizing that food would have to wait.

She had to find her missing dress first and then—properly clothed—she could locate some nourishment.

The dining room drapes were drawn back to admit sunshine despite his housekeeper's dire warnings about its effects on rugs and furnishings. The warmth and brilliance of sunshine was as necessary to Barclay as breathing, and this morning, as he sat perusing a copy of *The Times,* he felt more in need of the sun's energizing effects than usual.

Last night he had tossed and turned on the couch in his study before he awakened enough to make his way to his bed. There he lay sleepless and tense, thinking about his inescapable guardianship and his damnably attractive but ungrateful guest, who was sleeping soundly down the hall.

Of all the recent complications in his life, she was the most unexpected. The Fates had thrown Norah Capshaw into his path more than once and practically taunted him to involve himself in her plight. But she—like so many females before her—refused his company and carried her rejection even further, declining even his charitable aid. Still, he was attracted by her face and her determination to make her own way in a world that seemed set against her.

Now, as he perused *The Times* and sipped his coffee, he wondered what would become of her once she left his house that morning. Perhaps he could make an inquiry or two on her behalf through Anglesmith and his firm. If she was truthful about her education, they might be able to find her a position somewhere . . . governess . . . lady's secretary . . . tutor . . .

Movement near the arched doorway caught his attention and he found a frazzled-looking Norah Capshaw standing with her arms wrapped around her. It took a second for him to realize the oversize garment she wore was a man's dressing gown, though—shockingly—not *his*.

"Mr. Howard," Norah said, forcing the words to sound more emphatic than they felt. "I should like to have my dress back now, whatever condition it is in. Please tell me where I might find it."

"Your dress?" Her host sat forward in his chair, searching her suggestively rumpled appearance.

"That Murielle person took it last night and it hasn't been returned."

"Good Lord." He reached for the bell on the table and rang furiously. When the butler appeared he set the man to looking for Murielle and Norah's dress, then called for another place setting at the table. "Sit. You look ready to collapse. Did you not sleep well?"

She didn't move toward the chair he indicated.

"Well enough, considering the circumstances."

Upon a wave of her host's hand, a young footman hurried from the sideboard to lay out china and silver, then went back for a pot of coffee. Still, she stood apart, afraid to assume such service was meant for her.

"What circumstances? Were you cold or hungry? I gave orders that you be made comfortable."

"I was warm enough and the bed was adequate." A half-truth. It had been delightful . . . better than she had experienced in years. And the rich aroma of coffee at the table was making her dizzy. Despite her determination to maintain distance and decorum, she drifted a few inches forward to stare fixedly at the serving dishes on the sideboard. Her stomach growled so loudly she was sure he'd heard it. "However, I shan't feel comfortable until I am once again in my own clothes."

"*Sit.*" The power behind the word made clear that it was no longer a suggestion. He rose to nudge her to the place laid out at the table. She couldn't seem to resist. When she sank into the chair he held for her, he carried her plate to the sideboard and waved the footman away to fill it himself with ham, kippers, cottage potatoes, and buttery scones. He seized an egg, too, and planted the food before her before resuming his seat. Another flick of his hand had the footman pouring her coffee.

She grabbed the cup with two hands and buried her nose in it. The aroma and flavor burst on her senses with the brilliance of a noonday sun. She drank the entire cup in three huge and desperate gulps, then held it up for the footman to refill. A moment later she caught Barclay staring at her and lowered the cup, embarrassed by her desperation. How long had it been since she had a full meal? Forcing herself not to quail before him, she unfolded her napkin, picked up a fork, and closed her eyes as she inhaled the aromas of the food.

A whimper escaped her with her first bite, and a louder one with the second. She opened her eyes fully and found her host's chair at the head of the table empty. Glancing this way and that, she felt relief at no longer being under scrutiny and began to eat with an eagerness that would have shamed her at any other time.

Lord in Heaven, the food was good! No, *great*! Better than any she had eaten in her entire life. Barclay Howard had heaped her plate and disappeared so she could stuff herself in private. Perhaps the beast had a few sensitivities after all.

When there were only a few bites remaining, she slowed, sat straighter, and heaved a huge sigh. She was stuffed to the gills.

Please God, don't make me pay for eating so greedily.

The footman had left the silver coffee server on the table within reach and she poured herself another cup. Sitting back, she sipped that delicious brew and, a moment later, was startled by Barclay Howard's reappearance at the head of the table.

"Still hungry?" he asked. "There may be a few crumbs left."

She flushed, wondering how much of her gluttony he had seen.

"I am fine, thank you."

There was a hint of amusement to his expression as he looked her over, and she was somehow prodded to explain.

"With all the turmoil of yesterday, I didn't have time for meals. I was a bit hungrier than I realized."

"Glad to provide—" He halted and looked past her to the archway into the dining room. "What the devil are you doing here?"

A tall, fair-haired man strode to the dining table and stopped halfway between Norah and her rescuer. A tall, fair, *handsome* man . . . impeccably clothed and clearly at ease with barging in on Barclay Howard's breakfast.

"I came to check on you, having just heard about . . ." The man's voice was cultured and melodious. He halted, looking at her with widening eyes. "Am I intruding?" He looked at Barclay Howard in surprise. "Perhaps I should come back later with my condolences. I had no idea you had company."

"She is not company," Barclay Howard said, sitting straighter, unsettled by his visitor's presence. "She is . . . a . . . a . . ."

"Tutor," she supplied, trying to look generally in the man's direction without meeting his searching gaze.

"Miss Capshaw," Barclay Howard said, "ran afoul of some ruffians last night. I offered her your old room for the night."

"Which explains, in part, why she is in *my* dressing gown," the man said with a grin of bemusement. "I wondered where that was."

Norah sucked a breath and shrank back, looking down at the garment in horror. It wasn't even Barclay Howard's?

"Rafe Townsend, Barr's closest friend," the man introduced himself before Barclay Howard could do so and extended his hand for hers.

She found herself placing her hand in his and reddening slightly as he pressed it and gave a gentlemanly bow before releasing it.

"I should . . . um . . ." she said, before recalling a tenet of her ladyish education: *It is never the proper thing to make excuses.* "My dress was . . ."

"Soiled in the tussle," Barclay Howard supplied when she faltered. "Murielle was supposed to have cleaned and returned it. Don't know where she's gotten to."

"Odd. I have always known Murielle to be reliable," Rafe said, then turned to Norah to explain. "Before my marriage I stayed here routinely and made myself quite at home—to the point of leaving part of my wardrobe here. Barr was my landlord as well as my best friend."

Norah nodded, still scarlet from embarrassment. Townsend must have sensed her lingering discomfort for he turned to his friend.

"I came to see how you are, considering the loss of your grandfather."

His grandfather had died? Norah was pricked to realize that there was more to Barclay Howard than a hulking frame, a boatload of male privilege, and even the odd chivalrous impulse. He had *family.* She watched as a number of emotions seemed to mingle in his frown.

"The old cod turned ninety last year. It was his time," Barclay said irritably. "But he couldn't die without one last gouge at me."

"Oh?" Townsend looked alarmed.

"He's made me guardian of the new earl."

Townsend's jaw dropped. "The new earl? Who the devil is it? The successor—your uncle—didn't he die? Did he leave an heir?"

"He did. A boy I am called to Northrup Hall to take charge of."

Townsend stared at Barclay for a long moment, absorbing that. "You're now the guardian of a boy named the earl of your family house?" He gave a low whistle. "There's an unexpected turn of events. What will you do with him? Send him to school? Harrow is cracking good, and I imagine they'd find room for a young earl no matter what their enrollment."

"He's six years old. Still under nanny's care. Don't know if he's been tutored or prepared for much of anything. That is the first task . . . assessing the boy and getting him up to snuff for a school."

"So you'll have to find a . . . tutor," Townsend said, realization dawning. He turned to look at Norah with a mischievous light in his eyes. "How fortunate you happened to come upon one being attacked by ruffians last night."

Norah realized Barclay was now staring at her, too, and pulled the lapels of the dressing gown tight about her neck.

"Miss Capshaw tutors at an *adult* school." Barclay looked uncomfortable. "Not one for children."

"So, this"—Rafe gestured to the breakfast table—"is not an employment interview?"

The possibility struck Norah as ridiculous, then awkward, then downright devious—all within the space of a moment. Was that what her rescuer intended? Maneuvering her into becoming a child's tutor? If indeed there was a child, could that be his intention?

Barclay Howard was saved the necessity of a response when Murielle bustled into the room with Norah's dress draped over her arms.

"So sorry, miss." She actually curtsied. "One of the stains wouldn't come out wi' my usual fuller. Had to run across the square for help."

Norah rose immediately, excused herself, and headed for her room to change into her dress. Murielle followed with a stream of apologies and promises to "lace her up good and tight" and help with her hair. The maid made no remark on the furniture out of place just inside the door.

"So, Mr. Howard is preparing to leave for his grandfather's estate to take care of a child?" Norah asked as she was laced into her dress.

"Aye, miss. Wretched duty it is, too. Th' old earl were a strange one. Always threatenin' some'at or other." Her voice lowered to a gossipy whisper. "Threatened to cut 'im off if he don't take care o' the boy. Not that he's penniless, Master Barclay. His ma was a Montgomery . . . left 'im this house and a purse."

"A Montgomery." Norah straightened, remembering

that. It was a powerful lineage. And not one she would have expected of such a—

"Aye. Though they don' claim 'im. A throwback, they say." The maid shrugged. "Ain't fair, if ye ask me. He ain't wot he looks to be. Never raises a fist to nobody. But 'e's got a look what can scare the piss outta grown men."

Norah bit her lip. She knew that look and hoped never to see it again.

Five

"She is easy enough on the eyes," Rafe said as he followed Barclay into the entry hall later and waited for Haskell to bring his hat and gloves.

"What were you thinking, bringing up the tutor business?" Barclay said irritably. "She already thinks I have evil designs on her."

"You? Evil designs on a woman? Perish the thought." Rafe grinned. "You're a gentleman through and through."

Barclay gave a growl of irritation. "Not that anyone notices. Anyway, she's unmarried. What does she know about children?"

"Of course she knows about children—she's a woman. You've seen Lauren with our Garrett. Picked right up with him the day he was born and has been an authority ever since."

"That's your wife. She's a living, breathing wonder." The first woman he'd met who didn't run screaming from his wolfish grin.

"Yes." Rafe looked entirely too pleased to agree. "She is."

"What would make a woman like Miss Capshaw agree

to being dragged north to a gloomy old mansion?" Barclay's broad shoulders rounded as he jammed his hands into his trouser pockets.

Rafe chuckled. "That may depend on how nicely the proposition is put before her. Where does she tutor now?"

"She didn't . . . say." Barclay didn't want to reveal that Norah Capshaw was currently unemployed, or that he found her entirely too appealing. The longer Rafe stayed, the more likely both of those things would come out. "Don't you have someplace to be?"

"I can see you're taking this change of fortune remarkably well. Condolences and good luck, my friend. You know . . . should you need help, just send word and I will be there." Rafe clapped him on the arm, accepted his hat and gloves from Haskell, and headed out the front door.

Barclay made straight for his study and, once there, stood pondering the possibility that Fate had tossed the perfect answer to his problem into his lap. A tutor for the boy. A woman who was literate and determined . . . not easily intimidated . . . who needed work and likely had the knowledge and skills to solve his most pressing problem. Perhaps he was looking at it the wrong way. She had needs . . . he had needs. Fate seemed determined to put the two together.

He paced a few minutes, thinking.

He would simply be hiring a tutor to accompany him to his grandfather's estate to meet the boy earl and prepare him for a proper education. What could be simpler? Except . . . the tutor was lovely and desirable and distracted him mightily.

Yes, well, he might think such things about her, but clearly she had assessed him as well, and it wasn't too difficult to deduce from her warnings of last night what she thought of him.

If he offered her the position—*if*—this would have to be a strictly employer-employee relationship. Firstly, he had a duty to determine whether or not she was truthful about her education and qualifications as a tutor.

Bolstered by such reasoning, he headed to his book-shelves and perused them for a few minutes before selecting a couple of slender volumes and then a much thicker one.

Half an hour later, Norah descended the stairs in a restored dinner dress, with her hair tidied and her demeanor much improved. He watched with fascination as she entered the drawing room. The sway of her skirts and the easy grace of her posture stirred interests that he stuffed back into his deepest recesses, determined not to let them influence his decision.

"Where is Mr. Townsend?" She looked around the grand room, and her eyes widened as her gaze lingered on the piano.

"He had business. After wheedling his usual coffee, he departed." Barclay went to stand before the hearth with his hands clasped behind his back. "I have been thinking. Seeing as you have no employment just now, I may offer you the position of tutor to my ward . . . providing you prove qualified." He picked up one of the thin volumes and handed it to her.

"Go, stand by the window and read from this volume . . . first in French and then translated into English."

She studied the command, then went to the window and opened the small volume to the title page. The first passage wasn't difficult. She read fluently in French and translated easily into English. Voltaire had a way with words in both languages. He handed her a second book, containing Latin text. It was harder to read aloud, but she relaxed visibly as she read and then translated part of one of Cicero's discourses.

The larger volume he handed her was easier, being printed in English. It was a series of fables and folktales with moral lessons. He had her read several and divine the lesson to be learned from each story. She proved to be as good as her word . . . fluent in at least two other languages, well read, and with reasonable deductive powers.

When she finished she stood in the sunlight streaming through the window, clutching the volume to her, and waiting to hear his verdict.

Truthfully, he had lost the purpose of her performance somewhere between "The Fox and the Grapes." He'd had her stand before the window because he wanted to see the way her hair became a halo of strawberry-kissed gold in the sunlight. It tantalized his senses, and her voice resonated in his head and trickled down his spine like feathery fingers. He stared at her for a moment, struggling with his impulses, trying to regain mental footing.

Clearing his throat, he looked away only to have his gaze land on the piano. "Now, please play." He gestured to the keyboard. "Knowledge of the arts is a mark of a gentleman. Even a young pip of a gentleman."

He took a seat on the settee facing the grand piano, and when she asked what he wished to hear, he waved the question aside.

"Whatever you will."

She raised the cover and propped it up, took a seat at the keyboard, and after a moment began to play. A sonata . . . one he didn't recognize, but it was lilting and produced a dreamy aura about her as she closed her eyes and concentrated on infusing the music with feeling.

"Another," he commanded when she finished the piece. The second was a more spirited composition that required an energetic approach to the instrument. It made Barclay itch to move.

He bolted up to pace the room behind her, his heartbeat keeping time with the music. He was drawn to watch the bend of her waist and the movement of her shoulders as she played . . . the nape of her neck, the tiny curls that had escaped her upswept hair, and the energy of her hands as they commanded the keys. The lush nuances of her performance crowded and then overloaded his senses. He stepped back and smacked into the window seat, where he teetered, feeling oddly weak in the knees.

Alarm shot through him as he realized where these sensations were leading. The tightness in his gut and tension settling in his loins warned of a kind of attraction that would only complicate his life at best and lead to crushing disappointment at worst. He was not good with women, and if he were to execute his plans for his ward, he needed to be clearheaded and determined. In point of fact . . . he would need her to dislike him as much as he was coming to like her.

The final notes faded away and Norah Capshaw looked up and around the drawing room, puzzled to find herself alone. That is, until she heard him clear his throat and turned to find her rescuer standing with his legs spread and arms crossed—wearing a frown that could only presage a negative judgment.

"Do I not meet your standard?" she said, bracing internally.

"You'll do," he answered, studying her as if trying to read the future in her very bones.

To defend herself from such scrutiny, she scrambled to think of something that would divert his—*money!*—a most potent distraction.

"If I were to accept, what would be my wages?"

"Your living and seventy pounds per annum, paid monthly."

Her breath caught at the sum. She had been prepared to bargain. "And how long do you expect this tutelage to take? A year? More?"

"It will take as long as it takes," he growled. "I have no way of knowing, because I have never laid eyes on the boy." After a moment he added: "But I can guarantee you at least one year. If he is properly prepared, he may go to a good school at seven and a half or eight, I am told."

"So he is six years old now?"

"Yes. And has a nanny. You will not be troubled with dressing and feeding him and minding his schedule."

"A reasonable offer, Mr. Howard. I should like to think on it."

"I need your answer now," he said irritably. "There are arrangements to be made and we must leave in three days."

"We?" She straightened back one telling inch.

"It will be more economical for us to travel together." He glowered. "Not to mention, you will be safer from unwanted attention."

She took a deep breath and paced a few steps away.

What choice did she have? A lucrative position she was certainly qualified to fill. And she had no reason to stay in

London—not with a strange man stalking her. Why would she turn down such an offer?

Then she turned back and found him standing like a colossus, looking fierce and in control. That was the reason . . . that determined, overpowering man who gave her shivers and made her want to touch him to see if he were living flesh or chiseled stone. And yet those piercing eyes, that ironic smile, the unexpected hints of gallantry . . . made her want to puzzle out what kind of man lay inside that formidable exterior.

It was precisely such thoughts that made her hesitate.

But she had to face facts. She desperately needed an income.

"Yes," she said, hoping she wasn't making the worst mistake of her life. "I accept the position."

He swayed closer and stood just before her, searching her with an intensity that stopped her breath. She could feel his warmth and smell a faint bit of sandalwood and soap about him. She lifted her chin and found her gaze sliding into those autumn-forest eyes. A wave of anxiety washed over her. What was she getting herself in to?

He relaxed slightly. "Then we should collect your things and have you visit Hatchards for a selection of books and supplies. You'll stay here for the time being. If you need to take care of other affairs before we leave, you will have the use of my carriage."

"I need only to collect my things from Dallywell Street."

He looked thoughtful, then stern. "I'll accompany you. The Scotsman knows where you live."

"I don't—" She halted, realizing that her protests were not only futile, they were ill-advised. What if the man who followed her was still watching her old lodging? She would be foolish to turn down whatever protection Barclay Howard's intimidating presence might provide.

"I am grateful for the offer of your carriage and your accompaniment. I shall do my best to see that the little earl is well prepared for an education. What is his name, by the way?"

He looked surprised by the question and a bit annoyed as he headed for the hall.

"I have no idea. It's probably in the papers the lawyer brought."

Dallywell Street was buzzing with foot traffic, vendors' carts, and wagons making deliveries to shops down the way from Norah's lodgings. There was just enough room for Barclay's stylish carriage to weave between the agents of commerce and travelers, both mounted and afoot. But when they reached number 42, the place was quiet and seemed almost deserted.

"You needn't come up," she said, adopting his air of reserve.

"But I will," he answered shortly and exited the carriage.

Norah felt his gaze on her, assessing her anew in light of her modest . . . meager . . . lodgings, as she led the way to the third floor. She was apprehensive as they approached Goldie's door, but was surprised to find it not only unlocked, but also slightly ajar. She called to her friend as she nudged the door further open. There was no response and a moment later she understood why. The room was a jumble of overturned furnishings, scattered dishes, tumbled baggage, and clothes strewn thither and yon.

Her clothes. Her baggage. Her belongings.

She stood just inside the entrance, jaw drooping and eyes wide. Barclay Howard nudged her forward as he slid around her to investigate.

"What happened?" Norah put her hands to her throat as she scanned for signs of Goldie. A moment later her shock thawed enough for her to lurch forward, searching the chaos for her friend. "She's not here. Goldie . . . who took me in when I lost . . ." She halted, staring at her open trunk and boxes . . . her papers, books, and sheet music were scattered about.

"Someone's been searching for something," he said, his deep voice carrying an undercurrent of anger. "It's not hard to guess who."

She stooped to gather up some of her garments and then stood up, blood draining from her face. "He forced his way in and rifled through my belongings. What for? What could I possibly have that he would want?"

"Jewelry?" he suggested, stooping to pick up her small leather jewelry case and place in it some items strewn on the floor. "Though if he left this"—he held up a strand of pearls on one finger—"I doubt it."

She grabbed the necklace and pressed it protectively to her heart.

"It was my mother's. It's the only thing I have of her."

He set the little box on the nearby table and turned to the papers strewn nearby. He squatted to collect a stack and then paused, looking at one handwritten page.

"A letter . . . from a 'Gladstone Rivers.'"

He looked up with a scowl, and she paused, holding the necklace and an armful of clothing. She felt sullied, knowing that her pursuer had pawed through and examined her most personal possessions. Even worse, Barclay Howard was seeing all of her worldly possessions discarded as though they were worthless, even her beloved mother's pearls. She reddened at having to explain her connection further.

"He was my guardian," she said, depositing the garments she had collected into the open trunk and snatching the papers from him. "The lawyer my father appointed to look after me before he died."

"A lawyer for a guardian?" he said, scowling.

"He was a good man. And a faithful guardian." The lump forming in her throat as she gazed at Mr. Rivers's letter made it difficult to speak. Fighting the tears welling in her eyes, she turned away to collect herself. "He even . . . wrote to me at school."

Barclay rose, watching her rigid posture and frowning.

"Perhaps your father entrusted him with something valuable?"

"If so, surely Mr. Rivers would have conveyed it to me when I reached my majority."

"How long ago was that?" he asked, knowing it was impolite, but curious about how old she was. For the moment he refused to consider just how personal an interest the question betrayed.

She turned, and he could see her cheeks glistening and her lashes wet. Something in his middle slid lower, creating an emptiness in his core.

"I cannot see how that is pertinent to my employment, Mr. Howard." She raised her chin.

"It is not," he agreed gruffly. "But it may be pertinent to the fact that you are being stalked."

She blinked, absorbing that for a moment before turning away to retrieve garments strewn on the floor near the trunk. As she knelt to refold some petticoats and place them in her trunk, he picked up several items to hand to her, one of which quickly caught his eye. When she looked up he was dangling a pair of lace-rimmed drawers from one finger.

She gasped and snatched it from him.

"Perhaps you should wait in the carriage."

"I will not." His voice dropped and developed an edge. "Every time you are left alone, something bad happens." He folded his arms and broadened his stance.

"It is broad daylight."

"Which didn't keep the Scot from pursuing you before."

She straightened with a fierce look that surprised him.

"I have more hatpins in my trunk."

The protective way she cradled her garments in her arms gave him pause. Was she threatening him with stabbing again? Something beneath her determination struck him as more desperate than dangerous. He suffered a flash of insight: she wanted—needed—time to right her belongings without his scrutiny.

Curse him—his lack of experience with females was showing. He should have remembered that women had pride of their own.

"Very well." He went to the door, but stopped in the opening with his back to her. "But I won't go any farther." After a moment he muttered a face-saving excuse for not leaving her alone. "You'll need help carrying your things down the stairs."

By the time her trunk was stowed at the rear of the carriage and her few boxes were stacked on the front-facing seat beside him, Barclay had made a decision that he was certain she wouldn't like.

"Where are we going now? Hatchards?" she asked as she settled on the rear-facing seat, a respectable distance from him.

"We have another stop to make first. My attorney's office."

She frowned, but remained silent as they reached a majestic old building that stretched four stories above ground level. He excused himself, entered, and minutes later, returned with a slip of paper bearing an address.

"You should know," he said as the carriage set off into traffic, "we're going to your old guardian's office."

"My—Mr. Rivers? Whatever for?"

"Lawyers keep things. Whatever old Rivers kept may shed light on what the Scot wants from you."

Her mouth worked, but no sound came out as she digested that and the reasoning behind it.

He remembered not to show his teeth as he smiled.

"Thank me later."

Six

Two leather folios of papers, including her father's last will and testament and a modest-sized pasteboard box, were the product of their visit to Mr. Rivers's old firm. From his partners' attitude, it was clear they hadn't approved of Rivers becoming so involved with a client of such limited resources. After requiring Norah to sign a release, they produced the documents and the dusty box from their records room.

Norah was offered no assistance in reviewing the documents, nor space to open and examine the contents of the box. Clearly, the solicitors and clerks were eager to dispense with the interruption and return to their busy schedules. Barclay's scowl and forbidding countenance may have helped move things along. There were occasional advantages, he had long since learned, to having a predatory appearance.

Their next stop was Hatchards, the legendary bookshop that carried all manner of educational materials, including maps. He told Miss Capshaw to choose whatever she thought would be helpful in tutoring the boy and to choose a book or two for herself to pass the time while traveling.

When he suggested that she stopped dead at the door

to the shop, trying to hide her surprise. He reddened under his collar and explained.

"I prefer riding in quiet on a train."

He saw irritation rising in her eyes and realized he might have gone a step too far in implying he wanted no conversation from her on the trip. He opened the door and waved her inside the shop. Well, it was true. It also seemed to put more distance between them, which wasn't a bad thing.

In retaliation, Norah chose a number of books for her personal enjoyment, as well as several sketchbooks, pencils, and charcoal. If he warned her to stay silent, he would learn that silence suited her as well. She was quite capable of occupying herself with productive pastimes. It was almost a disappointment that he nodded at her considerable pile of selections, added it to his own, and paid for both without complaint.

"Reading," he explained in the carriage later, "has become something of a passion. I regret not coming to appreciate it earlier in life."

"What prompted your discovery of the joy of books?"

"*Ivanhoe*," he answered. "The book belonged to my friend Rafe." He rubbed his muscular thigh, drawing her attention there.

She had to jerk her gaze away.

"He was betrothed to Lauren Alcott at that time, and she was a devotee of Sir Walter Scott. She gave him the book, which he refused to read. I picked it up and read it myself. I was immediately engaged and read it more than once. When it was over I felt . . . bereft . . . and went looking for another printed adventure. I discovered . . ."

He halted, sensing her scrutiny, and looked out the carriage window.

She finished it for him.

"A whole world of adventure, amusement, and enlightenment?"

He cut her a glance that was hard to interpret.

But she nodded at him, recalling his admission from the previous night. He had confessed to having read "too many books," implying that they had an impact on him. She looked out the other side of the carriage, concerned that she found his story more appealing than was prudent. She needed to stop wondering about him and focus on the coming challenge of tutoring and shaping a young boy's mind. The less interaction between her and her enigmatic employer, the better.

Murielle was assigned to assist Norah in settling into her room and restoring her wardrobe to a proper condition. The woman chattered like a magpie about the rugged north country and the beauty of York Cathedral, called the Minster. That was how Norah learned the maid would be accompanying Norah and their employer to the old earl's estate . . . to assist Norah and coordinate with the Northrup House staff. The girl asked too many questions that Norah answered without thinking while she was busy examining the contents of the box she had acquired.

The contents of her meager inheritance began with tintypes of her parents, one dated not long after their marriage and move to London. Further down were portraits of them individually and of a plump baby dressed in a lacy bonnet. That very bonnet, which had yellowed with time, was found lower in the box. Just beneath that was a small velvet box containing a pair of wedding rings and a gold locket and chain that she had seen around her mother's neck in one of the pictures.

Her mother's locket. Her parents' wedding rings. She

could hardly see for the tears filling her eyes and threatening to spill down her cheeks. Such lovely faces, such promising lives—cut short by illness and misfortune. They would never know the love and longing she felt for them. But at least now she had something to remember them by and to see what she had lost.

She dismissed Murielle before the sobs escaped. It felt both wrenching and a relief to vent the emotions that had been piling up for months. She collapsed on the bed and sank her face into the down pillows to muffle the sounds and gave herself permission to cry her heart out . . . releasing all the tension and grief she had stored inside.

When her tears were exhausted she turned onto her back and stared up at the ornate ceiling. Whatever her life might have been, it was on a different course now . . . one determined by Fate and her own desperate choices. Accompanying Barclay Howard to his family estate to tutor his ward could either prove a disaster or a mercifully opportune new start. She thought of his grim expression as he talked about the duty set before him and realized that despite his sex and apparent affluence, he had no more choice in his fate than she did in hers. He dreaded this duty so much that he hadn't bothered to learn his young ward's name.

She took several deep breaths and made herself think of the possible benefits to be derived from her service at the Northrup estate . . . a good reference, a chance to make fresh connections, savings that would allow her to begin anew wherever she decided to go. She would have to find the good in her situation and cling to it. She would have to make it a good start to the rest of her life.

* * *

Barclay ordered dinner to wait for her, only to learn that she had asked for a tray in her room that evening. He imagined her relief at being spared his company and was first embarrassed, then annoyed, and finally relieved to be spared the tension he felt in her presence.

Don't stare. Don't ask personal questions. Don't make sudden movements. Don't smile too broadly. Watch your damned language. Don't stand too close. Having her around was like being stuck at a society ball where his manners were scrutinized by one and all . . . without the relief that would come when the evening was over. He would be in her company for the next who-knew-how-long. What the devil had he gotten himself in to?

As he exited his study late that night, he heard strains of music coming from the salon. He arrived at the doorway preparing for what he would find. Norah Capshaw was playing his piano in a mostly darkened chamber. A pair of beeswax candles were perched above the keyboard, lighting her in a soft glow that matched the dulcet tones she produced.

He folded his arms and leaned a shoulder against the arched doorway. Every gentle flight of melody wrapped itself around his senses and brought a welcome relaxation to his muscled frame. For the moment he allowed himself to drift with the music, wondering if it was her skill that captured him or just his own damnable longings. What was it about her that constantly brought him to the edge of his experience?

In all his dealings with the fair sex, even those rare times when they were paid to provide him companionship, there was an underlying wariness in women's attentions. He recognized it and understood it to some degree.

Awareness of his size and appearance had been drummed

into him from childhood. He was big, intimidating, and had a voice that sometimes rolled like thunder. He knew he was described as a bear of a man and had always worked to restrain his movements and gentle his manner. In his rare intimate contact with females he was careful to rein in his response and allow himself only certain aspects of release.

From her reactions, Norah Capshaw undoubtedly saw him much as the rest of society did. But her determination—or desperation—forced her to meet his formidable nature with her own inner strength. He smiled wanly to himself. That seemed to be his purpose on earth—drawing others' strength to the fore. If that was so, he would have to accept that he was a whetstone against which others honed themselves.

He didn't realize that in his ruminations he had moved forward into the darkened salon, toward the music and the woman who gave it life. He found himself standing behind her, drinking in the melody that invaded his blood and set everything in his chest aching. Her scent, her warmth filled his head, and he clenched his hands to keep from touching her.

Something alerted her to his presence, and when the piece ended she sat for a moment in silent expectation. When he didn't move or speak she rose and turned to face him. The candle glow made her hair into that halo of rosy gold that fascinated him. His mouth dried. He couldn't speak.

She stepped to the side of the piano bench and he matched her movement, closing the distance between them to mere inches. She watched him, not shrinking but clearly braced to defend herself from whatever he intended. He couldn't help a rueful smile.

For a long moment he stood looking at her face and into her clear eyes. Wellborn ladies never allowed him such proximity. He couldn't recall being this familiar with a female ever. But just now, all he could think of was touching that stray wisp of hair at her temple. When he raised a hand to tuck it back he saw her stiffen. His smile broadened as his fingertips brushed her cheek. She felt soft and warm, just as he expected.

Something in her changed and she stepped back, her expression tightening.

He felt a door had just slammed shut between them and told himself it was for the best. What the hell was he doing approaching her, touching her? Burlap was never meant to pair with silk. He swallowed hard and stepped back to allow her to escape.

"Go to bed, Miss Capshaw."

They traveled first-class on the train north, in a compartment large enough to allow Barclay to stretch out his legs and still avoid contact with Norah and the inquisitive Murielle. It had only taken a scowl from him to silence the maid's stream of chatter. Apparently she had come to London from Northumberland and was excited to be traveling back to her home country in such privileged accommodations.

Norah understood the girl's excitement; her own stomach was full of butterflies. She had dressed in her best—her only—traveling clothes and wore a simple hat that would provide warmth if the compartment wasn't sufficiently heated. Her gloves showed signs of wear, so she made certain to keep her hands in her lap or around a book.

Still, she glimpsed her employer studying her above the

edge of his book and was made nervous by his scrutiny. When Murielle whispered that she should find the necessary and exited the compartment, Barclay Howard lowered his book and gazed intently at his new employee.

"Interesting locket," he said, staring at her chest.

Her mother's locket lay nestled between the lapels of her jacket. She picked it up and studied it, intending to tuck it away again. But Barclay Howard sat forward to examine it and she felt the urge to explain.

"It was in the box I received from Mr. Rivers's office. My mother wore it in the pictures that were in the box."

He slid to the edge of his seat.

"So, the old fellow did have something in safekeeping." He reached for the locket and she stiffened, but allowed him to take the large, golden oval on his fingertips. "Fine work," he said, turning it over and spotting the delicate hinge on one side. "What is inside?"

"I wasn't able to open it," she said.

"I have a way with locks. Take it off."

"I don't know . . . it's old and may be fragile."

Her reluctance yielded to his intimidating expectation, and she worked the clasp at the nape of her neck. She was taut with anxiety as she handed it to him. He studied it for a moment, then pressed the edge gingerly with his fingertips. The latch didn't yield right away, but he was persistent, and just as she was about to protest that it could break, it opened in his hands.

The rim around what appeared to be a portrait inside popped up, and the picture it held curled up with it. Startled, he quickly turned the locket to keep the contents from falling. In alarm, she snatched it from his hands to see what had happened and found a miniature picture of her parents together, smiling.

"Just press that circle down," he said, leaning to peer at the raised rim and picture. "Gold is soft. It will obey."

When she hesitated he reached in to press her fingers over the frame and squeeze it in place. As he predicted, it stayed to hold the picture. She sat gazing at the image, but also at the hand cupping hers. The contact brought a surge of warmth in her core that surprised her. She scooted back on the seat, staring at the image, determined not to look at her employer. This was a gift from the Graces . . . her parents' legacy . . . a touching reminder that she was born of love and determination.

Barclay sat back on his seat, watching her react to a picture of what was likely her parents. A dozen emotions crossed her lovely features, and he wanted to ask her about them, about the beautiful locket, about her memories of her parents. But a second later he looked down at his leg and saw a piece of something yellow on his trousers. He might have brushed it off, but something about the texture made him pick it up to examine.

It was golden, flat but thicker than paper, and a bit rough on the surface . . . it looked like a flake of raw gold. Where on earth had that come from? A second later he looked at the locket Norah was replacing around her neck. Had this been in the locket? If so, it had fallen onto his knee when he forced it open. It had to have come from there, he realized. Flakes of gold didn't just drop out of the air.

"What is this?" he asked, holding up the piece on the tip of his finger.

She frowned at first, then sat forward and shook her head.

"It looks to me like a flake of gold ore." He drew it back to examine from different angles. "It fell out of your locket onto my knee."

"Really?" She transferred across the footwell to the bench beside him and scowled at the patch of yellow. "That came from my locket?"

"It must have. Gold ore doesn't just appear out of thin air."

"Are you certain that's what it is?"

"I studied some geology at university. You never know when you might need to know what metallic ore looks like. This looks like unrefined gold." He held it closer to her. "See the texture?"

She pulled his hand closer and viewed the piece from several angles before looking up at him. He saw curiosity and wonder in the blue-green pools of her eyes. He could have sworn her eyes were green as grass before. Where did that blue come from? A reflection from her dress?

"If it is gold, why would it be in my mother's locket?"

He shrugged. "A keepsake? Something to recall an adventure? Something to hope for?"

"I wonder if my father knew it was there," she said, holding out her hand. He dropped it into her palm, where she stroked it with a finger. "What should I do with it?"

"Put it back in the locket. Keep it there until . . ."

She picked up the locket and tried repeatedly to open it.

He took it from her and applied his thumbnails along the latch. It popped open, and he held it out for her to deposit the piece of ore.

"It seems I may have to call you every time I want this locket opened," she said, closing the piece and dropping it back between her jacket lapels. When she looked up he was leaning closer to her, no longer watching the locket. Her lips and cheeks were flushed and her eyes sparkled in a way that caused a hitch in his breathing.

"Norah," he said, his voice low and full of an urgency he didn't want to explain, even to himself. "I think—"

The door to the compartment opened with a clunk and banged against the seat near Norah. She started and he lurched back, feeling both annoyed and relieved that Murielle chose that moment to return. It kept him from saying something personal and foolish. But the worldly maid raised an eyebrow as she bumped into Norah while hurrying to her seat.

He fumbled with the book he'd been reading and finally located the ribbon that marked where he had left off. He cleared his throat and flicked a glance at Norah over the top of his book.

"You may want to go over the documents we retrieved from the lawyers' offices . . . see if there is any reference to your discovery."

"I shall," was her only reply as she buried her nose in her book.

It was Murielle's turn to clear her throat.

Northrup House was a sprawling stone mansion nestled in a rolling, autumn-kissed countryside. Great old English oaks with leaves now red and umber dotted the landscape, and stables and a number of stone outbuildings lay at the rear. The long windows of the house's front faced a broad gravel court that led to main doors that were large enough to accommodate a king's entourage.

But the closer they came in the hire carriage, the clearer it became that the grand old house had not been kept in a very grand manner. The weedy front garden hadn't been trimmed in at least a year and the lane approaching the main entry was full of ruts and holes that probably hadn't been filled in several seasons. Luckily, the weather had been dry of late or they would be axle deep in mud. Still, the carriage pitched this way and that, causing Barclay and the others to grip the sides and grit their teeth.

When they reached the front entry no one—not butler nor footmen nor a single household staff member—came out to greet them. That negligence darkened Barclay's mood, raising memories of slights and indignities he had suffered while growing up in his grandfather's uncharitable sway. He burst from the carriage the moment it stopped, handed Norah and Murielle down, and then headed for the doors with a stony set to his face. Norah winced at the sight and Murielle shrank behind her, muttering what might have been a prayer.

Inside the grand entry hall, chaos reigned. No one seemed to pay attention to the front doors being thrown open.

Barclay stopped dead at the sight of servants gathered around a form lying senseless on the floor. He strode for the group, causing them to part in surprise to admit him.

"What the devil is going on?" he demanded as he recognized the woman on the floor. "Mrs. Heybert?" The graying housekeeper roused at the sound of her name and shook her head, trying unsuccessfully to rise or even make her eyes focus properly. She sank back to the floor with a sigh.

"S-s-sorry, sir. Don't mean t-to-o—" And she was unconscious again.

"What happened?" he demanded as he knelt beside her to assess her condition. Murielle squeezed into the group and fished in her traveling bag for some smelling salts. Barclay lifted the housekeeper enough for Murielle's potion to do its work, then gathered the woman in his arms and carried her into the grand salon. The cavernous room was cool, dim, and a bit musty. It was an atmosphere that brought back unpleasant memories, so he ordered the drapes thrown back and the windows opened to admit fresh air. He placed her on a settee and again demanded to know what had happened.

One of the more intrepid parlormaids answered. "It were the little master . . . him an' his tricks. Slipped a slimy thing in her pocket, 'e did. It jumped up on her an' the shock made 'er faint."

"The little master?" Barclay frowned. "My grandfather's heir?"

"He's . . . a . . ." Mrs. Heybert tried to explain, but halted with her hand to her head.

"Bloody pill, 'e is," one of the older house women muttered. "Alwus playin' tricks . . . scarin' the life outta somebody."

Barclay turned to the woman, surprised to recognize her as a servant who had been there during his youth. "Cosey, yes?" She nodded and stepped back, looking like she regretted speaking. "Where is this 'little master'? I would see him straightaway."

She scowled. "'E run off soon as she hit the floor. 'E alwus runs off. Laughs and runs off."

Samuel, the butler, arrived with a bottle of smelling salts—too late to revive the housekeeper, but in time to chide the maid.

"Cosey, see to your duties." He scowled at the group. "All of you, return to your work." As they dispersed, he turned to Barclay with a bow.

"Master Barclay. I must apologize for the turmoil. I meant to turn out the staff and greet you properly, but at the last minute—"

"Where is he?" Barclay demanded, eyes narrowing as he towered over the graying head of the butler. There was no doubt about who was meant.

"Up a tree somewhere, I should imagine," Samuel answered with a scowl. "He takes to climbing trees whenever he has—"

"There's a thousand trees out there." Barclay gestured toward the gaping front doors. "Which ones does he favor?"

Samuel swallowed, facing the reined anger in Barclay's imposing presence. "Likely those to the east. They're old and some have lower branches."

Barclay jerked a nod. "See Mrs. Heybert to her quarters. Then have the luggage brought in and—if you haven't already—freshen some rooms." He turned toward the grand entry hall and found Norah Capshaw standing just outside the salon doorway, clasping her hands anxiously.

"Where are you going?" she asked, following him out the doors.

"After the 'little master,'" he growled. "It's time we met."

Seven

"He's just a boy, Mr. Howard." Norah seemed alarmed and sputtered. "A little boy. I'm sure he doesn't understand—"

The rest of what she said fell at his back as he exited the house and turned toward a large stand of spreading English oaks. When he reached the nearest trees he stood for a minute looking up, searching the half-bare branches. After a few moments he spotted movement in a towering grandfather of an oak and went to stand under it as he concentrated on finding the source of that disturbance.

It didn't take long for the motion to resolve into a small, boyish shape fifteen or so feet up. Shaggy hair, bare knees, scuffed shoes; the boy was perched in the crotch of a substantial limb and peering down at him.

"Boy!" he called up in thunderous tones. "Come down. Now!"

The only response was what sounded suspiciously like a giggle.

"I'm counting to five," Barclay said with a bit less rumble. As he counted aloud, he removed his coat and laid it over the lowest branch. He braced, looking up, with fists at his waist, wearing a deadly serious expression.

"Five," he announced loudly. "You come down or I'm coming up!"

"You can't," the boy said with what seemed to be a grin.

"Oh, but I can." Barclay quickly shed his vest and pulled himself up on one of the lower branches, grateful that the old tree had grown thicker and stronger in his absence. He looked up and smiled wickedly at the boy, showing his teeth.

Even a dozen feet away he could see the boy's eyes widen. Had no one ever challenged the brat's willful behavior? If not, it was certainly time for it. Determination set his face in a hard mask as he transferred to a higher branch, then to another. For a small boy such a climb might seem forbidding, but for a man of Barclay's height and dexterity, it was quite manageable.

A voice from below called to him to come down . . . then to be careful. It was Norah Capshaw's voice, though he wasn't certain at first who she addressed, him or the boy. He brushed it aside.

"Please, Mr. Howard. The boy will come down sooner or later."

"Sooner is better!" he called out.

The boy skittered higher, onto smaller, less secure branches.

"You can't come up here!" the boy yelled with a tremor of bravado. He glanced around him, looking less certain of his escape plan. He was likely reaching the limit of his previous explorations.

With each limb Barclay reached, the boy climbed one higher.

"You're just forcing him up!" Norah's voice was filled with anxiety. "It's not safe!"

He concentrated on the boy's upward scramble. Years

ago he had climbed this very tree again and again. The limbs were heavier now and the bark was rougher, but then, so was he. With every limb he advanced, the boy retreated by equal measure. Soon the "little master" was having to search frantically for a branch that would support him.

"Stay where you are!" Barclay ordered as the child reached a branch that sagged perilously under his weight. "You can't go any farther!"

The boy made one last, desperate lurch to a higher branch . . . one with no bark and even less strength. The branch drooped under his weight, and the boy sprawled and wrapped both arms and legs around it while searching frantically for something stronger. Teetering on the brink of disaster, he now made noises of distress . . . whining accompanied his efforts to maintain a hold on his perch.

"Damn it!" Barclay muttered, watching the boy's growing panic and feeling a bit of it taking root in himself. The stubborn whelp had gotten them both in a fix that could end badly if he didn't finish it quickly.

Branches now sagged under his weight as he stretched as high as he could reach. The child was still at least four feet beyond his grasp and bobbing precariously when a gust of breeze set the top of the tree swaying. Barclay felt it, too, and braced with his last secure hold on a branch. When he looked up the boy was struggling to hold on to two neighboring branches with both arms and legs, his face filled with fear.

"I'm coming to get you!" Barclay called to him against the gusts of wind. "Hold on."

Climbing any higher was too dangerous, he realized, as the limb dipped beneath him. The narrower branches above would never hold him. He searched the area below the boy and found a sturdier limb several feet down. He maneuvered toward it, calling to the boy.

"When I tell you let go and I'll catch you!"

But the boy only heard "let go," and his small hands no longer had the strength to hold on. With a cry he plummeted. Barclay lunged beneath him, praying that the branch below would hold, and caught him with one arm as they dropped onto that substantial limb.

The impact of landing knocked breath from them both, but Barclay recovered quickly and pulled the boy to his side. For a moment he couldn't move and realized the child was clinging to his shoulder and shirt with all his might. It registered that someone below—a woman—had screamed.

He looked down into the boy's pale face and saw uncertainty and lingering fear. The need to teach the boy a lesson evaporated . . . replaced by a need to get him down the tree to safety.

"I'll need my arms free to climb down," he said, hoping the boy would understand. "I'm going to boost you up . . . you need to climb onto my back, put your arms around my neck, and hold on. Can you do that?"

The boy nodded, his eyes large and luminous. Something in Barclay's chest tightened . . . something that had nothing to do with his thundering heart or the fight-or-flight rush of his blood.

Six years. That wasn't much time to learn about the world, especially when you didn't have a father to teach you.

Climbing down was trickier than he expected with the boy on his back. The child didn't weigh a lot, but by the time they reached the ground Barclay's muscles were burning and his hands felt raw. They both bore a number of scrapes and scratches. He dropped to the ground to find half a dozen people gathered and voices clamoring to know if the boy was all right. Only then did Barclay realize the boy's face had been buried in his back all the way down.

Six years old.

Named *Elias*.

Norah rushed forward to receive the child, who was shaking and crying. As she did so, an elderly woman in nurse's gray, panting and leaning heavily on a cane, reached them.

"Ellie! My boy! My sweet baby boy!" The old woman sank to her knees and opened her arms. The child rushed to her and nearly bowled her over with his embrace. Norah halted, watching the reunion, and glanced at Barclay, who was inspecting his hands and glowering at the state of his trousers and once-impeccable shoes. When he turned toward the voice and looked up, his expression was more shock than irritation.

"Nanny?" he said, stepping forward before he caught himself. "Nanny Broadbeach?"

The old woman looked up at the sound of her name.

"Who are you to treat my boy so wretchedly?" she demanded, squinting hard at him. "How could you be so mean?"

"Barclay," he answered, stiffening. "Barclay Howard."

The name rumbled around in the old woman's head until it struck a memory. "Barclay? Barr? My little bear?" Her voice became tremulous as she leaned toward him. She pressed Elias closer to her. "You're not him—you can't be him."

"I am, Nanny." He stepped closer, and the old woman

drew back her head. "And I'm here to take charge of . . .
your charge. I'm the young earl's guardian. Appointed by
my grandfather."

"The old lord is dead as a doornail," she said, looking
confused. "How could he set you over Ellie?"

"He left instructions in his will. Didn't anyone inform
you of it?"

Samuel stepped in, looking anxious. "The old lord did
indeed say that you would be young Master Elias's
guardian in the event of his death. We sent for the solicitors
as soon as his lordship passed away, and they took responsibility for contacting you." He looked with sad emphasis
toward Nanny. "Some of us must have forgotten."

Nanny looked like she was trying to get to her feet, and
Barclay bolted forward to help her. Once reasonably upright, she glared at him with suspicion and gathered the
boy against her other side.

Norah glimpsed a flicker of emotion in Barclay as the
old woman shook off his hands. He straightened and
looked down at the boy.

"Go inside, to your room, and don't come out until I
come to speak with you."

"I don't have to mind you," the boy said with insolence
bolstered by his nanny's sheltering presence.

"You do. I am your guardian . . . in charge of your well-
being and inheritance. By law you are obligated to be guided
and corrected by me until you reach your majority . . .
which, I can tell you, is a long way off." Barclay looked
down his nose and said sharply, "Go to your room and *wait*."

The boy looked up at his nanny, expecting her to intervene. He was visibly shocked when she didn't.

"Go to your room, Ellie. I'll be along shortly," Nanny

Broadbeach said with an air of sadness, giving the boy a shove toward the house. As he stomped toward his punishment, the old nurse turned and followed him slowly, supported by her cane and housemaid Cosey.

Norah watched Barclay looking after them and witnessed a turmoil of emotion in his face. She went to stand beside him, seeking to understand what had just happened.

"Who is Mrs. Broadbeach? And why is she in charge of the boy when she can barely walk?"

"She has been nanny to generations of Howards. Was pensioned off years ago." He stared after the old woman. "Apparently brought back."

She watched him gather his coat and vest and walk toward the rear of the great manor house as if he bore the weight of the world on his shoulders. She had thought he was being reckless climbing that huge tree after the boy. But, in fact, it was the boy who climbed recklessly until he reached branches destined to break under his weight. Barclay had caught him when he fell and had carried him to safety. Many men would have walloped a boy afterward for such headstrong mischief.

She lifted her skirts and ran after her employer, not knowing what she would say but sensing that he needed an ear. And there was no one else to share his thoughts just now.

"You grew up here?" she asked, falling into step with his long strides.

He glanced at her but kept walking. "I did."

"And Mrs. Broadbeach was your nanny?"

"She was."

She clasped her hands behind her back, imitating his posture.

"She's quite elderly now and her eyes are dim," she said. "I doubt she's able to keep up with such a spirited child."

"She was never one to keep up," he said tersely. After a moment of silence he added, "I climbed that same tree a hundred times. Fell out more than once. She tended me and taught me lessons until I was sent to school."

"Now she doesn't seem to recognize you," Norah said, immediately regretting that observation.

He stopped and looked around at the overgrown rear garden.

"Things change," he said with a grim air of acceptance.

When he began to move again she kept pace. She had a strong and confusing desire to touch him.

"You're not going to thrash him?" she said. "Surely he has learned his lesson today. I doubt he'll repeat that bit of mischief."

He cut a glance at her. "Don't know much about boys, do you?" He gave a hard sigh. "Perhaps bringing you here was a mistake after all."

The words stopped her, though he kept going. She fought a sense of embarrassment as she watched him assessing the plantings and the disarray of the garden. Then she turned and strode back to the front of the manor house, fists at her sides and determination brewing.

Barclay glanced back to watch her walk away, knowing he'd goaded her with his comment and trying to justify it. She needed to be kept at arm's length. That warm voice, her concern for the boy and for his own . . . he didn't need her poking around in his history and his feelings about it. It was better this way.

Later, Barclay trudged up the worn steps toward the third-floor nursery, trying to decide what to say to the boy to set boundaries and expectations. In the upper hallway he ran into boxes and a trunk that looked familiar. Down the hall, on the far side of the schoolroom, Norah stood in the hall with her arms crossed and a worried look, staring into a room that he recalled as being Nanny's old room. Raised voices wafting down the hall made clear there was a problem. He strode to the room and quickly learned what it was.

"It's my room. Always has been." Mrs. Broadbeach's voice was higher and hoarser than before but still recognizable.

"Of course it is, Nanny B," he declared, positioning himself in the doorway. "It is your room until you no longer want it."

"The staff brought my things up." Norah's voice came from behind him. "They assumed the tutor would occupy rooms on this floor, but none are ready, so—"

One of the maids stood beside the old woman's open wardrobe and a footman stood over the old lady's trunk, where he had been packing books and personal items.

"Take Miss Capshaw's things down to one of the guest rooms," he ordered them. "She will take a room on the floor below."

When he turned toward the boy's room Norah followed.

"The staff believed that I was intended to take her room," she said. "They told Murielle that Nanny Broadbeach can't manage the stairs, so she stays up here on the children's floor most of the time . . . allowing Elias to roam as he wishes. Now that I am here, they thought to move Mrs. Broadbeach's things down to more accessible accommodations."

"It's sorted now," he said. "Choose a room on the floor below, and when you are settled see to setting up the schoolroom. No doubt it requires work."

A moment later he reached the boy's room and stepped inside, closing the door firmly on Norah Capshaw's curiosity. He paused a moment, looking around.

The boy sat on a well-worn rug in front of a single bed, building something tall with an assortment of worn wooden blocks. Nearby was the iron brazier that had warmed many a morning for Barclay as a child. The walls were dingier than he recalled and the shelves and the books they held were dusty, but otherwise the room looked untouched by the passage of time. It struck him that probably no one had used the room since it was his . . . until now . . . until this boy, whose fate and future would be quite different from his.

"You must stand up whenever an adult enters the room," he said gruffly.

The boy looked up. "Why?"

It was more curiosity than challenge. Barclay had to think for a moment. The boy honestly had had no one to defer to in his life. The old earl had been confined to his bed for some time, and there were probably no visitors except physicians and nurses, who would have ignored a child.

"It shows respect for your elders and those who provide for you." He waited a moment. Then gestured for the boy to rise. Elias scowled and turned his attention back to his blocks.

"Now," Barclay said. And after another moment's

noncompliance, he added more force to his command. "*Now!*"

The window-rattling volume made the impression he intended. The boy scrambled to his feet and backed away. Barclay crossed his arms, looking stern, determined to make the boy take his words seriously.

"Things will go better for you if you listen and obey the first time."

"I don't have to do what you say."

"Oh, but you do," Barclay said, striding closer. "I am here to see that you are educated and disciplined into a man worthy of the title you will hold. It is your duty to obey my instructions and learn how to do what you must."

"I'm the master. Nanny says I am 'the little earl.'"

So, the boy knew that he occupied a privileged position here at Northrup, even if he didn't understand what it meant or why it was his.

"'Little' being the important word there." Barclay's face turned to granite. "Listen well: If you want to grow and learn what being an earl means, you will do as I say. I have brought you a tutor who will prepare you for school and see you are given the knowledge you need to make a good start in school and in life. Your task is to master yourself . . . your undisciplined ways . . . and apply yourself to your studies."

Elias thought for a moment; Barclay could see calculation in his eyes.

"I don't want to," he said, raising his chin.

"Don't want to what?" Barclay narrowed his eyes.

"Read an' such. It makes my head hurt."

The arrogant look on Elias's face was a perfect copy of the old earl's pugnacious expression. He had not realized that children could inherit attitude and mannerisms so totally from grandfathers. He edged closer to the boy, who tensed and looked ready to flee.

"If that is your choice, you should know," he said, in a voice that scraped the bottom of its range, "consequences will follow."

"You can't beat me," the boy said angrily. "Nobody can beat me."

Barclay allowed a long, slow smile to make his mouth into an arc.

"I don't *beat* children." And his lips parted in a fierce grin that bared his teeth and transformed his face into a predatory mask.

"I have other means of dealing with them." He made three sharp clicks with his teeth.

The child's face drained of color. He stood shocked to immobility as Barclay strode for the door and then turned for one last declaration.

"Just so you know . . . Nanny Broadbeach was my nanny, too. She made me study and mind my manners and treat others with respect. I will do that for you unless your behavior forces me to more extreme measures." He studied the boy's uneasiness. "Miss Capshaw is your tutor. You will obey her as you would me and apply yourself to learning whatever she decides to teach you. Furthermore, there will be no more pranks. Mrs. Heybert might have been seriously injured when she fell. I won't have you endangering the staff with your tricks."

And he stepped into the hallway and closed the door with a bang.

Norah Capshaw and Nanny Broadbeach stood together outside, waiting for the outcome of that meeting.

"Did you thrash him?" Nanny demanded in what was

probably her most forceful voice. "Ellie's not used to whacks."

"It shows." Barclay ignored Norah's beseeching look. "He's spoiled."

"No more than he should be, poor little thing," Nanny said, her determination suddenly overwhelmed by a flood of emotion that caused her voice to waver. "Growin' up an orphan with nobody to love him."

"No more than me, and you never let me by with such rude and defiant behavior." He leaned closer to give her a better view of his face. "Barclay. Once your 'little bear.'" He straightened. "You've gone soft, Nanny Broadbeach."

And he strode for the stairs.

Norah watched him go and wondered again at the puzzle he presented. Fierce and yet protective. Determined and yet conflicted. He had been an orphan here, too, and never spoke of Northrup without an expression of distaste. He didn't want to be here, among his tangled roots and what seemed to be less than pleasant memories. She couldn't help wondering what life had been like for him as a child who was termed a "little bear." That was hardly a description a nobleman would desire for his progeny. It couldn't have been easy for him.

Shaking off those musings, she headed downstairs to find a room. She called for the upstairs maid and then for Murielle to advise, but neither appeared. She wandered from room to room, peering into empty bedchambers intended for family members and esteemed guests while avoiding the ornate double doors that indicated accommodations designed for the master of the estate. Was that Barclay Howard now?

She settled on a corner room at the end of the east hall, beside the servant stairs. It had long, front-facing windows and was decorated in a delicate blue-and-white chinoiserie motif. The moment she stepped into the chamber she felt her tension ease. The mahogany bed stood under a silk canopy and was furnished with a figured damask counterpane that had faded a bit but lost none of its appeal. Unlike the heavy Tudor furnishings of other rooms she had seen, these were crafted in a delicate Louis Quatorze style that made her want to run her hands over every curve and figure. For a wardrobe there was a French armoire with mirrored doors, and nearby was a matching dressing table, complete with mirror and trays for brushes and toiletries. It was a lady's room, clearly.

Murielle found her and directed her trunk and bags to the room she was in. With no other direction, they decided this room would be hers. The girl helped Norah brush and put away her clothes, then set about arranging her dressing table and seeing to it that the washstand had water and fresh toweling. The housemaid Cosey appeared and insisted they allow her to air the room, dust, and change the bed linen.

Norah took the opportunity to climb the stairs to the schoolroom and inventory the books, maps, and other educational materials.

In the spacious but dusty schoolroom she was surprised by the range of books, the large slate board that hung on one wall, and the stacks of maps that detailed the geography of Europe, the Middle East, the Orient, and the Americas. She found a chamois rag and used it to dust the tables and shelves, then unpacked the books and supplies they had bought in London and positioned the tables to catch the best possible light from the north-facing windows.

Waving away dust motes in the air, she stood back to look at the room and assess its possibilities. All this for one child. A privileged child who thus far had grown up without much guidance or structure.

A noise behind her made her turn and she spotted young Elias standing in the doorway with a frown.

"Are you that tooder lady?" he asked after a moment.

"*Tutor*. My name is Miss Capshaw." She moved toward him with an outstretched hand, but he just stared at it, as if puzzled by the gesture.

"You can't be here. This is *my* room."

"It is your schoolroom, true. It is here we will study and discover things. You . . . about the world. Me . . . about you."

His scowl faded. "You goin' to study *me*?"

"I must, if I am to help you learn all you need before going to school."

"I don't want to go to school." Another scowl. "I don't have to."

Norah folded her arms and studied his attitude, glimpsing beneath it his uncertainty at the changes happening in his life. It was written so plainly in those large gray eyes.

"What do you know about schools?" she asked.

"They beat boys," he said. "And make you do things."

She smiled. "I think you've been misinformed. Schools are places of learning and growth. The boys at Harrow have tutors called masters and go to forms together . . . where they sit at desks and listen and read and study. Can you write your name?"

He ignored the question. "They steal your shoes."

"They may play pranks occasionally—like someone else I know—but stealing is a serious matter. They don't allow it. Are you worried you won't be safe at school?"

She took it as a good sign that he stepped inside the room and began to walk around, fingering the rolled maps in a basket and then the new books on one shelf. It was interesting that he singled out the new books. He had clearly paid attention to the things routinely in "his" room.

"They also play games and run races and sing at chapel services. Sometimes they go on trips to museums and, as they get older, they learn the secrets of the stars and science and mathematics."

"I already know numbers," he said, raising his chin.

"Really?" She smiled, watching the way the boy studied her face. "Can you show me on the slate board? Write out a few numbers for me?"

He looked suspicious as she went to the wooden chalk box and offered him a piece of chalk. It took a moment for him to accept it.

He did indeed know his ordinal numbers, though he wrote them out of order and large and his five looked very much like an "s."

"Did Nanny teach you your numbers?" she asked, smiling.

"Naw. Cook writes stuff on paper an' I saw her do it."

"So, you learned the numbers by yourself?" She feigned surprise.

"That"—he looked a bit sheepish—"an' Cosey made me count."

"What did you count?"

"Lemon drops." Then he looked up with new interest. "You gonna make me learn?" He brightened. "You gonna give me sweets if I do?"

"I am here to help you learn," she said, wondering if the spark she saw in his gray eyes was some part hope. "Can you write your name?"

His mouth pursed at the corners. "Yeah." He took the chalk he'd been toying with to the big slate board and, after erasing two starts with his fingers, produced a reasonable "E-l-l-i-e."

She frowned when she realized the boy had accepted what Nanny B called him as his name. "Ellie." If that girl-ish name followed him to school, he would never live it down.

"You know, your name is really Elias." She tapped her lips with one finger, thinking. "I think Nanny meant to call you 'Eli.' It's a more manly form of your name. That's what I'll call you. *Eli*."

She could have sworn he stood an inch taller as he nodded. That was when she noticed the dirt and scrapes on his hands. Had Nanny not seen to this? She could tell he tried not to flinch as she gently explored the damage.

"You scraped your hands climbing that tree." She rose from the chair and took his hand gently in hers. "We have to do something about that." He walked with her to his room, staring up at her all the way.

Eight

Dinner that night was delayed slightly while Barclay sent Samuel to fetch Elias from the nursery. From then on he decreed to Samuel, Cook, and the kitchen staff that the boy would dine with him to learn table manners and give a report on what he had done that day. By the time Norah and the boy arrived, Barclay's stomach was growling and his mood was darkening. Norah's presence brightened the dining room . . . until he saw that she held Elias's hand.

"Where would you have Eli sit, Mr. Howard?" she asked in a tone that made him feel it was more for the boy's benefit than for direction.

"On my right. Near me. We will converse over dinner."

She escorted the boy to his seat and started for the kitchen stairs. He stopped her with: "And you must join us, Miss Capshaw. The boy will have need of your assistance with table manners."

She was surprised to find a seat at a third place setting laid out at Barclay's left. He asked her to explain the courses and service to the boy.

The meal began with a tasty broth, which Elias sniffed but did not try despite Norah's attempt to make it sound delicious and necessary to prepare his stomach for what was to follow.

"I always have milk an' bread." The boy's mood was petulant.

"Sops are good enough for infants," Barclay said, frowning at Elias. "But you're no infant, and if you expect to grow, you need 'growing food.'"

"Try it, Eli," Norah urged. "You'll find it delicious."

The boy finally attempted a spoonful, then, a moment later, a second one, and then a third. When he looked up at Norah, he smiled.

Barclay told himself the boy was pleased to discover a delicious new taste, but sensed that his smile at Norah involved more than that. She was a pretty woman with striking hair and eyes and a calm, confident nature. When she won the boy over it might not be for purely dutiful or academic reasons. Even young boys, he recalled with a wince, were drawn to beauty. They could make themselves quite amenable when a lovely lady's approval was at stake. He himself had certainly done so when . . .

"Tell me, boy, what did you learn today?" He refocused on Elias as the next course was served. Elias looked up from the fork he was holding. His use of it was awkward despite Norah's coaching.

"I taught Miss Captain her numbers."

"Cap*shaw*," he corrected, glancing at her. "I wasn't aware she needed tutoring in numbers."

Norah gave the boy a narrow look and he corrected his statement.

"I showed her how I can write numbers." He slurped more broth.

"Ah." He nodded. "And do you know your letters A through Zed?"

The boy frowned. "A lot of 'em. She didn' ask me that."

"Do you know any words?"

"One. The stable boy wrote it in the dirt with a stick. P-O-O-P."

Barclay raised one eyebrow. "Easy to remember, I suppose, but that is one word that should stay in the dirt. You do know that it is 'poop'?"

Eli giggled, indicating he knew it well enough. The glint in his eyes as he looked to Norah said he expected a reaction from her. To her credit, she did not gasp or take offense, merely looked at him and then to Barclay.

"After dinner, Miss Capshaw will explain to you why such words are not allowed at the dinner table or in company," he told the boy. "You will not say or write that word. There is never cause to use it."

"What if I have to go poo?" Elias said in mixed provocation.

"You may whisper your need in other terms to Nanny or Miss Capshaw and then excuse yourself to a necessary. No more '*poop*.'"

Elias seemed to be suppressing a smile as he nodded.

Through a light supper of cottage pie and autumn vegetables, Norah coached Elias on forks and the proper use of a knife. He struggled with the flatware but seemed to like the pie and its golden, cheesy crust. When told to try the braised winter squash, carrots, and onions, he grimaced and adamantly shook his head. Barclay cut him a look.

"It's just as well," he said. "Vegetables make boys taste funny." And he smiled broadly, baring his teeth at the boy.

Elias's eyes widened and he looked at Norah, who was watching Barclay in puzzlement. Elias bit into a carrot and shuddered visibly as he chewed and swallowed. He didn't seem eager to repeat the experience. A moment later the "braaaaat" of a loud fart resounded in the room.

It was so startling and so odiferous that Barclay gasped and Norah couldn't help covering her nose, while Elias stared bug-eyed at them and then burst into a gale of laughter. He flipped and flopped in his chair, laughing uncontrollably while holding his stomach.

Barclay recovered first and growled the boy's proper name to no avail. He pushed back his chair, rose, and picked the boy up by the middle and slung him over his shoulder. He stalked for the main stairs while the boy gasped for breath and, after a moment, began to struggle and demand to be put down. Barclay refused to oblige until they reached the nursery, by which time Elias was screaming for Nanny and pounding on Barclay's back.

Barclay opened what he had known to be a linen cupboard with plenty of room for mischievous boys, shoved Elias inside, then closed the door, and—lacking a key— braced his back against it. Elias pounded and kicked the door, demanding release, but even when Nanny and Norah arrived, Barclay refused.

"He farted on purpose," he said, braving Nanny's horror and Norah's dismay. "It was a fart of defiance."

"He's a wee boy," Nanny B groaned. "Can't always control hisself."

"It's time he learned."

"You stuffed him in a linen cupboard," Norah declared, spurred on by what had become a stream of pleas and threats from behind the door. "What if he can't breathe in there?"

"He has plenty of air. I spent many an hour in that same linen cupboard and survived."

Barclay slid to a seat on the floor and stretched out
his legs before him, crossing his arms and ankles and looking utterly determined. No amount of pleading or guilt-in-
ducing admonitions would change his mind. The boy
needed to be taught a lesson . . . now.

When things quieted Nanny pecked on the door and
called to Elias. The boy replied in a small, tremulous voice.

"Don't let him eat me, Nanny," he cried. "I'll be good,
I promise."

Nanny drew back, more puzzled than anguished, then
tried again to reassure him. "No one's going to eat you,
Ellie."

But when the old girl looked daggers at Barclay, he
just smiled and showed his teeth. It was enough to give
Nanny B second thoughts.

"You have to let him out!" she shouted. "This is cruel."

"No crueler than when you did it to me," he said, settling in for a stay.

Nanny looked stunned as recollections fought through
the veil of age and she slowly crumpled. When her tears
appeared Norah gave her a handkerchief and bundled her
down the hall to her room.

"You mustn't work yourself into a state, Nanny."
Norah seated the old lady in her rocking chair. "I'll talk to
Mr. Howard. I know he doesn't intend to harm the boy."

The old lady dabbed at her eyes and squeezed Norah's
hand. A moment later she was staring off into some unseen
vista, seeming to no longer suffer anxiety for her charge.
Norah left her there with a blanket tucked over her knees
and headed back to the now-quiet cupboard on the far side
of the schoolroom.

Barclay hadn't moved and the cupboard behind the

door was quiet. She stooped beside Barclay, who didn't acknowledge her.

"This is not helpful," she said quietly. "The boy needs to trust those who care for him. This is no way to build that trust."

"He needs limits. He's never had them."

"Yes, but perhaps if you talked to him instead of threatening—the boy seems to think you might *eat* him."

"Can't imagine where he got that idea." But he couldn't help the satisfaction that played at the corners of his mouth.

Norah tightened her eyes to a glare. "Did you threaten him when you talked to him earlier?"

He flicked a glance at her. "I warned him there would be consequences if he continued such behavior."

"Hmm. And left the rest to his imagination?"

"Exactly."

She studied his strong profile, his thick hair, and the size of his arms as they crossed his chest. The boy was intrepid indeed to cross such a force. She thought for a moment. What did that make her—confident or foolhardy?

Whatever it meant she intended to see that the boy was cared for, as well as educated and disciplined. Her earlier interactions with him hinted that he wasn't a bad child, just strong-willed and used to getting his own way. Then another thought struck her.

"They really put you in this linen cupboard as punishment when you were a child?" she asked, settling to a seat on the floor beside him.

"Yes," he answered, sounding a bit tired and leaning his head back against the door.

"And Nanny B did it?"

"Yes."

"She must have changed quite a bit."

"Yes."

After a few moments he spoke again. "It's smaller than I recall." He went silent for a moment, then added, "But there's plenty of room in the aisle between the shelves. If he's smart, he'll use some of the linens to make a pallet and take a nap."

"Is that what you did?" she asked, trying to picture Nanny's "little bear" finding a way to make himself comfortable in the darkened closet.

"Yes."

"It must have been dark and scary. Were you afraid?"

He hesitated for a moment. "At first. But by the third time or so, I knew what to expect. And I knew I had to correct my behavior." He rolled his head to the side to look at her. "After a while it became a place to be alone to think."

"You hated growing up here?" she asked, knowing it was too personal to ask of her employer.

"It was all I knew."

"So you weren't unhappy?" She studied his face in the marginal light.

"It prepared me for life . . . taught me what to expect."

"And what is that?"

His voice deepened to a finger-tingling whisper.

"Disappointment."

The way he said it sank a weight into her stomach. She sought his eyes with hers and glimpsed in them a sense of acceptance that settled sadness on her mood. She couldn't help remembering the whispers she'd heard from the girls at school about "that Howard beast." She hadn't listened to much of it, but to hear them tell it, he was indeed capable of eating little boys. And well-bred young debutantes.

Wealthy young girls could be cruel in their judgments of one another, but their most cutting assessments came from their ignorance of all that lay outside their privileged world. None had ever suffered exclusion or deprivation, so how could they understand the effects of such things on others? And as to being different . . . the reddish tint of her hair and her green eyes had been enough to set her apart from the elite of her classmates. Other girls—those heavier, plainer, or less socially adept—were even less accepted than she. She had been anointed "the orphan" and was allowed to be "studious" and keep to herself much of the time.

She glanced at Barclay and wondered how old he was when his parents died, leaving him in his grandfather's care. Had he suffered a similar exclusion in his schooldays? Had his size and appearance marked him as unacceptable company then, too?

She considered the odd path that had brought her to be sitting on the floor outside a linen cupboard containing a six-year-old earl . . . beside "the Howard beast." Never in a million years would she have guessed she would be in such a situation only a week before. When her thoughts turned again to her pupil she roused and rolled up onto her knees to look back at the door and Barclay.

"He's been quiet for a long time," she whispered.

"Probably asleep." He seemed to consider the possibilities, then got to his feet and offered her a hand up. He put a finger to his lips for quiet and turned the cupboard doorknob.

Inside, Elias lay on a feather pillow and had snuggled under an old quilt pulled from one of the low shelves nearby. He didn't appear to have suffered much from his punishment. In fact, he seemed to have made himself at home, in much the way Barclay said he had decades before.

Barclay swung the cupboard door open wide and turned as if to leave.

"You can't just leave him there," Norah said, looking up at him. He narrowed his gaze and she raised her chin. "I'll carry him to bed."

She stepped into the cupboard, intending to collect the boy, then heard a growl and was pulled back out. Barclay took her place, knelt to gather the boy into his arms, and then rose and turned to her with a look of annoyance.

"Open his door," he said in a rough whisper.

Moments later he was laying the little earl down on his bed in the nursery. Norah took over when he stepped back and removed the boy's shoes, recoiling at the pungent, sour smell of his feet. She quickly covered him with a quilt and then stood back with Barclay, surveying their mutual challenge.

"The first thing tomorrow," she said, "he gets a bath."

She could have sworn Barclay chuckled, but when she looked up he was looking at her with that luminous glint in his eyes that made him seem so interestingly human. They closed the boy's door and then headed down the stairs to the upper hall.

"It's been an eventful day," she said, thinking of her corner room with its ladyish comforts and feeling eager to slip out of her traveling clothes and between some soft sheets. She hadn't known she would be expected at table for dinner, too, and hadn't had time to change into something more appropriate. She probably needed a good dusting, head to toe, and a bath as soon as it could be arranged.

"It has been," he said quietly.

"Arriving in the midst of uproar, climbing a tree and rescuing the boy, then putting him in a linen cupboard— hardly an auspicious start with your ward." She walked slowly in the dim light of the hall, needing to prolong the moment. He matched her pace, seeming in no hurry himself.

"But I did learn that he seems fairly bright and curious," she continued. "In the schoolroom he was drawn to the new books we brought and wanted to know what his lessons would involve. That strong will of his, put to proper use, could help make him a wonderful scholar."

"He won't need to be a scholar—he's an earl."

"But he'll need a wide range of knowledge about the world and the wisdom to know how to use his rank and power wisely."

"What he'll need," Barclay countered, "is a knowledge of men. Noblemen delegate. They must learn how to judge a man's worth and integrity, and then how to judge whether or not he is loyal enough to apply himself to the good of the lord and the estate."

"Does the same apply to judging women?" she asked, appalled by her bold curiosity a heartbeat later.

"Few principles apply to women. It's mostly trial and error." He appeared to be staring at his feet. "One man's pleasure can be another man's pain."

She looked up to find they were in the dimness near the end of the hall and her room and she stopped. "This is my room." She waved a hand toward her door. "I believe you said I could choose and this one suited best. It's comfortable and it's far from the earl's quarters and the rest of the family."

"I'm afraid you're wrong," he said with a wry smile. "*I* am the rest of the family." He motioned to the door across the hall from her room and his voice lowered. "And that is my room."

It took a moment for the sense of both revelations to become clear in her head. Dearest Heaven, she had chosen the room directly across from the one occupied by the very person she hoped to avoid as much as possible during her tenure here.

"Wh-why on earth is your room so far away from the rest of . . . the family . . . quarters?" She felt her throat tightening and knew it wasn't wise to look up at him, but she couldn't help it. He was now facing her, his arms at his sides, his eyes that dangerous liquid amber. She held her breath for a moment, wondering if he was getting closer or if it was just her imagining it.

"It was my room from the day I turned twelve. I've always . . . always . . . should just get this out of the way," he muttered, though the words were hard to distinguish. If she'd had time to sort them out—

His head lowered and his lips touched hers with gentle pressure that gradually deepened and spread to cover her mouth. His lips were on hers like—Sweet Jesus!—he was kissing her! She stood rigid, shocked to immobility, and drank in sensations unlike anything she had imagined.

Not even when she sneaked old Ovid's racy sonnets into her room at the academy and tried to glean from them the truth about the unthinkable between a man and a maid . . . had she guessed the warmth-generating pleasure of a man's lips on hers. Some things, she had learned recently, had to be experienced to be understood.

When he pulled back she simply stood looking at him, trying to make sense of the heat in her lips and the excitement in her breast.

"Apologies," he said, taking a step backward. "Bound to happen sooner or later. Curiosity and all that." He made a military-precise about-face and in three long strides entered his room and closed the door with a finality that jolted her out of her sensory haze.

She stood a moment longer, staring at his bedroom door, trying to put that unexpected kiss into a box labeled "curiosity" and unable to find one in her experience that would fit such sensations. As she stumbled into her room and leaned back against her door, she touched her tingling lips and knew beyond a doubt that the experience of that kiss—the lush feel of his mouth on hers—was going to sit stubbornly in the middle of her being until she decided what to do with it.

She shivered and felt gooseflesh rise all along her shoulders, chest, and arms. Her eyes widened and she licked her lips. Kissed. At long last she'd been kissed.

By her beast of an employer.

Nine

Barclay spent a miserable night, tossing and turning in the narrow bed he'd always been given in his grandfather's house, trying to rid himself of thoughts that caused a tumult in his blood and in more susceptible body parts. Down deep he had to have known that kissing her was a bad idea, but he still had managed to delude himself into thinking that doing it instead of obsessing about it would break the spell of her allure. Once done, the mystery would disappear and he could get on with more important matters.

The added bonus, he had told himself, was that she would be properly horrified. If she slapped his face he would deserve it, and she would avoid him like the plague afterward. But she didn't slap him. She just stood there with an expression of surprise, giving no hint of whether she liked it or hated it. For such a self-possessed female, it surprised him that she hadn't responded in one direction or the other. No female he'd kissed had shown ambivalence to the process. She behaved as if—

Dear God. Had she never been kissed before?

Boarding school, female academy . . . a short time

working in London . . . when had she had opportunity to experience such things?

Saints, he was a brute . . . taking advantage of her inexperience.

When she had a night to think about it she would be furious.

His only course was to avoid her . . . not think about her or that wretched kiss . . . spend as much time as possible out on the estate, seeing tenants, assessing the stables and livestock, and checking the farm steward's tally sheets. He would make time for the boy, of course . . . teach him to ride and care for a horse . . . take him fishing and on outings to learn about farming and about the nature it would be his duty to protect. He would probably just have time to give Elias a good start on such things before sending him off to school, but there would be time at holidays and in summers to continue the lessons.

He hauled himself out of bed, stretched, and rubbed his face. He deserved every sleepless minute he'd suffered, and he would have to find time and opportunity in the day ahead to apologize better for the affront.

She likely would be stiff and distant, efficient and unapproachable. He should be the same . . . until he had a chance to assure her that taking such a personal liberty would never happen again. And for a few days he would avoid her whenever possible and be sure to be circumspect in his behavior when he couldn't do so.

He made quick work of shaving himself and dressing before heading downstairs to breakfast. Riding clothes were the thing for being out and about with Fickey, the estate steward . . . boots being the footwear of choice. He would see what riding stock they had and if there was a saddle horse with some size; he might even take it out for a ride around the estate and tenants' farms. The more he thought about it, the more he realized he should probably search for a large horse with Norman blood to provide him with a proper mount while he was here.

Thus preoccupied, he was surprised to find his ward and Miss Capshaw in the dining room awaiting his arrival. They were seated on chairs against the wall, waiting quietly, and rose when he stopped in the doorway. Norah gave the boy a nudge that was less than discreet.

"Good morning, sir," Elias said flatly, looking down at his feet. Apparently he'd had some coaching since last night.

"Good morning, Mr. Howard," Norah said, looking in his direction if not actually at him.

What the devil were they doing here?

"Good morning," he answered with a dip of his head.

"I was uncertain whether you intended Eli to take all of his meals here with you or only dinners," she said, avoiding his eyes.

"I suppose because you're here, breaking fast together is not a bad idea this morning," he said, waving them to the table.

Norah ushered Eli to the same seat at the table he had occupied the previous evening. However, her seat was now beside Eli instead of across the table. Apparently she had requested the footman move her place to beside her pupil's . . . effectively putting the boy between them . . . a tactic Barclay didn't fail to note.

He ordered porridge for the boy, but Miss Capshaw suggested he be allowed an egg and some bacon as well, and he nodded to the servant.

* * *

He scarcely glanced at her, Norah realized as she but-
tered toast and saw to Eli's first lesson in egg etiquette.
Blast Barclay Howard's hide.

Admittedly, the kiss was probably less than he expected,
considering her lack of response. He had no way of knowing she had indeed responded . . . belatedly and in ways
he might have found shocking. She had spent half the night
reliving it, analyzing it, and trying to guess what prompted
such an urge—to kiss her in the darkened hallway between
their respective rooms. The product of all her sleepless cal-
culations was disappointing; she had no idea how the
man's mind worked and thus had no basis for deciding
what he intended.

All she knew was, it was improper and even potentially
dangerous for a young woman in her position, and she still
liked it. Damn it.

And when did she start using profanity?

She apologized to the Almighty, shook her head, buried
her nose in another cup of fragrant coffee. Now what
was it she planned to talk with her employer about over
breakfast?

"Ah—Eli's schedule—" she managed to recall. "Morning hours are most conducive to mental tasks. I should like
to have him study with me from nine o'clock to eleven
each morning except Sundays. Then I believe it would be
best for him to have some exercise before a midday meal."

Barclay Howard said nothing but seemed to be listening.

"In the afternoon he could spend another hour or
two with me, then be free to spend time at physical play,

creative arts, or exploring the estate until time to dress for dinner. Tree climbing is not the worst use of such time." She looked to Barclay and found him studying his half-empty plate with a frown. "Does that not meet with your approval, sir?"

"It sounds like a reasonable schedule. Do you think four or five hours a day will be enough to bring him up to snuff?"

"From what I have seen, I believe it will suffice. As he grows we will, of course, add hours for study, reading, and practicing computation."

At that, Elias looked up with alarm. "I have to read and do numbers every day?"

"Not all day. Just a few hours a day," she said, with a smile showing confidence she hoped would be contagious. To her thinking, the schedule she proposed was rather liberal.

"Nanny says I don't need to stuff my brainbox . . . I have servants to do numbers." He raised his chin with a look of condescension that would have done Henry VIII proud.

Barclay intervened in midbite.

"Nanny Broadbeach," he declared, "is a tired old lady who no longer has the strength or will to deal with a child. I, on the other hand, have plenty of both. And if you continue such insolent behavior with me and Miss Capshaw"—he punctuated his words with the fork he'd been using—"you will come to regret it heartily."

The boy's glare dimmed and he glanced up at Norah to see if she was part of his guardian's ultimatum.

She gave him a decisive nod, seconding Barclay's stand, and Eli's shoulders drooped. He pushed back his plate with a sullen look and slid out of his chair. Unfortunately, he chose the side nearest Barclay, who caught his arm and kept him from stomping off.

"Ask to be excused from table," Barclay said, leaning closer to the boy. When there was no response Barclay added, "So Nanny has failed to teach you even the most rudimentary manners. It goes like this: 'May I be excused, Miss Capshaw'?"

The boy submitted, turning reluctantly in Norah's direction.

"May I be excused, Miss Capshaw'?"

"You may," she said, watching Eli's response to Barclay's handling and recognizing in his approach a firmness that the boy apparently needed. Sentiment would have to be put aside for now. The little earl needed structure first. There would be time for hugs and laughter later.

Barclay thought about Elias's reaction to his new schedule as he strolled through the stable, assessing the horses and deciding what needed to be done there. The boy was certainly strong-willed and self-directed. He seemed to have a strong attachment to Nanny, which was not surprising, and in time would likely develop an attachment to Norah—Miss Capshaw. Damn it, he needed to think of her on a formal basis.

Steward Fickey pointed out a horse he thought might suit the new master of Northrup House, and Barclay spent some time running his hands over the seventeen-hand bay and studying her before deciding to try a ride. He needed some fresh air and time to reacquaint himself with the land and people of Northrup. As he rode out along a familiar cart road, he couldn't help wondering what was happening in the schoolroom with the all-too-ambivalent Miss Capshaw.

Did his kiss not even rate some outrage?

Norah went over the alphabet with Eli, finding he honestly did know most of the letters by name, though he had apparently picked them up here and there and didn't have them in order. When assigned to write out the letters three times in order, he huffed but complied. When that was done she had him make the sound produced by each letter, telling him that he could figure out how to say almost any word by sounding out the letters. It was like a secret code, she told him . . . one that few people knew and used. Even the grown-ups she had taught to read didn't know it.

By the end of that first session he could make nearly all the sounds the letters stood for on sight, and Norah was flushed with pleasure at his progress. He had an ear for sound and caught on quickly to the concept. But when she asked him to guess the letters in a few simple words she spoke, his enthusiasm waned. He became restless and began staring out the window.

She tapped his shoulder, recalling his attention, and told him she intended to ask Mr. Howard for a kickball, a skipping rope, and ball and bat for him to use in his exercise time. She had asked the staff about other children and learned there were a few boys on the estate who could be invited to participate in sporting exercise. Eli seemed unmoved by the notion. She realized that besides the stable boy, he had had little experience with other children . . . another deficit in his otherwise indulgent upbringing.

When schoolroom time was over she took a shawl and accompanied him outside for some exercise. He headed straight for a tree and climbed as far as he could before calling down to her and waving. She watched him and waved back, calling out to him to be careful. He just laughed and swung to a higher branch. She was starting to worry, remembering the previous day, but he began to climb down, and by the time he reached the ground he was grinning from ear to ear.

He ran around the main house to the rear gardens and disappeared. Norah walked the weedy paths, growing more anxious as he didn't answer her calls, when he sprang up out of nowhere, yelling "Boo!"

She stumbled back with a gasp, and he began to laugh.

"You rascal!" she said, recovering. "You scared me."

"I know," he said, clapping his hands. "Nanny always laughs."

"I bet she does." Norah frowned, but then rumpled his hair. "I didn't find it enjoyable, however. No more scares, Eli. *None.*"

He nodded with a twinkle in his eye.

The afternoon lessons were a review of what had come before and he seemed to have retained almost all they had covered. It showed heartening progress and laid groundwork for future gains. She closed out the afternoon session with a story from one of the books of fables she had purchased for him. He seemed to enjoy the story but was confused by the fact that the wolf ate the young rabbit after promising to carry him across the stream. It took a bit of explaining about what wolves were like and the fact that small rabbits were their favorite meal . . . a fact that young rabbits might not fully understand. The other aspect—creatures being true to their nature—was left for another day.

Eli didn't like the fact that there might be morals or

hidden meanings in stories. With boyish impatience, he wanted things spelled out plainly so he didn't have to use his "brainbox." Norah explained that understanding such stories taught him lessons about the world that he might not otherwise learn, and she challenged him to imagine himself as the little rabbit. What choice would he make and why?

He said confidently, "I'd never hop on a wolf's back."

"Even if he offered you a ride across a wide stream? Why wouldn't you?"

"Because I know what wolves are like. They eat little rabbits."

"Ah." Norah smiled. "But would you have thought of that before hearing this story?"

He thought for a moment, then scratched his head. "Yeah."

"Really?" She smiled at his boyish bravado. "Good for you. Most boys wouldn't think twice about accepting the wolf's offer . . . until they heard this story and learned this lesson. That's the reason we read and study such stories. We can learn valuable lessons without having to go through the pain of getting eaten up. Learning lessons from others' situations is a mark of maturing—growing up."

She bent to intercept his gaze. "Besides, some of these stories are fun."

He sighed, not totally convinced, but nodded.

Elias George Wellington Howard's life had changed, but he was determined to make his new masters reckon with his cleverness and return to him some of the privilege he had always enjoyed.

Miss Capshaw seemed a good enough sort. She didn't

shout or swat his knuckles like Nanny sometimes did. And she was pretty. He heard the servants talking about her and saying she was "a good egg" for respecting their history of service in the great house. They seemed to get along, though her maid was nosy and made a lot of "tsks."

He could put up with his tutor lady, but his big, tough-looking guardian was a different story. He couldn't imagine that gnawing on boys was permitted, even if they misbehaved. But the way he clicked his teeth and the fierce gleam in his eyes seemed like a threat to do that very thing. And after being thrown in a linen cupboard that first night, he wasn't sure his guardian paid attention to whatever rules there might be regarding young earls. There had to be some rules. There were rules for everything.

But after two days in the schoolroom, lesson-laden meals in the big dining room, a full bath and endless applications of soap and water, he was tired of politeness and obedience. It was time for a bit of fun . . . and just maybe something to make them see he had a few tricks up his sleeve.

The weather was unusually balmy for an early October day. Norah could see her pupil getting restless and staring out the window more often. By the time their afternoon lessons were over, she felt he needed something to vent his pent-up energy and probably a bit of frustration. To that end, she had inquired earlier about some things found in an old box in the notorious linen cupboard. Among them was a leather ball that had seen better days and was no longer as full of horsehair as it had been. She had given it to Samuel, asking him to clean and re-stuff it for Eli to use. The butler appeared as she was preparing to join her pupil on the rear lawn and handed it to her with a look of pride.

"It's like new," Norah said, smiling.

"A bit of whitewash and some boot black for the dark patches," he said. "We had some old horsehair stuffing from a chair in the attic. Your girl stitched it up smartly."

"Thank you. This is just what he needs to get rid of his excess energy," she said, clutching it to her and heading out the kitchen door.

Eli was delighted to have something to kick around and before long was pounding away at it, sending it shooting into the rear garden and occasionally flying through the air across the grassy lawn. Norah watched, calling out to him to see if he could guide it with just his feet—no hands allowed. He tried, but was soon using both again, kicking away and throwing it with all the power he could muster . . . which was what sent it sailing into the pond.

Norah winced at the sight of the ball floating on the water—then saw Eli racing to the pond's edge.

"Eli, no!" she called, momentarily frozen as he stepped out onto a mat of waterweeds and began to sink. He stretched his arms toward the ball, clearly still several feet away, and she tried to call him back as he crept farther out from the bank, in water well past his knees.

"Leave it—we'll have one of the workmen come to retrieve it!" But he glanced at her and then kept moving toward the ball. Her mouth dried as she headed for the bank. Could he even swim?

"Eli, listen to me—head for the bank right now!"

But it was too late. The boy sank fully under the water, arms flailing, but a moment later managed to get his head above the surface.

"Help! Help me! Miss Capshhh—" He went under again, and a moment later was back up and crying for help.

Norah had shed her shawl and was running as fast as she could. She was not going to let the boy drown while she was in charge. Tucking up her skirts, she looked for a way to reach him quickly and found an old log stuck in the weeds and pointing to Eli's location. She waded through the weedy shallows to that log, her arms out at her sides, alarmed by the cold water seeping into her boots. If only she had time to unlace her shoes—but every moment was critical to saving Eli's life. She called to him again and again, telling him to keep his head above the water, she was coming.

The log was substantial but slippery with pond slime that made her shoes slip this way and that. Eli splashed and flailed to stay above the surface. Her heart raced and her focus narrowed on Eli and his desperate cries. She stretched out her arms toward him and bent to keep her balance while calling to him to reach for her hands.

The log began to roll, and the next minute she was stepping frantically and flailing her arms to remain upright. The cold water smacked the breath from her when she hit the surface. Her skirts bloomed around her and began to fill with water. She cried out in shock and dug at the water to stay afloat, while she searched for the bottom with her feet. There was nothing but water beneath her, and a moment later she went under and kept going down while clawing at the water and trying to reach the surface. When she broke the surface she heard what sounded like laughter and turned in the water to find Eli climbing out onto the bank with a face full of glee.

"Help!" she called to him. "Get help!"

Panic seized her as she realized how far she was from

the bank and how little the boy on the shore understood her situation. She had never learned to swim and could barely open her mouth to call for help without inhaling water.

Dear God—she feared it would be her last prayer—don't let me drown!

Barclay had just returned from his ride and handed over his horse to one of the grooms when he heard Elias's cries. They seemed to be coming from the pond and alarm shot through him. Had the boy fallen in?

He broke into a run between the outbuildings—a shortcut to the water that was more lake than simple farm pond. He didn't have to think about the quickest route—something in his core remembered the path and pointed him straight for those cries for help.

He shed his coat as he came in sight of the water and was stunned to find Elias on the far bank, dripping wet but apparently safe. The one in the water was Norah! Galvanized by the sight of her struggling to keep her head above the surface, he plunged into the water and made for her with long, powerful strokes.

She had somehow managed to find one of the deeper areas of the pond and couldn't touch bottom. Hell's bells, even *he* couldn't touch bottom there! Moments later he reached her and held her up while she coughed and spat water. Frantically, she seized his shirt and shoulders and held on to him for dear life.

"I've got you—you're safe."

She was shivering by the time they reached the shallows. Her legs gave out as they reached the bank, and he picked her up in his arms and carried her out onto the autumn-dry grass.

"What the devil happened?" he demanded, realizing as he said it that he sounded furious. Hell, he *was* furious!

"Eli was kicking the ball . . . it went into the pond. I warned him not to . . . I tried to get him . . . the log rolled and pitched me in." She looked around for Eli in confusion. "I told him to go for help, but . . ."

Eli stood twenty yards away, his eyes wide and his face pale. The moment both of them turned to look at him, he turned and fled back toward the main house.

"Never mind him." Barclay turned back to her, running his hand over her face and wet hair, assessing her condition. She was cold and pale but breathing. He needed to get her inside and warm as soon as possible.

He slipped an arm beneath her knees and rose with her. She was heavy in her waterlogged clothing, but he gritted his teeth and for once was glad to own such a heavily muscled frame. She nestled her head against his shoulder as he walked steadily toward the house. He was in no hurry to put her down. Something about her safely in his arms felt right, and he refused to examine that. Instead, he looked down at her pale features and thanked the Almighty that he had learned to swim in the very pond where she had almost drowned.

The house staff had seen them coming and poured out onto the side court, demanding to know what had happened. Mrs. Heybert sent footmen running to carry a bathing tub to Norah's room and Cosey and the other parlormaids for hot water from the kitchen. Murielle rushed through the house ahead of them to lay out toweling and warm clothes on Norah's bed. Then she rushed to the nearest linen cupboard for blankets.

"Brandy" was Barclay's only order to Samuel, who was soon rushing up the stairs after them with a healthy dose on a tray.

Murielle tried to shoo him out of the room the moment he put Norah down on the blanket-draped chair she had prepared. He ignored the maid to take one knee beside the chair and hold Norah's icy hands in his.

"You'll be fine," he said, his voice taut. "A warm bath and some rest . . . you'll be good as new."

She shivered but tightened her hold on his hand and nodded.

"Thank you." She sought his gaze with hers, and those blue-green pools were open in a way he had never seen them. "That's three."

"Three what?" He felt her fingers release his slowly—sensing in her a reluctance to let them go.

"Three times you've rescued me," she said just above a whisper.

"I haven't kept count." No truer words were ever spoken. It never occurred to him to count such actions or see them as creating indebtedness for her.

"Still . . . thank you," she said with warmth and true gratitude.

Unsure how to respond further, he rose and transferred the brandy from Samuel's tray to her hands. "Drink this."

Moments later the bathing tub arrived, and Mrs. Heybert bustled in with maids bearing hot water to fill it. He withdrew across the hall to his own quarters to dry and change clothes. Catching his reflection in his shaving mirror, he cringed. He looked like a half-drowned rat . . . hair going this way and that, face harsh with worry, shirt wet and clinging.

It shamed him to hope that she would be so addled that

she wouldn't remember how disheveled he looked. He stripped off his wet clothes, spread them over the ancient wooden valet stand, and buffed his cold skin with the rough toweling until it was dry and feeling warmer again. He dressed quickly and once again told himself he should hire a proper valet. He had too many responsibilities now to concern himself with drying wet boots and rescuing his shirts and trousers.

He stopped dead, thinking of one responsibility in particular, and where the boy might be at that moment. As soon as he was presentable, he headed downstairs and found Samuel in the entry hall giving orders to the servants.

"Where is he?" he demanded.

The butler didn't have to ask who was meant.

"I am so sorry, sir. The young master engages in a bit of mischief now and again, but I cannot think he meant to harm Miss Capshaw."

"He done it before an' got clean away with it," Cosey said as she shifted her hold on the linen she carried.

"Got away with what?" Barclay scowled, but the maid was not intimidated by it, nor by Samuel's disapproving glower.

"He went out in the pond an' made like he was drownin.' Got Nanny B to wade out after him . . . got 'er good an' wet, then scampered out like he was fine all along. Nanny said it was just one o' his tricks and laughed about it. Then took th' grippe, she did. Was abed for three days."

A trick indeed, giving the old woman who doted on him the grippe. Barclay kept his face a mask of resolve as he turned again to Samuel.

"Where do I find him?"

Ten

Norah steeped in the tub with the warmth of brandy circulating through her veins, but her thoughts were on her narrow escape. The seeping cold, the water closing around her, stealing her warmth and then her breath. All was brown and murky as she fought to the surface, and then there was fear and frantic splashing . . . until *he* came.

His deep voice, his strong arms holding her up, his body moving against hers . . . she knew from the minute he touched her that she was safe. Still, she couldn't help a few tears and shivers as she clung to him. She couldn't recall what she said, but a moment later she was floating in his arms, feeling his warmth around her, and her shivering slowed.

All she could think now was that he'd rescued her yet again. He'd appeared out of nowhere to dive into the water and pull her out.

Moments later Murielle put a hand on her shoulder, saying the water was cooling and it was time for her to dry, put on warm clothes, and get into bed. They had taken down her hair and washed the pond water out of it. By the time she was in the well-warmed bed, she was drowsy and ready to sleep. And she prayed she wouldn't have nightmares about what had just happened.

Barclay tromped up the stairs to the nursery, his fists clenched and his jaw set like stone. He knew exactly where the boy would be and why he would be there. A word with several of the staff had confirmed the heir's penchant for mayhem. He was a trickster who took pleasure in fooling and scaring the people who looked after him and his inheritance. It was time he learned that his pleasure had limits, and that the consequences of his actions would someday—*today*—take him to task.

A glance at the vacant schoolroom and the boy's empty room assured him that the boy would probably have sought refuge where he expected. Nanny's door was partly open, and he found his old nurse in her rocking chair, hands in her lap, watching the door in expectation.

"Where is he?" Barclay said with a take-no-prisoners tone.

"My little Barr," Nanny said with a wistful smile. "Come, sit by Nanny." She waved to the sturdy stool by her feet.

Did she think he was still eight years old?

"I'm not here for a chat. I'm here for Elias."

"Aww . . . my Ellie's a good boy at heart. Just like you. Remember how you climbed trees an' wouldn't come down?"

No, he didn't remember refusing to come down.

"Never saw a quicker monkey than my little Barr," she said with a grin missing several teeth.

She ate only soft foods these days, Murielle had said.

"Frogs and lizards are one thing; drowning his tutor is another."

"Is she dead?" The old girl sat forward with widened eyes.

"No, thank the Almighty. But if I hadn't gotten there in time . . ."

"Just a silly trick, then." She sank back with a sigh. "A good boy at heart. Just needs somebody to make him a decent human."

Somebody with the strength of Hercules and the patience of Job.

"Regrettably, that task falls to me," he said irritably.

"Ohhh, good." She looked genuinely relieved. "You were always a good boy. Ate too much and snitched sweets from the pantry . . . hated your lessons . . . hid in the stables . . . always had horse manure on your shoes . . ."

Horse manure? That's what she remembered of him?

The brightness faded from her eyes, dissolving in cloudy memories.

He swallowed hard, trying not to remember the tenderness she had offered him when the rest of his life seemed bounded by stony walls. His boyhood here was as different from his ward's as night was from day. He'd bet his boots that Elias had never felt the strap or had his ears boxed.

"Boy, come out," he ordered in a voice like rolling boulders. Somewhere in Nanny's room the boy was crouched and listening, he was sure of it. After a moment he added, "*Now!*"

Elias climbed out from under the bed and stood looking small and defenseless. Barclay beckoned and pointed to the floor by his feet, ordering the boy to present himself. But it took Nanny's beckoning to make him round the bed and come close to Barclay.

"You and I have serious matters to discuss," he said.

Elias turned a flushed face toward Nanny B. "I don't want to."

"Your wants are not important at the moment." Barclay narrowed his eyes. "You have endangered the life and well-being of a Northrup staff member. You must stand and answer."

"He's just a wee boy," Nanny began plaintively. "He—"

"Wrong. He's the Earl of Northrup. And he is coming with me."

Quick as a flash, he grabbed Elias's arm and pulled him out the door. Barclay was determined, and no amount of grabbing stair railings, kicking legs, or pleading for help from maids and footmen could stay the consequences of Elias's deviousness. They did, however, collect quite a following as Barclay pulled him through the house. In the kitchen he finally gave in, picked up the boy, and slung him over a shoulder.

Barclay was only partly aware of the staff pushing out the kitchen door behind him and standing in small knots, muttering to one another.

"He's in fer a beatin,' sure e'nuff," the head footman said.

"Couldn't happen too soon," Cosey said with a vengeful air.

Mrs. Heybert leaned her head toward her male counterpart, Samuel, as they stood watching from the kitchen steps.

"Where do you suppose Master Barclay's taking him?"

"Someplace where nobody can hear," the butler said grimly.

Between struggling to breathe and pounding ineffectually on Barclay's back, Elias was soon out of breath and resistance. He got a frantic second wind when Barclay stopped by carpenter Hugo's toolshed, poked his head in, and asked for a hatchet.

"A hatchet?" The aged carpenter's eyes flew wide and focused on the boy thrashing and complaining on his new master's shoulder.

"A small ax will do," Barclay said calmly, allowing Elias to kick and vent his panic. The carpenter looked between him and his frantic ward and broke into a wry smile.

"I believe I have just the thing. She ain't been used in a while, but I kept 'er sharp as a razor."

The few intrepid souls who had followed him through the estate work buildings now turned and raced back to the house, no doubt to report to one and all that Master Barclay was last seen disappearing into the woods with the boy on his shoulder and an ax in his hand.

Barclay thought about his course with the boy as he shouldered his way through brush and small trees into the forest that comprised a good part of Northrup's preserve. The dappled sunlight coming through the trees revealed a little-used path he felt as much as saw. Elias had quit struggling but occasionally issued a whimper of discomfort that made Barclay wince. He didn't mean to cause the boy pain, but he didn't trust the rascal to walk with him to their destination.

Truth be told, he hadn't been there in years and wasn't entirely sure he'd recognize the place when he saw it. He began to pick his way more carefully through the trees, recognizing some grandfather oaks and glad to see saplings struggling up to the canopy the old trees spread around them. Nature was busy with renewal underway. A quarter of an hour later he stepped out into a clearing a hundred yards wide, dotted by stumps and edged by young trees of various ages.

He smiled, took a deep breath, and wiped sweat from his brow.

"I'm going to put you down," he said to the boy draped over his shoulder. "Take a minute to breathe and get your feet under you."

He lowered Elias to the ground and supported him with a hand on his shoulder until the boy shook off the touch and bolted back several steps. Elias looked anxiously between him and the hatchet he carried.

"Have a seat," Barclay ordered. When Elias looked frantically around the meadow, he thought to add: "Don't even think about running off. You're in the middle of a forest and could get lost for days."

Elias ignored the warning to dart off across the meadow and Barclay made no move to stop him. He held his breath as the boy stopped at the edge of the trees, looking uncertain. Twice Elias started to plunge into the trees, but twice he stopped, as if realizing the foliage was a barrier to the unknown. After a few minutes Elias turned and studied Barclay and the hatchet he had just embedded in a stump.

When he felt the tension beginning to lower, Barclay called to the boy: "Come and sit, Elias. We need to talk." And he took a seat on a nearby stump, resting his hands on his knees.

Elias came slowly, pausing along the way to study Barclay and the implement of mayhem he had planted in the stump. He finally reached Barclay and stood for a moment before Barclay waved to a smaller stump.

Elias took a seat there, frowning and uncertain.

"You, young man, are to someday bear a burden and a privilege that few men can bear with strength and integrity. You may not know the meaning of those words now, but in time you will learn."

"Nanny says I'm strong now," Elias said defensively and held up an arm and a fist.

"There are different kinds of strength, Elias, and you will need all of them to be a good earl. And you will need integrity, which is even more important than bodily strength. Integrity means having a core of goodness in you and acting on it for the benefit of others. It means speaking the truth and keeping your word. It means thinking and acting for the welfare of others, especially those in your care."

"Like children?" Elias asked, eyeing him.

Quick little rascal, turning that question back on him.

"Yes, like children." Barclay almost smiled. "It also means sometimes doing difficult or unpleasant things for the good of others. Like bringing you out here for a serious talk."

The boy scowled and lowered his gaze. Barclay hoped it meant the boy was using that "brainbox" to think about what he'd done.

"It is my task to turn you into a man of honor and integrity. The Almighty and some good food will turn you into a man of strength."

Those little shoulders had rounded and the boy clasped his hands between his knees. He looked so small and vulnerable. But Barclay knew willfulness and defiance still lurked beneath that exposed surface.

"But I'm the earl *now*," Elias said, trying to sort it out.

"You have inherited the title, true. But you will not be

issued a call to the House of Lords and recognized fully as 'your lordship' until you reach your majority . . . at twenty-one. That is fifteen years hence, and until you are at least eighteen, I will oversee and manage your estates in trust for you. That means I will care for them as if they were my own, and I am bound to do my best to see that they prosper for you. Meanwhile, you will receive the best training possible for your role as Earl of Northrup."

He could tell all this sounded awful to Elias and knew he had to make the importance of it clear.

"I advise you to take advantage of having time to learn and enjoy the fruits of my labor. You will learn to ride and drive horses, hunt, fish, shoot, read, study nature, and meet people who will give you access to power and wealth. You will need to be wise in choosing companions among your fellow nobles . . . will need to learn how to resist temptations."

The mention of temptations apparently sparked the thought of where Elias had heard that word used before.

"You gonna make me go to church? Nanny says I don't have to if I don't want to."

"Ah." Barclay did smile. "You will have to go some-times. Part of being a good earl is setting an example for your people. And going to services is part of being a good example. Plus—who knows?—you may learn some things there that will make your life better."

They sat for a moment in silence before Barclay brought up the incident that caused this confrontation.

"Now, as to your 'trick' on Miss Capshaw. Tell me what went wrong." When Elias didn't speak he prodded, "Tell me what you know."

Elias heaved a breath and looked at his feet.

"I . . . just played a trick," he said defensively. "She got in the deep water and kept going under. I didn't mean to—"

"She can't swim," Barclay said with escaping heat. "You didn't bother to think of such a thing, did you? And doing so put her in a deadly situation." He couldn't hold back the irritation he felt. "She damned near drowned, Elias!"

It was something of a shock to see prisms of tears in the boy's eyes when he looked up. The quivering chin might have been effective if the victim had been anyone but Norah. As it was, Barclay struggled to rein in his residual anger before continuing.

"Miss Capshaw is a good person. She is smart and educated and generous with her care and help. We are lucky to have her here. So you must quit playing silly, childish tricks that can get you and others into trouble and start showing some gratitude for what she will teach you."

He paused for a moment, wondering if any of this was sinking in.

"You do know how to say, 'I'm sorry'?"

The boy simply nodded, looking miserable.

"Then say it. As often as necessary and in as heartfelt a manner as possible. Today to Miss Capshaw, Mr. Samuel, Mrs. Heybert, and Nanny B—who loves you without measure for some incomprehensible reason.

"Those two words, 'I'm sorry,' truly meant, are what you owe people you have wronged. And you must be man enough to say them.

"The other two words you must master and use frequently are 'Thank you.' Gratitude for care and benefit must be shown to Miss Capshaw, Samuel, Mrs. Heybert, and any servant who helps you with anything. They are all deserving of your thanks because they make your house run smoothly and keep you well-dressed and well-fed. They till your fields and tend your orchards, care for your livestock, and train your horses. You cannot be an earl without them." He lowered his head to look into the boy's eyes. "*'I'm sorry'* and *'Thank you'* may be the four most important words you utter in the next ten years."

Eleven

He stopped for a moment, knowing this was probably the first time anyone had talked to Elias like this. It might take many more such talks to penetrate the thick shell of stubbornness around the boy. But "little Barr" was now "big Barr" and had tenacity in spades. He would see it done or die trying.

In that moment he felt an odd kinship with the boy and realized that was probably the key to his mission here.

"Now"—he rose and stared down at Elias—"as to your punishment for endangering Miss Capshaw . . . you need something that will make you think twice before doing such a thing again."

He went to the stump with the hatchet buried in it, freed the blade, and swung it at the stump with enough force that a large chunk of wood flew from the edge.

Elias bolted up and stumbled back, horror on his face. That fear was replaced by confusion when Barclay turned to him and offered him the wooden handle.

"Take this hatchet—go on—and bring the blade down on that stump until it is gone . . . or sunset, whichever comes first. You'll need two hands and have to think carefully about each swing—keep the narrow edge down at all times because the blade is bone-slicing sharp."

"Y-you mean I hit the stump with this?" He frowned, apparently thinking this was strange punishment indeed.

"Exactly. Like I just did. Give it a try." Barclay backed away a few steps. "You'll soon get the hang of it."

Elias gave it a couple of swings and downward blows that did nothing to whittle down the stump.

"Harder, please. That is old wood and won't split easily." He gave a huff of a laugh. "It's as stubborn as you are."

Elias squinted at the stump and then at the blade in his hands, summoning strength. He gripped the handle hard with both hands, lifted it above his head, and brought it down with all the force he could apply. A chunk of edge wood and bark flew off and he straightened, visibly pleased. Several more blows produced chips and chunks of wood. The little earl was breathing heavily when he paused and looked to Barclay with determination mingled with defiance.

"Keep going. There's plenty left to cut." Barclay sat down on a nearby stump to watch and make sure the boy wouldn't injure himself. To Elias's credit, he seemed able to turn stubbornness into action and continued to hack away at the stump well past the point that Barclay would have expected him to quit in a haze of fatigue and whining.

A full hour passed as Elias attacked the stump. His chopping gradually became less effective and Barclay watched, remembering his own early attempts at using a hatchet, then an ax in this very clearing. It was his brawn and determination that felled every tree that had come down to make the clearing. Some of the stumps memorialized a punishment, others represented his way of working off anger and frustration. He learned through experience that physical labor and exhaustion helped him cope with the difficulties of life in his grandfather's house, and he hoped it would do the same for his willful ward.

The autumn sun was starting down when Elias's swings of the hatchet grew weaker and gradually stopped. His shoulders rounded and he staggered over to a small stump and collapsed, looking at Barclay.

"My arms hurt. My hands, too."

Barclay nodded. "Good. They should after hard work. That is what some of your people feel every day as they work to make your estate run." He rose and beckoned to the boy. "Bring the hatchet."

Elias picked up the hatchet handle, though it seemed to take monumental effort, and followed Barclay without him having to say more. The trek back through the forest seemed to take forever, and by the time they reached the estate Elias was dragging both his feet and the hatchet.

Barclay stopped by Hugo's toolshed, where the veteran carpenter sat on a bench outside. He rose as Barclay and Elias approached.

"Mr. Hugo, this is Elias. He's just had his first lesson in chopping stumps. Thank you for the loan of the hatchet."

He motioned Elias to hand the tool back to Hugo and he did so, looking like the effort was exhausting.

"What do you have to say to Mr. Hugo?" Barclay said firmly.

It took Elias a moment to realize what was expected of him and he seemed resigned to comply.

"Thank you?"

"My pleasure, young sir. I'll keep it good and sharp for ye."

With a nod to the old man, Barclay led the boy to the

nearby well, where he pumped water and gave Elias plenty to drink.

Barclay walked slowly so that his ward could keep up. By the time they reached the rear lawn Elias was shuffling and Barclay was considering picking him up and carrying him the rest of the way.

Out of the kitchen door a robe-wrapped fury in a whirl of red-gold hair came flying, headed straight for them. Barclay was stunned as she planted herself before them with fire in her eyes.

"What the devil do you think you're doing?"

The moment Norah woke up, Murielle had been at her bedside with word of Barclay's startling action. After what seemed like forever, she reported to Norah that he was bringing the poor lad back to the house—who knew in what condition. Norah grabbed a robe—heedless of her recent weakness and disheveled state—and hurried to intercept them. At the sight of Elias's shoulders drooping and feet dragging, she gasped.

"You took a young boy out into the woods with an ax—"

"Hatchet," he said, and the correction only infuriated her more.

Norah fell to her knees before the boy, her hands flying over his head, shoulders, and finally his hands . . . where she counted his fingers. One, two, three—ten, he still had ten—though they were red and swollen.

"What did you do to him?" she demanded, glaring up at him.

Barclay looked surprised, then scowled at Elias.

"Tell her what happened, Elias."

"I chopped wood."

"What?" She looked at the boy, then at Barclay.

"We talked—guardian to ward—and then, as punishment for such a dangerous prank, he had to do some work."

"Chopping wood?" She was shocked, but honestly less than she expected to be. "That's dangerous."

"It can be. Fortunately, he was shown how to do it safely and was watched. He learned how to cut wood on a stump that needs to be cleared. Furthermore, he learned some important words he will need to use, starting today." He nudged Elias, who looked from him to Norah.

"I'm s'posed to say I'm sorry, miss." He dug the scuffed toe of his shoe into the gravel. "So, I'm sorry." Then he raised his chin. "But I didn't know you'd go in the deep part. And *you* can't swim." When Barclay crossed his arms and glowered, clearly expecting more, the boy added, "I didn't mean to hurt you."

She stood up and assessed that apology and his thin attempt at justifying his actions. "I thought I said, 'no more tricks.'"

"I didn't think it would . . . I just wanted t-to . . ." He halted, sensing that his excuses were not enough to excuse his actions, and his real reason for doing it was too embarrassing to admit.

"You wanted to get one over on someone who makes you do things you don't want to do. Is that it?" She trapped his gaze in hers and held it until tears welled in his eyes and he lowered his head. His confession was so quiet she barely heard it.

"Yeah, I guess."

"I guess so, too. That is hardly behavior befitting a young earl."

He seemed to take her words to heart and lowered his head even farther. "You need to go to your room, Elias, and Murielle will come to see that you wash before supper." The boy stuffed his hands hard into his pockets and headed for the rear door.

She watched him go, sensing that he truly was sorry. But it remained to be seen if his regret would temper his behavior in the future.

"Shouldn't you be in bed?" Barclay's voice intruded on her thoughts. When she looked up he was studying her.

Reddening, she pulled the robe tighter together at the neck. "I slept some earlier."

"You don't look fit to resume your duties." He nudged her toward the kitchen steps and, when she tripped, he was there to catch her. She thanked him awkwardly, pulled her robe tighter, and felt strangely akin to Eli. She had all but accused Barclay of abusing his ward and now cringed inwardly at showing such suspicion.

She climbed the steps into the rear hall in embarrassed silence.

He was at her elbow all the way, and when she stepped on her robe on the center stairs he kept her from stumbling and falling yet again. She flushed with humiliation. She knew she should probably say something—apologize for her suspicions—but she couldn't seem to find the words without revealing why she had thought what she had.

After all he had done . . .

"Here you are," he said when they reached her door. "I'll have a tray sent up for supper—if they haven't already planned one." He turned to leave, but soon turned back.

"Just so you know, I fully intend to see the boy to his majority . . . whole and hopefully improved."

She nodded, shamed by her reaction to his handling of the boy. Perhaps if he had stayed a moment or two longer, she would have found the words she needed, such as "I'm sorry for misjudging you."

But he was gone and moments later she was in her room again and in her bed, burying her face in her pillows, wishing she could bury the memory of her alarm and indignation six feet under. It seemed her bad luck hadn't changed after all. She had nearly drowned and then behaved like a madwoman toward her rescuer. What did she have to do to dispel the cloud of disaster that hung above her head?

The evening food and time to think set her on a course to make amends. If he could teach Eli to apologize, she could certainly learn the same lesson. She determined to find a time and place soon to apologize.

That night, well after the house settled down for the night, she left her room to check on Eli. Carrying a candle, she made her way to the boy's room and found him in his bed, sleeping soundly. He appeared to have received another bath . . . his hair smelled of soap and his neck had none of the sweaty lint it often carried in its creases. Whoever used that much soap and water on him deserved a medal for heroic service above and beyond mere duty.

She watched him for a moment, feeling a budding affection for the child. Headstrong and bright and sometimes devious . . . he could also be genuinely grateful and contrite. He had possibilities, this boy. And the challenge was to turn those possibilities into realities. She couldn't help feeling that whatever Barclay had done in the woods with him—*chopping wood? really?*—had been a good thing. Certainly the outcome was better than she expected.

She left the nursery floor and made it down the stairs just as Barclay was coming up the central stairs. It was late, but he was still in his dinner clothes . . . likely just coming from his study. She knew he liked to read at night after the house was quiet. She paused, focusing on his shirt, which was open at the neck.

A wave of unexpected memory washed over her: him in a wet shirt that clung to his big shoulders and chest . . . holding her close, carrying her with little effort. She stopped, and he stopped, too. Her robe was gaping a bit and she pulled it closed, trying frantically to think of something to say.

But he spoke first. "What are you doing out of bed?"

"I-I just needed to check on Eli. He's sleeping soundly."

"You expected worse?" His gaze traveled over her.

"No." She turned to continue down the hall to her room. "I just wasn't sleeping and felt a need to check on him." As he fell into step with her, headed for his room, she realized this was the best time to broach the subject uppermost in her mind. "I feel I must apologize to you for my behavior this afternoon. Murielle said you had taken Eli into the forest with an ax and I knew you would be angry at what he did . . ."

He stopped, his face enigmatic planes in the golden light.

"Half the house saw me do it."

"The staff was on edge, not knowing what you intended."

"House folk do like to imagine the worst."

"They don't know you well," she said with a rueful look. "Apparently I don't either. But I have been the recipient of your generosity more than once." She shifted her candle to the other hand. And looked up into his face. Sweet mercy, he was handsome. Or was it the intimate cloak of darkness surrounding them that made him seem so blasted attractive? That unruly hair . . . that broad chest . . . those amber eyes . . .

"I apologize for thinking that you would do anything but the best for your ward."

His face softened slightly and he nodded.

"I mean, I know he misbehaves and thinks only of his own comfort and pleasure, but he has more in his heart. I think, given time, he will make an admirable man."

"Hard to tell," he said, turning his face aside, "what kind of a man a boy will turn into. And even the best of men sometimes make mistakes." He looked uncomfortable, as if there was something he needed to say, and she waited, feeling an urge to touch him.

"I feel I must apologize, too, Miss Capshaw. I did not mean to make you uncomfortable the other night when I infringed upon your person."

"Infringed?" He sounded like he regretted kissing her . . . was apologizing for giving her one of the most fascinating and pleasurable moments of her life. The thought astonished her.

On impulse, she seized the front of his shirt and pulled him toward her. "Is that what you call this?" Rising onto her toes, she pressed her mouth against his in a way that couldn't be mistaken for anything but an intended kiss.

For a moment she held her breath and soaked up every possible sensation of his mouth against hers. Clearly she had caught him by surprise. He was still at first, then tilted his head to fit his mouth to hers. Their lips were mated, moving slightly, exploring, until she broke the contact and sank back on her heels.

"There. Now you've been *infringed upon*." Her voice was breathy and she was awash in sensations she would hold in until her dying day. She looked him in the eye. "Do I owe you an apology?"

"N-no." He stumbled back a step. "God no."

"Then neither do you owe me one." And on that note she turned and strode down the hall into her room.

Once her door was closed she slid down it to a seat on the floor. The impact of her behavior hit her.

What in blazes had she done? Was she losing her mind? The feel of his mouth on hers came back to her in waves that set her face and throat tingling.

She was suddenly appalled by her behavior. Was there a hoyden buried deep inside her . . . a being separate from her upstanding self? Were there two women spirits inside her, contending for her soul?

Barclay lay in his narrow bed that night, his arms behind his head, reliving that kiss and warning himself it was just a tit for tat from her. She wanted to give him a taste of his own medicine, and it worked. He was duly embarrassed to have taken such a liberty with her—a young woman in his employ and under his protection. The beast in him, he realized. Passions unexpressed boiling to the surface. He would have to do better. He managed to be rational and measured with the boy; he would have to apply the same restraint with Norah Capshaw.

But every time he closed his eyes he felt her lips against his and sensed heat stirring in his traitorous loins. If she only knew that the lesson she intended had the opposite effect. It made him curious about more and hungry for . . . oh, God, he was in trouble.

Several days went by without incident. Eli submitted to his lessons and occasionally even seemed to enjoy the time he spent with Norah in the schoolroom. He especially liked the stories she shared each afternoon, right before his free time. Twice he guessed the moral of the story, and Norah was so pleased she gave him a side hug and he beamed a smile at her. She had the feeling she was slowly winning him over.

In the afternoons Barclay arranged a pony for him to learn to ride. Eli was wary at first, but Barclay had him spend some time brushing and talking to the little mount first. By the time the pony was saddled and the boy was taught to mount, he did so without hesitation. Barclay walked alongside them as they went around the paddock, giving Eli hints and bits of horse lore. He seemed genuinely interested and by the third day ran to the stable in the afternoon and even brought a carrot for his new equine friend. The stableman commented that the young master was a quick learner, which brought the boy a huge smile.

The evenings were the hardest. Supper was reasonable; there was food and etiquette to occupy Norah and the boy. There were reading lessons and the new adventure of horsemanship to relate. But afterward, when Eli was sent to bed under Nanny B's supervision, Norah retreated to her room, avoiding Barclay as much as possible.

That was when she finally felt prepared to read the

letters and documents held for her by Mr. Rivers. And as it turned out, some of the material was quite enlightening.

"Mr. Howard," Norah said one evening as she approached his desk in the study, "may I have a word with you?"

Barclay lowered the papers he was reading, genuinely surprised by her approach. He had expected their communication would continue to be limited to the "Good morning" and "Good evening" it had been for the past several days. He waved her into a chair in front of his desk and she sat primly on the edge, holding a folio of papers. Her face was flushed and her eyes were bright with whatever she intended to bring to his attention. For a moment, facing her again, he held his breath.

"I have been reading the documents kept for me by Mr. Rivers and"—she could barely contain the news—"I may have some family after all."

He sat forward, searching her hopeful expression.

"That is interesting." He frowned. "I can't imagine why your guardian would withhold such vital information."

"When you see the letter to my father you may understand why. Apparently when he married my mother he was forced to break with his family. They did not speak after that. But a great deal of time has gone by and I would like to see if perhaps I can reestablish ties to them.

"It seems I have an uncle." She opened the folio and handed him a letter addressed to her father from his elder brother.

When he read it he paused over its harsh language and the ultimatum her father had been given. It didn't seem like her uncle was a man who would be amenable to reconciliation even twenty-four years later. But people could change, he told himself. Look at the relationship between his friend Rafe and Rafe's father, Horace. The old man was tough enough to chew tenpenny nails and Rafe had hated his bulldog style of doing business. Yet now they worked amicably side by side.

What sealed it for him was the hope in Norah's eyes. Whatever the outcome, she wouldn't be happy until she at least tried to establish contact with her estranged family.

"Perhaps a letter?" he said, handing the papers back to her.

"That was my thought. If they are agreeable, I could arrange a visit to their home in York on a Sunday, when Eli doesn't have lessons."

"That seems reasonable." He tapped his fingers on the chair arm, knowing his advice was probably futile. "Don't raise your hopes until you have a reply."

"Of course." She nodded. "I understand that there still may be hard feelings to resolve. I only hope they reside in the same place."

Norah's letter was posted the very next day, bearing wording that she had worked all night to perfect. For the next few days every rider or lorry that approached the house brought her to the windows or down to the entry hall. But on the eighth day after sending the letter she did indeed receive a response.

Barclay met her in the salon and sat opposite her while she read and reread her uncle's words.

"I'm afraid I may read too much into it," she said, offering him the letter. "Will you read it and give me your opinion?"

He read the single page twice and heard the same rigid

voice coming through the words answering her inquiry. There was an edge to the words, but also an avowed interest in meeting a long-lost niece. Her "Uncle Edgar" suggested a Sunday two weeks away and asked where she was staying and who had engaged her as a tutor.

Barclay studied her glowing face and retreated into his restrained persona. "Tell him you are a young gentleman's tutor. Beyond that, say little."

"I already told him about my guardian's death and that I have a position here in the north country." She seemed surprised, then a bit deflated. "Should I have been more cautious?"

"It seems reasonable in such a case."

"I don't expect an enthusiastic welcome. I am a stranger to them, after all. But I want to believe they offer goodwill, as his reply says."

He studied her for a moment, realizing that her feelings in the matter could be easily bruised. But something about her uncle's harsh letter to her father combined with the calculated politeness of his response brought out Barclay's wariness. Norah tried to hide the excitement she harbored, but he could feel it as if it were his own tremors of expectation . . . which in his experience often ended in disappointment.

"Two weeks—is that right?"

She nodded. "I don't know how far it is to York, or if there is coach service on a Sunday . . ."

"You won't need that," he said gruffly. "We'll take the Northrup carriage."

"We?" she said with puzzlement.

He adopted a granite-jawed stare that brooked no denial. "I'm going, too."

* * *

Late that same night a gentlemanly figure alighted from
a cab, ordered it to wait, and then entered a working-class
pub near the Cattle Market in the south of the city of York.
There he caught the eye of a ruddy-faced man in a checkered coat and flat cap and jerked his head toward the door
to a back room. The man joined him, and the pair were
ushered in to a small, poorly lit room where the smell of
sweat and old ale lingered.

"I found 'er." The man leaned close as soon as the
gentleman was seated across from him. "Slippery tart 'ad
some great bully helpin' her. Whisked 'er away afore I
could get me hands on 'er." He edged closer, his reddened
face intent on redress. "I'll get 'er, I swear to—"

"Save your oaths," the well-dressed gent growled. "I
know where she is—or where she will be in a fortnight."

His agent looked stunned. "Where?"

"My house." The gent smiled.

"How?" The Scot's face twisted with surprise that
turned quickly to outrage. "I searched high an' low."

"She contacted me." The gent chuckled at the irony of
it, enjoying his agent's embarrassment. "Seeking out long-
lost family. She says she is in Yorkshire, engaged as a tutor
for someone."

"Whadderya sayin'? Now I get nae money?"

"While the results of your efforts were disappointing,
you can still be of use." The gent reached into his greatcoat
and withdrew a pouch of coin. Handing it over, he narrowed his eyes. "You will need assistance for what I have
in mind. I assume you have acquaintances suitable for
'sensitive' work."

"Aye, I do, but—"

"You'll need to find a place where matters may be handled in private." He pointed to the pouch. "Use some of that. If you need more, contact me."

The Scot nodded and tucked away the money. "Ah ken jus' the place." He paused, fingering the bulge of the pouch through his coat. "Whaddya want done?"

"I'll tell you soon enough. Two men can keep a secret . . . only if one of them is dead." His fierce gaze made the Scot draw back an inch. Seeing that reaction, the gent laughed wickedly, rose, and left.

Twelve

Everything about the trip to York took longer than Norah expected, starting the night before with Barclay's order to her to pack things for an overnight stay at a hotel. She stood in shock when Barclay decreed that not only would he accompany her, Murielle would come to "attend to your needs" . . . a polite way of saying the maid would act as chaperone.

It was another surprise when Eli threw some things into a satchel belonging to Nanny B and dragged it downstairs, insisting he was coming, too. There was a bit of roaring on one hand and stubbornness on the other, but in the end Eli went stomping back upstairs and refused to eat supper. He was sent to bed early, and when Norah checked on him later he was fast asleep.

Barclay had had the Northrup carriage taken from storage and cleaned and had the top raised and a brazier prepared. The weather was turning colder and frost glazed the ground as the carriage was brought around that morning and the luggage was brought out. Eli watched from the small parlor window as they loaded the trunk at the back of the carriage and Norah could see he was still irritated at not being allowed on the trip. But he soon disappeared and she knew he would be in his room sulking.

"Do you think I am properly dressed?" Norah said once they were underway. Feeling self-conscious, she rearranged her coat over her knees. "I understand they are in the mercantile business and are prosperous. I want to make a good impression."

"You will," Barclay said, a sentiment that was echoed by Murielle.

There was little conversation after that, except for the maid's reminiscences of her one trip to the major city of the north. Candy, she said—Rowntree's chocolate and fruit candies—was everywhere. And she confessed to Norah that she came across Eli looking despondent and was moved to promise to bring him a special treat.

Norah smiled. Murielle wasn't known to have a soft spot for children, but lately Eli had sometimes managed to sneak past her judgmental side. The boy had a way of doing that—making people soften toward him even when he was less than his best self.

They stopped for food and to rest the horses at a small inn on the main road. When they returned to the carriage later Barclay noticed that the straps on the luggage trunk were loose and had the driver rebuckle them.

As they came closer to the city, they began to see evidence of the prosperity of the north's largest city; church spires in the distance, the tower of the old York Castle, and tall smokestacks attached to factory buildings along the rivers. Yet there was much green in the city proper as they entered the still-standing medieval walls. Murielle pointed out the sights she recalled . . . all of which Barclay knew and furnished some history about. He had been there several times in his university days. Knowing the city, he had secured them rooms at Grays Court, a handsome hotel situated between the old city wall and the York Minster.

Norah was surprised and delighted by the charming brick structure set in gardens that beckoned with colorful, cold-blooming flowers. When they exited the coach at the front court the doorman headed for the luggage. The moment the trunk opened, a cry issued from it.

Norah rushed for the rear of the carriage, but arrived after Barclay to find Eli's sweaty face and frowzled hair popping up from the trunk.

"What the devil are you doing in there?" Barclay rushed to pull him out and hold him up in the air—feet dangling as he squirmed.

"He was in there the whole time?" Norah asked, though the fact was obvious. She rushed to grab him by the shoulders when Barclay lowered him to the ground. "What on earth possessed you to climb in there? It took hours—you might have suffocated!"

"I . . . I w-wanted to come . . . I had to," Eli stammered, rubbing his face and trying to steady himself. "I never been anywhere but Northrup." He looked up at Norah. "I need to see geography . . . for . . . the maps . . ." Tears rolled down the scamp's reddened cheeks as he faced his shocked tutor and angry guardian.

The barely reined outrage in Barclay's eyes stunned Norah. The "beast" she had met that first day at the lecture hall was back. It was all she could do to gather the nerve to plead for his understanding.

"Really, Mr. Howard, it wasn't meant in defiance." She swallowed hard. "It was just the boy's curiosity overwhelmed him."

A moment later Barclay tore his gaze from hers to loom over the boy and capture his face in a big hand.

"You have punishment coming." He studied the fear in the boy's eyes. "There is no time to take you home, so you'll have to stay. But make no mistake, you have disobeyed a clear order and you will have to pay."

Eli gave a stiff nod. A moment later Norah collected him against her side to usher him with her through the hotel's entry. Shortly, Barclay appeared by them at the registration desk, his face like granite.

"It seems the brat made room for himself in the trunk by removing other luggage. *Mine*." He glowered such that Eli pressed back against Norah's skirts, seeking protection.

Norah glanced at the boy's widened eyes, assessing the genuine fear in them. Had he known the bag he tossed out was his guardian's? She screwed up her courage to look at Barclay. "We aren't staying long . . . and if need be, you can find something to wear in a local shop. We saw some along the way. Surely . . ."

There was a deadly silence that had her knees weakening.

"I cannot wear *anything* ready-made," he said fiercely, then turned his attention to the hotel manager waiting anxiously to greet them. When the arrangements were made to accommodate an extra person, he gave the boy and Norah a steely glare and stalked out of the hotel.

It didn't take very many inquiries in local shops to locate a tailor who might prove helpful. But the minute Barclay ducked into the front room of Boorman's, he found himself in the middle of a confrontation. The proprietor—a balding, fiftyish fellow in shirtsleeves with a tape draped around his neck—was dressing down a young man in a dapper suit. The younger man stood with hand clasping wrist, submitting to the tirade.

"Damnable slackard! If ye spent 'alf the time tending the shop that ye do fussin' with yer own kit, I'd have a decent trade! I told you before—sweep th' floor and dust th' shelves every day! An' bow to the trade—no matter who walks in!"

The proprietor seemed oblivious to Barclay's presence until the clerk focused on him and produced a taut smile. The clerk was tall, had dark hair, and had by any standard a striking face. Just as notable was his clothing . . . clearly bespoke and worn with the dignity of a robe of office. His reaction caused the proprietor to turn and greet their outsize patron with a drooping mouth. His speech changed dramatically.

"W-welcome, sir. What can I do for you this afternoon?"

Barclay looked from the proprietor to the clerk and then turned to the better-dressed underling.

"I am in need of a shirt or two." He straightened, barely clearing the low ceiling of the shop. "I am hard to fit."

Immediately, the clerk brought out a tape and began to measure Barclay's shoulders, chest, neck, and arms. He recorded the numbers and studied them. "I believe we can accommodate you, sir. We have a shirt or two in the making that can be altered. Would two days suffice?"

"Afraid not," Barclay said. "I need it tomorrow morning."

The fellow produced a handsome smile. "I'll see it done, sir."

Barclay assessed the clerk's gaze and saw in it a confidence that assured him it would be done as promised. He nodded.

"You will add a premium for the urgency." It was a simple statement but, like much Barclay uttered, came across as an order. "I am at Grays Court. Howard . . . Barclay Howard."

The clerk's eyebrows shot up. Apparently he knew that the name Howard meant something in York.

"Of the Northrup Howards?" he had the temerity to ask.

Barclay jerked a nod and moved toward the door, then turned back.

"I admire the cut of your suit. Who is your tailor?"

The clerk produced a satisfied grin.

"Myself, sir."

Barclay nodded, stored that away, and exited the shop.

The following morning Barclay awakened to the melodic tolling of the nearby Minster's bells, but was not especially pleased by the serenade. He had dined poorly the previous night and retired to a bed that seemed to be made of rocks. He knew it wasn't the mattress or the accommodation that caused his discomfort; it was the overall tenor of the trip.

Nothing seemed to be going right, and he sensed that what followed that day would not dispel the unease he felt. He feared that Norah's visit with her unknown relations would not be the joyful reunion she hoped for. Strange, how just a few words on a sheet of paper could give him such a distaste for her father's family. He had intuited early that it might be prudent to accompany her, but now he feared it could prove vital.

When there was a rap on the door of his room he answered it promptly and found Boorman's tall, lean clerk outside with a paper-wrapped package that could only be the shirt he had ordered. He stepped back and waved the fellow in.

"If you would like to try it, sir, I would make certain it fits properly." The fellow looked around the room, then stood ready to assist.

Barclay nodded, feeling a bit awkward, but removed his shirt and opened the package. The fabric was fine under his fingertips and the workmanship was clearly excellent. There was no need for a collar form, one was made a part of the shirt. He could tell as he slid his arms into the sleeves that it was superior work and would serve him well. His tension faded as he worked the mother-of-pearl buttons and found he had room to breathe, even at the stiffened collar.

"Your work?" he said as he stepped in front of the wardrobe mirror.

"Yes, sir." The clerk gave a nod and a taut smile.

Barclay turned to him. "With such skill, why are you working for Boorman? If ever a man was aptly named . . ."

"Personal circumstance," the tailor responded, then after a moment added, "Needs must."

"Ah." Barclay knew the meaning behind such terms. Too much time at the track or tables, losing. "And where did you learn tailoring?"

"At my father's knee. He had a shop in London."

"So you 'suit yourself' now."

That brought a genuine smile to the fellow's lean face. "I do."

"You have markers still outstanding?" Barclay asked, not sure why he was so curious or whether the fellow might answer him. But the tailor seemed an enigma and, being one himself, he was keen to know another. He folded his arms, considering the man.

"They are now paid." The fellow met his eyes for a moment . . . blue eyes, clear of malice and judgment. "A man of worth pays his debts."

"So he does." Barclay decided in that moment to offer him an alternative. "I have need of help. I am guardian to the Earl of Northrup and his estate. I have never had a proper valet and find myself needing one. You seem to know clothing and are well-spoken and presentable."

"I have no references." The fellow tensed visibly.

"I believe I am wearing one," Barclay said with a wry half smile. "Consider my offer while you make me two more shirts. I will need them day after tomorrow when we leave for Northrup."

The young man nodded with a smile. "I will think on it as I make your shirts."

"Your name?" Barclay said, certain he was making the one good decision he had made on this trip.

"Randville."

"Randville." Barclay turned the name over in his head. "Clearly worth his wage."

The fellow looked surprised by the comment, but nodded and left.

Barclay ruminated for a moment on his impulse to hire the man. He was not a valet, clearly, but Randville had good knowledge of clothes and how to assemble and keep them. Even if he stayed only a short time, he could organize Barclay's closet and set a standard of care for the staff.

As he finished buttoning his vest and slid into his coat, he recalled the event ahead and thought about how he would secure the boy while doing it. Then he smiled.

Murielle would certainly earn her wage today.

* * *

Norah scarcely heard the horror in Murielle's voice as she protested taking care of the mischievous little earl. She was equally oblivious to Eli's insistence that he was not a baby and didn't need a minder. She was busy reviewing the list of things she meant to tell her uncle and the things she meant to ask. Last-minute adjustments to her best blue wool day dress and reasonably fashionable hat, and a final brush of her short, dark cloak took the rest of her attention. Still, she was surprised when Barclay came to escort her to the Northrup carriage, saying it was time.

Butterflies fluttered in her stomach as they drove through a prosperous neighborhood where sizable houses were set behind front gardens that bore colorful autumn flowers. What if they didn't accept her? What if she was over-dressed or appeared shabby compared to their affluent tastes? What if they didn't even receive her?

But it was too late for such misgivings, she realized as the carriage stopped before a substantial, Palladian-style house and Barclay Howard assisted her down the step. She caught a glimpse of what seemed to be a woman's face at a front window, but in a blink it disappeared. No doubt they were curious about her and possibly suspicious about her reason for contacting them.

She and Barclay were admitted to a pleasant entry hall paved in black-and-white marble and ringed by gilt-framed paintings of people and places that most likely meant something to them . . . probably had meant something to her father, too. That thought settled some of her nerves. She was here to learn what she could about her father and whatever place she might claim for herself in the family that had rejected him.

An aged butler shuffled ahead of them to a long parlor,

indicating that the master and mistress would be down shortly. Norah looked around the well-furnished room, noting that the fabric of the drapes and upholstered furnishings looked fresh and rather expensive. There was a handsome mirror over each of two marble fireplaces and the air bore a faint scent of beeswax polish.

Norah perched on the edge of a settee to wait, clasping her hands tightly and feeling chilled. Barclay moved to a nearby window, his hands joined behind his back. He had a stonelike countenance that spoke of dour expectations and set her even more on edge.

A well-dressed man and woman entered the parlor and stood evaluating Norah, who rose the moment they appeared. The man was moderately tall with rounded shoulders and hair graying at the temples. The woman was very thin, with pinched features and hair done up in braids that looped around her ears—a style that hadn't been in fashion for some time.

"Norah Capshaw," the man said, stepping forward with a smile that looked somehow out of place on his lean features. "So you are my wayward brother's child." He looked her over thoroughly as he took her offered hand. "You don't favor the Capshaws. Though, on second glance, there is something of your father in the shape of your face. I am your uncle Edgar and this is your aunt Agatha."

Norah knew the instant their gazes caught Barclay's presence; their eyes widened and jaws drooped as he approached from the fireplace. She knew too well the first impression he made and turned to introduce him to the pair with a determined smile.

"My employer, Mr. Howard, generously volunteered to

accompany me on the trip to York. I am tutor to his ward, Elias Howard."

"Howard?" Edgar Capshaw looked taken aback by Barclay's imposing presence, but recovered. "Perchance the Northrup Howards?"

"The same," Barclay said, coming to stand behind Norah.

"Well, this is an unexpected turn," her uncle said with forced pleasantry. "When you mentioned being a tutor you neglected to say it was in a noble house. The Earl of Northrup is"—he paused, only now recalling—"recently deceased." He looked to Barclay. "But you cannot be—"

"I am the old earl's grandson and the new earl's guardian. Miss Capshaw was engaged to prepare him for school." When he offered Edgar a hand the man took it, though the handclasp was brief.

"A young earl." Agatha Capshaw gave Norah a sympathetic look. "Boys are quite active. I imagine he keeps you busy."

"He does," Norah admitted. "But he does well at his studies and a bit of spirit is expected in one so bright. In fact, he came along with us to see some of York."

"Where are you staying, dear?" Agatha asked.

"Grays Court, near the Minster," she responded, receiving a nod of approval from her aunt.

"A lovely place. The gardens especially."

There was a deep lull in the conversation, and Norah knew the time had come to ask about her father's life and background.

"I was hoping, in coming to meet you, to learn more of my father's family and background. Were there only two children in the family?"

"Two sons were our parents' allotment of offspring, it seems," her uncle said. "As it happened, our mother died young and our father was never in good health afterward. Your father's desertion was the final stroke to make him take to his bed. He died a year later."

Norah was struck by her uncle's vengeful tone. He clearly blamed his brother for their father's death. She couldn't reconcile the loving, considerate father she had known with a careless, willful son who abandoned his family to follow his passions. Tension deepened in her middle as she stored her uncle's opinion under "resentment" and continued. "I would like to hear about my father's schooling and activities while growing up. Perhaps you can tell me about his younger years."

The request seemed to lower some of the tension in the meeting and some recollections were shared. Her father had never showed interest in the family business concerns, Edgar was keen to point out. Instead, he occupied himself with hunting and fishing, most often at the family hunting retreat across the border in Scotland. He had an interest in horses and all manner of physical activity—was considered a capable sportsman. But why wouldn't he be, Edgar opined, given so much time to sharpen his skills at shooting and horsemanship?

Norah struggled to picture the father she had known in such roles and asked if they might have any pictures of him. Agatha retrieved a family album, and soon Norah was seeing for the first time the experiences that had been her father's early life. He was shown with favorite horses, prize fish, and shooting trophies. A number of the pictures showed him with his father . . . just the two of them looking relaxed.

Then came the darker parts of Edgar's story.

On a fishing trip into Scotland's Southern Uplands his brother ran across some heathen Scots named

MacFergus . . . who had a temptress of a daughter. Her uncle's voice grew clipped and cold as he recounted that her father fell under the sly wench's spell and planned to marry her without consulting his father or elder brother.

When he returned to York with her they were appalled to see the half-wild creature he intended to make his wife. It was a scandal . . . her one entry into local society was a disaster and she was considered untamed and unacceptable. Her father was given orders to take his beloved straight back to her home and leave her there. Clearly, he disobeyed.

"That is not at all the image I have of them," she said, her voice thick and full of emotion. She fingered the locket around her neck.

Barclay had retreated to the front fireplace, fearing that his presence might hinder whatever goodwill might develop between them.

But with each unpleasant revelation, he moved nearer to Norah, determined to provide whatever support he could. Truth be told, he was also curious about the pictures she was being shown and the truthfulness of the relatives' account. Everything about these Capshaws set his nerves on edge. By the time her uncle pronounced his low opinion of her mother—*the arrogant bastard*—Barclay stood behind Norah with his fists clenched behind his back.

When Norah turned her head he could see tears in her eyes. He was about to intervene when he saw she was holding her mother's locket. "I found this locket in a box saved for me by my guardian, Mr. Rivers." Her hands trembled as she tried to open it. "And the strangest thing, there was—"

"Let me." He surprised Norah into looking up as he rounded the settee. He had assessed the judgmental looks on the Capshaws' faces and thought of the mysterious piece of gold in the locket. "It seems that I am the only one who can open this piece."

He stood before her, holding the locket, looking into her upturned face. The strain of the visit and her relatives' hostility toward her father was visible in her pale features. He frowned as he pressed the latch in all the wrong ways, hoping she would understand that he wouldn't open it.

"He's never had trouble with it before," she said softly, clearly puzzled but struggling with more volatile emotions.

"I may have damaged the latch when forcing it." He straightened with an intent look at Norah, surrendering the locket to her fingers. "Another time, perhaps."

"Yes." Her disappointment was hard to watch. "Perhaps."

Agatha Capshaw unexpectedly offered an olive branch.

"I know it may be difficult for you to hear of your father's reckless behavior, my dear. It was a shock to your uncle and grandfather, too." The woman's tone was kind and she seemed to react to Norah's discomfort with womanly concern. "I do hope you will not hold these revelations against us. We can see that you are a young woman of education and refinement and we would like to count you part of our family despite your unfortunate origins."

As they left the Capshaws' home, those last four words rang in Norah's mind. *Despite your unfortunate origins.* They wanted her to know they still blamed her father for the estrangement and would accept her only on their own terms. It was not what she had hoped for. But in truth she should have been better prepared for their attitude by her uncle's letters.

During the ride back to Grays Court she was silent for a time as she went over the visit in her mind. She saw Barclay looking at her and turned to him.

"Why did you not open the locket? I wanted to show them the picture of my parents together—to make them see they had made a loving marriage." Her throat tightened as she uttered those last words.

"There is a mystery in that locket. That piece of gold ore. I thought it best not to let them know it exists until you know why it was put there."

She looked down at her clasped hands.

"You don't trust them," she said, part statement, part accusation.

"About as much as I would trust a fox to guard a henhouse." That blunt statement summed up his opinion of the visit and the people.

Her first instinct was to protest that they were probably being cautious regarding her claim of kinship . . . though why she would defend such unpleasant and judgmental people was a puzzle of its own. She recalled Barclay's statement that earls needed to be able to judge men . . . their character, loyalty, and trustworthiness. No doubt that came from hard-won lessons in noble society. He was cautious about making associations. She winced to think of how her own introduction to him was filled with judgment and insulting expectations.

"I could understand their caution regarding me; they are well-to-do. I am a poor relation. I have nothing to guard from them."

"Don't be too sure of that. You have been followed and

searched . . . someone wants something from you." He looked at her with a wry twist to one side of his mouth . . . a mischievous expression that always sent a trickle of pleasure through her. "Something more than fetching smiles."

She looked down but couldn't help the pleasure that washed her face with warmth and tugged at the corners of her mouth.

"What was your father's name?" he asked, watching her.

"Douglas Trenton Capshaw. Why do you ask?"

"Did it seem curious to you that your uncle and aunt never used his name during the visit?"

She frowned, thinking. "That didn't occur to me. I never think of him as anything but 'Father.'" Now, however, she thought about it.

A moment later she was startled by his hand closing around hers and taking it to the seat between them. When she looked at him he was staring out the carriage window as if he didn't want to have to explain what his hand had done.

The chill in her core began to warm. Taking a deep breath, she squeezed his hand and felt grateful that he had insisted on accompanying her and was honest with his assessment of her relatives' reception. His presence always seemed to make the world around her safer. "As safe as in a bishop's pocket," he had once said. She had thought it a boast at the time. But he had saved her more than once, and right now she sensed that such security was part of her growing attachment to him. She wasn't sure it was wise to depend on him—on anyone—for her safety and future. She had sworn to stand on her own two feet, and a year from now she would no doubt be glad she did, whatever the cost.

As the carriage turned into the short drive of Grays Court, she felt a sense of loss when he released her hand and spoke.

"I wonder if Murielle has any hair left on her head."

Thirteen

After dark that evening Edgar Capshaw descended from a cab in front of the Cork and Cleaver in the Cattle Market district. The Scot was waiting in the back room with a bottle of whiskey and a bellyful of impatience.

"Well?" he demanded before the merchant even removed his hat. "Did she come? Where's she now?"

"Grays Court." Capshaw picked up one of the small glasses on the table, scowled at the crusty film on it, and put it down again. "She came with a great bull of a man who claimed to be a Howard, of the Northrup Howards."

"A great bear of a bloke? A glare wot could light damp kindlin'?" The Scot scowled when Capshaw nodded. "Wot's he doin' here wi' her?"

"He's her employer, he says. Claims to be the guardian of the young Earl of Northrup. That's where she stays now, the earl's estate."

"I seen th' place. A bloody palace it is."

"We have to get her alone . . . find out what she knows." He tapped the scarred tabletop with gloved fingers, thinking. "Better chance here than at the Northrup estate. Did you find a place?"

"Aye. The ol' mill on Seyfarth Creek."

"I know it." He smiled, anticipating. "Then go watch the hotel. She'll be out seeing the city tomorrow. Follow and make sure you're not seen. Take her to the mill and let me know when you have her." He paused, recalling the big man who accompanied her. "Watch out for that Howard bloke. He claims noble connection but looks to be a beast."

"Aye." The Scot sneered. "I owe tha' big lug a Glasgow kiss."

"B-but there's candy everywhere—Murielle said so," Elias declared, his eyes misting. "She promised me some."

"That was before you stowed away on the carriage against Mr. Howard's orders," Norah said, wishing the sight of tears in a six-year-old's eyes was easier to ignore.

She stood in the reception area of Grays Court trying to enforce Barclay's order for the boy to stay at the hotel with Murielle and Miss Capshaw while he was out. She wasn't certain what his errand was or when he might return; he hadn't shared such details. And she had a query or two of her own to pursue.

"P-please, Miss Capshaw—I promise I'll be good an' write numbers and learn words an'—eat vegg-ettables every day!"

She was softening. Something in her felt his desperation to experience new things as if it were her own. Against her better judgment, she relented and asked the desk clerk where the nearest candy shop could be found. Murielle rolled her eyes, but minutes later the three were on the street and headed for what the clerk described as the place for "a jolly good treat."

The shop, called Sweetie's, proved to be even better

than advertised. Elias's face glowed with excitement as he ran from case to case filled with dark, fragrant chocolates, fruity pastilles, peppermint sticks, lemon drops, and all manner of edible wonders.

"Please, miss, can we get some? Pleeeease—"

Because that seemed to be the purpose of the visit, Norah nodded and allowed Eli to take her hand and lead her from one case to another. The clerk offered them samples and Eli was soon transported to a land where sugary goodness transformed him into a compliant child. She ordered several treats that were weighed out and put in pink-striped paper bags that echoed the color of the bright pink shop door and awnings.

"Three pieces," she declared to her charge as they left the shop. "Choose three to eat now, but the rest must be saved for later."

It didn't take Eli long to pick three candies to try. It was the first time Norah saw him try to prolong the pleasure of something . . . letting his choices melt in his mouth and linger on his tongue. She and Murielle indulged in a treat themselves as they walked to the venerable parish church where her parents were reportedly married.

Norah wanted to see firsthand the date of their marriage and their signatures on the page of the register. If she had time afterward she wanted to find a shop where sporting equipment was sold and purchase a new ball or two for Elias.

She felt a twinge of unease as they entered narrow streets in the old section of York and found herself glancing over her shoulder at other pedestrians and the upper stories overhanging the narrow streets. Nothing seemed amiss, and she chided herself for being nervous. Likely she had gotten too accustomed to the feeling of safety that

Barclay Howard's large presence provided. What happened to the woman determined to deal with her own troubles and make her own way in the world?

Meanwhile, Barclay sat in the outer office of Maren, Lister, and Dowd, formerly his grandfather's lawyers and now, for the sake of continuity, his own. He hoped to set eyes on the men who would provide him legal advice and support in the coming years. A secondary goal was to see Solicitor Westerman again and glean whatever information the man could provide regarding the Capshaws. He had long ago learned that few men held grudges that strong for that long unless motivated by money or status, or both. Knowing their circumstances might help him figure out their still-burning animosity toward Norah's father and, by association, Norah herself.

"Mr. Howard!" Henry Westerman hurried into the reception area to greet him with an outstretched hand. "How good to see you, sir! I wish I had known you were coming to York. I would have planned a dinner party for you with the partners. Two of them are in London just now and the third is at the local courts, attending hearings."

"A shame," Barclay said, meaning every word. "I had hoped to meet them. But in fact I came to see you. I need information that you may be able to provide."

He was shown into Westerman's office, a cluttered but comfortable room with oak and leather furnishings that spoke of a partner in the making. Westerman moved bundles of papers from the chairs before his desk and, with an apologetic smile, motioned Barclay into one of them.

"How may I help you, Mr. Howard?"

"You can give me whatever information you may have

about a family of merchants here in York. Edgar Capshaw and family have a mercantile concern that I am told is rather prosperous. What do you know of them?"

Westerman gazed intently at Barclay, while rubbing the wooden edge of his desk. "May I ask the reason for your interest in them?"

"The young woman I engaged as a tutor for my ward is related to them. She met them recently and they told her things about her father—Edgar Capshaw's younger brother, Douglas—that I would verify."

"The Capshaws and their mercantile concern are believed to be quite prosperous," Westerman began. "Not, however, the most pleasant of people." He took a breath and appeared to be measuring his words. "Ambitious and acquisitive describes the current owners. . . . They have entered into partnerships with other merchants that have been dissolved due to 'irregularities.' No one airs grievances openly, in part because the Capshaws are suspected of having associates in rough trade. But they are not popular in local society." The lawyer leaned forward with his elbows on his desk. "I speak in strictest confidence, you understand."

Barclay nodded. "That matches my own assessment. But my employee's late father, Douglas Capshaw—do you know anything of him and his scandalous marriage?"

"Only what I've heard. He was a decent chap: clever, amicable, and the apple of his father's eye . . . a favoritism that apparently earned the older brother's resentment. I know little about the marriage except that there was some contention concerning it. When the father became ill, the older brother seized the reins and has been in control since." Westerman's brow furrowed. "The younger Capshaw died, I believe."

"He did, leaving my employee an orphan at a young age. She had hopes to reconcile with the family."

"A hard road there, I imagine. Not the most welcoming sort." The lawyer's troubled look spoke volumes, but then he brightened. "And the young earl—how is he faring?"

"He is a challenge. Strong-willed and too clever for his own good. But he makes progress in his studies and seems to accept correction. He may make a lord of consequence someday."

Barclay left Westerman's office determined to caution Norah and to see to it that whatever someone wanted from her, they would not get. Her uncle seemed a prime suspect, but it was a Scot who pursued her to her lodgings in London and ransacked her belongings, and the Capshaws were not fond of Scots. Still, whoever wanted something from her was serious and could be capable of finding her at Northrup.

He would have to take measures to secure the estate, starting with some additional staff who knew how to handle themselves in dangerous situations.

Norah, Eli, and Murielle continued their walk around the center of York after visiting Holy Trinity Church, where Norah's parents were married. The dignity of the old church cast a spell over them, making them whisper and tiptoe as they trod the aisles and gazed at the beautiful windows. Norah found the deacon and asked to see the church register, which he gladly showed her.

Gazing at her parents' signatures on the marriage roster, she smiled through tears that filled her eyes. The sight brought her closer to their memory and she felt oddly at peace there. It was hard to leave, but Eli was becoming restless, and she surrendered to inevitability and exited with them to walk to a nearby square, where booths had been set up and street performers commanded a ring of spectators.

After purchasing lemon ices, they paused to watch a juggler who tossed balls, then bowling pins, and then balanced spinning plates on long sticks. Murielle was transfixed and Norah herself was so fascinated she lost track of time . . . and Eli. When the performer took a bow and announced the next act, she looked down to see Eli's reaction and found him gone. Assuming he had wandered forward to get a better look, she nudged her way to the front of the spectators only to find he wasn't there either.

More annoyed than concerned, she made her way back to Murielle, who was newly enthralled with some acrobats bounding into the street-side stage.

"Have you seen Eli?" she asked. "I can't locate him."

"Likely playin' his tricks, miss. He'll be close by," the maid said, reaching into a striped paper bag for another sweet.

Just then, Norah spotted a cone of lemon ice upended on the pavement near where Eli had stood. The boy had been so delighted by the treat—he would never have dropped it without a word of complaint and a plea for another. But there it was, and the sight of it coupled with Eli's absence alarmed her.

"Murielle"—she grabbed the maid's arm—"Eli's gone. I'm afraid he's gotten lost or something's happened to him."

The maid looked around in dismay, hoping to spot him. When she didn't see him she looked back at her mistress, who pointed to the cherished lemon ice melting not far away. The three had been the only ones enjoying that particular treat when the juggler's performance began.

"I'll go this way, you go that," Norah said, pointing to the sides of the crowd of spectators. "Call out when you find the little devil."

She ran around the edge of the crowd, stooping here and there to search for a pair of small feet wearing scuffed shoes. There was no sign of him as she cleared the crowd. With a sinking feeling, she stood at the edge of the square and called for him again and again.

A shrill cry came from across the way and ended abruptly, as if smothered. She ran toward the sound and spotted a figure at the mouth of an alley that opened onto the square. The alley's deep shadows made it hard to tell if that was the source, but she moved toward it all the same.

A moment later she made out a big hand across a small face and little legs kicking and she began to run. Noise from the growing crowd and the music that accompanied the acrobats drowned out her calls to Murielle.

It was Eli, she was certain, and the man holding him had a hand across his mouth, stifling his cries for help. She had no idea what she could do to free her pupil, but instinct took over as she rushed toward them and resolve filled her. She yelled for help, but there was no one close enough to come to her aid. There was no time to waste; the man was dragging Eli deeper into the shadows with every second that passed. She plunged ahead, telling herself she would find a way . . . she would free Eli even if it cost her her own freedom.

Near the brick wall at the intersection of alleyways the man stopped, and she drew close enough to recognize his flat cap, burly build, and checkered coat. She gasped as men lunged out of the shadows on either side of her and seized her arms.

"Let go of me!" She twisted and jerked her shoulders, managing to free one arm long enough to grab the hatpin from her hat. "How dare you?" A moment later that arm was captive again, only in a more punishing grip. She cried out to Eli, telling him to run when he could and tell Murielle to get help, but he seemed to be caught as fast as she was.

The men holding her clamped a hand over her mouth and uttered nasty threats about what they would do if she didn't cooperate. Panic filled her as the Scot dragged Eli flailing and writhing closer to her.

"Where is it?" he demanded. "Tell us an' ye go free."

The panic in Eli's eyes was all she could see for a moment. When she tried to speak the wretch covering her mouth removed his hand and she saw the only chance she had to escape. But what about Eli?

"I don't know what you want."

"Yer old man . . . he knew . . . an' ye owe it back to th' clans. Don' try to say he died wi' out tellin' ye where it lay."

"I was a small child when my father died. All he left me were a few documents and a couple of pictures. I'll give you everything he left me if you'll just let the boy go." She could see in the Scot's narrowing eyes that he didn't believe her and wasn't about to release Eli. She would have to take desperate measures. She had a weapon—a simple but effective one. She caught Eli's gaze and nodded to him, trying to tell him to be ready. "He has nothing to do with my father—he's just an innocent child—"

She jerked up her arm, surprising the bully on her right, and stabbed him in the face with her hatpin. A shocked second was all she needed. When he released her to grab his cheek and howl, she struck her other captor in the neck. He jerked back, spitting curses.

"*Run*, Eli!" She bolted back down the alley for the square, praying he was behind her. But the moment she reached the open square, calling for help, she whirled and saw to her horror that the Scot was hauling Eli down the intersecting alley and out of sight. The boy hadn't acted quickly enough! He was still captive!

"Eli!" she cried out, running back down the alley and finding it empty. Even the crossing alley was vacant. Where had they gone? She rushed one way and then the other, looking for gates and doors that could have provided escape, but everything seemed locked tight. She groaned in anguish and frustration. Help—she needed help!

Murielle came running down the main alley, calling her name, and she rushed back toward the square. Halfway, she met Barclay, too, who practically barreled her over before he caught and steadied her.

"What's happened?" he demanded, setting her back to look at her. "Where is Eli?"

"They've taken him," she said hoarsely, desperate to get it all out. "The Scot who followed me—he's here with some men and he seized Eli. He wants something he thinks my father had. I tried to tell him I don't know anything about it. I tried to get us free—stabbed them and ran—but Eli—they took him."

"Damn it," Barclay growled, his nostrils flaring and fists clenching. His shoulders seemed to expand and his face took on that granite-hard appearance that sent a chill through her. "He followed you here? How could that be?"

"I don't know." Her throat tightened. "But they have Eli.

I would turn over everything I have, if only I knew what the wretch wanted."

The silence from Barclay was worse than thunder.

"I'll get him back." His voice was as hard as his countenance. "If I have to tear York apart, brick by brick, I'll find him." He took her arm and pulled her back into the square.

"How?" She had to hurry to keep up. "Where will you start?" She shuddered as she felt his impenetrable resolve dragging her into a future filled with unknown dangers.

"I'll find a place."

Barclay stuffed Norah and Murielle in the carriage and they rode back to Grays Court in tense silence. Murielle kept an arm around Norah, who wiped tears from time to time. He stared out of the carriage, a muscle in his jaw flexing, his hands clenched on his knees. His mind worked furiously.

Could the Scot have followed them from London to Northrup House and then on to York? Even if he knew Barclay's identity, it would have taken time to scour the West End and find his house . . . his residence was not widely known. And they left London shortly after that first night, giving the bastard little time to locate them.

"Why take Eli?" he said aloud. "Do they know who he is? Or did they just see him with you and seize him to get you to comply?"

Another thought occurred. "Your pursuer is a Scot, likely familiar with the north country and the borderlands. Does he have connections in York?" A taut, disagreeable face came to mind . . . someone who wasn't adverse to weaseling profitably out of partnerships . . . someone who was reputed to be acquisitive and might see Norah as the key to an asset.

Was there a link between the two? His heart was beating faster. There had to be a way to find out.

The minute he stepped into the reception area of Grays Court the solution presented itself, along with two beautifully made shirts.

"Mr. Howard . . . I am here to deliver your order . . . and accept your offer." Randville, former tailor and just-hired valet, approached with a paper-wrapped package in his hands.

Barclay smiled with a ferocity that made the man stop short of handing over the promised garments.

"Excellent. Just the man I wanted to see."

Minutes later, Barclay and his new valet were exiting a cab and heading for the rear of the Capshaws' house.

"Tonight I need you to be more than a valet," Barclay said, watching his new employee's reaction. He seemed strangely calm for a tailor about to embark on a potentially hazardous task. "You're to watch Edgar Capshaw's house for a burly man in a flat cap and a checkered coat. If he enters, wait until he comes out and follow him. I need to know where he goes."

"What did he do?" Randville straightened his already perfect tie.

"Abducted a child." Barclay glowered. "My six-year-old ward."

"A child?" Randville scowled. "That's a despicable thing to do. Shouldn't you be contacting the authorities?"

Barclay turned his most wolfish and deadly look on his new manservant. Better the man see it now than later. He smiled, purposefully showing his canines.

"I *am* the authority."

Randville, to his credit, read his employer's dangerous mood.

"So you are."

"Watch the kitchen and servants' entrances . . . the man is hardly the sort Capshaw would want to be seen admitting through his front door."

"Understood."

"If he comes, follow him and then bring word of his whereabouts to me at Grays."

"What then?" Randville asked with a tilt of his head.

"Then we go and retrieve my ward." The flatness of his tone said there was no question of methods to be used or of failure.

"It should be noted, sir," Randville said, "I am not much for fisticuffs."

"Noted," Barclay said, appraising the man's lanky but seemingly agile frame. "I plan to do that part. I want you to free the boy and make certain he doesn't try to join in. He's a bit . . . spirited."

Randville produced a one-word assessment: "Interesting."

As they circled the house, locating doors and coal chutes the Scot might use, they moved with similar stealth. Once they located a rooftop vantage point for surveilling two promising entrances, Barclay pulled up the lapels of his coat to hide the white of his shirt and motioned Randville to do the same. They watched for a time before Barclay became restless.

"I need to head for Capshaw's offices," Barclay whispered. "There's a chance the Scot might try to contact him there. I'll check in at Grays for word from you. If there is none, I'll come back here."

Fourteen

Norah paced in her room at Grays Court, trying not to think about what was happening to Eli. Her heart ached as she recalled the fear and pleading in his eyes as the Scot held him captive. But here she was, doing nothing, depending totally on Barclay's determination and strength to recover him. Her thoughts migrated all too easily from her pupil's state to her employer's.

When he left he had that steely look on his face that always gave her shivers. His only clue to the boy's location was his own intuition about her uncle and what he'd learned from the solicitor he had consulted earlier that day. He wasn't forthcoming about what the man said, but it was enough to make him think Edgar Capshaw was capable of something as wicked as abducting a child.

Harshly worded letters, her uncle's local repute, and a mysterious flake of gold had led him to bet everything on that possibility. She prayed that his instincts and head-strong actions would be as productive as they had been since he first rescued her.

Stubborn man.

Well, she was discovering she had gumption of her

own. She had heard part of his conversation with the tall, lean fellow he'd hired as his valet and knew they would be watching her uncle's house for the Scot's appearance. He insisted she remain at Grays and out of danger, but she knew what her pursuer's minions looked like. What if one of them came to her uncle instead of the Scot himself?

The memory of Eli's frantic face haunted her. She couldn't just sit and wait; she had to do something. She paced for a few moments, then found herself standing before the wardrobe. She took a deep breath. What concealing clothes did she have?

A short while later, dressed in her dark blue woolen dress and carrying her cloak, she descended to the main reception desk to have the innkeeper send to a livery for a saddled horse . . . only to find there were two already waiting in the front court. The innkeeper informed her that the mounts had been ordered by her employer, who said he would return for them that evening. She smiled, informed the innkeeper that one was meant for her, and chose the smaller of the two.

She hiked her skirts and mounted with an ease that surprised her. She had been required to take lessons once upon a time, never guessing in what dire circumstance such an accomplishment might prove helpful. Resettling her skirts, she adjusted the reins with a faint smile and headed for the gate.

Murielle came running out of Grays main doors as she turned the horse toward the road. "Miz . . . please, miz . . . come back . . . wait!"

But Norah ducked her head beneath the branches just outside the gate and kept going. Fortunately, she had been so focused on meeting her uncle that she had fixed every twist and turn of the way to his house in her mind. That concentration served her well as she located the house and surveyed the lights coming from the windows. She rode past the entrance, doubled back, and rode past again. There was shrubbery—a small garden—on one side of the house, beneath an illuminated window.

A plan formed in her mind. Gentlemen liked to linger in a study after supper. Was that her uncle's private sanctum? Could he truly be involved in the Scot's vile deeds? If so, that was where he might reveal it.

She dismounted one house away, tethered her horse to a post in an iron fence, and crept to her uncle's house. A tree and shrubs in the garden provided adequate concealment as she slipped to the window. She stood on tiptoe to get a glimpse of the room, but even with her height was only able to see the ceiling. She was, however, able to make out the voices of her uncle and his wife. They discussed the merits of waiting for word from someone named Brody and they clearly weren't happy.

Brody—wasn't that a Scottish name? The idea sent a bolt of energy through her. Barclay might be right; they could be in league with the man pursuing her. If so, they were using him to find something her father had kept secret. Was that the real reason they resented him so—he kept something of value from them?

She thought of Barclay's refusal to open the locket and reveal the piece of gold. Thank Heaven he'd done so. It settled firmly in her mind: Even if her uncle and aunt weren't in league with the Scot and were merely arrogant, secretive, and high-handed, they were not people she could trust.

Moments later, the pair left the room and turned the gaslight down. Her hiding place was reasonably secure, but she had to know what was happening. She stepped out and looked up to see if lights came on in other windows. None were visible, but she knew there could be some on the other side of the house. While debating her next step, she heard voices from the front of the house and the sound of footfalls on pavement.

Creeping to the corner, she saw her uncle passing between the lamps that flanked the entrance gate. He turned away, headed down the street, and, when she swallowed her heart back into place, she slipped out to retrieve her horse to follow him.

Edgar Capshaw collected his mount from the livery stable and set off for the old mill on Seyfarth Creek. Every streetlamp, every dimly lit pub he passed marked a rise in his irritation. He hadn't heard from Brody and took that silence as a sign that something had gone wrong. Bloody ham-fisted Scot, he thought. Bash and roar was all he knew. If he could find the treasure without the man . . . but he could not afford to dirty his hands with the kind of deeds that might be required to find the lode.

It would have been so much simpler if the stupid girl had come without her brute of an employer—and a *Howard* at that. They could have offered her lodgings with them and simply whisked her away in the night, clean and simple. By now they'd have softened her up and gotten the information needed to make him the richest man in the whole north country.

The old stone mill on Seyfarth Creek stood in a decline from the surrounding land, making for a natural fall of water that had allowed the mill to serve the surrounding countryside for years. It sank into disuse when a larger, more modern mill was built closer to the city. Now even a new road had bypassed the crumbling stone-and-wood structure. Owned by who-knew-whom and frequented only by vagrants and those wanting not to be noticed, it was the perfect place to hold and persuade a young woman to reveal a secret. That was, assuming Brody had managed to nab the wench.

It was half an hour's ride and the moon was up, providing good light along the rutted road, when the ramshackle stone structure came into view. He noted horses tied at the back and soon added his to that line. The sound of water falling over stone was a strange counterpoint for the curses he heard as he entered through a rear door. There was a high, defiant cry that was silenced by an audible smack of fist on flesh.

"There's more where tha' come from if ye don' keep yer trap shut."

"That's e'nuff, Sully," came Brody's voice.

"Little shite bit me!"

"What the hell?" Capshaw broke into the milling room to find Brody sitting in a chair with a smirk while one of his henchmen stood near the old millstone nursing a bloody hand and a foul mood. The recipient of the blow he had heard sat in a chair nearby, wrapped in a coil of rope with his head lolling to the side and his mouth bleeding.

A child? His eyes flew wide. They were holding a *child*?

"What the hell?" He stalked closer to look at the small boy—no more than six or seven—then turned on Brody. "What in damnation is a child doing here?"

"We got wot we could." Brody thrust to his feet wearing a defiant look. "She dragged th' kid all over York today, so he's gotta mean somethin' to 'er. We'll swap the kid for the whereabouts of the lode."

"Idiot! Do you know who this is?" Capshaw shouted,

taking a swing at the Scot even though he was still feet away. "It's the bloody *Earl of Northrup*! You grabbed the kid who just inherited half of York! They'll turn out the whole bleedin' country to look for him and won't stop until they find him—and the idiots who abducted him!"

Brody's usually florid face paled as he glanced at the boy.

"Ye said to get 'er an' didna say how."

Blame never sat well with Edgar Capshaw.

"I swear—if the coppers don't string you up for this, I just may!"

He paced away and back, eyes darting over unseen images. There had to be a way out of the codswallop the Scot had made of his scheme. But try as he might, he couldn't think of a course that didn't involve doing exactly what Brody said: ransoming the boy for what she knew . . . then seeing that she disappeared quietly.

He stalked over to stare down at the child's wide eyes and bruised face and mouth. "So, you're an earl, are you? You'd better hope your tutor values your life more than she does her own."

"She does." Norah stepped out from behind a stack of scrapped lumber and broken stone. The shock of seeing Eli bound and bleeding had torn through her like a lightning bolt. Trembling with anger, she couldn't stop herself from confronting her uncle.

"Let him go this minute!" She started for Eli, but a motion of his hand sent his men to block her way.

The Scot laughed. "Why would we let him go? We got ye both now, an' he's worth a pile."

"I'm afraid that for once Mr. Brody is right." Her uncle backed away with a smirk, ceding the situation to the Scot and his minions. "Cooperate with us and afterward we can discuss your future."

"What is it you want from me?" She backed away a step, realizing now what a mistake she had made in revealing herself. The man who had struck Eli had just slipped behind her to close off her avenue of escape. Sweet mercy, she realized as her uncle's face twisted into a smirk of triumph, she had no way of getting word to Barclay or summoning other help. Her foolish bravery evaporated in the face of cold reality.

When they sprang at her, she fought furiously. But they knew what to watch for, and hatpins and bootheels were no match for brute force. They imprisoned her arms, smacked her hard enough to make her see stars and, moments later, she shared Eli's fate . . . bound tightly by rope and with a bleeding lip.

Her uncle watched it all with detachment, then pulled the Scot aside, where they consulted for a time. Her uncle didn't seem pleased with the result, but he nodded, turned on his heel, and strode out. The Scot turned to her with a wicked grin.

"Yer myne, lassie. All myne now." He swaggered closer and lowered his grizzled face to hers. "An' yer gonna tell me about th' gold."

Randville was not on the roof in the mews behind Capshaw's house where Barclay had left him. Muttering irritably, he surveyed the outbuildings and fences along the narrow lane as he crept to the Capshaws' back gate. The side garden was draped in gloom as he entered, and when hands reached out to pull him into deeper shadows, Barclay braced to defend himself. The sight of Randville's face stayed his fist and he took a deep breath.

"Why aren't you keeping watch?" he growled.

"Your quarry has flown," Randville answered. "He left a half hour past. Went straight to the closest livery and rode out. Hasn't returned."

"Damn it. He must be meeting the Scot somewhere else."

"There is more," Randville said, frowning. "When he left someone else followed him. I tracked Capshaw to the nearby livery and saw that same rider wait in an alley and slip out behind him after he passed."

"Someone else is tracking Capshaw?" Barclay was puzzled.

"Not just someone. A woman in a dark cloak that covered light hair." He raised an eyebrow. "I think it may be your lady."

"My lady? I don't have—" The sense of it broke over him like a pail of icy water. "Miss Capshaw? Impossible. I told her to stay at—"

"The woman at Grays Court with you," Randville said, confused. "She's a Capshaw?"

"Edgar's niece and potential victim." Barclay grabbed Randville's arm and urged him toward the street, no longer caring to hide their movements. "Did you see which way they went?"

Randville shook his head. "Afoot I could only go as far as the livery. They could have turned any of a dozen ways after that."

"Damned stubborn woman—she has half an hour's head start on us. Pray she has sense enough not to try to rescue the boy on her own."

"Where are we going?"

"To that livery. I have a horse. We need to get you one."

The liveryman was closing up when they arrived and wasn't of a mood to be helpful. Crossing his palm with a fiver persuaded him to find a horse for Randville and loosened his tongue. It seemed Capshaw boarded a horse at the stable and occasionally came to take the gelding out at night. He always came back within a couple or three hours, and the horse hadn't been ridden hard. The liveryman gave a sly grin as he ventured the opinion that the wealthy merchant most likely visited a fancy woman he had tucked away somewhere.

Barclay snorted. Capshaw didn't seem the passions-blazing sort.

As he saddled a horse for Randville, the man recalled that Capshaw sometimes smelled of drink when he returned. Barclay considered that. A club or hotel bar? By the time they were mounted and riding, Randville recalled a place near the Cattle Market, where Scots gathered to drink and gamble.

When they arrived at the Cork and Cleaver Randville grabbed Barclay's arm and suggested his employer stay back and let him go in alone. Barclay demanded to know why and Randville smiled.

"One look at you and someone will pick a fight . . . the house'll take bets . . . whatever the outcome, there'll be sore losers. And you may need to save your knuckles for more important battles."

It was reasonable, if annoying, advice. Barclay briefly wondered if he had made the right choice hiring a gambling tailor turned valet. He nodded, despite a lingering feeling that he could use a good dustup to clear his head and vent the steam in his blood.

And when did he start itching for fights? Normally he avoided bare-knuckle confrontations like the plague.

Having Randville go in alone proved to be a sound decision. He emerged later with word that a burly Scot named Brody had met with a gent a few days before and straightaway began asking about the old mill at Seyfarth Creek. Apparently, the place was abandoned by everyone but drifters who needed a roof over their heads and petty thieves looking for a place to hide. Every so often the county law took an interest and cleaned out the place . . . most recently a fortnight back. It was considered safe territory for now—just the kind of place someone might take an abducted child and conduct clandestine meetings to plot a ransom.

"I told you, I don't know anything about gold," Norah said weakly. How many times had he asked the same question? How long had he been at her to give him information she didn't have? Every denial earned her a shake, a yank of her hair, or a threat with a knife.

"Yer a stubb'rn one, ye are," Brody said, drawing back a hand.

"Don't you hit her!" Eli shouted. "You'll pay if you do!"

"Yeah?" The scrawnier of the two henchmen wheeled to seize the boy's hair and raise a bandaged fist. "Whaddaya gonna do 'bout it, runt?"

Eli braced for a blow even as he raised his chin to answer. "I'll have the law on you! I'm the earl!"

Guttural laughter diverted Brody's attention for a moment.

"Hear that, Brody? His lairdship here's gonna sic the law on us," the thicker, slower minion said.

Norah tried once again to get information from the Scot.

"What kind of gold are you looking for?"

"The spendin' kind," Brody snapped. "What other kind is there?" He looked her up and down, deciding. "Yer pa come back from th' west coun'ry wi' a pair of gold coins from th' prince's war chest. Gold meant to feed an army to free Scotland from th' bloody English."

"The prince? You mean Bonnie Prince Charlie?" She was truly astonished. That conflict was more than a hundred years old.

"Some o' the gold was found—th' rest is still hid somewhere in the hills an' crags." He leaned his face into hers. "Yer ol' man found it."

"My father was E-English," she stammered, stunned to realize how rich a prize they sought and how desperate they were to have it. "How would he know anything about it?"

"He hunted w' the MacFergus all over the Douglas an' up north by the Campbell when he took up wi' a lass from their clan. He found it. Th' coins are proof. Died a' fore we could make 'im tell where it was."

The implication struck her forcefully.

"You saw my father? You tried to make him tell its whereabouts?"

"Aye. Stubb'rn as yerself. Wouldna return th' gold to the rightful owners . . . nor even make things right wi' his blood kin."

"His kin? My uncle knows about this, too?"

"He's the one wot sent me after ye. Bastard thinks he'll

get the war chest an' keep it fer hisself. He'll think better o' it when he meets Duncan's crew." He lowered his face to hers and his putrid breath made her want to gag. "Yer goin' to tell me what ye know, lass, or yer pretty face won' be following ye to Heaven."

The abandoned mill matched its reputation as a crumbling home to an assortment of vermin . . . both four-legged and two-legged kinds. When they rode down the slope toward the structure, Barclay could see horses tethered at the rear, and his heart began to pound. He clenched his fists and tightened his gut. Where the devil was Norah? Had Edgar Capshaw led her here? His mount absorbed his tension and strained at her reins, desperate to run. He reined her back, but it was all he could do to keep from thundering down the road to take the place apart stone by stone.

But when rescuing abducted females, he discovered three years before, patience and stealth were the wiser course. Firearms were helpful, but there was something satisfying about using bare fists to beat the hell out of a man who had abducted a woman. He just hoped the Scot was a fists-on-flesh sort who had left his blunderbuss somewhere in the Highlands.

They dismounted, stowed their horses, and crept quietly toward the old building. Dim light came from holes in the walls that had once held glass, and as they flattened against the stone beside one such opening, they heard men's voices. From what Norah had said, the Scot had help . . . two at least, from the number of horses in the back. He prayed they had made it to the mill before Edgar Capshaw and Norah.

"I'll go in first," Barclay whispered, "and hold their attention while you get the boy." He winced. "Damn it—I didn't think—you may need a knife."

Randville smiled and produced a long and thin blade that in London's riskier precincts was known as a devil's toothpick. Barclay took a deep breath, both reassured and disturbed by his valet's possession of such a diabolical weapon. In the end, he nodded. "Call the boy 'Eli' and tell him he won't have to chop stumps if he comes with you. He'll know you're here to help. Get him to the horses as fast as you can."

"What if there are more than three?" Randville whispered, sheathing his knife inside his coat sleeve. The movement drew Barclay's gaze for a moment. Did he just put a razor-sharp knife—

"Then I'll be busier than expected," he answered, "and you'll have to watch your back." The rear door stood ajar, hanging half off its rusty iron hinges. Barclay pointed to them and smiled. Randville nodded, acknowledging that bit of luck.

With one last look at each other, the pair burst into motion . . . Barclay in the lead, Randville not far behind. Though alerted by the noise, the Scot and his men were still caught by surprise . . . apparently expecting it was Capshaw returning and thinking they were secure inside the old stone walls.

Barclay recognized the Scot right away and headed for him, only to run into a scrawny fellow with a club he didn't know how to use to full advantage. Barclay sidestepped a wide swing of it, then chose the moment the arc was at its end to lunge in with fists that stunned the fellow and knocked him back against the old grinding platform. Barclay wheeled on the Scot, ready to rush, but stopped dead at the sight of not one but two hostages. Norah—they had Eli *and* Norah!

The shock drove him at the one responsible, body set to ram and fists ready to hammer. The Scot had pulled a dirk during Barclay's hesitation and now slashed at him. Barclay didn't feel the steel raking his ribs.

Brody was muscular beneath that burly exterior, and once the dirk was wrenched away and thrown onto a pile of mixed rubble, they were almost evenly matched—head to head and fist to fist. They grappled for control, each going for the other's throat and trying to sweep their opponent's legs. Barclay's height gave him the advantage, though it was slim in the face of the Scot's rage. Brody used his head, literally, giving Barclay a head butt that made his vision swim for a moment. Seconds later Barclay returned the blow in kind and added several body punches that sent the Scot crashing backward. The wretch tripped on a broken beam, fell onto a nearby pile of rubble, and went slack.

Panting, Barclay turned to find his previous opponent getting up and beckoned tauntingly to him and his comrade. The pair rushed him at the same time, one swinging a truncheon and the other wielding a knife that was half the size of the Scot's dirk.

Norah was confused at first by the commotion. Her head ached and her jaw and lips throbbed with pain. She blinked in the dim light, praying that what she saw was not an illusion born of desperation. Barclay was here rushing Brody and his men, pounding them like a divine hammer meting out punishment. He was huge and agile—seemed to be everywhere meting out forceful blows. The cold fury in his face stunned her, but she had never felt so glad to see such vehemence in her life.

A moment later she felt her bonds loosening and looked over her shoulder with a start. The man cutting her ropes was the tall, lanky fellow Barclay had hired a day earlier as his valet. When she was free she found herself almost too stiff to rise. He glanced at the desperate brawl and pulled her to her feet. "Hurry!"

She looked over at her young pupil, who had been too exhausted to stay awake earlier but had come to abruptly when the fighting started. He saw her being freed and panicked, thinking he might be abandoned.

"Please, miss, don't leave me!"

"We have to get Eli," she said to Randville, turning toward the boy.

"I'll come back for him," Randville said, wrapping an arm around her shoulders and pulling her around the edge of the room toward the exit.

Barclay glanced her way and saw Randville helping her out as if she could barely stand on her own. He had seen Eli beside her, looking bruised, and the anger in him poured out in blows that bludgeoned the Scot's two henchmen until they went down and didn't rise again.

Chest heaving, he staggered over to Eli and lifted the boy's tearful face in an aching hand. "It's all right," he said, brushing tears and dried blood from the boy's cheek. "You'll be all right." The hope and relief in Eli's little face sent pain squeezing through his chest. He knelt and worked the knots of the ropes with hands so stiff and sore that he uttered a few curses before he remembered his ward's age.

"Sorry." He glanced at the boy with a rueful grin. "My hands hurt like hel—the devil."

The minute Eli was free he scooped up the boy and held him in a fierce, protective hug. The boy threw his arms around his neck and buried his face in Barclay's shoulder.

"I've got you now. You're safe." He swallowed hard. His voice came low and hoarse. "I'll always come for you, Eli. *Always.*"

He stood a moment, holding the boy tightly and surveying the wreckage he had inflicted on the bastards and their den. Then he turned and trudged down the passage that led outside.

He met Randville coming in and they exited together to find Norah sitting on a low stone wall that had survived the mill's decay. She shoved to her feet and stumbled toward Barclay, who opened his free arm and pulled her hard against him. She hugged him and Eli, even as Barclay held them both in a fierce embrace.

For a long moment no one spoke. When she looked up his face was filled with emotion. He drew his damaged right hand across her swollen cheek and ran his thumb gently over her split lip.

"The bastards," he said softly. "I should have sent them straight to Judgment."

She opened his hand to rest her cheek in it as tears filled her eyes.

"You came for us. I don't know how you found us, but . . . you're the answer to prayers."

Something swelled in his chest as he met her brimming eyes.

"You are, too."

He lowered his head to press his lips against hers very gently and was surprised that she pressed her lips harder against his. It didn't occur to him that they had an audience until the kiss ended. He looked around for Randville and found they were alone.

"Are you all right?" he asked. "They didn't—"

"No," she anticipated his meaning and turned her attention to Eli, rubbing the boy's shoulders. "Are you all right, Eli?"

He raised his head and bobbed a nod. "Did you see, miss? Did you see how Mr. Barclay fought 'em?"

"I did," she said, wiping her eyes and smiling up at him. "He was wonderful. A warrior angel . . . St. Michael in the flesh."

Barclay smiled, looking at her and then at his ward. It was amazing how in mere weeks they had come to mean so much to him. He would risk everything to see them safe. The vow he had just made to Eli broadened to include Norah . . . whom he was coming to care for in ways he hadn't thought possible. He pulled her back into his arms and lifted his face to the night sky, pushing pain and exhaustion aside to welcome the relief of the chill and quiet.

For the first time in a very long while he said a prayer of thanks.

Randville returned, breathing heavily, with news that the Scot had disappeared. Barclay turned Eli over to Norah, while he ran back inside. Together, he and Randville searched as much of the mill as was safe to explore, then bound the two groggy henchmen with the very ropes they had used on their victims.

"He's gone. Brody," Barclay told Norah when they emerged again. "I have no clue where he's gone, but I intend to make certain every bit of information about him is interrogated out of his accomplices."

That was when Norah saw the wetness on Barclay's

shirt and rushed to investigate. The blood spreading slowly across his side, looking almost black in the moonlight, made her gasp.

"You're hurt."

"It's a scrape, nothing more."

But it was *more* to her, and she bit and ripped a ruffle from her petticoat to wrap his side.

"I'm so sorry, Barclay." She looked at him, eyes filled with tears.

"It was worth every drop of blood in my body to get you two back safely." The somber tone of his voice said he meant every word.

"At least one mystery was solved," Norah said as he held her and Eli close. "They wanted to know the location of some gold he thinks my father found. Bonnie Prince Charlie's gold—from the Jacobite uprising. He kept saying my father knew its whereabouts and demanding I tell him where it is."

"Jacobite gold?" Barclay was truly surprised. "The man's daft."

"Possibly," Randville put in as he brought the horses over. "But in the Scottish borderlands 'the hoard' is considered very real. Only part of the prince's war chest was found. It's believed that the rest is waiting for the clans to gather and take up the fight to free Scotland again."

"Well, aside from their crazy notion of treasure," Barclay said irritably, "they've abducted and abused a lady of quality and an English nobleman, and they damn well are going to pay for it."

Fifteen

The ride back to York was cold and quiet, broken only by Randville's wry observation that the chill was probably good for swelling. Barclay managed a laugh and Norah smiled despite her injured lip. Eli, cradled securely on Barclay's lap, simply fell asleep.

Despite their fatigue and the need to tend injuries, their first stop in York was at the central police station. The report took what seemed like forever. Norah's and Eli's injuries were examined and recorded . . . along with the identity of their abductors. Constables were dispatched to arrest the men who lay bound and waiting at the old mill.

Norah had a few misgivings when describing her uncle's role in the incident. He hadn't intended to abduct Eli . . . though he had plotted to abduct her and use force to make her divulge the whereabouts of a long-lost treasure. But if he wasn't arrested as part of the scheme, Barclay said firmly, the wretch would likely try again. Thus, she detailed for the record her uncle's appearance at the mill and his instigation of the scheme that resulted in the little earl's abduction.

Detectives were sent to the Capshaw house, but soon

returned with news that Edgar Capshaw was reported to be away on business and couldn't be reached. That alibi, supplied by his wife, fooled no one. After a quiet consultation with Barclay the captain sent his men back to watch the house in the event Edgar tried to return home.

The sun was still hours from appearing on the eastern horizon as they stumbled back to Grays Court and found Murielle dozing in the reception room beside a low-burning lamp. She roused with a start and was horrified by Norah's and the little earl's injuries. She roused the inn's staff to send for a physician, and before long the injured had been treated, washed, and ensconced in warm beds under Murielle's watchful eye.

As she lay in her room, staring up at the shadows on the canopy, Norah kept thinking about what the Scot had said. Her father knew about hidden gold. Was that connected to the piece of raw gold in her mother's locket? The man implied that her mother's family, the MacFergus clan, had something to do with finding the treasure. But if her parents knew the location, why didn't they tell the authorities so it could be retrieved?

But retrieved by whom? The Scottish government? The British Crown? The hardheaded clans, who might try to use it to fund yet another rebellion?

She wanted so much to talk about it with Barclay, to hear his sensible and clearheaded logic. As she lay tense and sleepless, she kept thinking of the protective way he had held Eli, and how the boy had relaxed in his arms on the ride back to York. If only she could have been in his arms, too, and felt as secure as Eli did.

She recalled the fury he unleashed on their captors and closed her eyes to relive it again. He was fierce and surprisingly agile for a man of his size. Even without a weapon, he managed to subdue three men in a matter of minutes. Any worry she had felt for him was soon replaced by wonder. His movements were heart-stopping . . . his power astonishing. Her body came alive as memory took control.

She wanted to touch that power, to experience that strength and prowess in a direct and personal way. She no longer thought of him as a potential danger, but as a man of strength and integrity. A man whose lips were as soft as his broad chest and thick arms were hard. A man whose formidable body and determination formed a bulwark of safety for those in his care.

She wrapped her arms around herself, thinking of his amber eyes and often tousled hair. If only she could touch—

A knock came at the door, and Murielle's head popped up from the big, stuffed chair near the bed. When the door opened the light of a single candle preceded Barclay into the room and the maid rose to meet him.

"She's asleep, sir."

"I'll stay with her. Eli is asleep, too. You get some rest," he ordered. Murielle nodded with a sigh and left, stretching her back.

Norah's heart beat faster as he pushed back the window drapes to admit moonlight, then settled in the chair Murielle had vacated. She could almost feel his gaze, searching the bed shadows for her. It was only a minute or two before she could no longer contain the urge to look at him.

She turned her head on the pillow to find him watching her with an odd expression on his chiseled features.

"I didn't mean to wake you," he said softly. "I just wanted to spell Murielle and make certain you were all right."

"I'm fine," she said, realizing that his presence was responsible for that. "Just a bit chilled and unable to quit thinking about what happened."

"Understandable," he said, then paused. "You're cold?"

"A little." For some reason she was beginning to shiver.

He rose, and before she could protest, he picked her up, snagged a comforter, and carried them both to the chair. Once she was settled on his lap he pulled the comforter over her and tucked it around her. It seemed the most natural thing in the world to have her body pressed against his big frame that radiated heat like a hearth screen. Within minutes her tension melted into a lush feeling of comfort and belonging. He freed a hand to urge her head against his shoulder and she sighed quietly. This was exactly what she'd wanted . . . what she had envied when she saw Eli held the same way.

She knew she should sleep, but she was too caught up in the pleasure of his closeness to even close her eyes. With her head against his chest, she could hear his heartbeat . . . a slow, dependable rhythm that made her want to curl up inside him and wrap herself around his core the way she wanted him to wrap around hers.

"Barclay?"

"Um-hmm," he answered, sending delicious vibrations through her ear and cheek.

"Do you think the gold in the locket is just a coincidence or a hint that my mother's family knew something about the prince's treasure?"

"Good question," he said, leaning his cheek against the top of her head. "One that is hard to answer. The flake of gold was put there for a reason. But it's a big step from a small piece of ore to a treasonous treasure meant to topple thrones."

"Then it's a mystery still," she said just above a whisper. "The Scot—Brody—said my father hunted with my mother's family, the MacFerguses. Maybe they know something about the piece in the locket. I don't think I'll be able to rest until I learn why it's there."

"You need rest, Norah Capshaw." She could hear the smile in his voice. "Let me do the worrying. That's what I'm here for."

She raised her head and levered herself up against his chest. "That's what you're here for? To worry and see that I sleep?"

"Primarily," he answered, adjusting his position beneath her.

"Gallant. But I'm not sure I believe you." She lowered her gaze to his lips. At that moment nothing seemed more right than feeling his hard body beneath her and remembering the feel of his lips against hers.

"I think you may be here for something more interesting."

"And what would that be?" His voice had dropped to the bottom of its register and his eyes shone in the moonlight.

"This." She laid a hand against his cheek and tilted his head to just the right angle. Her lips touched his gently, searching for something she had glimpsed once and longed for every night since. As he responded, she felt it again, and slid her arms up his chest to wrap around his neck.

This was passion . . . pleasure . . . and it was irresistible. Small wonder people defied church and state and the rules of society to claim it.

"Let me know if it hurts," he said, touching the injured side of her mouth. His breathing was as quick and ragged as hers.

"It doesn't," she replied, realizing it was true. And remarkable.

As their kisses deepened, she became aware of every inch of bare skin beneath her gown . . . and then every inch of him that was pressed against it. She explored his lips, the taste of his mouth and skin, and the teasing flicks of his tongue that drew hers to do the same. Heat bloomed in her core. More; she wanted this and more.

Catching his head between her hands, she absorbed every angle, curve, and nuance of his expression. He smiled . . . a sensual and slightly wicked expression that sent a frisson of excitement through her. At that moment she saw a universe of possibilities in his face and responded without thinking, kissing him again, running her tongue over his teeth . . . lingering over his canines that made him seem so fierce and wolfish.

She didn't know where this was leading, but she knew it would be good and intended to see it through to whatever end would come.

Barclay knew from the moment he settled her on his lap exactly where this was leading, and he braced internally to survive the rise of need that threatened every ounce of his control. He was not wrong about the potency of the desire rising between them, though he was surprised by her wholehearted participation in it. He had intended to hold her and warm her . . . to give her back her sense of security and control. He knew she had a need to take charge, but—sweet Jesus—she had seized control of both her passion and his!

When she sat up her hair was tousled and spread over her shoulders like a silk waterfall. He gave in to the urge to sink his fingers into it and savored the way strands curled around his battered hands as he drew them along her shoulders. She was like a painting from an old Florentine master . . . vivid and shimmering in the pale light.

It struck him that she was not the least bit afraid of him. She met his lips with a desire of her own and touched him with a tenderness that showed in her eyes. Such beautiful eyes . . . pale and silvery in the night . . . windows on the longing and the pleasure she felt. There was no hesitation, no shame in her eagerness as her hands explored his chest and shoulders and threaded themselves into his hair.

His hands ached to explore her the way she touched him, and he surrendered to the urge to run them down her side and hip, then up to her breasts. Beneath her curves he could feel her response to his touch. He had never felt such a connection with a woman . . . never understood the possible depths and complexity of passion that could be shared. It was overwhelming. For a moment. One shattering moment.

Plunging into such powerful feelings jolted his mind back into a rational mode. For a moment he froze, taking stock of his arousal and intentions.

Just what did he expect from Norah Capshaw? Did he truly want to make her his lover? The vote from his well-primed body was a decided yes. But his mind and heart, the gallantry he had tried so hard to cultivate in his core, said there should be more or none at all. His hero, Ivanhoe, had refused to take advantage of the maid who loved him . . .

Why the hell was *Ivanhoe* poking a nose into his desires?

With pleasure now overpowered by a sense of duty, he withdrew his hands from her body to wrap his arms around her and hold her as he struggled to calm his racing heart and ragged breathing. She stilled as well—he could almost feel her searching his reaction. He owed her an explanation, and there was only one that made sense.

"I am charged with your welfare, Miss Capshaw," he said, unable to keep regret from his voice. "I would not force unworthy or inappropriate attentions on you."

She studied his face with understanding. "Then how about 'worthy' and 'appropriate attentions' toward someone who admires you and is wholly grateful to you?"

"Grateful?" Was that what lay under her response to him? The thought confirmed his instinctive restraint. "All the more reason to behave with consideration for your honor."

Norah could feel him tensing and realized that her words had put distance between them. Grateful? What in Heaven and Earth made her say such a thing? He was preparing to put her back in her bed and she was determined not to let that happen. She looked steadily into his eyes, baring her hope and praying it would be enough to make him stay.

"Then for my honor and well-being, just sit with me

like this and keep me warm." She forced a smile and hoped it covered the sense of loss she was feeling.

His deep breath and tightening embrace marked a surrender to her plea. With her eyes stinging, she lay her head against his shoulder. Did he still see her as a luckless young woman who was ignorant of the world and too vulnerable for her own good? Did he regard her only as a responsibility . . . just one more test of duty to be carried honorably? Worse still, did revealing her desire somehow diminish her in his eyes?

Those questions undercut hopes she had nourished in her heart. He rubbed her shoulder and she looked down to see him now clasping her arm. The abrasions on his hands were a reminder of the trouble she had brought on him and his precious ward. If it hadn't been for her questionable background and deceitful family, they wouldn't have been abducted . . . wouldn't have required rescuing . . . wouldn't have made him fight and damage those big, capable hands.

She had no right to expect him to defend her, or to endanger the well-being of the boy he was charged with guiding and protecting.

No right at all.

The truth of their situation came crashing through her fragile longings. The mysteries connected to her had put young Eli and Barclay both in peril, and despite Barclay's heroism and refusal to blame her for it, she felt increasing guilt. Even as she lay safe in his arms, she was plagued by the thought that she should remove herself and the questions surrounding her troublesome heritage from their lives. She had hoped her time at Northrup would be a fresh start for her, but now it was clear that she wouldn't be free to begin a new life until she settled the matter of the gold and ended the vicious pursuit by her father's family.

Her luck, she realized, had not really changed at all.

It was devastating enough to realize she was so ill-fated. She could not, would not bring her dismal fate down on Barclay and Eli.

It was all she could do to hold back the tears when he tucked her back into her bed. As soon as the door closed behind him, she let her emotions and tears flow freely. And as the first gray light of dawn filtered into the room, she rose stiffly and began to pack a small valise. She knew what she had to do.

Barclay was groggy as he trudged downstairs to the dining room the next morning to find Eli and Murielle having a late breakfast. When he asked after Norah Murielle mumbled something and would not look up from her plate. He scowled and asked again.

"She's out on an' errand, sir," Murielle finally said, though she didn't look happy about it. Her response smacked of a half-truth, which was annoying. It took a minute for him to realize that such vagueness should be investigated.

"What kind of errand? Her uncle is still abroad in the area—it's not safe for her to—" He narrowed his eyes in a way that probed the maid for secrets. "Where the devil is she?"

"At the train," Eli said, defying a fierce glare from Murielle.

"What train?" he demanded of the boy. "We're not—she's going somewhere?"

Twisting her hands, Murielle looked up ruefully. "I wasn't supposed to say . . . not 'til later."

"Where?" Barclay thundered, feeling his gut tighten. *"Where?"*

"To her ma's folk," the maid said, flinching. When he turned on his heel she gazed after him, calling, "She told me not t' tell!"

The station was filled with people, the hiss of steam, and the smell of coal smoke, oil, and steel. It wasn't hard to find her among the drab winter clothing and the sea of flat caps and bowlers; her hair shone like a beacon . . . which alarmed him as he rushed toward her. Was she asking to be abducted again?

When he seized her arm she turned on him with her valise raised to strike. He raised an arm to prevent being walloped, and a second later she lowered her bag.

"What the devil do you think you're doing?" he growled, oblivious to the stares of people boarding nearby passenger cars.

"I-I'm going to see my mother's family," she said, yanking her arm free.

"Without me? Are you mad, woman?" His glower was enough to make grown men go weak in the knees, but she squared her shoulders.

"Yes, without you." She raised her chin. "I've caused you and Eli quite enough trouble. I have decided from now on to sort out my muddled family matters by myself."

In the middle of a growl, he realized people were stopping and staring at the "beast" who seemed to be pouncing on a defenseless young woman. He straightened up and lowered his voice.

"Don't be daft. You've become a good influence on the

boy, and if something happens to you, I'll never hear the end of it. Not to mention finding and wearing in a replacement would be a bloody headache. You know how 'the little earl' can be." He swallowed and glanced away, as if uncomfortable with such persuasions.

"Not to mention, it will be an arduous trip for you into perilous countryside—who knows what hazards you may encounter? It would be madness to attempt it alone and ill-equipped."

"I am not ill-equipped. I have sensible shoes and a warm cloak."

The stubborn set of her jaw said that she truly believed it. She glanced over her shoulder at the small engine and weathered passenger cars that soon would be headed across the Scottish border.

He gave a huff, stepped behind her, and nudged her toward the station house. He counted it a victory that she didn't just wheel around, bash him with her bag, and then run off to board the departing train.

"Where are you taking me?" she demanded.

"Back to Grays," he grumbled, "where we will have a civil conversation about your decision to abandon us in favor of a daft expedition to find answers about a treasure that may or may not exist."

"I'm not treasure hunting," she snapped. "I'm trying to learn what it was that my father and mother were trying to tell me."

In the terminal they found Randville scanning the ticket area for signs of her. He broke into a smile at the sight of Barclay ushering her briskly toward the main doors.

"You found her," he said, tugging the brim of his hat in deference to her as he joined them.

"In the nick of time," Barclay said, giving her a narrow look.

"You will come to regret becoming his accomplice in abducting me again," she said to Randville as Barclay pulled her out to the carriage.

"Again?" One of Randville's eyebrows rose.

"This is the third time," she declared as she was lifted by the waist and set on the carriage step.

"Second," Barclay corrected, straightening his coat and giving her skirts a discreet nudge meant to hurry her into a seat. He took in Randville's confusion and addressed it as he climbed aboard, too. "That first time the coppers got her before I could take her away. So the first time was really after the riot at the music hall."

Randville's gaze darted between the two as he dropped into the rear-facing seat. "Interesting."

The ride back to Grays Court wasn't long but seemed interminable to Norah as she sat under Barclay's frown and Randville's covert curiosity. She should have known better than to trust Murielle to keep a secret, especially from her employer.

The minute she stepped out of the carriage at Grays, Eli came running out and threw his arms around her.

"Miss—don't leave us. We need you. We have to read more stories . . . an' play with th' new ball . . . an' get more sweets . . ."

His voice was muffled by her skirts, but she got the gist of his plea and it went straight to her heart. She disengaged his arms and stooped to meet him face-to-face.

"I'm sorry, Eli." She took his face between her hands. She hadn't expected tears from her troublesome pupil.

"I need to see if I still have family and I think you and Mr. Barclay should—"

"Come, too!" It was a genuine wail. "I wanna come with you to Scottslund. I never been there!" Then he seemed to think she needed added incentive. "I can help make sure th' bad men don't get you."

She couldn't help glancing up at Barclay, who stood with legs spread and arms crossed, looking like the resolute colossus he sometimes was. His intense gaze seemed to say, *See there—even the boy gets it.*

She looked from Barclay back to Eli, then to Murielle and the enigmatic Randville. It surprised her to realize they were all genuinely concerned. Then Barclay cleared his throat and ordered Murielle: "Pack up." There was no room for misunderstanding. "We're all going."

Sixteen

Transportation west took a day to arrange. They first intended to take the carriage, but were soon advised it would be too large for the roads in the Southern Uplands that were home to Norah's family. They arranged horses and a small cart to be ready at the end of their train journey and did some additional shopping to be certain they had clothes warm enough for outdoor travel.

The train itself was small and spartan . . . wooden seats with padding long-since flattened and no first-class amenities. Eli eagerly watched the countryside at first, but soon grew disenchanted with the sameness of the view. In time he fell asleep with his head on Norah's lap and became the envy of everyone else in the party. When you are six—each sighed privately—you get to nap almost anywhere and anytime.

But not even Eli was able to nap on the road at the end of their train ride. From the rail terminus the roads became narrow tracks used mostly by farmers headed for market and flocks of sheep that flowed like noisy clouds of wool from pasture to pasture. Twice they came to a small collection of buildings that contained cottages, a church, and a tavern of sorts—seated beside a stream. At each they stretched their legs, found a bit of refreshment, and confirmed that they were indeed on the road to a place called Hesterwaite.

The farther they traveled into the rising hills, the more the folk at the farms and clusters of cottages they passed turned out to stare at them. Strangers, Barclay observed dryly, were a rarity in many parts of Scotland. When they stopped to ask permission to water the horses and where they might find some food, the folk stared anxiously at Barclay and nodded permission, then crossed themselves and backed away.

Norah found herself growing saddle sore and wishing— not for the first time—that she had come alone. Murielle bore the discomfort worst, moaning and generally behaving as if she was being carted to her execution. Eli, on the other hand, was full of energy and excited by virtually everything he saw. Flocks of sheep, men repairing stone fences, young girls herding geese and ducks, and cheesemakers carrying cloth-wrapped rounds to market all had him gawking, asking questions, and acting like a curious boy.

Randville, who drove the horse cart, seemed to accept the jostling and monotonous pace with a stoicism that would have made Marcus Aurelius proud.

As day and spirits waned, Barclay dropped back to ride beside the cart and entertain its occupants with tidbits from the book he had read on Scotland. Norah watched him telling quirks of culture and legend and had to smile. When that finished he launched into a tale of a knight in the time of the crusades, who helped ransom and free his king . . . setting an example of loyalty and daring for generations to come. The book was *Ivanhoe*, he declared, by the famous Sir Walter Scott . . . who happened to come from Scotland.

Barclay was a wonderful storyteller, Norah realized as she watched and listened . . . so good, in fact, that even Murielle forgot her discomfort for a while. When he described the battles and dangers of Ivanhoe's mission, he held them all spellbound with the dramatic rise and fall of his voice and his colorful language. No one gave thought to the oncoming night until dusk fell and there wasn't a dwelling in sight.

Fortunately there was something of a moon that allowed them to make it to a farmstead located beside a small brook. Barclay dismounted and approached a squat, wattle-and-daub structure that charitably could be called a cottage. When he rapped on the rough plank door it opened quickly to reveal a stout woman with frizzy hair and a rolling pin raised in her hand. At the sight of him she screamed. It was not an ordinary ladyish scream of distress; it was more like a gathering of banshees having a good howl.

She slammed the door and Barclay staggered back, stunned by such a reception. He stumbled to his horse and looked to Norah, who had dismounted and now stood blinking with confusion.

"Perhaps if I tried—" Randville stepped down from the cart.

"No," Norah said, coming to her senses. "I believe this requires a woman's touch." She headed for the cottage door with shoulders squared—fully prepared to do battle with the resident harpy.

When she rapped on the door and called out to the woman with determinedly pleasant tones, it was a few moments before the portal opened a crack. She smiled and planted her booted foot against the bottom of the door as she introduced herself.

"My name is Norah Capshaw. I believe I have kin somewhere around Hesterwaite and we're trying to find them. Could you please tell me if we're on the right road?"

The crack of the door widened just enough for the woman's face to fill it. She looked Norah up and down, then opened wider.

"Capshaw, ye say?" The name must have made a connection in her head. She peered out at the entourage behind Norah. "Cain't be too careful nowadays. Haints an' demons all over th' roads." She looked past Norah to Barclay and the rest of their party. "Yer man gimme a fright."

"I apologize for startling you. Mr. Howard and his ward, the Earl of Northrup, are seeing me to my family's farm. But night overtook us. If you can, please tell us if we're near the village of Hesterwaite. The journey is taking longer than expected and we need to find lodging."

"Ain' no inn in Hester. No call fer it." The woman focused on the cart and glimpsed Eli. "Ye got a wee lad wi' ye?"

"Yes. He is the young lord of Northrup, from west of York. Mr. Howard is his guardian."

Behind her, Barclay bowed and Eli jumped out of the cart to get a better view of what was happening. When Norah called to the boy and beckoned to him to join her, he ran quickly to her side.

"Your lordship," she addressed him with purposeful formality, "I would have you meet . . ."

"Maudie Douglas," the older woman said, pulling out one side of her skirt as she made a dip that caused her to wince.

Eli smiled his best six-year-old smile and surprised

Norah by bowing to the woman with a flourish. Maudie grinned, showing a few teeth missing, clearly delighted by the boy's manners.

Thus they secured lodging for the night. Norah, Eli, and Murielle were invited in to share the hearth with Maudie, while the men were consigned to a stable built into a cave-like opening in the slope below the cottage.

She gave the men blankets and told them there would be clean straw for bedding. Before long the cottage contingent was sipping warm broth and drowsing before a peaty fire, and the men were feeding the horses and sharing a flask of brandy in the company of inquisitive cows.

Maudie, it turned out, had been widowed for two years and worked her farmstead with the help of a nearby son and grandchildren. She offered the travelers her bed, but after seeing the difficulty she had moving about—"th' lumbago," Maudie explained—Norah declined and said they could use a couple of blankets instead. They stretched out on a rag rug before the hearth and were soon fast asleep.

The next morning Norah gratefully accepted a soupy oat porridge as breakfast and gave Eli a warning look that said he should do the same. But being six years old, he missed the finer points of her example and said that he didn't want "sop"—that he would have eggs and toast instead. Maudie, to her credit, chuckled and said she'd rather have eggs, too, but her last hen died months ago. It took Eli a minute to connect loss of hen with no eggs, demonstrating just how privileged his life had been.

Norah started to explain, but Eli frowned and declared he would get Maudie some hens so she could have eggs whenever she wanted them.

Norah bit her lip to keep from smiling but nodded to Maudie, who chuckled and ruffled the little earl's hair.

The men ate quickly and then prepared the horses for the day's journey, which, according to Maudie, shouldn't be more than half a day. Hesterwaite was a few miles farther on, and they should be able to find directions to the MacFergus farm from there.

Taking leave of Maudie, they set off on a second day of bone-jarring travel. The sun was high when they reached the small village of Hesterwaite, which proved to be a score of houses, a smithy, a tavern, and a pair of shops, one offering dry goods and the other grocery items. They stopped by the tavern for food and information and found the locals tight-lipped regarding the MacFergus clan. The tavernkeeper scrutinized Norah and probed her claim to be related to Daniel and Maureen MacFergus, to the point that Barclay intervened and the fellow hastily withdrew.

Norah insisted they visit the local shops next so she could purchase a gift or two for her family. There, peppermint sticks caught Eli's attention. Peppermint, Murielle put in to support his plea, was good for the digestion and they might need it when eating Scotland's "foreign food." While shopping, Norah asked quietly about the MacFergus family and found the merchants just as closemouthed as the tavernkeeper.

It was in the smithy and livery that they finally were able to learn the way to the MacFergus holding. As they talked, Norah grew uncomfortable with the way the old stable man, who called himself Clyde Bannock, scrutinized her.

"Ye kin to th' MacFergus clan?" he said, scratching his bald head.

"I am told so. My mother was Constance MacFergus,

and she is listed on the marriage roster as coming from Hesterwaite."

The old fellow grunted. "Ye got the look of 'em, sure e'nuff."

He pointed them to the road through the village and out along a track bearing north and east "a ways." When they came to a cairn of stones topped by a sword hilt, they should turn off to the east and continue on the track to the MacFergus place. And he warned them to wrap up warmly because the place was known to be windy.

Norah's stomach was tied in knots as they came over a rise and spotted an assembly of stone structures in the distance. The buildings seemed to be perched just under the crest of a hill, and in the valley below were sheep, goats, and the occasional cow grazing near what appeared to be a stream. There was not a tree in sight, but there were plentiful hedgerows that were still green—likely juniper, Murielle ventured. And the liveryman was proved right; the breeze became a chill wind as they made their way up the gradual incline to the buildings.

Norah insisted that she go first and make herself known to the MacFerguses. Barclay tried to accompany her, but she reminded him of Maudie Douglas's first reaction to him. He had to admit that Norah might be more easily welcomed.

She dismounted, straightened her hat, and smoothed her cloak, then went to what seemed to be a main door. There were chickens and ducks on the loose and smoke coming from a chimney, but there was no immediate response to her knock on the iron-bound door. After a minute she glanced over her shoulder to see Barclay with arms folded and an I-told-you-so scowl. She tried again. And again.

Just as she was about to give up and search for someone in the outbuildings, the latch scraped and the heavy door swung open. A woman stood inside, wearing a plaid skirt, a full apron, and a messy bun. It took a moment for the woman's coloring to register with Norah . . . she had red-blond hair that was showing white around her face, but her skin was light and unwrinkled, with a smattering of freckles. Her features were oddly familiar and her widening eyes were a bluish shade of green. The woman gasped, put a hand to her heart, and staggered back a step.

"Jesus, Mary, an' Joseph—she's—back from the dead!"

The next minute her eyes rolled back and she crumpled into a heap on the floor.

Norah sprang forward just in time to keep the woman's head from smacking stone. She sank to her knees and rolled the woman onto her back, calling to her and patting her face.

"Ma'am . . . ma'am . . ." She looked around frantically, seeing what appeared to be a second room with a cooking hearth and a worktable that identified it as a kitchen. "Help! Is anyone there? This lady needs help!"

She thought she heard footsteps inside, but moments later it was Barclay and Murielle who appeared. Murielle had her traveling bag and quickly provided smelling salts, while Barclay entered the kitchen and called for someone to provide help.

When the woman winced at the astringent smell under her nose and jerked her head back, Norah breathed a sigh of relief . . . until the woman looked up at her with renewed shock.

"Connie girl—ye come—home," she whispered, though

something in her gaze changed the longer she stared at Norah. Her eyes cleared after a moment and Norah supported her as she struggled to sit up.

"Are you all right? I didn't mean to frighten you," Norah said, feeling strong waves of emotion competing for expression. She already knew on some level who the woman was and why she had collapsed. "Are you Maureen MacFergus?"

"I am." Maureen reached up to touch Norah's cheek with a hint of wonder. "Ye must be our Connie's wee lass."

Norah bit her lip, eyes stinging. "Constance was my mother."

"Ye favor her mightily." Maureen shook her head in wonder. "Heaven be thanked—it's like seein' my sweet girl reborn."

"That means . . . you're my grandmother," Norah said softly, barely able to believe she was uttering those words or that finding her family had finally happened. She reached for Maureen's hand and squeezed it.

Tears welled and spilled down both faces as the longing of decades became reality.

A moment later Maureen was up on her knees, hugging Norah for all she was worth, laughing even as tears rolled. Then she pressed Norah's head to her shoulder and nearly deafened her granddaughter as she threw back her head to yell: "MacFergus, get yer wooly arse in here—quick! Our Connie's daughter 'as come home!"

There was movement somewhere past the kitchen, evidenced by heavy footfalls, the squeak of hinges, and the slam of a door. A moment later a burly typhoon of a man with a thick head of graying hair and a great red beard laced with white came barreling in from the kitchen. He stopped dead at the sight of Maureen rising from her knees with a joyful glow to her face. He inhaled sharply as he beheld Norah, then let out a yell that might have been heard all the way back to Hesterwaite.

He sprang at Norah and, before she could retreat, scooped her up in his arms and whirled her about. She couldn't tell if he was laughing or crying, but his bellowing was loud and certainly celebratory.

Emotion erupted in her and she began to both laugh and cry as she was swung with her feet off the ground— around and around—like a beloved child.

This was the welcome she had dreamed of and had literally prayed for all her life. Maureen and Daniel MacFergus—these were her grandparents, her blood, her heritage. It didn't matter that they were delirious and even crazy wild in their acceptance . . . she plunged head-long into their open arms and hearts and drank in all the joy and belonging they had to offer. For the moment she was not the proper and educated young woman whose task was to mold a young nobleman's mind and behavior; she was a hungry, love-starved child who had found that most vital of connections in a pair of earthy Scots who celebrated her for just being alive.

Barclay watched from the open doorway as the old couple hugged Norah, whirled and danced her around, and touched her hair and face with unabashed pleasure. They behaved like they were drunk with joy, the pair of them. And part of him envied every excessive bit of pleasure they were experiencing.

How different would his life have been if someone— anyone—had wanted him and greeted him with such exuberance? Watching the joy and release in Norah, he wanted to take her grandparents' place and feel that cloudburst of emotion with her—wanted to touch her face and let down her hair the way they were doing, wanted to adore and envelop her without reserve or reason. His entire body ached with the need to hold her and share every—

It was in that moment that he realized that for good or for ill, he had likely fallen in love with Norah Capshaw.

He leaned on the doorframe, fixed on the meeting that might prove the balm to Norah's heart but might become a crushing blow to his. Having found their granddaughter, how could they let her go? Once her questions were answered, would she feel an obligation to take her mother's place in their lives as well as their hearts? Would she abandon him . . . and Eli's future . . . to pursue her own?

As the initial storm of emotions settled, Daniel and Maureen caught sight of Murielle, and he could see in their faces the moment they spotted *him* in the doorway. Their eyes widened and their jaws dropped as they pulled Norah into their arms again—this time for apparent safekeeping.

"Oh, my manners," Norah said, peeling their arms from her when she realized what was happening and putting herself between her grandparents and him. "I would have you meet my employer, Mr. Barclay Howard, guardian of the young Earl of Northrup. I am the boy's tutor. He—Elias Howard—came with us. He is outside in the cart right now."

Her grandfather scowled as he looked Barclay up and down.

"Who, ye say?" he demanded, crossing his arms.

"Howard," Barclay answered for her, stepping fully into the dwelling and trying not to take offense at the older man's blatant and somewhat combative suspicion.

"Barclay Howard, grandson of the late Earl of Northrup and guardian to the young earl."

"Howards." Daniel drew a breath that expanded his barrel chest and stroked his wiry beard. Clearly he was recognizing in Barclay a force to be reckoned with. Then he looked to his wife. "Do we hate 'em?"

Maureen bustled into the kitchen and could be seen running her hand down a list tacked to the wall just inside the doorway.

"Nah," she said, watching her husband's reaction. "No Howards."

Her grandfather's manner changed in a heartbeat. A grin burst through his coarse beard. "Well, o'course not. She'd have better sense than to come home draggin' a cheatin' Campbell or thievin' Rayburn.

"Come in, man, an' wet yer whistle." He held out a hand that Barclay stepped forward and accepted, even though he wasn't sure why. "Maurie girl, break out th' ale!"

"'The MacFergus' has spoken," Maureen said with a hearty laugh that let Norah know that both she and her employer were accepted.

Norah dragged Murielle into the kitchen with her to help Maureen, who was already hauling tankards and cups down from a shelf. Something in a large iron kettle on the brick hearth smelled very good, and there were fresh loaves of wheat bread cooling on the worktable. Maureen rolled a small wooden barrel out from under a set of shelves at the far end of the room and used a mallet to hammer in a tap.

Voices rose in the front room, and by the time they

carried in cups and tankards of ale there were several additional people in the room.

An older couple stopped to stare at Norah with amazement. They were introduced as the MacFergus's younger brother, Angus, and his wife, Diedre, who had moved from the farm into Hesterwaite when Angus's health declined. They told her they had known Constance from a babe to a woman and were adamant that Norah was the spitting image of her mother at the same age.

Two strapping, slightly older men were introduced as the MacFerguses' sons, her mother's younger brothers Griff and Cam. They and their wives, Dara and Lucy, worked the farm, tended flocks, and raised crops down near the river. Norah hadn't found just grandparents but a whole family! And every one of them offered a hand or a hug and a warm welcome.

When Eli was introduced as the young Earl of Northrup there was silence for a moment. Then Maureen boldly stepped forward like the grandmother she was, gave him a thorough hug, and proclaimed him the handsomest earl she'd ever seen.

Laughter warmed the room as Eli beamed with pleasure and took advantage of the heady mood to ask for a taste of ale. Over Norah's objection, her grandfather granted his request, and the boy turned a bit green before managing to swallow it. Barclay clapped his ward on the back, advising him to let that be his last taste of ale for a decade or two. Eli appeared to take that advice seriously as he shuddered and tried to wipe the taste from his tongue.

Tall, elegant Randville entered soon after, having seen to the horses as the MacFergus suggested. There was a stir of interest among the females present and a bit of competitive chest-puffing from the men. Even Maureen's eyes sparkled as she leaned toward Norah to whisper, "Where'd ye get such a handsome man? He don't look like any servant I ever seen."

"Mr. Howard has a way of convincing good people to work for him," Norah responded, studying Randville from a new perspective. He was something of a specimen, she supposed. But not nearly as muscular or as devastatingly male as Barclay.

When she saw Barclay look at her grandfather with a twinkle in his eyes, she felt like she was seeing the very soul of him shining through them. He was a man among men and other men sensed it straightaway. Good men were drawn to him and men of flawed character avoided him. At that moment she realized that she would always compare the men she met to her enigmatic employer. And she had a feeling that all others would be found wanting in the comparison. And women? Would it be too selfish to thank God that they had been too vain and shallow to see the true value of his strength and stalwart heart?

Barclay Howard deserved the best life could offer, and what a travesty that he had seen so much disdain and disappointment instead.

There was more hugging and drinking as children of various ages arrived from their chores, some bringing milk fresh from their cows. The younger boys and girls were shy when introduced to Eli, but not so shy they wouldn't invite him out to see their pet lambs and rabbits and their newest litter of pigs. Norah took a nod from Maureen as assurance it would be all right and nodded to Barclay, who waved him off with them.

Soon the younger women hurried home to bring back soda bread, cheese, and shortbread they made regularly from old family recipes. After a bit Maureen enlisted her daughters-in-law to help dish up the fragrant lamb stew that had been brewing on the hearth.

Some of the folk ate in the kitchen, others in the front room of the cottage on hinged tabletops that were let down from the walls. It was clear they shared food regularly in such an arrangement and enjoyed the talk and camaraderie. They had questions about the trip and York and the Howards' home at Northrup.

Eventually, the younger MacFerguses left to return to their work and the excitement and tension both subsided. Talk stopped when the MacFergus asked Norah about her mother and father . . . how she found their home . . . and why no one had bothered to let them know where she was or how she was faring.

It seemed such an obvious question now; why hadn't someone let her know she was not alone in the world? She felt a hollowness in her chest as she sat between her grandparents, holding their hands, and could only shake her head.

"I was sent away to school after Papa died. I was told by my guardian that I didn't have other family, but that I could count on him. He was a good man, but I think he only knew what my father told him. I can't think why Papa wouldn't tell him about you and send me here to live with you."

The MacFergus and Maureen exchanged speaking glances.

"He did wot he thought best for ye, lass," Maureen said, patting her arm. "Here, lovie, have a sip o' my special honey brew."

Before she knew it, Norah had drunk a whole tankard of honey wine that Maureen swore was the finest she had ever made. After that she had trouble keeping her head up and everything seemed odd and funny. She giggled shamelessly at her grandfather's stories and laughed at Barclay's recounting of anecdotes from the book he'd read about Scotland. Later, she was vaguely aware of Maureen and Murielle helping her to a bed alcove off the kitchen, removing her boots and covering her with a blanket. When she surrendered to sleep it was with a smile on her face.

By the time the moon was up and the ale was spent, the only one fully upright was Randville . . . and he'd had one tankard too many himself. These Scots were prodigious drinkers, he thought, and weren't shy about insisting guests enjoy their beloved brew, too. He watched his employer consume enough ale to float a frigate and still maintain a semblance of control, which was a good thing because the MacFergus gestured expansively in the middle of a story and knocked a tankard of ale all over Barclay's trousers.

His formidable employer graciously waved blame aside despite the fact that they were his only pair of trousers and the fabric was already strained by his riding horseback in them for two days. Barclay declared Randville would know how to take care of it. Then, when the MacFergus declared he would see them to a bed and Barclay bent to pick up Eli, his overly fierce grip on his sleeping ward indicated that he might be more affected by drink than it seemed.

Randville plodded along behind Barclay and the MacFergus, who carried a lantern and led them to the stable where he earlier had stowed their horses. He hadn't noticed the modest tack room at the end of the horse stalls. There was a cot at the back and a bench that would make a bed for Eli. Horse blankets would have to do, the

MacFergus said, until tomorrow, when Maureen could fix up some beds proper.

Randville took Barclay's trousers, rinsed them, and hung them out in the chilled air to dry before collapsing onto an unoccupied pile of hay and falling instantly asleep.

Seventeen

The MacFergus trudged back to the cottage and stood for a moment outside, breathing the cold air and re-covering. By the time he entered the front room his mind was working well enough to meet his wife with a sem-blance of clarity.

"Th' big fella can put it away, sure e'nuff," he said, trudging through to the kitchen for a dipper of water. Maureen followed with folded arms and a thoughtful ex-pression.

"Whadda ye think, Daniel?"

"Why'd she come?" He paused, then gulped another draught of water before answering. "Hard to say. Seems eager fer fam'ly. That could be the truth o' it. No denyin' she's Connie's."

"Aye, but she says she come up an orphan w' no one to look after her. Her da never told her 'bout us . . . thinkin' to protect his wee lass. He worried so. But now she got this beast of a man and th' lad they say is earl o' some-thin'." She sighed. "I got the feelin' there's more to it."

"Then likely there be. Yer feelin's are never wrong.

We'll know soon e'nuff." He gave her a tired smile. "T' bed wi' ye, Maurie lass. We'll sort it on th' morrow."

It was midmorning and the sun was well up when Norah was awakened by the sound of movement and giggling in the kitchen, where she was sleeping. When she rolled over to squint through her headache, her burning eyes widened at the sight of the MacFergus holding his wife hard against him and whirling her around in the kitchen. Her jaw dropped when her grandmother's feet touched the floor and she kissed her husband ardently. Norah's eyes slammed shut, but the image was burned into her mind. The pair of them were acting like . . . youngsters . . . newlyweds . . . lovers. At their age? It was embarrassing to see.

She didn't realize she was sitting up until her grandmother murmured something and gave her grandfather a playful shove that made him laugh. He followed his wife's gaze to Norah's reddened face and burst into a wicked grin.

"Aye, our lassie! How ye farin' this fine morning?"

"I'm . . . faring . . . fine, I think." Norah threw back the blanket and slid to the floor beside the cupboard bed. But she swayed and put a hand to her forehead. "A bit dizzy."

"Ahh, that's the tail end o' yer gram's honey wine. Th' stuff takes gettin' used to. In future, stick to th' ale . . . it's safer."

She walked slowly toward the big table on the far side of the room, testing her balance and finding it returning. "I need to wash my face . . ."

Her "gram" pointed to the door and she hurried out to find the necessary. Afterward she used the outdoor pump to wash her hands and splash her face with icy water that brought her fully awake. Hugging herself in the cold, she started back inside but had to skirt a small herd of goats headed out to pasture as she went.

The warmth of the glowing hearth and the smells of sizzling bacon and baking oat cakes enveloped her like a hug. She breathed deeply, letting the aromas permeate her senses, then she smiled as she joined her gram at the worktable.

"We got extra mouths to feed," Maureen declared, smiling at her. "Yer ma was a good hand at oatcakes an' mornin' bread."

"I've not had much practice at cooking, but I'll try. What can I do?"

"We need more flour from th' larder." Maureen gestured to an empty crock that was rimmed with flour dust. "Over there." She pointed to a door on the far end, near the bed alcove.

Norah opened the door and stepped down three steps into a cold chamber that had been chiseled out of rock and was lined with plank shelves, crocks, bags of milled grain, bottles of oil, wine, and canned goods. What little light there was came from a narrow window set high in the far wall. There was a second door in the larder, but she barely noted it as she looked for an open bag of flour. There didn't seem to be one, but she did find a smaller bag that had part of the word "flour" stamped on it. A partial bag, she thought as she seized it and carried it back up the steps into the warmth of the kitchen.

It occurred to her that the bag was especially heavy and when she untied the top was surprised to find yet another bag inside . . . made of what looked like sheepskin. She scowled, thinking it strange, but untied it as well and poured some of its contents into the big wooden bowl her grandmother was using to make what looked like scones.

A glint of light caught her eye and she froze, staring at the lumpy powder and spotting tiny clumps of yellow . . . familiar-looking yellow. Her mouth dried.

"I don't think this is flour," she said quietly.

"It's not." When she looked up her grandmother was standing nearby, staring at the contents of the bowl. "You got . . . the wrong bag. That's—" With sudden intensity, she moved to whisk it away.

Norah stepped between her grandmother and the bowl, her heart skipping beats and her head suddenly light on her shoulders.

"It's not cornmeal or oats or barley," Norah said. "It's . . . it's . . ."

"Dust," Maureen said, reaching past her for the bowl.

"There are pieces of yellow in it. Flecks of gold." Norah seized one side of the bowl to keep her grandmother from moving it. Then she looked up at Maureen. "I need to know where this came from."

"That's none o' yer concern, girl," Maureen said sharply. "Ferget ye ever saw it. Speak no word of it t' anyone." Again she tried to seize the bowl, and again Norah prevented it.

"I have a right to know," she said shortly. After a long moment eye to eye with Maureen, she released her grip on the bowl and pulled her mother's locket from her jacket. Her grandmother fixed on the piece with what could only be called recognition.

"That was our Connie's," she said on an indrawn breath.

"My mother's. Inside is a piece of gold." She tried unsuccessfully to open it to show Maureen.

After watching her fumble Maureen brushed her hands aside and opened it herself. Her jaw dropped at the sight of a small piece of gold ore resting on a portrait of her daughter and son-in-law.

"She took a piece . . . in her locket," Maureen murmured, her stiff shoulders rounding and features filling with emotion.

"Took it from here?" Norah asked, glancing at the bag on the table. "This is where it came from? She took it when she left with my father?"

Maureen nodded and nudged Norah aside.

"I have to talk to th' MacFergus." She headed straight for the larder and closed the door behind her. Norah could hear a latch being slid home on the other side and was confused that her grandmother would seek her grandfather inside a cold, dank—

The door . . . the other door. She went over her movements in the larder and recalled that unusual feature. A second entrance—or exit—that led to where?

Barclay heard Eli rising and running outside but squeezed his eyes tighter shut, refusing to move and hoping the boy would relieve himself someplace appropriate. The parts of him beneath the thick horse blanket were fairly warm, but he couldn't feel his nose and he could have sworn there was ice on his eyelashes. The cold distracted him from the ache in his head and the sourness in his stomach.

He lay for a few minutes trying to recapture the peace of sleep, but it eluded him. The light coming through the open entry to the tack room was bright enough to be annoying and he finally sat up. He was wearing his suit coat, shirt, undershirt, and long drawers, but the chill of his legs said he had lost his trousers on the way to sleep. It came back to him in bits and pieces . . . drinking with the MacFergus . . . wet trousers . . . Randville taking them. He'd have to find them before he could locate his ward.

He looked down at his silk drawers . . . one of the few extravagances he permitted himself, sartorially speaking. Bright pink, surprisingly warm, and eminently washable, they were all that had kept his stout wool trousers from rubbing his legs raw during his two days in the saddle. They probably could do with a scrub. He would hand them over to Randville, once they were back in York.

He stepped into his short boots, didn't bother with the laces, and left the tack room in search of his valet. Jerking his shirt down over his nether parts, he called for Randville but got no response. There were voices in the distance, and down the slope behind the house there seemed to be a haze of fog or smoke or both. Sheep were scattered over the shallow valley and he spotted a small clutch of goats with a couple of male figures headed his way. He squinted and realized one of those fellows was his newest employee.

He looked down at himself and his pink drawers. Never mind that they were the height of fashion for underclothing for well-dressed London men . . . he could just imagine what the Scots would think of them. He pulled his shirt even lower, but there was still plenty of pink showing.

Randville arrived with a pile of something dark in his hands. It took another minute for Barclay to realize it was stringy—fabric—black fabric that looked like—

The remains of trousers. Horror bloomed in him. *His!*

He croaked out a reaction: "What happened to . . . are those . . . ?"

"Your trousers, I fear." Randville winced at the anger that curled Barclay's hands into fists.

"What in infernal blazes happened to them?"

One of the MacFerguses came running up behind Randville with a strange look on his face. "Apologies, sarr." He halted with a nod, glancing in surprise at Barclay's colorful drawers. "It were tha' wicked nanny—Jezebel. Eats ever-thing that don't eat her first."

"Last night I hung your trousers over the sill of the tack room window to dry," Randville explained ruefully. "This morning when I went to get them they were gone. I checked high and low, but—"

"We passed by takin' th' goats out to pasture," Griff MacFergus—Barclay recalled the name—explained with a grin aborning as he took in Barclay's fashionable drawers. "Demon she-goat grabbed 'em an' had 'em half ate afore I saw she had something. Couldn't get 'em away from her 'til yer man Randall come to help."

"Randville," Barclay corrected, feeling utterly exposed.

"Yeah, Randall."

Bracing, Barclay looked down at his pinks, desperate for a substitute. Randville's pants were much too slim, and this Griff MacFergus wore heavy canvas work overalls—again, much too small. There wasn't a man on the place comparable to him in size that he could borrow from. He groaned, wheeled, and headed back into the stable to retrieve his horse blanket.

When he stepped out again Randville and the younger MacFergus flushed guiltily, like they might be stifling laughter. His face stiffened as he wrapped the blanket tighter around his lower half and struck off for the cottage. Please God, let him find something to wear before the MacFergus saw—

That prayer was quickly answered in the negative. The MacFergus came barreling up the slope behind the cottage and stopped dead at the sight of Barclay clad in a horse blanket, below which pink drawers could be seen. He burst out laughing, and his reaction seemed to give permission for the other men present to vent their amusement.

Barclay gave the old man his most terrifying glare, which didn't dampen the Scot's mirth one bit. His humiliation was complete when Norah and her grandmother rushed outside to see what was happening.

Maureen laughed and Norah's eyes widened like saucers on Barclay's makeshift attire.

"One of your cursed animals ate my trousers," Barclay declared with considerable heat. "When I left Northrup I had no idea I would be gone so long or might meet up with ravenous goats, so I brought no others with me."

Norah bit her lip to keep her laugh inside and then looked to her grandmother for help. "Is there a tailor or seamstress nearby where we could have something made?"

Maureen shook her head. "Folk 'ereabouts stitch their own. But nobody in these parts stitches English Sunday breeches." She studied Barclay and then her husband, who was enjoying his big guest's dilemma much too openly. With a determined look, she walked around Barclay, surveying every inch of his tall, brawny form.

"'E looks ta 'ave abou' the same girth as the MacFergus." She turned to Norah with a glint in her eye. "Ye think?"

"I suppose," Norah answered, folding her arms and watching her grandmother take charge of the situation.

"Then I got a fix fer yer trouble, Master Howard. Come along inside . . . warm yer bones an' break fast whilst I get it fer ye."

"Aye, if any can fix ye"—the MacFergus boasted, brushing dust from his coveralls and waving them to the cottage—"it's me Maurie lass."

Inside, Norah helped Barclay to a bowl of porridge, some

tasty sausages, and a tankard of what her grandmother called "morning ale." His clear discomfort didn't diminish his appetite . . . he ate as if he hadn't had nourishment in weeks.

Norah served her grandfather and herself some oat porridge and then sat down beside Barclay, hoping to have a word with him about what she had found in the larder. Her grandmother had come back from consulting the MacFergus with a serious air, and when Norah asked what was said Maureen frowned and shook her head, forestalling that conversation. Now it seemed that with Barclay's raw mood and her grandfather's wicked enjoyment of his predicament . . . her employer would have little patience for news about her quest for answers.

Shortly, Maureen reappeared with a thick blue-and-green-plaid draped over her arm. She approached Barclay and held it up by what appeared to be a waistband . . . a pleated skirt . . . a kilt. The MacFergus's feet, which had been propped on a stool, hit the floor. He sputtered and turned red. "Wot the devil, woman?"

"Because ye lost yer breeches due to our flock and need to cover yer nethers," Maureen declared, "the MacFergus will offer ye a bit o' honor—our Douglas plaid—to wear."

"The hell I will," the MacFergus roared. "Me braw an' best kilt—'ave ye lost yer wits, woman?"

Maureen narrowed a fierce glare on her tempestuous mate and didn't blink in the silence that followed. The MacFergus knew defeat when he encountered it. He stiffened, clearly outraged, but backed away.

"Mus' be somethin' better," he muttered.

"None tha' fits our Norah's big man 'alf so well," she responded. A moment later she pulled the horse blanket from Barclay, over his feverish objections and proceeded to wrap the kilt around his waist and settle it firmly on his hips. Once it was pinned and fastened she stood back beside Norah to appraise the fit.

"It fits," Norah said, still reeling from hearing her gram refer to Barclay as *her man*. "Looks like it was made for him."

But in fact it was a tad shorter than was customary and contrasted boldly with the pink drawers that reached his ankles.

"That's na right." Maureen shook her head. Before anyone could ask what she meant she was behind Barclay and invading the rear of the kilt to pull down those offending drawers. He stood thunderstruck for a moment, then tried to bat away her hands while sputtering. He did manage to keep from cursing and to keep his feet under him . . . which allowed his colorful drawers to drop around his ankles. Maureen yanked down the rear of the kilt and smoothed it over his rear with a practiced hand.

"There ye be." She stepped back beside her fuming husband. "Makes a fine, braw sight, it does. E'en wi'out a belt."

Norah was both surprised and appalled by her grandmother's daring. Even more astonishing, Barclay made no protest and gave only cursory resistance to such unheard of familiarity. He didn't chide or shove her, just stood braced with burning cheeks and horror-filled eyes.

With everyone present holding their breath there wasn't a hint of laughter in the cottage.

"Are his legs supposed to be bare like that?" Norah asked, tilting her head this way and that to examine his appearance. "It's cold out there."

"Ach, we'll get 'im knit hose," Maureen said. "They be plentiful."

His eyes glowed like molten gold and his lips pulled back over his teeth. She sensed an explosion coming on. "It's temporary, Mr. Howard," she said, wishing she hadn't been so saucy in her earlier comments. "You need wear it only until we can get you some trousers made somewhere."

Barclay felt like a keg of gunpowder with a lighted fuse. He lurched back, swayed, and caught himself before stumbling. Stepping out of his short boots, he shook off his drawers before jamming his feet back into his boots. Then he turned on his heel and strode out the door.

Every nerve and muscle in his body was straining for violent release. He tied his boots and then began to run. He had to spend this volatile energy before he did something drastic—like flatten two women, a crusty old Scot, and a goat with a taste for bespoke trousers.

It wasn't their fault, he told himself again and again as he climbed the nearest hill and went running down the other side. It was happenstance that his trousers were ale-soaked, washed, and hung out to dry in the path of an omnivorous horned she-devil who took them for a tasty treat.

And Norah's grandmother was probably earnest in trying to find him something to wear . . . though she clearly took wicked pleasure in offering him the MacFergus's best kilt. In truth, the old boy's girth made his clothes the only thing that would fit on such short notice. His eyes narrowed vengefully. It salved his pride a bit to see the blustery old cod pricked in the process.

Another hill, then another, and another . . . he was likely

a mile or two from the MacFergus holding before his bile was spent and he realized he was sweating in the chill wind and needed to stop for a short while. He found a large outcropping of rocks atop a craggy hill and sat down, tucking the voluminous yardage of the kilt under his bare buttocks and around his bare legs. What kind of men wore clothes that left their legs and nether parts bare to the elements? It was a wonder their johnsons didn't freeze and break right off.

The frosted valley below and the serene hills that grew steeper the farther they went made an impressive sight. The rugged, even harsh beauty of it seemed a perfect match to the peculiar folk who inhabited it.

They were mad, the lot of 'em . . . right down to the bleedin' livestock. But the mad MacFerguses were Norah's family, and she was grateful to find them and have them accept her. She deserved that happiness and belonging. He refused to do anything to ruin her budding relationship with them . . . even if it meant sleeping with horses, wearing a skirt, and eating haggis on Sunday.

Once again he prayed that when they left Norah would be going with them. In the soft soughing of the wind it struck him that he'd prayed more in the last four days than he had in years. Was that because he was becoming more devout or more desperate? In previous years he hadn't had anything as precious as Norah Capshaw in his life to pray about.

He was so embroiled in thought that he didn't hear the rustle of dry grass and the sound of feet on stone until someone was close at hand. He turned on his seat and was stunned to see Norah striding toward him with her hair free and flowing and her long cloak billowing in the breeze. He rose, batting down kilt pleats lifted by the wind and feeling a surge of pleasure at the sensual and uninhibited sight she made. A volcanic urge to pull her hard against him set his limbs trembling. She was mere feet away before he could speak.

"What the devil are you doing here?"

Eighteen

"I came to see if you're all right." Norah stopped to take in his wind-ruffled hair, his coat's upturned lapels, and the way the kilt wrapped around his bare legs . . . shapely, muscular legs that were exactly ones she might have given him in a fevered dream. She wanted to touch them . . . those broad shoulders . . . that silky, tousled hair . . .

"You followed me?"

"It wasn't hard." She brushed her wind-tossed hair back from her face. "You were visible across the hills . . . you weren't hard to locate." She glanced down. "And I have good walking boots."

He looked at her trim lady boots while she looked down at his much larger gentleman's boots . . . then slowly back up. She couldn't help admiring the shockingly handsome fit of her grandfather's prized kilt. She wished for a moment he would grin at her and show those teeth that always made her shiver.

"My gram wasn't wrong," she said, finally meeting his gaze. Intensely golden, like precious amber . . . it was mesmerizing. "It looks fine on you."

"I feel naked," he said gruffly, scratching his three-day stubble.

"You don't look naked. You look like a magnificent specimen of Scottish manhood."

"Which would be fine if I were a Scotsman, but I'm not." He stiffened visibly and looked down at his exposed legs. "I'm bloody cold."

"Want to share my cloak?" she said, opening the front of it to him.

He reddened and looked away.

"I won't bite," she said with a soft smile.

"But I might," he muttered. "At least that's what people think."

His customary determined-and-self-assured manner had deserted him. He was adorable like this . . . on edge and uncertain. Nothing she had done just now should make him uncomfortable. Then it must be his own thoughts and feelings that unsettled him so.

"A ravenous beast who wears silky pink long drawers." She couldn't help a chuckle. "You do have secrets, Mr. Howard. Who would guess that beneath that formidable exterior you have such fanciful tastes." Her gaze slid down him. "And such handsome legs."

He reddened more, genuinely embarrassed by her appraisal.

"Silk drawers are the rage on Saville Row," he growled. "The tailor I employ insisted they were warm and durable—color be damned." He exhaled and his voice dropped. "Insisted on wrapping burlap in silk."

At that moment she wanted to touch him, absorb some of that discomfort from him. Whether it was her bold grandmother's influence or the simple fact of being out of her normal element, she discarded her usual restraint and opened her long cloak to wrap it and her arms around his ribs. She felt his surprise and braced for a rebuke that never came.

Instead, after a moment he wrapped her in his arms and pulled her hard against his body. He felt cold to her at first, but after a moment warmth grew between them, and she felt a subtle relaxation in his frame. She lay her head against his chest and his deep breathing matched her own. He smelled of damp wool, sweat, and all things male.

They stood together, wrapped in each other's presence for several minutes before she looked up and saw him watching her with a look she had never seen on his face. She recognized the emotion that crept into his eyes: tenderness. And she returned it.

A moment later his lips descended on hers as she rose onto her toes to meet them. It was the sweetest contact she had ever experienced in her life. When it ended she smiled and settled back onto her heels, hugging him harder.

"You're a magnificent man, Barclay Howard. I can't imagine a wiser or more honorable employer . . . or a more caring one. I wish I could make you see yourself as I see you."

"No need to butter me up, Norah Capshaw," he said. "You've already got what you wanted."

"And what was that?" She frowned at his dismissal, confused.

"Your family. Your home." He loosened his hold around her. "People who want you."

She studied him for a long moment.

"It may be greedy of me, but I want more." She had a reckless urge to spill her thoughts, but managed to hold back *wanting him*. "I came here to get the truth about the men pursuing me, my mother's family, and the mystery of that piece of gold in my locket. I never imagined finding a real family and being welcomed into it. But the mystery I came here to solve gets deeper by the day."

His arms loosened around her, but hers tightened to hold him.

"I need your counsel. Something strange happened and I don't know what it means." She searched his face and saw in it an interest that said she should continue. "This morning as I was helping Maureen make breakfast, she asked me to get more flour from the larder. The bag I brought her turned out to contain gold dust. There were larger flakes of ore in it . . . though none quite as big as the one in my locket. I showed her the locket and the piece of gold and asked where it came from."

"What did she say?" he asked, watching her intently.

"She admitted it was gold dust, then said she had to talk with the MacFergus and spirited away the bag through the larder. She had just come back to the kitchen when we heard the confusion in the yard and rushed out to learn you'd lost your trousers. It seemed like she didn't want to talk about it. But they'll have to tell me something about it now that I've seen it."

"So you want me to help you confront them and learn the truth."

She studied his tension and realized he thought that was all she truly wanted from him. Restraint was not serving her interests just now.

"If you will," she said softly. "But right now, I want you to do something more important."

"And what is that?" he asked, lowering his arms altogether, leaving her holding him.

"Kiss me," she said, pouring a world of feeling into

those risky words. "Then tell me why you've kissed me three times before."

It was as blatant an invitation, as bold a declaration of romantic interest as a woman could offer. She held her breath for a moment, searching every nuance of his posture and expression. It seemed to take forever for him to respond, but the fact that he didn't try to escape her arms gave her hope.

"Why would you ask such a thing?" he said.

"Because it's important to me." She prayed her earnest desire to know showed in her face.

He swallowed hard, looked around the craggy hilltop as if composing an answer, then brought his gaze back to her.

"That first kiss—you were pretty and I was—curious."

She nodded and continued to look at him expectantly.

"The second time . . . I had been so worried when they took you and was trying to warm you . . . it was dark and you were . . . so . . . ." He cleared his throat. "It just seemed the most natural thing to do."

"Natural." She raised an eyebrow. "Go on."

She noted that one of his hands came back up to her waist as he stared into her face. Would he not admit wanting it, wanting her?

"Just now, you were unexpected and looked so fresh and lovely with your hair down and swirling free." He brought his other hand to her waist. "You looked like the blessed wind itself breathing life into the hills . . . into me. I was suddenly warmer and my heart beat faster. When I felt you wrap your arms around me . . . I just . . . wanted to kiss you."

"So, do you want to kiss me again?" she asked, feeling a stirring in her body that she prayed he shared.

"God help me"—his head bent lower—"I do."

She met his lips and tightened her arms around him. It was such a light and careful kiss that she wondered if he thought she was made of glass. After a moment she broke that contact.

"Kiss me harder," she said, raising her hand to cup his head and pull it down. He did kiss her harder, more hungrily, and her face and throat heated and her breasts began to tingle. But after a moment she felt him pulling back again and sensed caution returning to his response. It took a minute for her to realize what he was doing.

"I won't break. I promise."

"You don't know what you're asking," he said against her lips.

When she opened her eyes he was staring at her with the strangest mixture of longing and anxiety.

"Try me, Englishman. I'm stronger than you think."

And she raked his bristled chin with her teeth. It was light and playful, but it got the message across. A moment later she was being crushed against his body, lifted into the air, and swung around and around. When he set her back on her feet he gave her a kiss that reached so far down into her soul that she grew dizzy. She couldn't tell up from down or her body from his—she was spiraling on an updraft of pleasure that took her breath and seemed to melt her very bones.

His hands roamed her body, finding every sensitive curve and mound she possessed, setting them on fire. She had the sense that her clothes might be nothing but charred remains if this went on much longer . . . which would be hard to explain to her newfound relations.

He pulled her over to the boulder and sat down, taking her with him. Her cloak draped around them as she settled onto his lap and caught his face between her hands.

* * *

"Did that fulfill your requests?" Barclay looked into her clear eyes.

"Mostly."

"Only mostly?" He laughed. "Sikes—you're hard to please."

"Not really. I just wanted to hear you say you liked kissing me."

"Is that not obvious?"

"Words, Barr Howard. Females put great stock in hearing them."

He studied her for a minute, turning that over in his mind. She was bright and beautiful and filled with all manner of praiseworthy traits . . . earnestness, dedication, courage, determination, caring, dependability, thoughtfulness . . . the list could go on and on. But he knew in his deepest heart that praise wasn't what she wanted, and he wasn't sure he could or should tell her how he truly felt about her. So many things could change . . .

Then she trapped his gaze in hers. It was like a truth spell . . . impossible to resist.

"I love kissing you and being with you," he confessed, stroking her hair and tucking it behind her ear. It was hard to stop there, but he took a deep breath for steadiness and expelled it quietly. "You have a decision to make soon, and I want you to make it according to your own mind and heart, not out of any sense of obligation or because of a pleasurable diversion. Sooner or later we'll find the key to your mystery, and then you will have to decide where your heart lies and where you belong."

"I already—"

He pressed fingertips against her reddened lips.

"Not yet. Learn what you need to learn here, then you can decide whether your future lies here with your family or . . . elsewhere."

He wrapped her in his arms and simply held her for a time.

A pleasurable diversion was all that happened between them? How dare he kiss her and thrill her like that and then turn all gallant and self-denying? What was the matter with him? Did he not care for her the way she did him? Was he afraid of persuading her to go back to Northrup and having her yearn for her family and become miserable? Did he honestly not trust her to make decisions about her own life?

As they walked back to the cottage together, her disappointment battled with reason. He wanted her to decide whether to stay in Scotland or go back to Northrup without being influenced by the flare of passion between them. But why was the desire she felt not a proper factor in making her decision? She had come to respect and to care for him and no small part of that caring was the desire she felt for him.

His reluctance to reveal his feelings was infuriating. It smacked of him not trusting her to know her own mind and make her own decisions . . . even withholding information that would have a major bearing on those decisions.

Echoes of the free-love lecture where their fates first crossed rose in her memory. Women were entitled to make decisions for themselves . . . to decide who to love and when to love someone. And she damned well had decided!

Sorry, Lord. She scowled, not entirely repentant. There should be a language dispensation for women in such vexing circumstances.

What she had heard in the lecture and from the women in jail afterward had made more difference in her thinking than she realized . . . though it had taken time and additional experience to make her see it. She wanted Barclay in every way a woman could want a man.

And what was wrong with that?

The truth of it settled over her—she loved Barclay Howard. Big, powerful, noble, courageous, and clueless Barclay Howard.

It struck her that the standard he held for himself was based on that blasted Ivanhoe—he had admitted as much on the trip here. But his idol was a fictional character of preposterous gallantry, who ended up with a shallow, self-interested wife instead of the lovely and noble-hearted woman who loved him and helped him again and again. Was that what he wanted for himself? A proper stick of woman to share his life? A vain, status-seeking ninny? She was on the edge of becoming furious with him.

As they approached the MacFergus house, she fell back a few steps and watched Barclay's determined stride and the manly sway of his borrowed kilt. His gait said he was making peace with his new attire. Her eyes lost focus for a moment. She wanted that sway and everything that went with it—that gallant heart and insightful mind, that handsome body and dutiful spirit. And taking a page from her feisty maternal grandmother, she should not hesitate to use a bit of conniving to get what she desired.

With a smile, she set her feet down in time with his and her bottom swayed in a way Barclay Howard would soon have to reckon with.

Dinner was started and the smells wafting from the kitchen invited Norah to offer help while Barclay asked after Eli and Randville. The boy earl was following an older lad around at his chores and Randville had taken a horse into Hesterwaite to see if he could find fabric for some trousers. Murielle was at daughter-in-law Dara's house learning to make cheese . . . a smelly business no one could imagine her enjoying.

While Norah volunteered to peel and pare sundry root vegetables for the pot, Barclay snatched a hunk of fresh bread set on a rack by the open window to cool.

"Wheat loaves," he said, munching on a hunk with great relish. "Interesting—I thought Scots eat oatcakes."

Maureen paused in the middle of tasting from a large kettle hanging over the fire, then went back to her task. "Blame the MacFergus. 'E got a taste fer it when tradin' our wool an' wants it." She gave Norah a wink. "Let 'im have it, I says. He's gettin' old and 'as bad teeth."

Norah couldn't help chuckling, but neither could she help thinking that there were other things in the larder that sheep farmers couldn't normally afford . . . including French cheese, bottles of Bordeaux wine . . . *a bag of gold dust*. She glanced at Barclay, who groaned with pleasure as Maureen handed him a small crock of fresh butter.

"And you make butter and cheese?" His eyes widened with delight.

"Th' MacFergus says wheat bread's no good wi'out butter," Maureen said with a long-suffering sigh.

It was a busy hour before dinner, and the MacFergus sons came to pick up crocks of stew to take home to their families. That left the MacFergus and Maureen to sit down with Norah, Barclay, and Eli. And when bread was served a jar of honey appeared to make it a sweet treat.

Barclay asked Eli to recount his activities for the day, and he did so with enthusiasm. He was fascinated with milking goats and cows, enjoyed feeding the piglets and chickens, and proclaimed himself quite helpful when it came to splitting wood for kindling . . . due to his vast experience with a hatchet. Just as Norah started to express concern that he was wielding such a blade unsupervised, he turned to Maureen and asked how much one of her chickens would cost.

Norah looked to Barclay, who seemed equally puzzled.

"Why would ye be wantin' to know that?" Maureen asked.

"I need chickens for Miss Maudie. She likes eggs but doesn't have any hens. I promised I'd bring 'er some."

"Miss Maudie?" Maureen looked to Norah, then Barclay. "Ye mean Maudie Douglas? Lives a ways south o' Hesterwaite?"

"The same," Barclay said, slathering butter and honey on another piece of bread. "We stayed there one night on the way here."

"How is she?" Maureen asked, seeming concerned.

"Fine," Barclay said. "Some lumbago that comes and goes."

"Her son comes each day to help her," Norah said. "Odd . . . you know her, but she didn't recognize your name or know where you live."

Maureen exchanged glances with the MacFergus, who sat back from his dinner and scratched his belly thoughtfully.

"There be reason fer that," he declared. "Folk hereabouts know t' keep our name quiet. Don't want strangers prowlin' about th' place."

Strangers. Prowling. Norah looked at Barclay and shooed Eli from the table to go outside and find the other children. He grabbed a crust of bread, dipped it in honey, and ran out munching.

"There is something you should know," Norah said, drawing their attention. "When I lived in London a man started following me and tried more than once to drag me into an alley. He found out where I was staying and ransacked my belongings looking for something. I had no idea what he wanted and it was frightening to be pursued so fiercely.

"When Mr. Howard offered me a position as tutor for Eli, I accepted, thinking that leaving London would put an end to it. But when I went to York to meet my father's family, the same man—a Scotsman named Brody—was there looking for me. He abducted Eli and then me, demanding that I tell him the location of a treasure . . . gold that was part of Bonnie Prince Charlie's war chest. He said my father found it in the hills and had coins that proved it.

"I tried to tell him I knew nothing about it, but he didn't believe me. I doubt Eli and I would have survived if Mr. Howard hadn't rescued us."

She sat for a moment, gathering herself for the question that had brought her to their door.

"I never revealed the piece of gold in my locket to Brody, but I know it must be connected somehow to this mystery. And this morning I found gold dust in a flour bag in the larder. Gram said the piece in my locket came from here . . . that my mother took it with her when she left with my father." She looked from her grandmother to her grandfather, both of whom were sitting as rigid as poles, with eyes downcast.

"I need to know where the gold in my locket came from and if you know anything about my father finding the Jacobite treasure."

Sometime in the telling, Barclay had taken her hand and now held it tightly, reminding her that she was not alone in her query. She wondered if his heart was hammering the way hers was. Her grandparents had welcomed her with open arms, and in telling the whole story just now she had just confessed to possibly bringing trouble to their doorstep.

The MacFergus looked at Maureen with a question in his eyes and she took a deep breath and nodded.

"Ain't Jacobite gold, lass," he said gravely. "'Tis ours. Come from our land, our stream—an' betimes—burrowed out by our hands."

Nineteen

Hesterwaite was not much of a market for draper's goods. Only one shop carried ready-made fabric, and the sewing notions they stocked were rudimentary. The bulk of their woven choices were light canvas, primitive-looking plaids, and low-grade, locally produced linens intended for cheap undergarments.

Randville stared at the dismal selection that took up less than two shelves in the shop. "Haven't you anything else—perhaps held back for a special customer—that might make a gentlemanly pair of trousers?"

The shopkeeper, who was donning his coat and seemed eager to leave for his dinner, scowled and shook his head. His daughter leaned on a nearby counter with a flirtatious smile and gave Randville a sly nod. He was determined to keep his mind on the business at hand and selected a few notions he would need. But he couldn't dismiss the feeling that the buxom maid was hinting at something her father didn't wish to reveal.

The shopkeeper exited his shop a few steps behind Randville, who turned away toward the tavern, where he'd been told he would find meat pies worth the price. The shopkeeper's daughter appeared around the corner of the shop beside her father's and beckoned to him. She led him down the alley to a side door to their shop, where she showed him the remains of a bolt of fine black woolen that had probably been ordered for mourning clothes for an Upland family. He learned her name was Mollie, and as she measured what was left on the bolt, she slyly inquired why a man so "braw" and city bred was after such cloth. He told her the truth: a friend's trousers had been ruined and he intended to have them replaced. He neglected to mention he would be doing the stitching himself.

They settled on a price, and after she wrapped the cloth in brown paper she held it away from him with a glint in her eye that said he owed more than money. A kiss and a frisky pat on the bum later, he was headed for the tavern with true relief that the shopkeeper hadn't returned early from his midday meal.

The tavern pies were every bit as good as advertised. With delicious hot food and a tankard of ale in his belly, Randville mounted his horse, tucked his package under his arm, and headed back to the MacFergus holding. It had been a while since he'd made a proper pair of trousers, but measuring, cutting, and stitching fabric were skills no one born into the tape-and-thimble trade would soon forget.

As he rode along, feeling good about finding a way to make up for the loss of his employer's trousers, he began to whistle a catchy tune.

Brody was about to give up on finding them when he looked up from a tankard of dark ale in the local tavern and spotted a man he'd seen before . . . a face he'd not soon forget. He lowered his head to peer beneath his flat cap at the tall fellow who had accompanied that Howard brute to the old mill. It took days for his ribs to recover from the beating he got, and with every painful indrawn breath he had vowed to find both the woman and the bastard who snatched her from him and exact revenge.

He had managed to track them from Grays Court to the train depot and then to the end of a short line that led into the Southern Uplands. From there his search had proved miserably unproductive. There was nothing of value in these godforsaken hills. No inn for a good night's sleep and no village shops or even a decent tavern until he came to this cursed place they called Hesterwaite. Whoever "Hester" was, she had lived and probably died in the poorest squat of a village in all of Scotland.

Here, everyone he asked denied knowing a MacFergus family, and even the offer of hard coin didn't seem to improve their memories. He was about to head back to his rebel cohorts to report his failure when he spotted that unforgettable face. He finished his ale, counted to ten, and then followed the handsome bastard outside.

The MacFerguses' story started out believable enough.

Long ago, back before most records were kept in the Uplands, a MacFergus bought some land for his son with savings from a lifetime of thrift and sacrifice. After a couple of hard winters and dry summers, the first MacFergus was digging the stream channel deeper, hoping to slow the water and allow it to pond for his sheep, when he caught a glint from something in the water. He plucked a nugget of gold from the stream and carried it home to his wife.

The pair decided to keep their find a secret and to

search the stream for more. It wasn't long before they had a small bag of nuggets and grains that had washed downstream from the nearby hills. After a while the fortunate MacFergus made a trip to Glasgow and quietly exchanged the gold for coin and the coin for much-needed goods and supplies.

After a time they collected enough gold to buy more land and discovered it, too, contained a smattering of ore. And when they chiseled out an additional cellar they found a small streak of ore and mined it as they expanded their living quarters. Everything they touched seemed to lead to more gold.

But with the gold came problems. There were likely taxes of some kind on mining and, being thorough Scots, they didn't like the notion of having to pay again for something found in land they had already paid for. Also, it wasn't like they could walk into a store in Glasgow and pay for goods with gold dust or raw nuggets. They had to somehow convert the gold into something spendable without word of it getting out.

It took a bit of skullduggery to find someone who knew the ins and outs of refining gold and had access to stamping molds that could be used to make official-looking coins. When the canny engineer they engaged set up a small minting operation for them, he decided he liked one of the MacFergus daughters enough to not only keep the secret but also to make the holding his home. For a whole generation the man minted coins when necessary and taught the MacFergus sons the secrets of his trade.

Later came another problem. It seemed the stamping molds their engineer provided bore a thistle on one side and the profile of a man on the other. It was a full decade before they realized that those were the markings used by some Jacobites who collected and remelted gold coinage in support of their desired regent, Bonnie Prince Charlie.

The MacFerguses were horrified to learn they had been stamping seditious images into their coins for decades. They halted straightaway and found a way to give their coins more acceptable images . . . those of antique Spanish "eights."

There were, however, already a number of those traitorous coins in circulation. For years folk in the area had known that when trouble struck they could turn to the MacFergus family. Dependable and good Christian folk, the MacFerguses helped their neighbors with everything from paying for medicines to helping farmers buy livestock, to doing chores for injured farmers, to hiring a teacher to help the village children learn to read and write. A discreet coin pressed in a palm here and there with an accompanying finger pressed to lips asking for silence were all it took.

The family were known as hardworking and dutiful sheep herders, and if anyone asked, no one could quite recall how to reach their holdings.

Barclay listened to the story with slow-growing horror. By the time the MacFergus and Maureen finished, his stomach was in knots and his face must have borne an expression equivalent to the Grim Reaper's on Easter Sunday.

Not only were Norah's family wildly inappropriate at times and potentially mad as hatters . . . they were bloody criminals! They mined a precious metal and minted their own money! In previous years they'd have been hanged—now they'd merely be sent to prison forever if their scheme was uncovered.

"You do know that you're counterfeiting money in Her Majesty's kingdom?" he blurted out, fists clenched and gut in turmoil.

"No, no, no, lad. We ne'er forged a thing," Maureen said with a forgiving smile. "We just melted down th' gold we found—our gold—and poured it into a shape we could use."

"Really, Mr. Howard, to say such a thing—" Norah began.

"Under British law the right to mint and issue coinage is reserved to the monarch and her appointed government. By your own admission you have been minting coins and distributing them, using them to pay for goods and services. That's counterfeiting!"

"They ain't counter-fit," the MacFergus declared, bouncing a fist on the table. "They're real gold. Nothin' fake about 'em. They're ours to keep an' use as we see fit."

"But you said you have given such 'coins' to neighbors and friends, is that not true?" Barclay continued, facing Norah's red-faced grandfather.

"They did so only to help them out of difficulty." Norah put her hand on Barclay's arm, urging restraint. "It's not like they're living like kings and queens here. In fact they've been quite modest in their use of the coins. Generous and charitable in their use of the bounty the Almighty has given them."

"So, they're playing Robin Hood," Barclay declared, worrying that he was the only person within twenty miles who knew enough to realize they were violating one of Britain's most fundamental legal standards. Forgery and counterfeiting were seen as undermining the government and the very foundations of society and, as a result, was dealt with quite harshly. He was desperate to make them see the truth.

"If word gets out and they get caught, it won't matter who they helped or how little they circulated their coinage." It struck him like a slap in the face: "Good God—word of it is already out! They may not know that you minted the coins, but Edgar Capshaw, Norah's uncle, and his henchmen have seen gold pieces that Douglas Capshaw had in his possession, and they may even have collected more over time as they looked for it."

Norah was stunned. "You think they believe the coins my family produced are part of the prince's missing hoard?" She seemed to melt as the reality of the situation became clear. "My uncle will stop at nothing to get his hands on that gold. And he thinks I know where the rest of it is." She gave Barclay a desolate look. "Sooner or later he'll find me."

"You're safe here, Norah," he said, turning her to face him. He smiled for her, trying to mask his anxiety at the mess they were in.

There was no way to know just how far the MacFergus coins had spread and just who else might be trying to locate the source. Brody escaped from the mill and Capshaw was likely still at large. Every day those two were free was a day Norah was in danger of being taken and forced to tell all she had just learned.

There had to be something they could do to ensure her safety, and to see that her grandparents were not punished for their precious metal enterprise. He put an arm around her, filling with determination to see things put right for her.

"Aye, well, ye may as well see the rest of it," Maureen

said, rising and giving Norah and Barclay a rueful look. "Come wi' me." She paused at the kitchen doorway to stare at her husband. "You, too, MacFergus."

Norah and Barclay followed her reluctantly into the cool, dark larder, with the MacFergus close behind. Norah looked around them, wondering how many of those barrels, casks, bottles, and bags held what was marked on the outside and how many were filled with something more dangerous than dry gunpowder. The next second she was ashamed of such suspicion. These people were her flesh and blood, her family who had used their good fortune in generous and charitable ways. Barclay had been right to call them Robin Hoods. They took from Mother Earth and gave to their needy neighbors and helped their fellow Scots—

Maureen opened the second door Norah had spied in the larder, and she was surprised at the size of the portal. It had seemed much smaller when she glanced at it before. Barclay barely had to bend his head to clear it. They stepped down into a hallway that had been chiseled out of bedrock and contained stairs leading downward . . . into what? A second cellar? A cave? A mine?

Her grandmother opened another door at the bottom of the steps. When they stepped inside both she and Barclay gasped.

Their destination was a rectangular room of sizable proportions, furnished with tapestries on walls that had been mortared and plastered. There were stuffed chairs, a broad, stuffed couch, and a handsome reclining bench on one end and bookshelves filled with volumes, a library table, and a number of comfortable-looking chairs on the other. There were no windows, however; light was provided by wall sconces and oil lamps on the table and a sizable desk. The stone floor was covered by Persian carpets and two ottomans were upholstered with exotic animal skins.

"Wh-what is this place?" Norah had to force the words out.

"Home," Maureen said with a rueful smile. "Couldna let the space go to waste once th' mining was done. So we made it a livin' place."

"Aye." The MacFergus stepped to his wife's side. "Spent a few o' our coins to bring some comfort here. Me Maurie lass deserves a soft place t' park 'er bones after all she done."

There were two other doors, one leading off to spacious and well-furnished bedchambers, one of which looked to be the master's quarters and the other a simpler but still comfortable room with a big, soft bed. The second door led to a storage room in which old cottage furnishings and rusty iron tools and ceiling braces sat beside two shelves stacked with bags heavy enough to make the boards bow.

Norah gravitated toward the canvas bags and touched one. The contents were round, flat, and hard as rocks. *Or gold.*

A chill went through her and she turned on her grandparents.

"Are these . . ."

"Aye," Maureen said with a sigh. "A number of 'em have the old thistle and Prince Charlie stamps."

"Kept meanin' to melt 'em down," the MacFergus explained, "but charcoal be dear, an' the furnace only takes small batches . . ."

"So you just kept them here?" Barclay sounded strangled. "This is no humble Robin Hood setup—this is a Bank of England job!" He jammed his hands on his waist and spread his legs, bracing for the impact. "There must be twenty or thirty bags of gold coins here."

"Forty-three," the MacFergus corrected with a stubborn puff of pride in his barrel chest. "We 'ad some good years, we did."

"Sweet Jesus help us," Norah muttered.

It was a genuine prayer, but Barclay wagged his head.

"I doubt even the Almighty's Son would want to tackle this one."

At that very moment Brody was creeping back to his horse on the hill overlooking the MacFerguses' holding.

The fire in his eyes said retribution was close at hand. He hadn't seen the girl or that Howard brute . . . but he saw the kid runnin' around the place. And if the kid was there, the other two couldn't be far away. They came all the way to the Southern Uplands for some reason, and he had a hunch it had to do with his search for the gold.

The chit claimed not to know anything about it, but first chance she got she scurried off to a sheep farm in middle-of-nowhere Scotland. The wench knew more'n she let on. This time he needed proper help gettin' the truth out of her and he knew right where to get it.

That same night, Norah, Murielle, and Eli were invited downstairs to the comfortable second bedroom in the fine underground house the MacFerguses had created. Barclay slept under goose down on the stuffed couch in the great room, while Randville was assigned the cupboard bed at the end of the kitchen.

Randville watched the family and his employer disappear into what he thought was a larder and took it as confirmation of his deduction that all was not as it seemed here. He could have sworn that the MacFergus had purposefully gotten them drunk on the previous night, though he couldn't imagine why. They had nothing worth stealing and were clearly not a danger to the family. In the end he admonished himself to be grateful for a full belly and a soft bed in a warm kitchen. For some reason as he went to sleep, his gambler's mind was invaded by images of bright, shiny coins arrayed in stacks on a card table.

The next day the MacFergus took Barclay and Norah to his sons' homes, where they discovered a similar deception of appearances. Rooms had been carved out of the rock beneath the structures to form useful spaces for the family . . . that connected belowground to those used for the family's covert gold operation. From the road above no sign of the chimneys was visible and the outbuildings and pole sheds supposedly for animals accounted for most other underground air outlets and access. Barclay had to hand it to them: The layout and disguise were ingenious.

As he and Norah walked over the hills later that afternoon, the sun warmed their shoulders and the sky was a trouble-free blue. But her mood was subdued and it was clear she was worried about the danger to her family. He took her hands, pulled her close, and tried to reassure her that they were probably in the last place on earth her uncle would look for her.

"You know how hard it was for us to find your grandparents. We'd still be wandering the backroads and hills if the liveryman hadn't relented because you had the look of a MacFergus. I can't imagine your nasty uncle persuading anyone around here to help him find your mother's family. And I suspect that Brody wretch gave up after the dusting he got at the mill and headed for easier pickings."

She nodded, reassured somewhat on that account.

"But what do we do about all the Jacobite-marked gold my family has stored below? If it's discovered, they could be accused of Jacobite leanings and charged with helping to fund another rebellion against British rule. The whole family could go to prison."

"Counterfeiting can be life in prison, but treason is still a hanging offense," Barclay said, and immediately wished he could take it back. Norah's face paled.

She groaned. "We have to do something."

Twenty

"We are doing something," Barclay said. "Griff is firing up the hearth to begin melting them down. Heaven knows how long that will take to heat—starting from cold."

"Let's go see." She headed for the cottage with her skirts swaying.

Barclay lagged behind slightly to appreciate that tempting sight, then found it impossible to scrub from his mind.

Minutes later they stood in a large, cavelike chamber, watching her uncle Griff oversee the slow, smelly, and painstaking process of stoking a charcoal fire hot enough to raise the temperature of a thick iron cauldron to gold's melting point. The equipment—designed to produce a small batch at a time—could only handle melting eight or ten coins at once.

As they waited, she looked around the small foundry, finally realizing how much work the family's illicit enterprise entailed. This place and those bags of gold were the result of generations of grinding labor. To just throw it all away without trying everything possible to salvage it would be an insult to their entire ancestry.

"You see?" Barclay said as they watched and waited. "It takes far too long to melt those coins and recast them." He exhaled heavily. "And there's more of them than we thought. Almost twenty bags. If your grandparents are caught with such a lode, there isn't a magistrate in England who would believe they're innocent of counterfeiting and trying to overthrow English rule. I know it seems horrible to consider, but they need to get rid of those 'Jacobite' coins now. Bury them . . . throw them in a northern loch . . . pound them back into dust . . ."

Norah touched his muscular hand and it opened to reveal one of the tainted coins. She took it from him and, on impulse, bit it, testing the tradition of verifying gold content in such a manner. When she looked there were definite toothmarks visible. His words struck home.

"Why can't we do just that . . . pound the pieces flat and get rid of the images that way?"

Barclay looked at her in dismay. "Do you know how long that would take? How much muscle power it would involve?"

"No," she said brightly. "I haven't a clue. Do you know?"

He frowned, thinking, and had to admit: "Not really." He looked to Griff, who had stepped away from the hearth to see what they wanted.

Her uncle met his questioning look. He had heard their exchange.

"Don't ask me, lad. Been makin' the damn things fer years. Don't know nothin' about *unmakin'* 'em," he declared.

Norah's conclusion made far too much sense: "Shouldn't we find out if it's possible before consigning hard-won gold to oblivion?"

* * *

Barclay had little hope for her solution but picked up a small anvil and moved it to a worktable near the cooling platform.

She spotted a hammer, picked it up, and before he could react laid the coin on the anvil and gave it a rap. The result was off-center and the impression of the circular hammerhead was not especially deep. The images were still visible, if distorted.

"It will take more power," she said. Eyeing his muscular arms, she handed him the hammer. "You try it."

He hefted the hammer, scowled, and then exchanged it for a bigger, heavier one lying in a nearby tool box. If she wanted better results, he thought, he'd bloody well give them to her. After one wicked hard strike, the gold was thinner and the images were a jumble of lines.

"Again," she said, eyes sparkling.

After two more heavy blows there was a dramatic change in the shape and appearance of the gold. She snatched up the warm disk to examine the glow his efforts produced.

"You did it!" She threw her arms about him, hugging him hard and fighting the tears pricking her eyes. "Barr, you're an alchemist! You transformed tainted gold into circles of . . . pure sunshine!"

That was the way the MacFergus found them, holding each other tightly, having just finished a breathtaking kiss.

"What the devil?" he demanded, glancing at Griff, who grinned.

They showed him the result of their experiment, and

he ran back along the passage and up the steps to the house, calling for Maureen.

The next day Barclay and the MacFergus men took turns pounding traitorous images out of their "Jacobite gold." Some were more adept than others at what they termed their "goldsmithing." In the end, it was Barclay who supplied much of the power to render the gold no threat to the family's future. He was so occupied with the transformation of the gold that when Randville tried to locate him for a fitting of his new trousers, he was nowhere to be found.

"What the blazes is going on here?" Randville muttered, stalking from cottage to stable to barn and back to cottage with a pair of basted trouser pieces across his arm. There was a sharp, acrid smokiness in the air and a low hum he couldn't identify that seemed to come from beneath his feet. Something strange was going on here and he intended to find out what.

In the cottage he laid out the fabric on the drop-down table where he worked and headed out to find his employer. He stalked down the hill toward the stream, scattering sheep as he called, "Mr. Howard!" again and again.

At length he heard his own name called and wheeled to find his employer coming toward him around the side of the hill. The man looked like he'd just crawled out of a river—face and forearms wet and steaming in the cold air, shirt soaked and sticking to his muscular frame, and those knit hose the MacFerguses provided rolled down to reveal damp legs. He was breathing hard, and Randville sensed he wasn't happy at being dragged away from whatever he was doing.

"I need to fit your trousers," Randville said, arms folded and legs spread in unconscious imitation of his employer's stance.

"Trousers?" Barclay frowned, then seemed to shake off his irritation. "Don't think I need 'em. I'm making peace with the skirt."

Randville narrowed his eyes. "You hired me as a valet but refuse to give me 'valet' work. The first thing I was tasked with was a dangerous rescue and the second made me a driver for a lady's maid and a six-year-old earl. If you don't want me to replace your trousers, what is it you want me to do?"

Barclay studied that question as if he was wrestling with an answer.

"Does it have to do with Miss Capshaw and the men who abducted her?" Randville asked. "They tried to make her tell them about a missing hoard of gold. Does that have something to do with this place?"

"What makes you think that?"

"Miss Capshaw's folk are odd and secretive. They have a two-room cottage with one bed closet in the kitchen, but somehow they sleep seven people at night. Either there is more to the place than it seems, or the MacFergus and wife are capable of miracles rivaling the loaves and fishes. Also, Miss Capshaw stands in the upper field and scans the surrounding hills like she's concerned about something . . . maybe worried that Brody bastard will appear again."

"She does?" Barclay looked as if that was unwelcome news. He took a deep breath. "You are an astute observer, Randville Worth." He looked around, blew a heavy breath, and made a beckoning motion. "Walk with me."

* * *

"It does have to do with what they wanted from her," Barclay said as they walked along the cart path that led to the main track. "That's the principle reason we came here. She wanted to find her grandparents, but also to know why Brody and her uncle believed she knew the location of that treasure. They told her that her father had pieces of 'Jacobite' gold from a lost part of the prince's war chest. They believed he found it and that he must have relayed that information to her somehow. He hadn't."

"Some of that I gleaned from your conversations," Randville said.

"She was raised an orphan and believed she had no family. When she finally met her uncle, Edgar Capshaw, he had her kidnapped and watched as she was brutalized. . . . She is still recovering from that. She felt she had to come here to learn the truth about her father and the Jacobite gold. But when she got here she found two grandparents who opened their arms and hearts to her." He gave a huff of a laugh. "They've got cabbage for brains, the both of them. But . . ."

"They care for her. As you do." Randville clasped his hands behind his back as he walked. "So, did she learn about the gold?"

It took a minute for Barclay to digest that his feelings for Norah weren't exactly a secret, then continued.

"This is where I have to make a decision. I don't know you well, but you've been loyal and helpful, and my instincts tell me you will continue so." He halted and looked Randville in the eye. "Yes. She found answers here. But it's a strange tale and not mine to tell. I'll talk to Norah, and if she agrees, she'll tell you herself."

Randville thought that over for a minute before deciding. "Good enough."

Barclay headed back to the warmth of the cottage with one thing on his mind. If his feelings weren't a secret from Randville, it was a good bet Norah knew about them already. And what was he going to do about that?

Each day the number of bags of dangerous gold was reduced by one, and Barclay confided privately to Norah that though it was exhausting, it was also good for venting frustration and thinking. She reached for his hand, traced his developing calluses, and asked what he thought about.

"I once thought my hard experiences in my grandfather's house were a test of sorts . . . somehow judging my worthiness. They were strenuous and often seemed cruel. But now, putting the physical strength they developed in me to good use, I begin to wonder if those experiences were meant to prepare me for things I would need to do someday." He gave a soft laugh. "Like pounding illegal coins into golden doilies."

"Maybe a bit of both." Norah smiled, touched his face, then stretched up to give him a kiss on the cheek. "You are such a wise man."

That was when he told her about his talk with Randville and asked her to speak with him and tell him the rest if she felt comfortable doing so. He reminded her of the man's role in her rescue and left her to her own thoughts.

She watched him walk away and admired once again the sway of his kilt. She sighed. If only he would watch her the same way.

Later that day, at dinner, she noted the fatigue in Barclay's face and made her decision. Afterward she took Randville aside and told him about her family's gold problem. He was shocked at first and then silent, and then nodded and said he would do whatever was required to help. Trusting that she had made the right decision, she met his gaze.

"I think Barclay and the MacFergus men could use help."

That evening Randville literally fell into his cupboard bed. His nimble hands, used to shuffling cards or directing a needle, were stiff from wielding a hammer. And his shoulders, arms, back, and even legs were on fire. Maureen had supplied a willow-bark tea concoction to all who needed it, and Randville drank two cups. He didn't fall asleep so much as he passed out. And it was all to do over on the following day.

"At this rate," Barclay announced to the MacFergus over their midday meal the next day, "it will take two or three weeks to flatten them all." Every man present let out a groan.

Miles to the west on the craggy coast of the Firth of Clyde, a dozen men, some in filthy breeches and others in faded plaids were gathered in a cave around a weak fire. They held out hands and feet, seeking what comfort the struggling flames could provide. Copper hoops and straight iron bands were strewn further back in the cave, evidence of the barrels and crates they had taken apart for firewood. Empty wooden bowls, discarded rags, and cups and tinware were piled against one wall. Against the other lay a heap of blankets beside a line of old hunting rifles arrayed like an antique armory. The place smelled of filthy bodies, spent ale, and desperation.

"Tha' be the last o' it, Duncan." A short, scrawny fellow

handed a tin cup of watery brown liquid to a shaggy fellow seated on a barrel lid and staring into the flames.

"We'll find it soon," Duncan muttered, accepting the coffee. "Then we'll have plenty o' coffee. An' mornin' bread an' pies an' lamb shanks."

It was a promise repeated so often around that desolate campfire that it had lost meaning for most of the men. They eyed each other and a couple of them covertly shook their heads as they avoided their leader's gaze.

This group of revolutionaries intent on freeing their country from England's domination had spent more than a year together in this cave, waiting for the promised gold that would buy them supplies, ammunition, and recruits to the cause. Prospects for their cause had dimmed with delays in recent months, such that when their lookout came rushing in from the top of the cliff, the dispirited group scarcely bothered to look up.

"It's Brody comin'! There's a bloke wi' him an' they be leadin' a packhorse!" the fellow said, looking to Duncan with a bit of hope animating his thin face.

Duncan was on his feet in a heartbeat.

"Cursed fool knows better'n t' bring a stranger 'ere."

He headed for his gun, and moments later a dozen armed revolutionaries greeted Brody and a man they knew by name but had never seen in the flesh . . . one Edgar Capshaw.

The next several days passed quietly at the MacFergus holding. Norah resumed Eli's studies with the books from the secret library. The other children learned Norah was reading stories and begged to be released from chores early to join her and the little earl. She discovered they had been given little time for schooling and began to teach numbers and words in earnest to a receptive group.

For her part, Murielle spent time in the kitchen with Maureen, discovering that she actually liked some aspects of cooking—especially making sweets. Eli, when not attending sessions with Norah, ran with the other children over hill and dale, through pastures and up rocky crags.

Despite the occasional scraped knee and scrap with the other boys, he seemed to love it. For the first time in his life he had other children to play with, learn with, and even fight with. Every morning he bounded out of bed and rushed outside with no dread of the cold despite his short pants and the long socks he had to wear. His face glowed with health when he came into the cottage, and he ate everything he was served without a complaint. The trip to "Scottlund" was doing him a world of good.

One day Norah heard the other children call him "Earl," as if they thought it was his name, and asked him about it.

"Yeah, I'm Earl," Eli said happily, taking an offered piece of shortbread and running out to help the others so they could finish chores by story time.

Norah told Barclay about it and he laughed. Together, they marveled at how happy Eli was here. Despite his horrific encounter with Brody and his henchmen, he now seemed exempt from the worries of grown-ups and just enjoyed exploring the world of friends and farm. Norah said a prayer, hoping that nothing would happen to dim his pleasure at discovering the broader world . . . or her happiness at having found a family and a man to love.

It was only a day later—just over a week since they'd arrived at the MacFerguses'—that the first threat to that happiness arrived.

* * *

Strangely, that threat was brought by a friend . . . news of strangers in town who didn't seem to be what they said they were. Liveryman Clyde Bannock rode out from the village to tell the MacFergus that two men wearing riding clothes, packing long guns, and riding damn good horses had just spent an afternoon in Hesterwaite.

"They claimed to be huntin', but didna carry gear to make camp and was purse-mouthed at findin' no inn in Hester. They went by th' tavern an' filled their bellies good, then on to MacCready's shop an' looked about. One dropped a gold piece on th' counter an' went red-faced as 'e picked it up. Like it was a mistake."

"Aye." The MacFergus thus far was not impressed. "So?"

"Tha' Mollie be sharp. Said the fella was watchin' 'er—to see if she reco-nized it. She didna like the smell of tha' and snuck in behind 'em at Dougie Newton's shop. Damned if th' fella didn' do the same mistake there. Come ta' find out, he done it in th' tavern, too."

Clyde thanked Maureen for the ale she set before him and drank thirstily as the MacFergus sent for Norah, Barclay, and his two sons.

"Wha's queer about it," Clyde said after repeating his tale for the gathered group, "is Mollie says it were a thistle on one side o' the piece. She didna see th' other." He took a finishing gulp of ale. "I tell ye, tha' Mollie's sharp as a razor. 'We mebbe simple folk,' she says, 'but we ain't stupid.' She an' her pa figure they was gov-ment, lookin' fer somebody . . . er somethin'."

The MacFergus thanked him for coming by and Maureen sent respects to his wife and gave him a jar of honey and a round of their best cheese from the larder. The minute he was gone the MacFergus's face lost all trace of geniality.

"Now wha' could a pair o' gov-ment boys be lookin' fer if they be dangling a thistle coin as bait?" he snarled.

"Jacobite treasure," Norah said, looking dejected.

"Or counterfeiters," Barclay said, looking at the MacFergus.

"Or rebel nests," Randville added from the doorway.

All three were threatening prospects. Barclay glanced at Randville, who—as it turned out—wielded a surprisingly mean hammer as well as he stitched a fine pair of trousers. He was a man of surprising talents.

"What do you think?"

The gambler-turned-tailor-valet-rescuer-cart driver-and-now-goldsmith exhaled deeply and looked from Barclay to the MacFergus, Griff, and Cam.

"I think this means we've got to work faster."

Three days and five bags of gold rendered safe later, Barclay, Randville, Griff, and Cam were exhausted and aching in places they hadn't known they had. Norah, Maureen, and Murielle worked hard in the kitchen to keep them fed, but not even hearty farm food could make up the prodigious amounts of energy they expended as they pounded gold coins into thin, flat circles they hoped to later melt down and recast into small, ten-ounce bars.

"Ten troy ounces is the size most frequently traded on the metals exchange in London," Randville had advised as they worked together in the hot, steaming foundry. The others stopped to stare at him. "They're also quite portable, and in some areas—for some purposes—they're actually spendable."

"How the hell do you know that?" Barclay demanded, resting for a moment on his hammerhead.

Randville looked a bit chagrinned, then straightened and wiped sweat from his face with his sleeve. "I have at times—in a previous career—taken a bar of gold as either surety or payment. Which at times necessitated turning it into a more liquid asset. Which in turn led to an acquaintance with the metals exchange."

Barclay grinned and wagged his head. "Someday I'm going to have to hear your life story."

Norah went for a walk every afternoon and, despite the chill wind, found it calming and peaceful. She made it a point to stay within sight of the MacFergus cottages and barns but had chosen a spot on a rocky crag to sit and watch the surrounding valley and the track from Hesterwaite.

That weedy, overgrown road remained empty most days, which was why it was a jolt to see two men riding along it and stopping at the cairn marking the entrance to the MacFergus holdings. Clyde Bannock's report came rushing back to her: two men in riding clothes, good horses . . . and though she couldn't see them straightaway, she had a feeling there would be long guns somewhere about their saddles.

Her heart was thumping as she hurried down from her perch to the lane that ended by her grandparents' cottage. She paused, folded her arms, and waited as they approached. They halted and one dismounted, tipping his hat to her and producing a smile.

"Good afternoon, miss. We're looking for a farm owned by the MacFergus family. Have we found it?"

"You have," she said, praying her expression registered mild curiosity. "The MacFergus is my grandfather."

"Excellent. And would he be about just now? We've come all the way from Glasgow to speak to him."

"Ach, that be a trek," she said with as Scottish an accent as she could muster. The man's face registered surprise.

"Are you from around here?" he said. "I ask because you don't sound Scottish."

"I am visiting my grandparents, the MacFerguses. I'm from York."

"And your name, miss?" The man stepped closer and scrutinized her, though his manner was determined friendliness.

"May I ask why you want to know, sir?" She stiffened.

"I must inform you, we are here on official government business, and it would help to know who we are talking with."

"Government business? That sounds important." She eyed him and then the man still on a horse. "I am Norah Capshaw, tutor to his lordship, the Earl of Northrup, who is running around here somewhere." When the man looked puzzled she explained: "His lordship is six years old. He and his guardian, Mr. Barclay Howard . . . also of the Northrup Howards . . . elected to accompany me on this visit." She smiled and produced a confidential tone. "His lordship has never been to Scotland before and was so eager to come." She looked at them expectantly, and he introduced himself and his companion: Gerald Brett and Morgan Ralls. She turned and beckoned them with her to the cottage.

Maureen called the MacFergus in from the stable and offered the men refreshment. Eli came running with a couple of older boys and was introduced, given shortbread, and shooed away. Shortly after Barclay arrived, having rinsed and toweled off evidence of his strenuous activity. Brett and Ralls were suitably intimidated as Barclay gave each a potent handshake and explained he had been help-ing erect another shed for the family's sheep to use in the coming winter.

This visit was not entirely unexpected. They had heard from a passing neighbor that two men were canvassing the countryside, being direct in their queries, asking about the source of several gold coins that had made their way to Glasgow officialdom.

"Treasure huntin', are ye?" the MacFergus said genially, leaning back and linking his hands across his belly.

"In a manner of speaking," Brett answered. "We're hoping to find the source of some gold coins that were minted many years ago." He pulled one from his coat pocket to show them and Maureen's eyes lighted.

"It's a bonnie thing," she said, reaching tenuously to touch it, then frowning. "What's so special about it?"

"It was part of a Scottish rebel hoard, from over a hun-dred years ago. Part of it was never found . . . until now."

"Ye found 'the hoard'?" the MacFergus said with sur-prise. "Ye know, I 'ad a turn lookin' fer it." His face fell. "Got nothin' but an achin' back an' sore shanks fer me trouble. Who found it?—th' lucky bugger."

"That's what we'd like to know," Ralls said. "The gold belongs to the Crown now. It may be that whoever found it has leanings toward Scottish independence and wants to use it to start trouble."

The MacFerguses showed the perfect amount of shock and disapproval at that news and the men seemed to relax. After asking a dozen questions about the part of the treasure that was found long ago and listening raptly to the agents' information, they expressed fascination and invited the men to stay for dinner. As the men took leave, the MacFergus obliged Brett's request for directions to a neighboring holding.

"That was a close one," Barclay declared as they stood watching the men turn onto the track leading back toward Hesterwaite.

"Now we know the coins have reached the government offices in Glasgow," Norah said, taking his hand.

"Some in Hester mayn't be as closemouthed as Clyde and Mollie," the MacFergus said. "We best look to our defenses an' double our efforts to get rid of th' gold." He looked to Barclay. "Got a hammer fer me?"

Maureen nodded ruefully and patted her husband's beefy hand.

Twenty-One

Days later, nearing dusk, four men claiming to be coming from a hunt in the Galloway Hills appeared in Hesterwaite. They needed supplies for the trip home, they said, but when Clyde Bannock asked each where he was headed, three of the four gave entirely different answers. That bit of evasion and the lean, hardened look of them put him on guard. When he asked about their lack of hides from the hunt they went silent.

Shortly two other men arrived to join the party. They had just visited the tavern and declared that the food looked to be acceptable. One was a burly Scotsman, the other clearly English in dress and speech. They paid Clyde appropriately, flashing a memorable gold coin briefly, and asked about the hunting thereabouts . . . seeming oddly disinterested in the answer. Soon the whole group returned to the tavern for food.

Clyde waited a short while before calling on Mollie. He couldn't leave the livery with patrons waiting, but she could carry word to the MacFerguses. He provided a mount, and within moments she was racing along the track toward their hold.

Barclay, Randville, and the others had just ended their workday, washed up in the pump house, and were headed to their respective cottages for food when a rider with streaming dark hair came pounding up the lane. They stopped dead at the sight of a buxom wench reining up and hastily dismounting.

"The MacFergus," she panted, and they led her into the cottage, where the patriarch was enjoying a tankard of ale before dinner. Norah, Maureen, and Murielle stopped in the midst of dishing up stewed meat and vegetables to see who had arrived.

"Mollie girl." Maureen saw the girl's reddened face and hurried to take her hands. "What's brought ye here in such a rush?"

"Clyde sent me." She looked to the MacFergus and that big fellow who had been in her father's shop a fortnight before. When she spotted Randville in the doorway she smiled. "There's men in town . . . sayin' they been huntin', but they got no game to show fer it." She rolled her eyes. "Same lunkhead story as them others. But this be a tough an' salty lot, wi' a Scot an' a Englishman payin' th' bill. Flashed a piece of gold like th' others. But ain't askin' questions." She rearranged her short cloak, gave Randville a brief look, and licked her lips.

Norah watched as Maureen and the MacFergus thanked her, admonished her to hurry home before full dark, and sent her off with a bottle of French wine and a round of Dutch cheese.

She could scarcely breathe. Brody and Edgar Capshaw . . . here . . . together. And they had brought other men, tough and salty men . . . bone breakers who would do anything for money. They were likely worse than the pair Brody had employed before. Barclay had that smacked-with-a-gauntlet look again, and Randville, beside him, looked like he'd had the air let out of him.

"If they're not asking questions," she said, her voice dry, "that means they already know where to find me."

"And they'll come for you soon." There was barely contained fury in Barclay's voice now as he stabbed the air with his finger. "You're not to leave this house tonight, Norah Capshaw. You do not set foot outside, even in daylight, without me by your side."

Maureen pinched the bridge of her nose, working to hold back tears. The MacFergus pulled her into his arms and looked to Norah with patriarchal determination.

"Listen t' yer man, lass. He'll see ye come to no harm." Then he looked to Barclay and Randville. "I'll tell my lads an' we'll post watches. They could come t'night." He looked to Maureen. "Break out th' guns."

Soon every man on the place and a couple of the older youths of hunting age were gathered in the cottage's front room, checking and loading a shotgun or rifle. They were quiet as they worked, except for comments on the best place to watch the road and whether they ought to post a lookout on the track for early warning. It was decided to use the youths as lookouts along the Hesterwaite track because they were used to running the slopes in the dark after stubborn sheep. The men would go up in the crags overlooking the hold and around the hills above the cottages.

"A pity we couldn't bring those government fellows together with this mob—have them go at each other," Randville said as he checked his derringer, then stocked his coat pocket with shells for the shotgun he'd been assigned.

Norah, watching them load guns from a bench against the wall, was struggling with guilt and feeling helpless. If only she could do something to prevent the people she loved from getting hurt. Randville's words rumbled around in her head until they began to resonate and combine with her own thoughts. She straightened, her mind racing and her heart rushing to keep up.

She rose and grabbed Barclay's arm, her eyes flitting over a plan as it developed in her head. "That's it! They want the Jacobite gold and we're trying to get rid of a ton of it. Let's give it to them!"

Everyone in the room froze except for the dropping of jaws.

"Not all of it—obviously—but enough to make it seem they've got the Jacobite treasure they've been hunting." She looked to Maureen and the MacFergus. "It would take care of the problem of how to get rid of it, and they would have no more reason to pursue me or discover you."

She halted, seeing the shock on her grandparents' faces. If the stakes hadn't been so high, she would have been ashamed to suggest it. She had nerve, asking them to pay a prince's ransom for her safety. But it wasn't just her life on the line . . . the MacFergus, Maureen, Griff's and Cam's wives and children . . . there were three generations of MacFerguses to protect.

What were a few bags of tainted gold compared to peace-of-mind and safety for generations to come?

Barclay was the first to recover from the shock.

"If they get the gold, what will they do with it? Brody

said the clans would use it to restart the rebellion. If we let them have it, we'll be aiding and abetting treason."

Randville was the only one smiling just then. "Not if we let the government boys know where the group is . . . that they have the gold and plan to use it for traitorous purposes. They'll be arrested before they can do anything seditious."

"Oh my God," Maureen said, letting the possibility unfold fully in her mind. "It could work. We give some o' the thistle gold to th' bastards and then sic the law on 'em."

"But how do we make it happen? They might be a tad suspicious if we just invite them in and hand over a fortune in gold," Barclay said. "'Here ye be lads—go overthrow the queen'!"

Norah bit her lip and gripped the edge of the table where guns lay ready for a storm of violence that she could not allow to be unleashed.

"We have to convince the wretches they've won," she said, narrowing her eyes. "And there's only one way to do that."

Barclay looked at her with dawning alarm. "I'm not going to like this, am I?"

"Probably not," she said with a small but determined smile. "They have to get the gold as payment . . . of a ransom . . . for me."

"Oooh no!" Barclay bellowed. "Are you crazy, woman?"

The cottage erupted in chaos—everyone had an opinion and they seemed evenly divided between going with Norah's plan and locking her in the downstairs storage room for a month or two. But everything that was proposed, only led to more reasons that her idea was the only one that would get rid of the tainted gold *and* ensure a safe outcome for everyone on the holding.

In the end Norah won the right to be kidnapped and ransomed with Jacobite gold that would undoubtedly land her kidnappers in trouble.

As night fell, watches were posted and guns were dispatched. Orders were to shoot close to make it seem like a true defense, but to make certain Norah wasn't anywhere in the vicinity of the shot.

Her role was to fight her abductors convincingly until the wretches dumped her in their camp, and to spew enough bold threats to make them believe Barclay and her grandparents might try to rescue her . . . before ultimately confessing that the MacFerguses had found the prince's gold.

Chances were Brody and Capshaw were camping somewhere in the cover of the forest at the start of the Galloway Hills. Preparing for her role as victim, she donned a quilted petticoat, a quilted underbodice, and proper layers on top of them. Swaddled so, she feared she wouldn't be able to fend off her abductors if she had to. But Randville visited her in the downstairs parlor and slipped her a long, slender dirk in a leather pouch that she could tie to her leg or stuff in her bodice and use to cut her bonds if worse came to worst. She gave him a kiss on the cheek and he reddened and excused himself quickly.

Barclay walked out to the stable with her, going over the plan and reassuring her that he and Randville would have her in their sight at all times. Tracking their movements as well as protecting her was their task. Randville would carry back word of their location to the MacFergus, who would in turn carry word of men carrying Jacobite gold to Brett and Ralls.

If anything dangerous occurred, Barclay said, he would come for her no matter the timing. She had seen him take on unfavorable odds before and knew that he could handle himself with his fists, but that was little assurance. There would be guns this time, and there was no guarantee that they would escape from this venture unharmed.

When they arrived at the stable she put her arms around him and pulled him close. Despite her earlier show of bravado and determination, a lump of anxiety remained in her core. Things could go wrong, and if they did . . .

"Barclay," she said, looking up to his shadowed face, "I want you to know—I want to say something now in case—"

He stopped her with a finger against her lips. "It will work out."

"But I want you to know—"

"I'm mad about you, too, Norah Capshaw," he said, his voice low and resonant. "Isn't that what you wanted to say, that you're mad about me?" She swallowed hard and nodded. "I love you, too, lass. With all my heart.

"It's taken some getting used to, the notion that you might really want me, but I finally quit worrying about your taste in men and just accepted it. I want to be with you and care for you and share with you for years to come." He stared into her eyes, so luminous in the moonlight. "So, don't do anything foolhardy and courageous," he said. "There's only room for one white knight in this family and that's me."

"You *are* my white knight, Barr. I swore I didn't need one, but . . ." she said, tears pricking her eyes. "Wait—what do you mean, 'family'?"

"We are family. Right here. Right now. I'm taking you on, and the whole mad MacFergus clan with you. After all this is over . . . I want to find a church and stand up before God and everyone and promise to spend my life with you."

"Are you proposing to me? Now?" she gasped.

"Sort of." He grinned, showing teeth she knew he seldom revealed.

"Then I'm accepting. Sort of." She tightened her arms around him. "To know for certain, you'll have to ask me again . . . later . . . with flowers and champagne and maybe violins."

He looked thoughtful for a moment. "I think those could be arranged."

"I want you, Barclay Howard." She rose onto her toes to give him a blistering kiss that she memorized and prayed would not be their last.

"I want you, Norah Capshaw," he said against her lips afterward, "despite your villainous, greedy family connections and your Robin-Hooding, generous family connections. I love you just as you are. Stubborn, independent, determined . . . generous, caring, beautiful, brave . . . passionate . . ."

He released her and stepped back, studying her in the moonlight, capturing every beloved line and curve of her face to hold in his mind. Letting her go was hard—perhaps the hardest thing he'd ever done. But he had to trust her, to let her walk the path she had so adamantly chosen.

And he had to be there—her Ivanhoe, her white knight—to see her safely home again.

The half-moon was high and the air was cold when Norah went on her first walk. Maureen, the MacFergus, and Murielle gathered in the front room of the cottage to wait with her until it was fully dark. Barclay, Randville, and her two uncles were already stationed outside at vantage points that allowed them to see the cluster of buildings and nearby land.

The ransom was ready—eleven bags of gold coins, dirtied as if they'd been buried and then stuffed into a wooden box with iron bands securing it. It made for heavy lifting, so it was decided that Barclay, the MacFergus, and Griff would deliver it together when the time came. Randville would go separately and be ready for any kind of double-cross.

Everyone sat in silence, in honor of her dangerous mission . . . which she found nerve-racking. She finally asked for some of Maureen's honey wine and it was quickly provided. The potent drink nudged her back from the edge of her nerves, but also combined with her extra garments to make her flush with heat.

"I'm roasting," she said, fanning her face and reaching for her long cloak. "I may as well get started. There is no guarantee they will come tonight anyway."

Just before she stepped out the door her grandfather gave her a kiss on the forehead, as if blessing her for whatever was ahead. It caused a tightness in her throat and she wondered for the tenth time if making herself bait for a crazy trap was truly necessary. And for the tenth time she answered herself, "*Yes*."

She draped her cloak around her shoulders as she left, but purposefully left her hood and hair down over her shoulders, to make certain she could be seen and identified. She was to walk the path leading around the hill to her uncle Griff's house, ostensibly to borrow some sugar for making shortbread.

She made it to Griff and Dara's cottage and went inside for a brief time, then exited with a small bag in her hands. She paused and looked up at the moon for a few moments, then continued back to her grandparents' cottage . . . unhindered. When she opened the door her grandparents and Murielle descended on her with hugs and tears—grateful she had not been taken.

But that only meant she would have to try again later.

No one slept well that night, with the exception of Eli, who could sleep through a typhoon when he was tired. If he had any inkling of what was happening, he certainly didn't show it. By the next morning the adults were groggy and desperate for coffee and oatcakes with honey, but Eli was oblivious to everything but the prospect of running out to be with the other children. He gave Norah a hug as he left and, in her heightened state of emotion, it brought tears to her eyes.

The sentries, including Barclay and Randville, came in for food and reported that all was quiet on the track and in the valley. Barclay gave Norah a rueful smile and, after filling up with oatcakes and sausages, stretched out on one of the benches around the walls and fell instantly asleep. Randville joined him, but Griff and Cam went home to eat and rest.

For Norah it was a long afternoon of pacing, over-thinking, and hand-wringing. When she could stand it no longer she picked up Maureen's basket in the kitchen and announced she was going out to gather eggs. The hens were caged at night and freed each morning for feeding and exercise . . . which meant that sometimes eggs were found in patches of weeds around and behind the hen-house. Norah retrieved the eggs laid inside the main coop, then stepped outside to search the weeds and tall grasses that had escaped the attention of the sheep and goats.

She was bending over to collect an egg when she heard a footstep and the rustle of dried grass. The children were always running around here, playing hide-and-go-seek or bullyhorn—she had the passing thought—just as something came down over her head. She was grabbed by the waist and held while her flailing arms were wrenched behind her back and tied.

Shocked and struggling to breathe against the rough fabric over her face, she gasped and let out a scream that was stopped by a hand clamping across her mouth and digging into her cheeks. Her cries sounded only in her own head as something was tied tight across her mouth and around her head, forcing her jaw open and preventing her from making sounds louder than groans and furious squeals.

She was thrown over something—a shoulder perhaps—and carried. Whoever had her struggled to carry her as she bucked, fought to free her hands, and tried to roll off whatever she rested on. She was smacked hard on the rump and furiously ordered to "Shut th' hell up!" When she continued to resist there was more cursing and an even harder blow to the back of her head that stunned her.

After what seemed like forever there were garbled voices and it seemed they were on more level ground. She was slung on her stomach over what seemed to be a horse and her feet were tied together. She had trouble getting her breath and tried rocking from side to side, hoping to find a position that allowed her to take in more air. She could tell there was movement and heard sounds from other horses and men's hushed voices. She was tied by shoulders and legs to the mount and when it began to move every step the animal took caused a stab of pain that knocked air from her lungs and muddled her senses.

It was them, she realized, fighting through the fog in her head. They had come for her midday—in broad daylight—a time she had assumed it was safe to venture out alone. Barclay would be furious with her. But she was just gathering eggs. Damn it! How could she have been so stupid?

Then it struck her—Barclay was inside—sleeping.

No one saw her being taken! No one knew she'd been abducted!

Barclay woke with a dry, grainy feeling in his eyes and an ache in his shoulders. It had been a long night of watching and worrying while tucked into a cold stone crag overlooking the hold and he was truly exhausted. The front room was empty except for him.

Sounds of movement, kettles banging, and scraping came from the kitchen, so he rose and headed that direction. The hearth was glowing and Maureen was adding chopped potatoes and onions to a great iron pot hanging from a crane. She looked up and gave him a smile that clearly had fatigue behind it. He returned the same.

"You're awake," she said.

"I am." He yawned and stretched, something he would never have done in front of any woman he knew. Except maybe . . . "Where is Norah?"

She paused and looked around. "She went out to collect eggs."

"Went out? By herself?" Barclay was suddenly fully awake. "How long ago?"

"Umm . . . a quarter of an hour?" As she studied his

concern, it was clear she began to feel it herself. "Maybe longer. I was searin' th' meat."

"I told her not to go outside unless I was with her," he said irritably, heading back into the front room to get his jacket and woolen scarf.

"An' does she always do what you tell 'er?" Maureen said, knowing better. He ignored her comment, already thinking ahead.

"Where's Randville?"

Maureen wiped her hands on her apron and reached for her shawl. "Haven't seen him since he ate. I'll help you look for her."

As they checked the stable, Barclay bellowed for Randville again and again. There was no response. Maureen hurried to the henhouse and stopped dead beside the small, slat-built structure. A few feet into the flattened grass beside the chickens' roost was her egg basket on its side.

"Barclay!"

He ran to join her and found her staring at eggs strewn on the ground. As he moved closer, it became clear that more than one set of feet had trampled grass and crushed eggs Norah had collected. The broken and flattened grasses made a trail leading from the henhouse up the slope, toward a rocky outcropping. He was in motion before Maureen's strangled cry pierced the chilly silence of the valley.

"They took 'er. Damn their evil eyes—they've got 'er!"

He climbed the slope, following that line of disturbed grass, half praying, half cursing as it ran out on a rocky area. But he was able to pick up the trail again in the shorter scrub vegetation that took over in the poorer soil above. In a couple of barren patches, he glimpsed the fresh impression of a bootheel. A deep impression. They were carrying her.

Where the hill flattened out he paused to catch his breath while studying evidence that hooves had packed down the half-frozen sod. He ran around the edge, looking for hoofprints leading down the far slope of the hill, and finally spotted the flattened grass that marked the passage of several horses.

Six men, Mollie had said, which meant six or more horses. That many hooves would leave a significant trail across the hills. Frustration boiled up in him as he realized he had made a mistake rushing after them on foot. He needed a horse—and a gun and at least one other set of eyes and fists. Damn it—he'd let emotion get the better of him. And he would be making a second mistake if he rushed back to the cottage without learning all he could right now.

He spotted a rocky prominence not far away and headed for it. The climb wasn't difficult, and he stood for a time on top, shading his eyes with his hands, searching the rolling hills and occasional crags of rock that broke up the landscape. He could see nothing that looked like half a dozen men and one furious captive moving toward the west.

Another waste of time, damn it! He started down and heard what sounded like someone calling his name.

"Howard . . . Barclay Howard!"

He located a dark figure racing up the hillside below him and after a moment recognized Randville. He started toward the valet, but Randville waved him back and shouted for him to head straight for the MacFerguses'.

"Run—I'll catch up!"

Trusting that advice, Barclay did exactly what Randville

said. He ran along the crest of the hill, then headlong down the slope above the hold. By the time he was nearing the yard he heard footsteps pounding behind him and glanced back to find Randville hard on his heels. The man ran like a deer—long, graceful strides with his arms in effortless synchrony and a calm expression as he breathed in time with his body's movements.

The valet-turned-astounding-runner slowed to keep pace with Barclay for the last hundred yards.

"Saw the pass . . . through hills . . . we need horses."

"Where?" Barclay panted, jogging to a stop and bending over to brace against his knees. "Where are they taking her?"

"With that direction—has to be Galloway." Randville explained between gulps of air: "I saw them carry her . . . up the hill . . . right after they took her." He was recovering quickly. "She didn't make it easy for them."

Barclay straightened and headed for the cottage with a fierce look. "That's my girl."

Twenty-Two

Norah lost track of time as she was carried across hills and down rough trails. At length she felt them slowing, and it wasn't long before they stopped and voices grew louder. She was taken down from the horse and dragged across rough ground, where she was dropped in a heap that at least one of her captors found amusing. He laughed as he took what proved to be a strip of leather from her mouth and a cloth sack from her head.

She blinked at the light and tried to sit up, but her ribs and stomach were killing her and her hands behind her back felt numb. One of the rough-looking men dragged her to a nearby tree and propped her against it. The world slowly righted itself in her senses.

She was in a clearing in the midst of a stand of mixed-age trees. She saw horses being led to a line at the edge of the trees, then her attention caught on a figure dressed in black—a suit. She squeezed her eyes shut and when she opened them, her uncle Edgar was stooping in front of her with a pleased expression.

"You did it proper this time," he said, clearly talking to

someone else. A ruddy face appeared over his shoulder—drink-bloated skin, flat cap, and snakelike eyes filled with vengeful pleasure.

"Brody." She tried to speak, but it came out a dry rasp and he gave her a vicious grin.

"Told ye." He answered Edgar. "Warn't nothin' to it. Quiet as a tomb . . . we crept right in."

"Sorry to host you again under such trying circumstances, Niece, but you do make reunions difficult to arrange." He smiled at his own cleverness. "Let's not beat about the bush, shall we? You know what we want and you must know where it is by now. Your mother's family were with your father when he found it. You may not have known before, but I'm sure by now they've enlightened you on its whereabouts. After all, wasn't that the reason you came here . . . to learn where the gold is?"

She opened her mouth to speak but could barely manage a croak. Edgar looked annoyed but called for water. One of the hirelings brought him an earthen jug and he poured the contents over her mouth. Water splashed her cheeks as it ran down her throat, but she managed to collect several swallows. When she opened her mouth for more her uncle gave a smirk and filled her mouth more neatly a second time. Then he stoppered the jug and tossed it aside, signaling that there would be no more water or other consideration for her.

"They'll come for me," she ground out. "Barclay and my grandfather and uncles will find me, and when they do you'll pay."

"No, you stupid chit." Edgar rose to stand above her, emphasizing his power over her. "It is your family who will pay—if they want to ever see you again."

He strode away, taking Brody with him to talk with another man whose unkempt and ill-fed appearance marked him as one of the bone breakers hired for the job of retrieving a fortune in tainted gold. They paused, looked to her, and then parted ways. Her uncle went to sit by the fire, produced a silver flask, and took a long drink, while Brody came to her to gloat and threaten.

"You got away last time, but I'll see ye dead afore I let ye slip through me fingers again." He leaned close enough for her to smell that he, too, had been drinking, but she refused to admit her rising anxiety.

"Nobody knows where ye be. Ain't nobody comin' for ye. It's just you an' us, wench. The sooner ye tell us th' truth . . . the sooner ye'll go free." He let her mull that for a moment. "Where is the gold? Where do th' bastards 'ave it stashed?"

"I don't know. But if I did, I'd never tell you," she spat in defiance.

He struck her with a half-closed fist and then again with the back of his hand. The man they talked to earlier leaped forward to grab his arm and prevent a third blow.

"E'nuff," the man said sharply.

Brody looked up with barely contained anger, but the man's glower caused him to back down. Norah's wits were reeling as Brody stalked off, but she managed to understand that Brody hadn't challenged the man who'd intervened. That meant he had to be someone of consequence, despite his rough appearance. She looked up at him with eyes aching and face throbbing, and he turned and walked away.

She was grateful to be left alone for a time and lay her head back against the tree and closed her eyes to rest. The sounds of the forest were soothing and she was grateful to be able to breathe freely. Despite the pain in her face, wrists, and shoulders, she was able to drift off to sleep on a prayer that Barclay truly was out there, but that he hadn't seen what just happened.

The man they called Duncan retied her hands to the front and gave her some of the gamy stew and brick-hard bread the men shared around the campfire. Then he tethered her to a rope and freed her feet so she could step into the bushes to do the necessary. When she was pulled back to the tree where she was kept, it was her uncle who held the rope. The look on his face said it was time for another round of questions and demands. This time she would have to give him something more than defiance.

He squatted beside her, looked her over, and focused on her bright, unbound hair. "Your father was stubborn . . . that must be where you get it," he said. "I threatened to cut him off and he said that he and his wife would get along fine. His 'business' couldn't have been making much, but they were living well. I searched his room when he came home for Father's funeral and I found the coins. It took a while to figure out what they were and learn there was more of them waiting to be found.

"He swore he didn't know anything about the Jacobite gold, but I knew he was lying. After that Scottish tart of his died I tried again to get him to tell me, but he refused. Me, his own brother." He seemed outraged by his younger brother's lack of respect for their family ties. "Later I met Duncan and Brody. Brody tried to make Douglas talk, but he was a bit too forceful and . . . my brother couldn't even manage to heal properly . . . something about his ribs and lungs. So when he caught the consumption . . . well, you know the rest."

Norah listened to her uncle casually reveal his part in her father's death. He spoke of it so calmly, so matter-of-factly. The world began to spin. He had robbed her father of a life he desperately wanted and had stolen a beloved parent and a childhood from her. Yet he felt no remorse, no shame for his actions. The blame was all on his "stubborn" brother.

He was fascinated by the pain and anger rising in her and didn't notice her hands clenching, moving to the side and coming up.

She swung at him with every bit of force she could muster and connected forcefully with the center of his face. Knocked back on his arse, he howled and brought the rest of the camp running. A minute later her uncle was being led away with blood pouring from his face. Another set of blows from Brody and some nasty curses attempting to consign her to Hell were her punishment. Angry satisfaction helped buffer the pain until it began to subside. After a while she leaned back against the tree.

Not a bad exchange for the pleasure of drawing first blood from her despicable wretch of an uncle.

After that no one bothered her until well after dark. The campfire was down to glowing coals and the forest was filled with the rattle of dry leaves, the scamper of night feeders, and the hoot of owls starting to hunt. Norah was glad to have worn such warm underclothes. She scraped together fallen leaves to cushion the bony roots beneath her and found herself listening to the men, trying to make out what they intended.

They were rebels drawn from several clans, determined to find the gold and use it to keep their cause alive. The one they called Duncan left the fire, and as he knelt on one knee beside her, she braced, expecting more demands. But he held out her cloak and nodded to her to take it. She did so, nodding in return, pulled it around her shoulders, and drew up her feet inside it.

"Ye got guts, woman. I give ye that," he said. "But ye know this canna go on. Each day wot passes will be worse for ye. Tell us wot ye know an' go back to yer man and yer life."

"You really think my uncle will let me go?"

He tilted his head one way and then the other and then shrugged. "Ye did bloody the man's nose. It's hurtin' him bad."

"He had Brody kill my father. It's not half of what he deserves."

He studied her and her reasoning, then looked away.

"Has yer fam'ly no thought fer the Cause?"

"Independence?" She wasn't sure how to answer that. "I don't know. They've never talked about it to me." She caught a glint of light in his eyes. "Surely you don't think my uncle and Brody are believers in Scottish sovereignty. They're here for the money, not the fate of Scotland. My uncle made that clear before, when he and Brody were holding me and my six-year-old pupil hostage." She saw him react. "You didn't know? This is not the first time he's kidnapped me."

"In any war for freedom there are casualties," he said stiffly.

"You can be sure Edgar Capshaw and Brody will not be among them. Months from now, they'll be strutting along a fashionable street in New York or Paris in fancy clothes bought with the gold you and your men will have fought and bled for."

She caught his gaze, sensing this was the moment to put their plan in motion. "If my grandparents think like you do—that my life is merely a pawn in a game—why would they hand over the treasure to you? On the other hand, if they value love, family, and life as their faith demands . . . they may pay any price to have a beloved grandchild back in their arms."

"Ye sayin' they have the treasure?" He drew back, studying her.

She pulled the cloak tighter around her and looked away.

"Promise me they won't touch that gold," she said quietly.

He glanced at the fire, then at the two men her condition targeted.

"I promise."

"Then yes. They have it."

Clouds of greenwood smoke curling in some trees drew Barclay and Randville toward the camp they sought the next morning. Barclay's heart was thudding and his mouth was dry as they crept through undergrowth toward the sound of raised voices. He had just paused to check the load in his gun and retie his boots. Beside him, Randville did the same. Their gazes met and both nodded.

He had to see Norah, had to know if she was all right. It was more important to him than anything else. And it meant taking a terrible risk.

Before they reached the edge of the camp he waved Randville to circle around to the other side, near where Norah was held. Randville nodded and crept silently from tree to tree. When he'd had time to reach his position, Barclay took a deep breath, raised his rifle, aimed, and stepped out into the open.

"Capshaw!" he bellowed, sending a shock through the camp.

Norah's uncle and Brody were on their feet in an instant, looking in every direction for the source of that voice. Brody, like the rat he was, skittered straight for Norah and put a knife against her throat. The other men not already on their feet rose with guns in hand but had no target until Barclay called again.

"We've come for Norah," he called, having to resight on his target each time he spoke. "Give her over and you'll leave this place. Don't give her over and you'll be here 'til Judgment Day . . . six feet under."

He could see Edgar's ugly smirk at his partner's quick thinking.

"I don't think so, Mr. Howard. I think it is your pretty little tutor who will lie here until the trumpet calls . . . unless you hand over the gold they found. It belongs to the clans and should be returned to them."

"That's what you plan to do, is it? Hand it over to the clans? Why do I find that hard to believe?" Barclay called.

"Yer outnumbered!" Brody yelled, dragging Norah closer and pressing the blade of his knife harder against her throat. "Ye haven't a chance, Howard!"

"Oh, I didn't come alone." He nodded and a shot rang out, and the sound of dry branches breaking above let them know he had aimed high. The hired men whirled and one soon signaled he had a bead on Randville.

"We could kill you both without blinking," Edgar said, his tone icy. "But that would be a terrible waste. I'll give you a chance to live—and carry our demand back to those ignorant sheep farmers she calls family. Bring us the treasure . . . the Jacobite gold . . . and she goes free."

"And if they won't give it up?" Barclay said with deadly calm.

Edgar spread his hands at his sides with insolent pleasure.

"Then she dies."

As those words faded, he uttered an addendum. "We'll come to that grubby little hole they call home and find it ourselves. And we'll see there are no witnesses . . . starting with that little 'earl' of yours."

Barclay wanted to pull the trigger so badly his fingers twitched. Hell, his whole body twitched! Instead, he lowered his gun and watched as the hirelings lowered theirs upon a nod from a man in the group.

"I'll carry your demand," Barclay said tightly. "But if you harm a hair on her head, you'll have hell to pay." He shifted his gaze to Norah, whose face looked drawn and eyes looked defiant despite the dark smudge around one of them. He had a feeling that smudge wasn't dirt.

"Tomorrow," Edgar declared. "Where the road from Dumfries to Galloway crosses the track to Hesterwaite. Midday."

Barclay stepped backward, clamping his jaw fiercely, and then melted back into the brush. At a safe distance he turned to run and spotted Randville coming his way— silent as a deer on the damp leaf pack.

They took off for their horses at a lope, and Barclay muttered: "I *hate* this plan."

Norah's family had gathered at the MacFergus's cottage when Barclay and Randville returned. They rushed to him for word of Norah's well-being and he assured them she was all right, in spite of his misgivings. After a word with Eli, Barclay sent him out with the younger children but told him to stay close to the cottage.

The ransom was ready. The chest of "Jacobite" gold had been set in a pony cart, draped with canvas and concealed beneath a layer of straw and bags of oats. It was as ordinary a cart as could be found in the Uplands, but in its confines lay the key to all their futures.

The MacFergus had spent a tense hour with the government men, Brett and Ralls, the night before at a neighboring holding. He presented them three gold pieces like the ones they held, and wove a story of a group of rough and well-armed men invading their holding to get supplies. They paid for them with those coins, saying that with that payment they would expect supplies or assistance whenever they returned. The MacFergus confessed that he hadn't disabused them of the notion that he would help them.

"Where are they now?" Brett had demanded, clearly pleased to have such information.

"Don't know where the brigands camped," the MacFergus said, "but Barr Howard, snuck ou' behind 'em ta see where they went."

Ralls grabbed his hat and a small wooden case and left immediately to find a telegraph line to send a message to Glasgow requesting support. That was a clear indication that they believed the MacFergus. Brett promised to wait at the tavern in Hesterwaite for word of their location and thanked Daniel MacFergus for his honesty and sense of duty to the queen.

The MacFergus grinned all the way home. Clearly he hadn't lost his gift of gab. Things just might work out.

* * *

Barclay paced and grumbled and couldn't bring himself to eat while the MacFergus was gone. They had to wait until morning to take the gold to Capshaw . . . it wouldn't do to look eager to hand over a small fortune in gold. It should take time to convince her family, arrange a cart, load it, and drive it to the meeting place. Griff and the MacFergus would come with him, while Randville would ride separately and approach from a different angle to cover them in case of a double cross.

Norah's face haunted him whenever he closed his eyes. Her intense expression, her speaking gaze—so calm despite Brody's punishing hold on her. A small part of him wanted to throttle her for risking herself so, while the rest of him wanted to bull his way into that camp, pick her up, and hold her tight for the rest of his life.

Why hadn't he just damned well proposed the other night? What the hell was he waiting for? *Idiot.* He vowed to remedy that the minute he had her safely back in his arms.

Sometime in the middle of the night he must have dozed off because Maureen startled him awake well after sunrise with a steaming cup of coffee in her hand.

"Why didn't you wake me earlier?" he said, accepting the cup.

"Ye needed sleep," she said, giving him a pat on the shoulder. "Pull yerself together, lad—I'll be feedin' ye shortly. The MacFergus didna sleep well either."

With a shave, a fresh shirt, and a brush of his jacket and kilt, he was soon wide awake and starving. He ate quickly, and Maureen informed him Randville had taken a horse and gone ahead to scout the area. Barclay shook his head, amazed at his valet's capable nature and unstinting participation in this risky venture. What had he done to acquire such loyalty from the man? Someday he would ask. But today he needed to depend on it and pray all went well with the ransom exchange.

If so, their part of the plan was done. They would retire to the MacFergus holding and let the authorities do what authorities did. Rebellion-tainted gold would no longer be their problem. He and Norah would be free to—

Not yet. He wouldn't tempt fate by planning too far ahead.

Norah's second morning of captivity began differently. She was awakened by the sound of men moving around the campfire and the smell of coffee, but it seemed to her they were in a better mood. A pair of Duncan's men even joked with each other.

As soon as she was fed and given the chance to visit the bushes, her uncle came to tell her that she'd better pray her relatives wanted her back and decided to pay the ransom. If they did, she might be home by nightfall. Brody was more direct: She'd best behave if they brought the ransom or she'd bloody well regret it.

As the sun rose in the sky, Duncan's men led her to a horse, helped her up on it, and tied her hands to the saddle. The reins, she learned, would be handled by one of their number. Warned by Brody, they were taking no chances that she might try to cause trouble.

She made note of the fact that they had packed up their simple camp and appeared to be leaving the Galloway forest altogether. What would happen if they didn't get the ransom? She worried that Barclay or the MacFergus might decide to try something recklessly heroic at the last minute. But she told herself they knew it had to be done this way and that she had to be the bait to get the gold transferred to the rebels.

She squinted against the bright sun as they emerged from the trees and headed for a road visible in the distance. And she prayed.

More than an hour later, their party paused on a hilltop overlooking the intersection of a main road and a primitive track that was similar to the one they had taken to Hesterwaite. Duncan and one of his men rode ahead, scouting the area and planning their stations. He placed his men strategically behind rocks and in drifts of tall weeds and grasses.

Brody declared to her uncle that Duncan's experience in the military made him invaluable . . . he would have every point of entry and exit covered. And the new guns Edgar had provided the rebels would see that nobody in the ransom party left the site alive if they didn't hand over the treasure "quick an' clean."

Hearing that, her expression crumpled. She realized his statement had been meant for her ears when Brody caught her moment of emotion and laughed. It was yet another form of torture—the rotten bastard.

But in fact there was one area Duncan and his men— trained in the military to always claim the higher ground— had overlooked. There was a low, damp area thick with dried cattails and marsh grasses on one side of the site. Randville lay in it, covered by vegetation, and watched Edgar's hirelings choose higher vantage points . . . perhaps setting a trap for Barclay and the MacFergus contingent.

He could see Norah on the rise above him, and it was clear from her slumped posture and bowed head that she was under duress. He watched the men untie her from the horse and lead her to a large rock, where she was ordered to sit and they spent a moment at her feet—likely tying them again. She raised her chin and turned her face away.

Randville shook his head in wonder. She was an extraordinary woman, to have proposed this scheme and then volunteered to be both its pivot point and its victim. Small wonder she had not only won Barclay's heart, but seemingly had chosen the "Howard Beast" to hold hers. She had the core of a blessed Amazon! After knowing her, he would never look at women the same way.

A short while later he heard the plod of hooves and the creak of cart wheels, and the ransom to secure her freedom and its mounted escort rolled into view.

Twenty-Three

Barclay exhaled the breath he'd been holding when he saw Norah seated on a large rock, alive and apparently well. Three men—two on horseback—stood near her watching the ransom approach. Only three? He scanned the area for more. There had been six the morning before, so he had to assume the others were nearby—probably with guns pointed at their hearts. Were they riding into an ambush?

Griff pulled the cart off the road and into the field and stopped near the kidnappers. The MacFergus and Barclay, also on horseback, evened the odds for the moment, and they had brought two additional saddle mounts for Norah and Griff to ride on the way back.

"About time." Edgar looked Barclay over thoroughly, noting his rifle and the dirk stuck in the top of his hose. Then his gaze fixed on the cart and his eyes narrowed. "You brought it?"

Barclay didn't answer as he swung down to the ground and threw back the canvas and its straw camouflage. He could have sworn that he saw Edgar quiver at the sight of the chest.

Brody dismounted immediately and stood looking at the contents of the cart like a starving man looks at beefsteak.

"Check it," Edgar commanded, and Brody lunged for the cart and the lid of the chest, while the man called Duncan stalked over cautiously and removed his worn gloves. "Open it!" Edgar snapped with tension that made his voice go higher.

There was no padlock. The lid raised with a creak of iron hinges to reveal a heap of old leather bags. Edgar made a sliding dismount and hurried to the cart to inspect firsthand the treasure he had spent years pursuing. Brody had produced a small knife and was already cutting open one bag. All three men went still at the sight of shining gold coins.

Duncan thought to pick one up and bite it to verify its content. He tested a second and a third before seizing the bottom of the bag and upending it, scattering gold coins all over the contents of the chest. He picked random coins to test the same way. Then Brody and Edgar each grabbed a bag, tore it open, and poured out the contents—testing those the same way. None failed.

It was the true treasure. Edgar and Brody looked at each other with lustful pleasure, dug their fingers into the piles, and let the coins slide sensuously through their fingers. Genuine gold! And theirs!

They grabbed and opened bag after bag, finding the same magnificent color and the same seductive, metallic yielding.

It was Duncan who picked up the coins to inspect the images. He touched the thistles reverently, then nodded and closed his eyes briefly.

"They're genuine." He opened his eyes to look at Barclay with astonishment. "I hardly dared hope." He searched the MacFergus's and Griff's faces, seeing in them anger banked beneath strict control. "How could you just hand it over like this?"

"Don' know much abou' fam'ly, do ye?" the MacFergus said, giving him a look of equal parts disgust and pity. "Cursed gold be more burden tha' boon." He shook his head sadly. "Ye'll see."

Barclay kept looking at Norah. It was all he could do to keep from rushing to her and ripping away her bonds. Their gazes met, and he could have sworn her mouth turned up into a smile meant only for him. Then she looked down and began to sift through and straighten her petticoats.

"How many bags?" Edgar demanded, frenzied in his desire to know how rich he would be. "*How many?*"

Barclay tore his gaze from Norah to give him an icy look. "Eleven. At least sixty coins in each. Perhaps as high as seventy." He jerked a nod toward Norah. "You have what you wanted. Release her." His face hardened. "*Now.*"

Brody looked up with a smirk. "Take yer filthy bitch an' go."

Barclay wanted to put a fist through that smug face but told himself the wretch's reckoning was already in motion. Instead, he rushed to where Norah sat and slid the knife from his hose. "Are you all right?" he asked, forcing himself to cut her bonds instead of grabbing her into his arms. Strangely, the ropes around her feet had already been cut. "Can you walk?"

She nodded. There were tears in her beautiful eyes and a dark, puffy ring around her left one. The right side of her mouth was swollen but didn't seem to have bled. Thoughts of what she'd endured at the hands of her uncle and his brutes brought anger roiling out of his depths. For a moment he trembled with the urge to pound the pair of them into vulture food. But she reached up to touch his face, as if she sensed what he was thinking, and shook her head.

"Let's just go. Now. Please."

He wrapped an arm around her waist and helped her to the horse tied behind the cart. "Can you ride?"

"To heaven's gate," she smiled through her tears, "if I'm with you."

He helped her up, gave her the reins, and then nodded to the MacFergus and Griff. The MacFergus turned his mount and Griff scrambled from the cart to take his place on a horse beside his father.

Barclay stepped back to the side of the cart and leaned close to Brody for a moment. His mouth moved, and whatever he said gave Brody a start. As he turned to his horse, the furious Scot wheeled and raised a pistol aimed at Barclay's broad back.

A shot rang out and Brody jerked back and then crumpled. Edgar gasped and instinctively crouched low to avoid the same fate, then spotted Norah nearby and rushed around the cart to pull her out of the saddle. She raised Randville's dirk and stabbed it hard into his forearm. It scraped bone as she withdrew it and her uncle screamed like a banshee.

Barclay grabbed her mount's halter, yanking the horse into motion, and yelled to her and the others, "Ride!"

Brody's blood had spattered the coins at the edge of the cart. Edgar staggered back, holding his wounded arm and staring in horror at the blood seeping through his fingers. Duncan recovered enough to grab his rifle from his horse and take aim at Barclay.

A second shot came, dropping Duncan to the ground. Out of nowhere three men appeared and rushed to defend their leader, taking aim at the riders racing away across the hills but firing wildly. Duncan cursed and ordered them to cease firing and bind him up. They did so, relieved to find his wound clean and simple. When they asked what to do about Brody, Duncan stared at his sprawled form, then at Edgar's bloody figure.

"If he's breathin', throw 'im in the cart. The other one can come if he can ride." His face hardened as he looked at the treacherous pair that would now be more burden than help. "We've got gold to move."

When they were well away and had slowed down Norah turned to Barclay. "What did you say to him?"

Barclay gave her his best wolfish smile. "I just gave him a little farewell promise . . . from you." He took a deep breath. "It was Randville who took him down."

"Randville?" she asked. "I didn't see him there."

"That was the point." Barclay reached for her hand. "You don't think we'd go into such danger without an ace in our pockets, do you?"

She smiled at him and then at her grandfather and uncle as they rode. Her family had risked so much and saved her. She was free and was feeling the chilled wind in her hair and the sweet breath of liberty in her lungs.

After a few minutes the MacFergus dropped back to reach for her hand. Studying the damage to her face, he demanded to know how she truly was.

Emotion welled inside her at the genuine concern in his face. She was suddenly crying and trying to explain to all of them that the tears were just relief. Apparently they weren't convinced. Barclay directed them into the shelter of an overhanging crag and pulled her down from her horse and into his arms.

He held her while she cried and gripped his big body tightly . . . as if she was drowning and he was saving her again.

She needed to be somewhere clean and safe and warm . . . somewhere Barclay could hold her and make her forget for a time the ugly business of being bait in a trap set for evil men.

"Are you all right now?" he asked after a while.

"I'll be fine." She wiped her last few tears with the heels of her hands. "Curse Uncle Edgar. If it hadn't been for Randville's dirk . . ." She fumbled through her skirts. "Did I leave it behind? I can't remember—"

"We'll get him another one." He loosened his hold on her to look in her face. "I believe my valet saved both our lives today."

She looked to the MacFergus with prisms of liquid in her eyes. "Thank you." She withdrew from Barclay's arms to walk into her grandfather's. He held her for a while, stroking her bright hair, seeming as warmed by her affection as she was by his.

"Yer so much like yer ma, lass." His eyes were wet as he released her. "She'd be proud to see th' braw and brave woman ye've become."

Griff brought out a canteen of water and offered to stand watch if she wanted to sit and rest a while. She smiled but wagged her head.

"I just want to go home, get warm, and sleep for days."

* * *

But what she got was an explosion of joy as they rode onto the holding and up to the cottage. Every MacFergus on the place rushed to give her a hug or a handshake . . . occasionally a whirl or a kiss on the cheek. Eli gave her fervent hugs and told her he was happy the "boogermen" didn't want her anymore. She laughed and hugged him back while Barclay corrected once again, "*Boogeymen.*"

Inside, she was handed a cup of honey wine and food that made her feel stuffed after a few bites and drowsy. She was not allowed to sleep yet, however. She was ushered downstairs, put into a bathing tub scented with rose oil, and allowed to soak her aches until the water cooled.

Maureen and Murielle trundled her into bed before allowing Barclay to come to see her. He sank onto the bed with her and pulled her into his arms. She sighed and snuggled against his chest.

"This is what I wanted. All I thought about . . ." She closed her eyes and finally was able to relax into the pleasure of his strength around her.

When she was sound asleep he slipped from the bed and crept up the stairs where the MacFergus and Maureen were cuddled by the hearth in the front room. It was dusk and the light was soft and rose-colored.

"She's sleepin'?" Maureen asked, sitting up straight.

"She is," he answered. "I'll go check on her in a while."

"She's been through a trial an' come out daisies," the MacFergus declared, appraising Barclay's distracted manner. "An' wot abou' ye, lad? Ye look like ye sat on a hill o' ants."

"I made a promise to Norah and I want to keep it, but . . ."

"What kind o' promise?" Maureen came to the edge of her seat.

The MacFergus gave him a knowing smile. "Now, wot kind o' promise would a lad make to a lass, Maurie?" He shoved to his feet and jammed his hands on his hips, looking positively patriarchal. "Ye got somat to ask me, lad?"

Barclay faced him with a similar smile. "I certainly do."

Norah was confused when she awakened and found herself alone in her pitch-black room. It was a disappointment, but she pulled the pillow he'd used close and buried her nose in it, letting his scent compensate for his absence. She was safe and warm and he was there with her . . .

She fell back to sleep and dreamed of horses and gold coins and Barclay's arms around her. It seemed so real that when she awoke, she still felt the press of his arms around her waist. She wrapped her arms around her middle with a smile and drifted off again.

When she woke for the third time she felt like she'd melted and become part of the featherbed itself. She had no idea how long she'd slept or whether it was night or morning. After a bit she felt for the candle on the stool by the bed, lighted it, and decided to dress and find something to eat. Where there was food there would probably be Barclay.

Murielle must have seen the light. She hurried in to help Norah dress and brush her freshly washed hair until it glowed. It was hard being patient for such things after being held prisoner in a cold, damp forest. And she couldn't imagine why Murielle insisted she wear her best blue dress . . . though the maid said it would make her feel better after her daylong sleep.

"I slept an entire day?" she asked, and Murielle nodded. "Ye needed it. And yer eye is lookin' much better."

Upstairs, the kitchen was abuzz with people, sounds, and smells. She paused at the sight of Dara and Lucy and Great-Uncle Angus's wife, Diedre, helping Maureen prepare what looked to be a small feast. She grinned, figuring it had something to do with celebrating the successful transfer of the gold and her safe return. Someone was setting up plank tables outside the front door, and both hearths were blazing, providing warming and additional cooking areas for those who gathered. She could have sworn she heard a fiddle somewhere, issuing short strains of toe-tapping music.

She moved through the group accepting hugs and exchanging greetings as she looked for Barclay. Someone snagged her hand in the front room and she looked back to see Barclay smiling at her. He led her to a bench, lifted her up to stand on it, then took both her hands in his. All around them things got quiet, and she felt ridiculously conspicuous standing there. Maureen and the MacFergus pushed through to the front of the group and watched with undisguised pleasure as Barclay cleared his throat and spoke.

"Norah Capshaw, I made you a promise a bit ago. I am about to fulfill that promise . . . with your grandparents' permission and blessing." He went down on one knee, and there was a titter of excitement among the guests. Eli battled his way through the throng with an armful of late-blooming heather that was drooping . . . probably in need of water.

"Here it is. We all found some, even Audrey an' Droopy Gus." He thrust the lot into Barclay's hands and then looked up at Norah standing on the bench and scowled, warning, "They make me get down." Maureen grabbed his shoulder and pulled him back to stand by her.

Barclay thanked Eli, arranged them in his hand, and held them up.

"I had a little help, as you can see," he went on. "Fortunately, you slept long enough for us to prepare. But these are for you. The promised flowers."

She accepted them, biting her bottom lip, guessing where this was headed and wanting to savor every moment. It wasn't exactly what she had dreamed of; it was a homier, more loving, more heartfelt version. Somehow . . . in this place, in this moment . . . it was perfect.

Murielle appeared at Barclay's side with a tray holding an open wine bottle and two metal cups.

"Champagne was requested, but we were short on time, so I hope you'll take French wine as a substitute. And of course . . . violin music. We just happened to have a fiddle player on hand."

From near the door came the notes of a folk ditty played by none other than her uncle Cam. She could see people grinning and heads bobbing in time. Tears pricked her eyes as she looked down at the most handsome and loving and unpredictable man she had ever known.

"Ask me, dang it!" she said, blinking frantically. "I'm gonna start bawling here!"

Laughter washed around them as he rose.

"Marry me, Norah. And make me the happiest beast in the British Isles."

She made him wait a heartbeat.

"Yes, you silly man! I'll marry you . . . anytime, any-where!"

She stooped to throw her arms around his neck and plant a long and thorough kiss on him. He lifted her down and she felt her heart nearly bursting with joy and pleasure. She would have her love—her sweet beast—her white knight—for the rest of her life. In that moment she prayed, *Please let our lives last forever*.

He whirled her around, laughing and stirring a giddy mood in the family and friends gathered. The music began in earnest and people began to dance here and there, swinging one another around and singing along with the tune.

"I hope you meant what you said." He had to practically shout to be heard above the ruckus. She frowned lightly, showing her confusion. "The anytime, anywhere part. Because I'm proposing that we get married right here . . . right now. I know it's not a chapel wedding and you won't have a white silk gown and a garland of roses in your hair . . . but we'll be married with your family and mine here . . . filled with happiness and hopes for us and sharing our fun. What do you say?"

"Your family is here? Where?" she asked.

"There!" He pointed at Eli, who was running around on the bench, daring anyone to tell him to get down. She laughed and gave herself over to her mad MacFergus side.

"We need a parson!" She looked into the glowing amber eyes she had come to love and trust. "I'm of a mood to say *I do*!"

As it happened, the parson of a neighboring town who rode circuit into the Uplands was just completing his ride when the MacFergus caught up with him earlier in the day. Asked him to do the honors in a hurry . . . with a handful of gold coins for his collection box . . . he was glad to oblige.

"Wait!" Norah said with a flash of memory. "There's something I need from my bag."

When she returned the parson had called the assembly together and climbed on a bench so all could see. It turned out he was a married man himself and had a few lovely things to say about the institution of marriage and about being a spouse.

When he started the vows Norah produced a pair of gold wedding rings and asked if Barclay would mind using her parents' rings for the ceremony. He smiled and nodded, taking the small one to put on her finger as part of his vows. She put the larger one on his finger during her vows, though it fit only partway. He suggested she put it on his smallest finger where it would be secure, and she did.

In mere minutes Barclay Howard and Norah Capshaw had said earnest vows and were united in holy matrimony. They signed the small book that served as the parson's register on the circuit, and had Maureen and the MacFergus sign as witnesses. Food came out on platters and in bowls. Ale was poured and distributed by the older youths and girls, and the French wine was shared by the bride and groom and older guests. When most guests had had their fill, the music started up, and people stepped outside—even in the chilled evening—for room to dance. Before long Norah was being whisked hither and yon by partners she knew and ones she didn't. But she kept plenty of time for Barclay, who claimed not to be the most graceful of dancers but knew how to make her feel like the happiest bride in Christendom.

It was all such a whirl that she barely noticed the passage of time until Barclay caught her hand, drew her close, and proposed yet again—that they slip away and get some rest—among other things.

She hugged Maureen and the MacFergus and gave Randville a kiss on the cheek. They would have made it downstairs to begin their honeymoon if two riders hadn't been spotted coming up the lane at exactly that moment.

In the evening light it was easy to recognize the two government agents who had come days before to inquire about some gold coins. Gerald Brett and Morgan Ralls looked like they'd been through a battle. Their riding clothes were ripped and spotted, their hats were missing, and their boots were covered with dried mud and leaf debris. But their faces, for all that dirt and disarrangement, were filled with pleasant surprise as they dismounted before the cottage and spotted the MacFergus and Maureen coming to meet them.

"T' what do we owe this honor, good sirs?" The MacFergus gave them a gracious nod.

"I fear we've arrived at an awkward time, sir," Brett declared, taking in the festive gathering.

"Ach, na such thing," MacFergus said. "We be celebratin' the weddin' of our eldest gran'daughter. Ye met 'er . . . Norah Capshaw."

"Goodness. We mustn't intrude." Ralls turned toward his horse.

"Nary a bit o' it," the MacFergus said, grabbing his arm to stay him. "Ye come fer somethin'. Get on wi' it, then stay for food an' ale. We got e'nuff ta feed th' county!"

Brett looked at his partner and the decision was quickly made.

"We came to report that the information you provided was . . . most helpful," Brett informed them. "With the assistance of the local constabulary and a small military contingent, we were able to track down and arrest a rebel group moving a large amount of coin to their stronghold near Ayr. It seems to be part of an old Jacobite war purse . . . a substantial sum they intended to use to start up old grievances and conflicts. I would have you know, there will be an expression of gratitude from Her Majesty's Government."

"Sakes, that's wonderful," Maureen said, beaming. "Ye got the wretches who came and threatened us."

"Did they put up much of a fight?" Barclay asked as he and Norah joined the group.

"Sadly so," Ralls informed them. "But right prevailed and the lot will be in prison for a long time. It turns out, two of the men were fugitives from York who had abducted a young nobleman a couple of months back. I doubt they'll see daylight again as free men."

The festivities were still in full bloom despite the end of day. Lanterns had been lit and placed around the plank tables and another keg of ale was rolled out. Norah watched Barclay carrying a small keg of brandy from the larder for Maureen and caught the sway of his kilt.

He had begun to walk like a proud Scot, with the long, rolling stride, potent heel strike, and sensual sway in his shoulders. She watched him walking back to her with a look in his eyes that sent a plume of heat to her core.

The moment he was within reach she grabbed his hand, pulled him into the larder, closed the door, and kissed him for all she was worth.

He tasted like good brandy and wedding cake and salty male need, and she wanted it all. He lifted her against him and she locked her arms around his neck, so intent

on covering every inch of his sleek jaw and muscular neck
with kisses and nips that she hardly realized he was carrying her down the stairs.

A single oil lamp had been left burning on the library
table and he grabbed it on the way to the bedchamber they
would share. Kisses and touches turned into skirt, petticoats, bodice, and stays on the floor . . . beside a coat, linen
shirt, knit hose, and, almost, a kilt. She wouldn't let him
take it off until he kissed her and let her run her hands over
his body as she had ached to do so many times.

She had known he was big and solid and shaped like a
blessed Greek sculpture. But she hadn't guessed how the
experience of physically exploring and claiming that body
would affect her.

"I have to be the luckiest woman alive," she said with a
whimper of pleasure as she ran her hands over him and
kissed his ribs and rubbed her tingling body against his.

"That's possible," he said, making a sizzling noise as
she raked her breasts over his stomach. "Betrothed and
wedded on the same day. You saved a bundle on clothes,
flowers, wedding breakfast, champagne . . ."

She laughed and gave him a playful swat. "It's not the
wedding I wanted, it's the marriage. And this." She stroked
his cheek. "I wanted this very much, Barr."

He closed his eyes as she stroked . . . lower . . . but when
he spoke one of them opened to see her reaction.

"Are you going to call me what my nanny used to call
me? Because in moments like this it could tend to put a
damper on my . . . enthusiasm."

She chuckled and pulled him toward the bed.

"I think we can find a way to enlarge your enthusiasm."

He growled from deep in his throat, picked her up, and

climbed onto the bed with her. A heartbeat later they were lying together, facing each other, facing their new life together.

"I love you, Barclay Howard. And I'm going to love living with you," she said, looking into his amber eyes.

"I love you, Norah Capshaw. I will until you're old and gray and snore loud enough to rattle the windows."

She laughed. Hard. When she finally sobered he was looking at her with that heart-stopping longing on his face that made her want to take him into her body, her heart, her very soul.

And she did.

Epilogue

Six months later

Barclay sat on the side of the great canopy bed in his London town house, looking a bit forlorn. They had been in the city for a week shopping, seeing the sights, introducing Eli to new friends and favorite places. It was fun and interesting . . . seeing so many things with Norah for the first time and appreciating them afresh through Eli's eyes. But he dreaded tonight . . . and this posh, white-tie evening wear, extra-starched shirt, and bloody stiff collar Randville insisted he wear.

"I miss my kilt," he said, looking very much like Eli at the moment.

"I do, too," Norah said, turning on her seat before her dressing table mirror to give him a smile. She knew he was dreading this . . . a party to celebrate their marriage and introduce them as a couple to a select number of people from London's prominent social and business communities.

"But Rafe and Lauren have done so much and extended their good name to see us included. I confess, I'm excited to meet people you know and dance with—"

He made a choking sound.

"What? You're an excellent dancer." She gave him a flirtatious smile. "Especially when you waltz."

"I can do it with you," he grumbled. "Your angelic grace somehow blesses my big feet. But please—for the love of mercy—don't let anyone else rope me into galumphing around a dance floor."

"If you insist." She laughed and left her stool to come and circle his neck with her arms. "Barr Howard, I have never, ever seen you galumph . . . anywhere or anytime. And I'll punch anyone—man or woman—who tries to say you do."

He drew a deep breath and squared his broad shoulders.

"I suppose I'm safe, then." He ran his hands suggestively over her pearl-bedecked blue bodice and the breasts mounded above it. "Have I told you how luscious you look in this?"

"Four times," she said. "And you still can't have your delightfully wicked way with me until we come home tonight."

He sighed. "You're a hard woman, Norah Howard. Must be the Capshaw in you."

She gave him a smoky-eyed promise as she draped her pearl-littered shawl around his neck and pulled him out the door.

They rode in Barclay's smaller town carriage to the Townsends' impressive Palladian house, and Norah could feel Barclay's tension increase in the way he held her hand. She knew what gossips and ignorant schoolgirls had said about him in the past and was fully prepared to flatten anyone who made a snide or disparaging comment in his direction. And if it came to such an extreme, she would withdraw from London to Northrup and spend her days happily raising a raft of little Barclays to set the world to rights.

She looked at his profile in the dim light from the street-lamps, remembering her first ride in this carriage . . . the way he had rescued her from Brody . . . the fascination she felt for the power this big, forbidding man exuded. She was every bit as fascinated by him tonight as she had been then. But now, he was hers.

The house was ablaze with lights and a line of carriages was forming behind them as their driver inched toward the massive front doors. They soon were welcomed into the house . . . hat, gloves, and cloak removed . . . and were sent to the upstairs ballroom, where Rafe and Lauren greeted them warmly and insisted they help receive the other guests.

Rafe Townsend and his lovely wife, Lauren Alcott Townsend, had been wonderful to them ever since they arrived in London. They'd hosted a family dinner, a picnic to introduce Eli to some children, and had a group of lady friends in for tea with Norah. This evening's celebration was the culmination of a campaign by Barclay's best friends to see him received into society as he deserved. For that Norah would be eternally grateful to them.

Honestly, she was a bit nervous herself, this being her first society event. She had seen and heard classmates prepare for such affairs . . . choosing gowns and hairstyles and jewelry . . . brushing up on dance steps and gossiping about handsome suitors. But being an orphan and on lim-ited funds, she had never attended such a gathering herself. She felt her heart fluttering as she was introduced to Lord and Lady Clemmons, Retired Admiral Everson, Marcus and Eugenie Bedlington, the Earl of Sumner and his lady wife Colette . . . the list went on and on.

The guests' eyes widened on her and grew still wider on Barclay. For his part, he nodded to the ladies, shook hands with the gentlemen, and smiled graciously through it all. Norah sensed a relaxation in his manner and glanced at him with visible pride. He was the best-looking man in the room—with the possible exception of their handsome host.

Then came an introduction that tested Barclay's composure.

"We met some time ago," the thin blond deb with an ill-fit bodice declared. "Lorianna Bascom-Roberts." She held his hand a bit too long, staring. "At Rafe Townsend's birthday celebration, I believe."

"We did?" He managed a smile. "Lovely to see you again, then."

The girl flounced off to join a pair of other young women, and it was clear from their repeated glances his way that they were talking about him.

Norah caught his free hand behind her skirts and squeezed it with an I-told-you-so smile. This time he took a deep breath and smiled back.

By the time they took the dance floor, the room was buzzing about the dramatic change in Barclay Howard and the remarkable warmth and beauty of his wife. The pair seemed perfectly matched. The grace and presence they brought to the dance floor drew every eye in the ballroom and occasioned a number of covert sighs. A second dance, also a waltz, had some ladies consoling themselves that they might have been Mrs. Howard if they'd have known Barclay would turn out so well.

When that dance was finished Lauren Townsend borrowed Norah for a bit of refreshment while Rafe steered Barclay into his study for a cigar and a brandy with a number of other gentlemen.

While in the ladies' retiring room, availing herself of the facilities, she heard that Bascom-Roberts female holding forth about how Barclay had pursued her relentlessly, and she was hoping he would not resume his reckless ways now that he was wedded to that . . . "What *was* her name?"

Norah stepped from behind the screen, straightened her skirts—drawing the group's attention—and smiled calmly.

"Norah. Norah Capshaw Howard." Her eyes flashed. "And I can say with certainty that if Barclay Howard had pursued you ardently, he would have gotten you. And that clearly is not the case."

At that moment their hostess exited the attached bathing room and asked if she was ready to return to the party. She put her arm through Lauren's and sailed off, glad she hadn't needed to punch the chit. She had forgotten how delicate and full of artifice London debs could be.

A late arrival to the party was waiting when she returned to the ballroom, and the minute Norah saw the young woman she felt a rush of memories returning. Margaret Keppler had been at boarding school with her, and for one year they shared quarters at the Trinity Academy in Oxford. Margaret had left the academy to work in a mission field in Africa and Norah had lost touch with her. Here she was . . . looking warm and approachable . . . accompanied by a man wearing a clerical collar.

The moment their gazes met, they rushed to greet each other, and there were hugs as well as smiles while they quickly shared events and name changes. She was

Margaret Keppler Ross now and her husband—once a missionary in Africa, where they met—served a large parish in Kensington.

Norah introduced Margaret and her husband to Barclay, who was genuinely interested in the couples' background and experiences abroad. They talked at length and laughed, and when Norah suggested Barclay ask Margaret to dance he hesitated for only a moment. It turned out Margaret had been the best dancer in their class at boarding school, and she and Barclay had a lovely turn around the floor.

Lauren Townsend was next to take the floor with Barclay while Rafe escorted Norah in a dance.

"I don't know what you did to my friend Barr, but I think half the men in London could use such a treatment," Rafe said, watching the pleasure radiating from her.

She pinked with delight. "I assure you, he worked a miracle with me as well. And of course there were those mad but fabulous Scots in my family tree."

By the time they climbed into their carriage to go home it was very late and both Norah and Barclay were tired and yet too full of impressions and dancing and delicious champagne to quite settle down. She put her head on his shoulder and they talked all the way home, reveling in the success of their London debut.

"Such nice people," Norah said. "So many good people."

"Probably because Rafe and Lauren are such good people themselves. Did I ever tell you that Lauren was abducted by smugglers before she and Rafe were married?"

"What?" She sat up in amazement.

"I went with him to rescue her . . . there was a sea

battle . . . a ship ran aground . . . the pair of them almost drowned."

"Spill it, Howard," she said, seizing his hands.

He began the story in the carriage and continued telling it as they climbed the stairs to their bedchamber . . . where Eli was waiting for them to return. He wanted to hear the story, too, so Barclay allowed him to climb onto the bed and listen—after eliciting a promise from him to go straight back to bed afterward.

Norah and Eli were spellbound, though Norah wondered if the details might have been embellished. She fully intended to ask Lauren the next time they were together. By the end, it was clear that pirates and smugglers were going to join the "boogermen" Eli sometimes encountered in his dreams.

When Barclay returned from tucking Eli in again, Norah was in her nightclothes and snuggled deep into the covers of their big bed. He shed his clothes quickly and joined her, sensing from her flannel nightie and cuddly behavior that wild, delirious mating was not on the schedule.

With a tired smile, he wrapped his arms around her and pulled her close. She nestled against him with a contented murmur.

"What was that?" he asked, kissing her temple.

"I asked if you like children," she said. He had the feeling she was more awake than she seemed. It was a wifely question that could prove to be quicksand for a man.

"If you mean Eli . . . he has grown on me and I care a great deal about him. But do I *like* him . . . ? Give me another couple of years on that one."

"I mean children in general." She opened her eyes to look at him. "And perhaps children we might have."

Oh, this was worse than quicksand. He swallowed hard.

"Norah Capshaw Howard . . . are you trying to tell me something?"

"Possibly."

"Possibly what?" He sounded horrified and wished to take it back. Too late.

"Expecting." She turned in his arms. "It's early . . . I'm not sure yet, but I've seen signs. . . ."

He rolled onto his back as if dropped from an enormous stork.

"A baby?"

"That's generally what husbands and wives make," she said, rising on an elbow to watch him take the news. "If it's true . . . this time next year, you might have a son or daughter to adore and carry around. Wouldn't you like to have a son?"

"Of course. Someday." He was still in shock.

"And Eli would have little cousins to play with. I think he'd like that. Little Barclays."

His eyes were suddenly saucer-sized.

"Oh God. What if he's like me?"

"If he's like you . . . he'll chop stumps with Eli . . . and we'll raise him to be a white knight like his father." She glowed at the prospect.

But he had a terrifying thought.

"What if it's a *girl* . . . and *she's* like me?"

She paused for a moment, then smiled and posed her own question.

"What if it's a girl . . . and she's like *me*?"

He looked into her eyes and she could feel the tension easing in his body as he lay against her.

"Then she'll be beautiful and bright and stubborn and

daring," he said softly. "And someday she'll need a white knight."

She stroked his hair and kissed his forehead.

"She'll be your daughter, too." She gave a throaty laugh as she rose onto an elbow and spoke against his lips before sinking into a heart-stopping kiss. "Maybe she'll *be* a white knight."

Author's Note

I hope you enjoyed Barclay "the Beast" Howard and Norah "the Tutor" Capshaw! They were such fun to create and bring together. As often happens, the hero of the next book showed up in this one. Randville Worth. But that's another story.

There are a few nuggets of history I'd like to share:

The Southern Uplands of Scotland historically have been the source of gold and even precious stones. There was never a "49er" rush like the one in California or the one in South Africa. The precious mineral deposits were more modest, but definitely there. To this day, the Southern Uplands and the Galloway Forest are a sparsely populated part of the British Isles. It was fun to bring that fact together with:

The legend of Jacobite gold. The rebellion of 1745 that tried to secure independence for Scotland and set Bonnie Prince Charlie on the throne was a failure militarily and politically, but it lives on richly in legend. The story goes that Prince Charles's war chest—gold from France and Spain—was broken up and sent to possibly four different places. Some of the gold was reputedly sent to loyal clans to reimburse their soldiers and their purchase of arms. The majority of the treasure was found not long after the rebellion was quashed and the rest was declared missing, became legendary, and has been the focus of treasure hunters for generations of Scots. Research and folk stories place the hidden treasure in obscure locations, but the best scholarship locates it in Loch Arkaig in Northern Scotland. Some claim it has been found and was paltry, others claim it is still buried (drowned) in a Highland loch.

I took a bit of liberty here, though it is said that some of the treasure and some contributions from nobles and even from other countries that backed the rebellion were melted down to make a Scottish coin honoring Bonnie Prince Charlie.

Finally,

Free-love lectures (as they were called) were indeed held in London during the mid and later 1880s. There was a new and growing movement to liberate women from "property" status to full human rights during that period. Participating, even as an attendee at one of these meetings was risky, especially after the arrest and prosecution of the publishers of the "birth control" pamphlet. Women attendees were indeed arrested for violating "moral decency," and I thought it might be fun to have big, powerful Barclay attend a free-love lecture with one set of expectations and leave in a paddy wagon because he tried to help a prickly young woman who needed rescuing. Imagine what they will have to tell their children about how they met:

Him: "Well, I was at this free-love lecture, looking for a date, when your mother came in to escape a masher who was trying to drag her into the nearest alley. The coppers showed up and arrested us all . . . We spent the night in jail . . . and even after I bailed her out, she refused to look at me."

Her: "I ducked into a lecture to escape a tenacious masher who'd been following me all day and found myself in this Women's Rights rally. When the coppers showed up this big, beast of a guy pushed me out a side door, supposedly to 'rescue' me. I stabbed him with my hatpin and ran, but the police caught me and I spent a night in jail. The big man was arrested, too, and ended up paying my fine. Next thing I knew—HE was following me, too!"

Come see me at BetinaKrahn.com for news on my next book . . . which, if the stars align properly, will be Randville Worth's story of adventure and love. Happy reading!

**Looking for more Betina Krahn? Don't miss
her captivating Regency historical romance
Sin & Sensibility series, beginning with . . .**

A GOOD DAY TO MARRY A DUKE

**From award-winning, *New York Times* bestselling
author Betina Krahn comes a beguiling new romance
brimming with her signature wit, timeless sensuality,
and thrilling romance—as desire proves to be
a great equalizer . . .**

Daisy Bumgarten isn't thrilled to be trying to catch a
duke's attention while dressed like a flowerpot caught
in a swarm of butterflies. But, after all, when in Rome
(or in this case London society) . . . Since her decidedly
disastrous debut among New York's privileged set, the
sassy Nevada spitfire's last chance to "marry well" lies
across the pond, here in England. If she must restrain her
free spirit, not to mention her rib cage, so be it. She knows
she owes it to her three younger sisters to succeed.

Now, under a countess's tutelage, Daisy appears the
perfect duchess-in-training. Until notorious ladies' man
Lord Ashton Graham, a distraction of the most dangerous
kind, glimpses her mischievous smile and feisty nature—
and attempts to unmask her motives. Daisy has
encountered snakes on the range, but one dressed to
the nines in an English drawing room is positively
unnerving—and maddeningly seductive. When a veiled
plot emerges to show up Daisy as unworthy of the
aristocracy, will Ashton be her worst detractor? Or the
nobleman she needs most of all?

*Available from Kensington Publishing Corp.
wherever books are sold.*

Prologue

New York State, 1888

This was the moment she had been waiting for, her time to shine.

She had the perfect horse—seventeen intimidating hands and black as midnight—and the perfect riding habit—scarlet coat with a black overskirt that hid her trousers, and a saucy top hat cocked at an eye-catching angle—

The Bellington Hunt had gathered in the estate's stone-paved court and the barrel-chested hunt master was making the rounds, glad-handing the men and flattering the few ladies who would soon be riding over hill and dale in pursuit of a fox and a pack of baying hounds. The morning was brisk and sunny, with wisps of mist lingering among the stately oaks that dotted the grounds. The horses snorted and stepped sharply, anxious to be off, while the riders laid wagers on who would be first at the kill and quietly appraised the saucy young thing holding the reins of a strapping black stallion.

They were staring at her, so she lifted her chin and stared

right back. And when the hunt master introduced her to nearby gentlemen, she thrust out her hand and gave them a shake they'd remember. She glanced at the other lady riders and thought: *Sidesaddle Sadie's, every one of them. Have to be hoisted up and tucked into stirrups like babies in buggies. Well, no mounting block for me, no sir! The minute that horn sounds, they'll see Daisy Bumgarten's a horsewoman who don't need coddling. I'll throw this soft bunch of city boys some gen-u-ine competition.*

"Daisy!" Her mother's fierce whisper penetrated her concentration, and Daisy looked down instantly to make sure her skirt didn't reveal what she wore beneath. Her mother gave her reddened cheek a kiss and straightened her hat to a more demure angle, giving the impression of a doting mother come to see her daughter off. Daisy knew better. She had come to remind her daughter how much was riding on this opportunity.

"Don't stare." Elizabeth Bumgarten gave her arm a covert squeeze. "Remember your manners. Rein in that beast of yours and hang back. Stay in the middle of the pack—try to keep company with the other ladies. And avoid fences. No proper lady could keep her seat going over a fence."

"Mount up!" the hunt master bellowed. "We're soon away!"

Every horse and rider in the yard was suddenly in motion, including Daisy.

"Be sure . . . use the . . ."

Mounting block. Daisy didn't need to hear it to know what her mother intended as she led her horse through the press and around that confounded contraption. With a quick look over her shoulder to be certain she was out of sight, she grabbed the saddle and jumped up to slip her boot into the stirrup. Swinging her leg over the saddle, she smiled. *Let's see any of these other gals mount half so slick.* She pulled her skirt up to tuck out of the way. The horn blew, the hounds tore off at a wicked pace, and a shout went up as the riders bolted out of the yard and across the nearby field. Daisy's last coherent thought before excitement seized her every sense was that her mother hadn't even noticed she was using her western saddle.

The horses were lathered and smelly, the riders were windblown and red faced, and the hounds barked triumphantly as they jumped around the dismounting riders in the same courtyard two hours later. The male hunters vied with bourbon-bold bluster for recognition of their prowess on horseback. Hip flasks—silver and monogrammed— were passed around, and one found its way into Daisy's hands. She grinned at its owner, tilted it up, and took a long, fiery swig of Kentucky's finest.

Raucous male laughter burst around her as she swiped her mouth with the back of her sleeve and thrust the flask back into her benefactor's hand. She'd done it—she had led the pack and jumped half a dozen fences and proved her mettle in grand style. And they toasted her performance in true camaraderie with their best liquor. She was too busy basking in the heat of their admiring gazes to notice the rush of footsteps behind her. It was only when her mother snagged her arm and spun her about that she realized she was in trouble.

"Daisy, dear, you must be exhausted from such exertion. You simply must come along to rest and change for tea," Elizabeth Bumgarten said through lips pressed as tight as barrel staves. Her eyes were intense and her grip was fierce. Daisy allowed herself to be dragged away from the rest of the hunting party, praying that her mother hadn't witnessed that impulsive gulp of bourbon. The heat of the draught lingered nicely in her throat and belly, fortification that would no doubt be necessary.

She was escorted firmly through the mansion's main hall, up the grand, carved, mahogany staircase, and around a gallery to one of the rooms set aside for the visiting ladies.

The China blue bedchamber was filled with wrapped dresses hung from wardrobe doors and was piled with valises, hatboxes, and small trunks. Discarded tissue, recently shed shoes, tins of perfumed powder, ribbons, and hairbrushes littered the floor and dressing tables. Mercifully, it was empty of ladies and ladies' maids just now, so no one else would hear the blistering Daisy was about to receive.

"How dare you present yourself to these people in that— that—" Her mother glared at Daisy's overskirt, which was still turned up in front and tucked at her waist, and then at her woolen trousers. Daisy half expected the fabric to burst into flames. "What in Heaven's Holy Name did you think you were doing dragging those things along?"

"I can't ride sideways, Ma. I damn near killed myself the last time I tried. *You* try takin' a fence on one of those death traps." Recognizing the mistake of mentioning fences, she lifted her chin. "Unless you'd rather I just wore a damned skirt and let my naked legs show?"

"How dare you use such language with me?" Her mother backed her against the wall beside an open wardrobe and leaned in, an inch from Daisy's nose, where she inhaled sharply. "You've been *drinking*!"

"Just a nip. To get the blood flowin'." Daisy winced. She sounded too much like her beloved Uncle Red just now, and she was fairly sure her mother wouldn't miss the similarity.

Elizabeth blanched and her mouth worked without sound. A moment later both her voice and her color returned with a vengeance.

"You know we're here on sufferance. If Mrs. Barclay hadn't intervened to get us an invitation—this is our one chance to show we're more than just a bunch of raucous, ill-mannered western—"

A gaggle of feminine voices burst into the stuffy chamber, and a second later the mahogany door swung open to the sound of Mrs. Townsend-Burden's grating, high-pitched laughter.

"Did you see the woman's face?" she crowed. "Purely mortified."

"Rightly so," said a voice as yet unfamiliar, but betraying the tortured vowels of Boston proper. "And those bloomers. Good God—even Amelia Bloomer has given those up by now."

"They're not bloom—" Daisy's whispered protest was cut off by her mother's hand across her mouth. The gowns hanging from the wardrobe doors hid them, but they wouldn't go unnoticed for long. Spotting the open doorway to the adjacent bathing room, Elizabeth impulsively yanked Daisy into the white-tiled chamber and pressed a finger to her own tightly clamped mouth, ordering silence.

"And riding *astride* with the *men*," the Townsend-Burden woman continued. "Brazen creature."

"Uncouth is what she is," came a third voice. "Where is that girl of mine? These shoes are killing me." That plummy, distinctive voice lowered. "No doubt she's given the men more than an eyeful this day."

The laughter was sharp as cats' claws.

"Did you see her this morning before they started out? Not waiting to be introduced . . . smiling, laughing, and shaking hands like . . . like a *man*. Mark my words: that one knows too much."

"A hussy, that's what she is. Far too bold to be anything else."

Daisy's chest tightened as she watched the fire in her mother's eyes flicker and damp. She wanted to look away, but the pain she read in Elizabeth's face kept her riveted. This was what her mother had brought the family to New York to do. For the last three years Elizabeth Bumgarten's every action, every hope, every expenditure had been focused on getting them into society, on getting her girls well fixed in the world.

Daisy had mostly ignored or pretended amusement at her mother's aspirations and the lessons, fittings, and exposures to "culture" that resulted. In truth, she had resented them and the implication that because she and her sisters were new to moneyed life, they were somehow inferior and had to work to become worthy of notice. Deeper still, she had chafed at her mother's constant watchfulness that said she was not to be trusted around men. Thus motivated, she had found ways to escape most of her mother's attempts to transform her.

Until now. Until she heard her mother's fears and dire assessments coming from the mouths of others, ridiculing her mother's attempts at her daughters' betterment and naming Daisy a hussy—a judgment that was a bit too close to the bone.

"Just goes to show what money cannot buy," the third woman said, her cultured tones dripping disdain. "Breeding, manners, and good taste. The chit and her pathetic mother will never set foot in my ballroom, I can tell you that. On that Mr. McAllister and I quite agree."

With the drop of that name and the mention of a ballroom, the identity of the third guest was made clear. Mr. McAllister. *Ward McAllister*. Even Daisy knew that name. That meant their third detractor could be none other than Mrs. John Jacob Astor herself. The queen of New York society. The creator and self-appointed keeper of the Four Hundred. She had apparently deigned to attend the "boring country house party," after all.

Daisy watched her mother's shoulders round and her face redden with humiliation. The verbal scalding went on until the ladies' maids descended to help their mistresses freshen for tea.

By the time the women exited the chamber, Daisy and her mother were pressed back into a corner behind the porcelain water heater, having missed detection by the slimmest of margins. Daisy stepped out cautiously and peered into the bedchamber, which now resembled the workroom at the rear of a dressmaker's shop. When she turned back, her mother was staring at her with a desolate look.

"It seems you've gotten your wish," Elizabeth said bitterly. "You won't be troubled with manners and prissy clothes and 'expectations' ever again."

"It's not too late," Daisy said anxiously. "I'll behave. I won't look at a single man and I'll use my best Sunday manners. You'll see—"

"I have already seen. And so have *they*," Elizabeth said,

her voice low and choked with anger. "As of this day, we are social pariahs. But know this, girl—you have not only ruined my hopes, you have ruined your sisters' as well. Their reputations, their expectations are forever tarnished by your headstrong, selfish behavior." She strode toward the bedchamber, but paused in front of Daisy for one last salvo.

"I hope you're proud of yourself."

One

London, two years later

"You don't have to do this, girl," Uncle Red said as they paused on the front steps of the Earl of Mountjoy's palatial London home.

"Yes, I do." Daisy struggled for breath against her wickedly tight corset. She had worked fervently for the last two years to come to this moment. A little suffocation and a few spots before her eyes were a small price to pay for climbing onto the social register. A girl had obligations, after all—sisters to marry off and a mother with badly bruised pride.

This was going to make everything she had done wrong, right. She was going to marry a nobleman—a top nobleman—and take him home and watch Mrs. Astor choke on "that Bumgarten tart's" good fortune. Assuming, of course, that she survived the night in this damned corset.

"You want a nip to brace you up?" Uncle Red patted the conspicuous bulge in the breast pocket of his coat. His concern was downright sweet, considering his own duress . . . being stone-cold sober and stuffed into a cut-away with a starched collar that was choking him sense-less. But if anyone could sympathize with a body it would be Redmond Strait. Her blustery, ruddy-faced uncle had a sentimental streak about as wide as the massive silver vein he'd discovered in Nevada.

"I'm fine, Uncle Red. Truly." She lied through her teeth; she could really use a nip just now. "Couldn't be better. My feet are positively itching for a dance."

Red sighed at her determined expression and took her at her word. The minute they handed over their invitation to the liveried footman, he smacked his mouth thirstily and struck off in search of the nearest punch bowl.

Daisy paused at the bottom of the great expanse of marble steps leading up to the ballroom, dreading the climb in an elaborate gown that had to weigh fifty pounds and made her look like she'd been caught in a florist shop explosion. Silk flowers were stitched to embroidered vines running riot over her narrow satin bodice and half bare shoulders—not to mention those absurd butterflies the countess had insisted on plastering all over her. She looked down at her waist, grabbed an eye-catching blue insect, and tugged until the threads that held it gave with a pop.

With a fierce sense of satisfaction, she gathered her skirts to proceed, but then someone clutched her elbow.

"Come with me, Miss Bumgarten." Lady Evelyn Har-grave, Countess of Kew—Daisy's sponsor and guide on her matrimonial quest—had eyes narrowed to slits and lips frozen into an icy smile. The force she used in spiriting her protégée out of public view told Daisy she was in trouble.

The countess ushered her down a long hallway and into a dimly lighted room filled with stuffed bookcases, heavy leather furnishings, and the smell of old cigars. As the door closed, the countess turned on her.

"Where in Heaven's name are your gloves?"

Daisy sighed and produced lengths of limp kidskin from the folds of her dress. She was in for it. The English were obsessed with gloves, wore them morning, noon, and night—sometimes ate in the damned things.

"I believe I have made myself perfectly clear on this matter." The countess yanked them from her and smoothed the wrinkles caused by her moist hands. "Ladies never appear in public without gloves."

"They make my arms feel like sausages," Daisy said as the countess held one out for her to insert her hand.

"They wouldn't if you—" The countess bit off the rest, but Daisy finished the comment in her head: *didn't have such unladylike arms*. She couldn't help it that her body had what old Chuck Worth in Paris had called "a remarkably physical aspect." She'd spent much of her life wrangling horses, carrying saddles, and hefting bales of hay back at her home in Nevada, and three years of city living in New York before she headed to Paris and London hadn't been enough to soften all of her contours.

The countess struggled with the row of tiny leather-covered buttons, paused suddenly, and looked up with splotches blooming in her cheeks.

"Where are your butterflies?"

"I felt silly in them, so I—I—"

Daisy opened her other hand to reveal the squished blue silk. The countess's mouth opened and worked, but produced only a gurgle. Daisy wondered if she were strangling on her own juices.

There's a thought.

"We paid a small fortune to have those hand painted

to resemble rare and exotic specimens." The countess
snatched the faux insect and tried to restore it, then stopped
dead. "There are supposed to be two in your coiffure and
two more at your shoulder. What the devil did you do with
them?"

Daisy wished the woman would just come out with a
good, old-fashioned "hell's fire" or "damnation" and get
it off her chest. Her blanches of disappointment were far
too much like Daisy's long-suffering mother's. With a huff,
she opened her reticule to reveal the four crumpled butterflies she had removed on the way to the ball.

The countess closed her eyes briefly and looked as if
someone were lighting a pyre around her feet.

"You have engaged me to assist you in your quest,
Miss Bumgarten. I cannot do so if you refuse to follow my
advice." She drew back irritably. "I shall be waiting by the
stairs to accompany you, should you decide to cooperate."

Daisy watched the door close and then glowered at the
gloves and butterflies.

"I'm a grown woman." She tossed her reticule onto a
nearby chair and started to button the wretched accessory.
"I shouldn't have to walk around frumped up like a god-
damned flowerpot!"

"I agree." Deep male tones startled her.

She clasped a hand over her racing heart and looked
around to find the top of a head sticking up behind the
back of a sofa.

"What are you doing there?" she demanded.

"Escaping a certain young lady's irate mother. At least,
I was before you and your governess barged in."

"The countess is *not* my governess." Daisy drew herself
up with true indignation. "Eavesdropping is—you might

have had the decency to say something, announce your presence."

"And miss such a fascinating conversation?" A face wearing a wince appeared. "Oh. I see what you mean about the flowerpot."

He began to rise. And rise. Daisy found herself watching a tall, broad-shouldered man unfold from the sofa . . . longish hair, arresting face, elegant evening clothes that sat casually on a leanly muscled frame. What she could see in the dim light gave her a very bad feeling. Well, not so much bad as wicked, the kind that started just behind her navel and curled upward and downward into alarmingly excitable territory.

With a flush, she jerked her gaze back to her glove buttons and tried to concentrate on stuffing the buttons through the loops. But he moved around the sofa toward her and she soon found herself looking up . . . and up . . . and up. He came to a stop barely an arm's length away, and she took a half step back.

He was tall and dark and—her heart tripped over the obvious—handsome. His face was framed on strong, patrician bones; he had a long, straight English nose; and his curved mouth bore a decidedly sensual cast.

"I agree with you, by the by. The butterflies look theatrical."

Tall, dark, and clever.

In other words, trouble. She groaned privately. Men who eavesdropped and commented boldly on a lady's appearance had no scruples. Much less what the Brits called "proper sensibilities." Men like him believed that rules were made for other people.

When he reached for her hand and began to fasten her glove, she felt a tingle in places she wasn't supposed to know that ladies possessed. She tried to withdraw her hand, but he held it fast.

"It's almost impossible to do these one handed." He slid buttons through loops with long, expert fingers. She glanced up and away, but not before she caught the way his dark hair lay in smooth, feathered layers. No sticky pomade there. Nothing but soft, silky—

She shook herself mentally, refusing to listen to the siren call of her own wayward impulses. She had come to England to marry a duke, and marry one she would. If it killed her.

Why, then, was she allowing this cad—the British equivalent of a "varmint"—to behave so presumptuously? Another of the Brits' favorite words: "presumptuous." The Brits were a wordy bunch.

"I believe I can manage the rest on my own," she said, yanking her hand back and refusing to look at him again.

He took a step back, spread his coat to prop his hands on his waist, and watched as she smoothed the glove and fumbled with the buttons.

"You're American," he said, and she could tell from his voice he was smiling, probably the same superior expression she'd seen on so many English aristocrats. "But not from Boston."

"Thank God," she said from between clenched teeth. The damned buttons were putting up a fight. "Nevada. That's out west."

"I know where it is," he said. "Next to California."

"Give the man a prize," she said irritably, regretting it the minute the retort left her lips. But he just laughed in low, mesmerizing tones that made her bones and determination both soften.

"At that rate, you'll be here until the closing dance." He

brushed aside her resistance to finish her buttons. This time she looked up, which turned out to be a bad idea. He had long, dark lashes that she could almost *feel* against her skin. "If I'm not mistaken, that is a Charles Worth gown."

"It is."

"Not his usual work." One eyebrow rose.

"It was made specially for this ball."

"I imagine so. The duke is known to be a nature lover."

She reddened. He knew exactly the point of her having bought and worn such an extravagant dress and was far too amused by it to suit her.

"So am I," she said defiantly. "I love flowers. And butterflies."

"Ah, yes. The butterflies. In your hair, were they?"

As the last button was fastened, she jerked her arm back and looked around for a mirror. The best she could do was a dark picture under glass that allowed her to see her reflection. She carried her reticule to the console below the picture, where she managed to settle two butterflies back into her hair and wrap the dangling threads of a third around some seed pearls in the flowers at her shoulder. She must have groaned aloud, because her fashion critic laughed. When she looked up, he stood nearby with a gold stickpin in hand.

"Try this." His grin raised both hackles and gooseflesh.

"I couldn't possibly." She dropped her gaze and found the butterfly she'd applied hanging to one side, as if it had expired from the indignity of having to appear on that dog's dinner of a dress.

"Well, I could," he said, taking the butterflies from her and stabbing both through with the stickpin. She watched in disbelief as he pulled out the shoulder of her bodice, jabbed the pin through a flower, and threaded it through from behind.

When the butterflies were secured, his hand remained in audacious contact with her liberally exposed skin. He ran the backs of his knuckles slowly around the neckline of her bodice. She froze; unable to protest, unable to even swallow as he reached the exposed top of her left breast and paused, stroking, sensitizing that all too susceptible flesh.

She raised her chin to tell him just how vile his behavior was, but he was leaning close enough for her gaze to get caught in the hot bronze disks of his eyes . . . worldly eyes that advertised understanding of a woman's deepest desires and the promise of pleasures well practiced and perfected. Unfortunately, there was more as well: humor, intelligence, and a piqued bit of sensual curiosity. A deep tremor of interest rocked her, awakening nerves and raising an alarm.

She should be kicking him like a Missouri mule, should be giving him a painful lesson in how American girls dealt with "bounders." But, truth be told—tall, dark men with bad intentions had always been her weakness, and he was taller and darker than most, and from what she could tell, his intentions were spectacularly bad. Right now every muscle in her body was taut with expectation and her lips ached for contact of a sort she'd sworn to forgo until she had spoken respectable vows.

"There," he said with a wry smile, lowering his hand. "If you can overlook the fact that those two appear to be mating, you'll be fine."

"Mating?" Her eyes flew wide as she realized what he'd done. "You, you—" She caught herself before she uttered a curse and drew a fiercely controlled breath instead. "What is her name? This mama you slunk in here like a polecat to avoid."

His grin dimmed and he paused a moment, studying her. She had caught him off-guard.

"A gentleman does not discuss the ladies in his life."

"Is that so?" she said, lifting her chin as she headed for the door. "Well, I'm sure I'll recognize her when I see her. She'll be the one with the shotgun"—she raked him with a look—"and the horse-faced daughter."

Connect with

Visit us online at
KensingtonBooks.com
to read more from your favorite authors, see books
by series, view reading group guides, and more.

for sneak peeks, chances to win books and prize packs,
and to share your thoughts with other readers.

facebook.com/kensingtonpublishing
twitter.com/kensingtonbooks

Tell us what you think!

To share your thoughts, submit a review,
or sign up for our eNewsletters, please visit:
KensingtonBooks.com/TellUs.